AND I
DARKEN

AND I
DARKEN

KIERSTEN WHITE

CORGI BOOKS

CORGI BOOKS

UK | USA | Canada | Ireland | Australia
India | New Zealand | South Africa

Corgi Books is part of the Penguin Random House group of companies
whose addresses can be found at global.penguinrandomhouse.com.

www.penguin.co.uk
www.puffin.co.uk
www.ladybird.co.uk

First published 2016

001

Set in 12pt Centaur
Printed in Great Britain by Clays Ltd, St Ives plc

A CIP catalogue record for this book is available from the British Library

ISBN: 978–0–552–57374–0

All correspondence to:
Corgi Books
Penguin
80 Str

For Noah

———◆———

Te iubesc

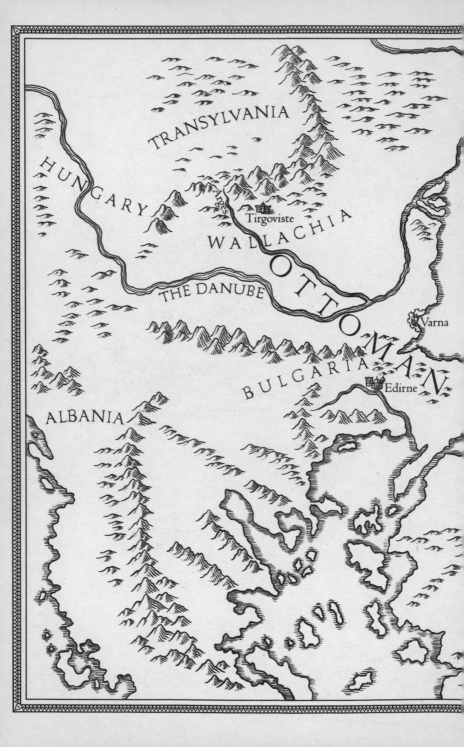

THE BLACK SEA

Constantinople

EMPIRE

Amasya

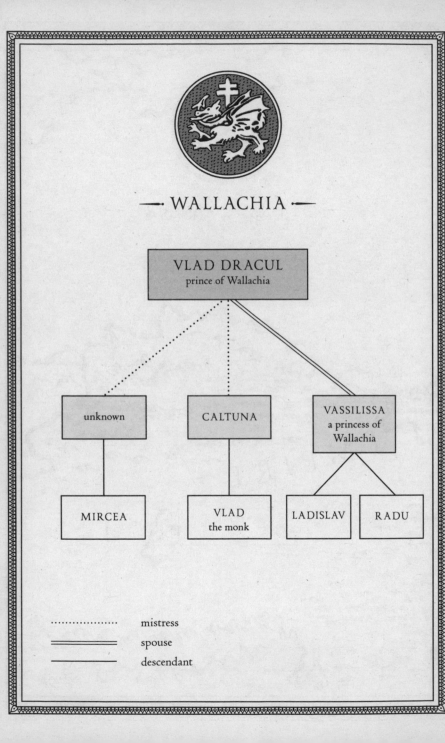

— WALLACHIA —

VLAD DRACUL
prince of Wallachia

unknown	CALTUNA	VASSILISSA a princess of Wallachia

MIRCEA	VLAD the monk	LADISLAV	RADU

.... mistress

========= spouse

————— descendant

— OTTOMAN EMPIRE —

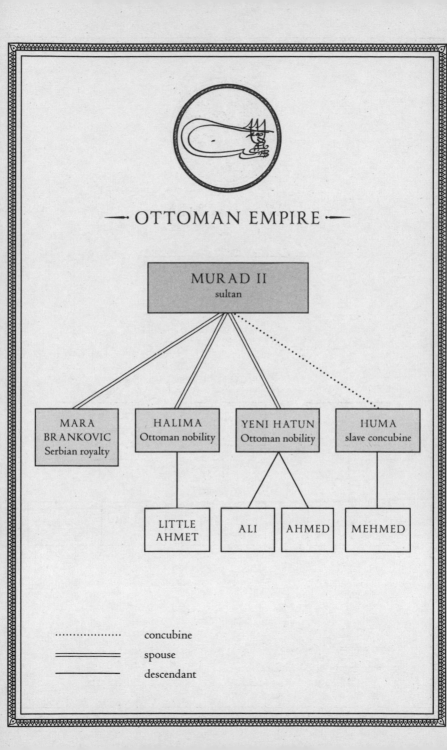

MURAD II
sultan

MARA BRANKOVIC
Serbian royalty

HALIMA
Ottoman nobility

YENI HATUN
Ottoman nobility

HUMA
slave concubine

LITTLE AHMET

ALI

AHMED

MEHMED

.... concubine

========= spouse

————— descendant

1

1435: Sighisoara, Transylvania

VLAD DRACUL'S HEAVY BROW descended like a storm when the doctor informed him that his wife had given birth to a girl. His other children—one from his first wife, now nearly full grown, and even a bastard child from his mistress, born last year—had been boys. He had not thought his seed weak enough to produce a girl.

He pushed through the door, into the close, heavy air of the tiny bedroom. It stank of blood and fear and filled him with disgust.

Their home in the fortified hill city of Sighisoara was a far cry from what he deserved. It sat next to the main gate, in the suffocating press of the square, beside an alley that reeked of human waste. His retainer of ten men was merely ceremonial, rendering him a glorified placeholder. He might have been the military governor of Transylvania, but he was supposed to be the ruler of all Wallachia.

Perhaps that was why he had been cursed with a girl. Another insult to his honor. He was in the Order of the Dragon, sanctioned by the pope himself. He should be the vaivode, the warlord prince, but his brother sat on the throne, while he was governor of Saxons squatting on his own country's land.

Soon he would show them his honor on the end of a sword.

Vasilissa lay on the bed, soaked in sweat and moaning in pain. Certainly the weakness that took root in her womb had been her own. His stomach turned at the sight of her, princess now in neither demeanor nor appearance.

The nurse held up a squalling, red-faced little monster. He had no names for a girl. Vasilissa would doubtless want something that honored her family, but Vlad hated the Moldavian royals she came from for failing to bring him any political advantage. He had already named his bastard Vlad, after himself. He would name his daughter the same.

"Ladislav," he declared. It was a feminine form of Vlad. Diminutive. Diminished. If Vasilissa wanted a strong name, she would have to bear him a son. "Let us pray she is beautiful so we can get some use out of her," he said. The infant screamed louder.

———•———

Vasilissa's royal breasts were far too important to suckle from. The wet nurse waited until Vlad left, then held the babe to her common teats. She was still full of milk from her own child, a boy. As the baby latched on with surprising fierceness, the nurse offered her own prayer. *Let her be strong. Let her be sly.* She looked over at the princess, fifteen, lovely and delicate as the first spring blossoms. Wilted and broken on the bed.

And let her be ugly.

2

V LAD COULD NOT BE bothered to be present for the birth of his second child by Vasilissa: a son, a year younger than his sister, practically chasing her into this world.

The nurse finished cleaning the newborn, then held him out to his mother. He was tiny, perfect, with a mouth like a rosebud and a full head of dark hair. Vasilissa lay, glassy-eyed and mute, on the bed. She stared at the wall. Her gaze never even drifted to her son. A tug on the nurse's skirt brought her attention downward, where tiny Lada stood, scowling. The nurse angled the baby toward his sister.

"A brother," she said, her voice soft.

The baby started to cry, a weak, garbled sound that worried the nurse. Lada's scowl deepened. She slapped a dimpled hand over his mouth. The nurse pulled him away quickly, and Lada looked up, face contorted in rage.

"Mine!" she shouted.

It was her first word.

The nurse laughed, shocked, and lowered the baby once more. Lada glared at him until he stopped crying. Then, apparently satisfied, she toddled out of the room.

3

IF VASILISSA SAW HER daughter wrestling on the floor with the dogs and the nurse's son, Bogdan, the nurse would lose her position. However, since the birth of Radu four years ago, Vasilissa never left her rooms.

Radu had gotten all the beauty their father had wished on his daughter. His eyes were framed by thick lashes, his lips full, his gentle curls kissed with a hint of Saxon gold.

Bogdan screamed as Lada—Ladislav, now five, refused to answer to her full name—bit down on his thigh. He punched her. She bit harder, and he cried for help.

"If she wants to eat your leg, she is allowed," the nurse said. "Quit screaming or I will let her eat your supper, too."

Like her brother, Lada had big eyes, but hers were close-set, with arched brows that made her look perpetually cross. Her hair was a tangled mass, so dark that her pale skin appeared sickly. Her nose was long and hooked, her lips thin, her teeth small and—judging from Bogdan's angry cries— quite sharp.

She was contrary and vicious and the meanest child the nurse had ever cared for. She was also the nurse's favorite. By all rights the girl should be silent and proper, fearful and simpering. Her father was a powerless tyrant, cruel in his impotence and absent for months at a time. Her mother was every bit as absent, withdrawn and worthless in their home, incapable of doing anything to help herself. They were an apt representation of the entire region—particularly the nurse's homeland of Wallachia.

But in Lada she saw a spark, a passionate, fierce glimmer that refused to hide or be dimmed. Rather than trying to stamp out that fire for the sake of Lada's future, the nurse nurtured it. It made her feel oddly hopeful.

If Lada was the spiky green weed that sprouted in the midst of a drought-cracked riverbed, Radu was the delicate, sweet rose that wilted in anything less than the perfect conditions. Right now he wailed at the nurse's pause in spooning the thin gruel, sweetened with honey, into his mouth.

"Make him shut up!" Lada climbed over her father's largest hound, grizzled and patient with age.

"How should I do that?"

"Smother him!"

"Lada! Bite your tongue. He is your brother."

"He is a worm. Bogdan is my brother."

The nurse scowled, wiping Radu's face with her apron. "Bogdan is not your brother." *I would sooner lie with the dogs than your father*, she thought.

"He is! You are. Say you are." Lada jumped onto Bogdan's back. Though he was two years older and far bigger,

6

she pinned him to the ground, jamming her elbow into his shoulder.

"I am! I am!" he said, half giggling, half crying.

"Throw Radu out with the chamber pots!"

Radu wailed louder, working himself up to a fit. The nurse clucked her tongue, picking him up even though he was much too large to be carried around. He put a hand in her blouse and pinched her skin, which was loose and wrinkled like an old apple. She sometimes wished he would shut up, too, but when he did speak it was always so sweet it made up for his tantrums. He even smelled nice, as if honey clung to his mouth between meals.

"Be a good boy," the nurse said, "and you can go sledding with Lada and Bogdan later. Would you like that?"

Radu shook his head, lip trembling with the threat of more tears.

"Or we could visit the horses."

He nodded slowly and the nurse sighed with relief. She looked up to find Lada gone. "Where did she go?"

Bogdan's eyes widened in fear and indecision. Already he did not know whose wrath to fear more—his mother's or tiny Lada's.

Huffing, the nurse tucked Radu onto her hip, his feet bouncing against her legs with every step. She stalked down the hall toward the narrow stairs leading to the bedrooms. "Lada, if you wake your mother, there will be—"

She stopped, holding perfectly still, her fearful expression matching Bogdan's own. From the sitting room near the front of the house, she heard voices. Low voices. Men's voices.

Speaking in Turkish, the language of their oftentimes enemy, the Ottomans.

Which meant Vlad was home, and Lada was—

The nurse ran down the hall and burst into the sitting room to find Lada standing in the middle of the room.

"I kill infidels!" the child snarled, brandishing a small kitchen knife.

"Do you?" Vlad spoke to her in the language of the Saxons, the tongue most spoken in Sighisoara. The nurse's Saxon was crude, and while Vasilissa was fluent in several languages, she never spoke with the children. Lada and Radu spoke only Wallachian.

Lada waved the knife at him in answer to the question she did not understand. Vlad raised an eyebrow. He was wrapped in a fine cloak, an elaborate hat on his head. It had been nearly a year since Lada had seen her father. She did not recognize him.

"Lada!" the nurse whispered. "Come here at once."

Lada stood as tall as her short, stocky legs allowed. "This is my home! I am the Order of the Dragon! I kill infidels!"

One of the three men accompanying Vlad murmured something in Turkish. The nurse felt sweat breaking out on her face, her neck, her back. Would they kill a child for threatening them? Would her father allow it? Or would they simply kill her for being unable to control Lada?

Vlad smiled indulgently at his daughter's display, then bowed his head at the three men. They returned the bow and swept out, acknowledging neither the nurse nor her disobedient charge. "How many infidels have you killed?" Vlad's voice, this time in the melodic romance language tones of Wallachian, was smooth and cold.

"Hundreds." Lada pointed the knife at Radu, who hid his face against the nurse's shoulder. "I killed that one this morning."

"And will you kill me now?"

Lada hesitated, lowering her hand. She stared at her father, recognition seeping across her face like milk dropped in clear water. As quick as a snake, Vlad snatched the knife out of her hand, then grabbed her by the ankle and lifted her into the air.

"And how," he said, her upside-down face level with his, "did you think you could kill someone bigger, stronger, and smarter than you?"

"You cheated!" Lada's eyes burned with a look the nurse had come to dread. That look meant injury, destruction, or fire. Often all three.

"I won. That is all that matters."

With a scream, Lada twisted herself up and bit her father's hand.

"God's wounds!" He dropped her on the floor. She tucked into a ball, rolled out of his reach, then crouched, baring her teeth at him. The nurse cringed, waiting for Vlad to fly into a rage and beat Lada. Or beat *her* for her failure to keep Lada tame and docile.

Instead, he laughed. "My daughter is feral."

"So sorry, my lord." The nurse ducked her head, gesturing frantically at Lada. "She is overexcited upon seeing you again after so long an absence."

"What of their instruction? She does not speak Saxon."

"No, my lord." That was not quite true. Lada had picked up Saxon obscenities and frequently yelled them out the window at people in the busy square. "She knows a bit of Hungarian. But there has been no one to see to the children's education."

He clucked his tongue, a thoughtful look in his shrewd eyes. "And what of this one? Is he as fierce?" Vlad leaned in to where Radu had finally peered outward.

Radu immediately burst into tears, burying his face once more in the nurse's shoulder and shoving his hand beneath her cap to wrap it in her hair.

Vlad's lip turned up in disgust. "This one takes after his mother. Vasilissa!" he shouted, so loud that Radu was terrified into silence interrupted only by hiccups and sniffles. The nurse did not know whether to stay or leave, but she had not been dismissed. Lada ignored her, wary eyes fixed on her father.

"Vasilissa!" Vlad roared again. He reached out to snatch Lada, but this time she was ready. She scrambled away, crawling under the polished table. Vlad rapped his knuckles on it. "Very good. Vasilissa!"

His wife stumbled into the room, hair down, wrapped in nothing but a dressing robe. She was worn thin. Her cheekbones jutted out under grayed, empty eyes. If the birth of Lada had nearly killed her, Radu's had drained whatever life she had left. She took in the scene—Radu tearstained, Lada under the table, and her husband, finally home—with a dull gaze.

"Yes?" she asked.

"Is that how you greet your husband? The vaivode of Wallachia? The *prince*?" He smiled in triumph, his long mustache lifting to reveal thin lips.

Vasilissa stiffened. "They are making you prince? What of Alexandru?"

"My brother is dead."

The nurse did not think Vlad looked much like a man in mourning.

Finally noticing her daughter, Vasilissa beckoned to her. "Ladislav, come out from under there. Your father is home."

Lada did not move. "He is not my father."

"Make her come out," Vasilissa snapped at the nurse.

"Can you not command your own child?" Vlad's voice was as clear as a blue sky in the freezing depths of winter. The sun with teeth, they called those days.

The nurse shrank further into herself, shifting so that Radu, at least, was out of Vlad's sight. Vasilissa looked frantically to either side, but there was no escape from the room. "I want to go home," she whispered. "Back to Moldavia. Please let me."

"Beg."

Vasilissa's tiny frame trembled. Then she dropped to her knees, lowered her head, and took Vlad's hand in her own. "Please. Please, I beg of you. Let me go home."

Vlad put out his other hand and stroked Vasilissa's lank, greasy hair. Then he grabbed it, wrenching her head to the side. She cried out, but he pulled tighter, forcing her to stand. He placed his lips against her ear. "You are the weakest creature I have ever known. Crawl back to your hole and hide there. Crawl!" He threw her down, and, sobbing, she crawled from the room.

The nurse looked steadily at the finely woven rug that covered the stone floor. She said nothing. She did nothing. She prayed that Radu would remain silent.

"You." Vlad pointed at Lada. "Come out. Now."

She did, still watching the door Vasilissa had disappeared through.

"I am your father. But that woman is not your mother. Your mother is Wallachia. Your mother is the very earth we go to now, the land I am prince of. Do you understand?"

Lada looked up into her father's eyes, deep-set and etched with years of cunning and cruelty. She nodded, then held out her hand. "The daughter of Wallachia wants her knife back."

Vlad smiled and gave it to her.

4

1446: Tirgoviste, Wallachia

Radu tasted blood in his mouth. It mixed with the salt from the tears streaming down his face.

Andrei and Aron Danesti kicked him again, their boots sharp against his stomach. Radu rolled onto his side, curling in on himself, trying to become as small as possible. The dried leaves and rocks littering the forest floor scraped his cheeks. No one could hear him out here.

He was used to being unheard. No one heard him in the castle, which, after six years, still felt like a home only when he was in his room with his nurse. His tutors were engaged in a constant power struggle with Lada, and Radu's exemplary work often went unnoticed. Lada was always either studying or off with Bogdan, and she never had time for him. Their older half brother, Mircea, forced Radu to seek out hiding places to avoid his blunt comments and even blunter fists. And his father, the prince, went entire weeks without acknowledging his existence.

The pressure built like steam until Radu did not know

whether he was more terrified that his father would never notice him again, or that he would.

It was safer to go unnoticed.

Unfortunately, today he had failed at that. Aron Danesti laughed, a sound sharper than his boots. "You squeal like a piglet. Do it again."

"Please." Radu covered his head as Aron slapped his cheeks. "Stop. Stop."

"We are here to get stronger," Andrei said. "And no one is weaker than you."

At least once a month, all the boys ages seven to twelve from boyar families—*boyar* was a word for nobility, to be said with a twist of the lip and a sneer if Lada were speaking—were left deep in the forest. It was a tradition, one most of the adults laughed at indulgently. A game, they called it. But they all watched with narrowed eyes, seeing who emerged first, looking as though he had been merely out for a stroll rather than tired and scared like a normal boy.

The Danestis, who had traded the throne back and forth with the Basarab family for the last fifteen years, were particularly interested in how Aron and Andrei, both a year older than Radu, fared. They were not overfond of the Draculesti usurpers.

Radu was the son of the prince, a Draculesti, the smallest boy and the biggest target. He was never the winner. And today, for the first time, he wondered whether he would make it back at all. Terror clawed in his throat. His breath came in short, painful gasps.

Andrei grabbed Radu, fingers digging into his arms as he dragged him up to stand. His mouth was against Radu's ear, breath hot. "My mother says your father wishes you had never been born. Do you wish that, too?"

Aron hit him in the stomach, and Radu gagged.

"Say it," Andrei commanded, his voice cheerful. "Say you wish you had never been born."

Radu squeezed his eyes shut. "I wish I had never been born."

Aron hit him.

"I said it!" Radu screamed, coughing and struggling for breath.

"I know," Andrei said. "Hit him again."

"My father will—"

"Your father will do what? Write the sultan to ask permission to scold us? Ask my family to donate to the throne so he can afford a switch to whip us with? Your father is *nothing*. Just like you."

Radu had braced for another blow when Aron's shout made him open his eyes. Aron was spinning in a circle, trying desperately to dislodge Lada. She was not supposed to be here, but somehow her presence was unsurprising. She had jumped on the boy's back, clasping her arms around him and pinning his arms to his sides. Radu could not see her face through her tangled drape of hair until Aron twisted to the side, revealing Lada's teeth sunk into his shoulder.

Andrei shoved Radu away and rushed forward to help his cousin. Lada released Aron, jumping off his back and crouching down. Her eyes narrowed. Andrei was eleven, the same age as Lada, but bigger than she was. Aron stumbled to a tree and leaned against it, crying and clutching his shoulder.

Lada smiled at Andrei, her teeth coated in blood.

"You demon girl, I—"

Lada stood and slammed her hand into Andrei's nose. He screamed, dropping to his knees and sniveling. Lada walked after him, then kicked his side so that he fell onto his back. He stared up at her as he choked on the blood streaming from his nose. She put her foot on his throat and pushed, just enough to make his eyes bulge in panic.

"Get out of my forest," she snarled.

She lifted her foot and watched, eyes hooded, as Andrei and Aron put their arms around each other, all traces of bravado gone. They ran.

Radu wiped his face on his sleeve, leaving behind a mess of blood and dirt. He looked at Lada, standing in the middle of a shaft of light that filtered through a gap in the thick branches. For once in his life, he was grateful for her vicious temper, for her strange instinctive knowledge of the best way to hurt someone with the least amount of work. He was so tired and so scared, and she had saved him. "Thank you." He stumbled toward her with arms outstretched. When he was hurting, his nurse folded him into herself, sealing him away from the world. He wanted—needed—that now.

Lada hit him in the stomach. He doubled over in pain, sinking to his knees. She knelt next to him, grasping him by the ears. "Do not thank me. All I did was teach them to fear me. How does that help you? Next time you hit first, you hit harder, you make certain that your name means fear and pain. I will not be here to save you again."

Radu trembled, trying not to cry. He knew Lada hated it when he cried, but she had hurt him. And she had tasked him with something impossible. The other boys were bigger, meaner, faster. Whatever made Lada better than them had skipped him entirely.

He spent the long, miserable walk out of the forest trailing his sister, wondering how he could be like her. The boyars sat waiting under tents, gossiping as servants fanned them. Mircea was there, talking with Vlad Danesti, and his expression when he saw Radu's face indicated that he approved of the damage to it. And, perhaps, he wished to do more.

Radu stepped more fully behind Lada; all other eyes were on her anyway. The boyars were astonished to see the prince's daughter walk out of the forest with her head held high. No one was surprised to see Radu filthy and bloodied, although he wasn't as bloodied as Aron and Andrei. In their haste to flee Lada, the Danesti cousins had gotten lost and had to be rescued.

After that, the forest lessons were canceled, and the boyar families whispered among themselves about the prince's daughter. She had always outpaced the boys her age with riding skills and demanded to be taught everything her brother was, but this was far more public. Rather than scolding Lada, their father laughed and boasted of his daughter, as wild and fierce as a boar. If it had been Radu who had come out of the forest victorious, would he have even noticed?

Radu heard it all, hiding behind tapestries, waiting in dark corners. He had seen Aron and Andrei watching him, but after two weeks they had yet to catch him alone. When adults were present, Radu could smile and charm and remain safe.

Lada had been right. She had not saved him. The looks in his enemies' eyes when they saw him made that clear.

So he waited, and he hid, and he observed. And then, one crisp autumn evening, he made his move.

"Hello," he said, voice cheery and bright enough to light up the twilight.

The servant boy startled, jumping as though struck. "May I help you?" His shirt was nearly worn through. Radu could see the sharp lines of his collarbones, the brittle length of his skinny arms. They were probably the same age, but Radu's life had been much kinder. At least as far as having enough food.

Radu smiled. "Would you like something to eat?"

The boy's eyes widened in wonder. He nodded.

Radu knew the value in being overlooked, because he himself was so often unseen. He led Emil, a servant so lowly he was invisible to the boyars he worked for, to the kitchen.

———

A rash of thefts plagued the castle. After every feast attended by the boyar families, someone would notice a necklace, a jewel, a personal token of value missing. It reflected poorly on the prince, so Vlad declared that whoever was discovered to be behind the crimes would be publicly lashed and indefinitely imprisoned. The boyars muttered angry, ugly things beneath their breath, and Vlad skulked through the castle, eyes narrowed and shoulders stooped beneath the weight of his shame at being unable to control his own home.

Several weeks later, Radu stood on the inner edge of the crowd as Aron and Andrei, faces covered in tears and snot, were tied to a post in the middle of the square.

"Why would they have stolen those things?" Lada watched, her mouth turned down in curiosity.

Radu shrugged. "All the missing items were found under their beds by a servant." A servant who was no longer painfully underfed, and considered Radu his best and only friend in the world. Radu smiled. There had been no real reason to wait as long as he had, delaying the punishment of his enemies and prolonging his father's embarrassment. The anticipation had been delicious, though. And now, the reward.

Lada turned to look at him, suspicion drawing her brows together. "Did you do this?"

"There are other ways to beat someone than with fists." Radu poked her in the side with a finger.

She surprised him by laughing. He stood up straighter, a proud grin at having surprised and delighted Lada bursting across his face. She never laughed unless she was laughing at him. He had done something right!

Then the lashings began.

Radu's smile wilted and died. He looked away. He was safe now. And Lada was proud of him, which had never happened before. He focused on that to ignore the sick feelings twisting his stomach as Aron and Andrei cried out in pain. He wanted his nurse—wanted her to hold and comfort him—and this, too, made him feel ashamed.

Lada watched the whip with a calculating look. "Still," she said. "Fists are faster."

5

1446: Curtea de Arges, Wallachia

DURING THE HEIGHT OF the summer of Lada's twelfth year, when plague descended with the insistent buzz of a thousand blue-black flies, Vlad took Lada and Radu out of the city. Mircea, their torment of an older brother, was in Transylvania soothing tensions. Lada felt gloriously visible riding by her father's side. Radu and the nurse and Bogdan rode behind them, and her father's contingent of guards farther back still. Her father pointed out various features of the countryside—a hidden trail up the side of a mountain, an ancient graveyard with long-forgotten people marked by smooth stones, the way the farmers carved out ditches to pull water from the river into their crops. She drank in his words with more thirst than the greedy soil.

Stopping briefly in the small green city of Curtea de Arges, they paid their respects at a church her father had bestowed his patronage on. Normally, Lada chafed under religious instruction. Though she attended church with her father, it was always a political duty of being seen, being observed, allowing one family or another to be closest to them as a matter of prestige. The priests sang soporifically, the air was cloying, and the light was dim, oppressively filtered through stained glass. They were Orthodox, but her father had political ties to the pope through the Order of the Dragon, so it was even more important that she stand up straight, listen to the priest, do everything exactly as it needed to look to others.

It was a performance that set Lada's teeth on edge.

However, here, in *this* church, her father's name was carved into the wall. It was covered in gold leaf and positioned next to a massive mosaic of Christ on the cross. It made her feel strong. As though God himself knew her family's name.

One day she would build her own church, and God would see her, too.

They continued traveling along the Arges River, which sometimes was narrow and violently churning, sometimes as wide and smooth as glass. It snaked through the land until reaching the mountains. Everything was a green so deep it was nearly black. Dark gray stones and boulders jutted out of the steeply rising slopes, and beneath them the Arges wandered.

It was cooler here than in Tirgoviste, a chill that never quite burned away clinging to the rocks and moss. The looming mountains were so steep that the sun shone directly on the traveling company for only a few hours each day before shadows reclaimed the passes. It smelled of pine and wood and rot—but even the rot smelled rich and healthful, unlike the hidden rot of Tirgoviste.

Late one afternoon, near the end of their journey, their father reached up to an evergreen tree that was growing sideways off a boulder. He broke off a sprig, smelled it, then passed it to Lada with a smile. It was a smile that made her feel as full and dizzy as the mountain air did. A peaceful smile. She had never seen such a smile on her father's face, and being the recipient of it made her heart beat with a frenzied happiness.

"We are that tree," he said, then rode ahead.

Lada pulled on the reins to make her horse, a docile and dull-brown creature, pause. She studied the tree squeezing life out of stone. It was twisted and small but green, growing sideways in defiance of gravity. It lived where nothing had any business thriving.

Lada did not know whether her father meant the two of them, or whether he meant all of Wallachia. In her mind, the two had become indistinguishable. *We are that tree*, she thought, holding the richly scented sprig to her nose. *We defy death, to grow.*

That evening they came to a village snuggled between the river and the mountains. The homes were simple, spare, nothing compared with their castle. But children ran and played in the lanes, and bright bursts of flowers were nurtured in tiny plots. Chickens and sheep roamed freely.

"What about thieves?" Radu asked. In Tirgoviste, their animals were kept carefully penned, with someone assigned to watch them at all hours.

Their nurse made a sweeping motion with her arm to encompass the whole village. "Everyone knows everyone. Who would steal from their neighbor?"

"Yes, because they would be immediately found out and punished," Lada said.

Radu gave her a frowning sort of smile. "Because they care about each other."

They were served food—warm, round loaves of rough bread, chicken blackened on the outside and scalding hot on the inside. Perhaps it was the travel, or the smell of green things all around, but even the food here tasted richer and more real to Lada.

The next morning Lada woke early, the straw under her cot poking through her shift and into her back. With the nurse snoring, and Bogdan and Radu curled up in the corner like puppies, Lada slipped out the window.

The cottage—cozy and neat, the nicest in the village— was built against the tree line, and it took only a handful of steps before Lada was enveloped in a new, secret world, filled with green-filtered light and the constant droning of unseen insects. The ground beneath her bare feet was morning-damp and littered with striped slugs the size of her index finger. Mist clung to sections of the trees, greeting her with almost sentient tendrils. She climbed straight up, picking out a precarious path, winding her way with slow progress toward the top of the nearest jutting peak of solid gray stone.

There were ruins up there, an ancient fortress long since fallen. It teased her with glimpses through the fog, calling to her in a way she could not explain.

She had to get to it.

She climbed down a small ravine, and then straight up the face of the rocky peak. Her feet slipped, and she pressed her face against the stone, breathing hard. Hammered into the stone were the rusted remains of pegs that once must have held a bridge. Lada grabbed one, then another, until she heaved herself up and over the crumbling remains of a wall.

She crossed the foundation, jagged bits of brick and mortar digging into her feet. At the very edge, where even the wall had fallen away, nothing was left but a cobblestoned platform hanging over empty space. Her heart pounded as she looked down at the Arges, now a tiny stream, and the village, mere pebbles for homes. The sun crested the opposite peaks, falling directly on her. It turned the motes in the air to gold, and the mist into brilliant rainbow droplets. A spiky purple flower growing in the old foundation caught her eye. She plucked it, holding it to the light, then pressed it to her cheek.

A sort of rapture descended on her, a knowledge that this moment, this mountain, this sun, were designed for *her.* The closest she had come before to the exultant feeling—both a burning and a lightness in her chest—was when her father had been pleased with her. But this was new, bigger, overwhelming. It was Wallachia—her land, her *mother*—greeting her. This was how church was supposed to feel. She had never experienced the divine spirit within a church's walls, but on this peak, in this countryside, she felt peace and purpose and belonging. This was the glory of God.

This was Wallachia.

This was hers.

After the sun had nearly crossed the canyon and was preparing to disappear behind the mountain, Lada made her way back down. It was harder than the climb up, her feet less sure, her purpose less driving.

When she walked back into the village, footsore and starving, it was to a severe scolding from her frantic nurse. Radu pouted that their whole day had been ruined, and even Bogdan scowled because she had not taken him with her.

She did not care about any of them—she wanted to tell her father how she had felt up on the mountain, how her mother Wallachia had embraced her and filled her with light and warmth. She was filled to bursting with it, and she knew her father would understand. Knew he would be proud.

But he had not even noticed her absence; and at dinner he was cross, complaining of a headache. Lada tucked the flower she had held on to all day beneath the table. Later that night, she pressed it into the small book of saints her nurse had packed for her, next to the sprig from the evergreen tree.

The next day her father left to attend to business elsewhere.

Still, that summer was the best of Lada's life. With her father gone, so, too, was her driving desperation to please him. She splashed in the river with Bogdan and Radu, climbed rocks and trees, tormented the village children and was tormented back. She and Bogdan created a secret language, a bastard version of their native tongue, with Latin, Hungarian, and Saxon mixed in. When Radu asked to play with them, they answered him in their garbled, intricate language. Oftentimes he cried in frustration, which only served to prove they were right to leave such a whining baby out of their games.

One day, high on the side of the mountain, Bogdan declared

his intention to marry Lada. "Why would we marry?" Lada asked.

"Because no other girls are fun. I hate girls. Except for you."

Already Lada understood, in a vague and fearful way, that her own future revolved around marriage. With her mother having long since returned to Moldavia—or fled there, depending on which gossip Lada was unable to avoid overhearing—there was no one she could ask about such things. Even the nurse simply clucked her tongue and told her *sufficient unto the day was the evil thereof,* from which Lada could only understand that marriage was evil.

Sometimes she imagined a shadowy figure standing at a stone altar. She would hold up her hand, and he would take everything she had for himself. She burned with hatred at the very idea of that man, waiting, waiting to make her crawl.

But this was Bogdan. She supposed if she had to marry anyone, it would be him. "Fine. But only if we agree that I am always in charge."

Bogdan laughed. "How is that any different from now?"

After delivering a sharp punch to Bogdan's shoulder, Lada was seized with a sudden and urgent need to eliminate the nightmare of the shadowy man. Here, on this mountain, everything was perfect. "We should marry right now."

"How?"

"Give me your hand."

He obeyed, hissing with pain as she drew her knife across his palm. She did the same to her own hand, then grasped his in hers, the warm wetness mingling between their small, dirty hands. "On this mountain, with my mother Wallachia as witness, I marry Bogdan forever and no other."

He grinned, his big ears glowing red, backlit by the setting sun. "On this mountain, with Lada's mother who is made of rocks and trees watching, I marry Lada forever and no other."

She squeezed his hand harder. "And I am in charge."

"And you are in charge." They released each other and, with a puzzled and disappointed frown, Bogdan sat on the ground. "What now?"

"How should I know? I have never married anyone before."

"We should kiss."

Shrugging with indifference, Lada put her lips against Bogdan's. His were soft and dry, warm against her own, and this close his features blurred, making it look as though he had three eyes. She laughed, and he did, too. They spent the rest of the afternoon with their noses smashed together, telling each other how monstrous they looked with one eye, or three, or whatever other tricks their vision played.

They never spoke of their marriage again, but it took weeks for their palms to heal.

When, after an infinite passage of golden and green days, they finally returned to Tirgoviste, it felt like the opposite of a homecoming. Lada ached for what they had left behind. Someday she would go back to the Arges and rebuild the fortress on that mountain, to live there with her father and Bogdan. Maybe even Radu.

It would be better than Tirgoviste. Anything would be better than Tirgoviste.

6

1447: Tirgoviste, Wallachia

RADU, ELEVEN YEARS OLD and still small for his age, kicked at the hard-crusted snow. He was cold and bored and angry. Lada and Bogdan screamed joyfully as they flew past him, the old metal shield barely holding the two of them. They tumbled off at the bottom of the hill, careering to a stop on the banks of the river. It had taken them ages to hike out here, with the heavy, stolen shield dragged behind them. Even though Radu had helped bring it, they would not give him a turn.

As Lada and Bogdan carried the shield back up the hill for another round, they jabbered in their secret language. The one they still thought Radu could not understand.

"Look at him." Bogdan laughed, his doltish ears violently red in the cold. "I think he will cry."

"He always cries," Lada answered, not even bothering to look at Radu.

This, of course, made Radu's eyes sting with tears. He hated Bogdan. If that stupid oaf were not here, it would be

Radu going down the hill with Lada, Radu who shared her secrets.

He stomped off through the snow, the reflected sun dazzlingly bright. If they caught him with tears in his eyes, he would claim it was the light. They would know the truth, though. On the banks of the river, the water was frozen for as far as he could see. Several children played nearby, some around his age. He edged closer to them, trying to appear as though he were merely going in that direction anyway.

He wanted them to ask him to join.

He wanted it so badly it hurt more than his frozen fingers.

"I have a honey cake for whoever dares go to the middle of the river," the oldest boy declared. His shoeless feet were wrapped in cloth, but he held himself as straight as any boyar child.

"Liar," answered a little girl with long braids trailing from the shawl clutched around her head. "You never have any food, Costin."

The boy lifted his chin, pride and anger visible in the set of his mouth. "I can go farther out than any of you. I dare you. Who is brave enough?"

"I am," Radu said. He immediately regretted it. Cautious by nature, ever fearful of being hurt, Radu shied away from risk. It was part of what Bogdan and Lada mocked him most for. Going out onto a frozen river was not something he would ever choose to do.

He nearly backed away when he heard Bodgan's loud whoop of joy behind him. He stepped forward instead.

The group looked over, only now noticing him. Costin's

eyes narrowed as he took in Radu's fine clothes, lingering on his leather boots. Radu wanted to be his friend. More than that, in a way Radu did not even understand, he wanted to *be* Costin. He wanted to look others full in the face, unafraid, unashamed, even with nothing to his name.

Costin's upper lip pulled back, and Radu was seized with a sudden fear, worse than that of facing the frozen river. He was afraid Costin would ignore him, or tell him to leave. He was afraid these children would look at him and know he was not worth their time.

"If you go farther than I do, you can have my boots," Radu said, his words tumbling out in desperation.

Costin's eyebrows rose, and his expression grew sly. "Do you swear?"

"On all the saints."

The children looked equal parts aghast and impressed with Radu's brash and inappropriate declaration. It was a very big swear, as there were more saints than Radu could ever remember. And he knew he was not supposed to invoke them for something like this. Radu stood straighter, mimicking Costin's aggressive stance.

"And what if you go farther than me?" Costin's tone indicated he thought it impossible.

Radu smiled, going along with Costin's obvious lie. "The honey cake."

Costin nodded, and they stepped from the bank to the river. This close to shore, the ice was an opaque white and littered with small pebbles. Radu shifted his feet hesitantly, trying to get a feel for how his boots might slip.

Laughing, Costin glided forward, sliding his cloth-wrapped feet along as though he had done this a hundred times before. He probably had.

Studying Costin, Radu continued to slide forward. He began making better progress, though he still lagged far behind. That was fine. Radu did not actually want to beat the boy, since he was certain Costin had no honey cake to offer. When people could not meet expectations, they got either ashamed or angry, Radu had found. He suspected Costin would be the type to get angry, and he wanted to be his friend, not his enemy.

He had another pair of boots at home, anyway. Nurse would scold him, but she would not tell his father. And she was always kind and gentle to him after a good scolding.

They had gotten several body lengths from the riverbank when a loud crack echoed around them. Radu froze.

Costin looked back, dark eyes flashing, chin lifted. "The middle is this way, coward." He took another few steps and, with a shattering sound, fell through the ice.

"Costin!" Radu shouted, edging toward the break. The boy bobbed back up, scrambling for a grip on the ice. Radu dropped to his belly and scooted forward. He could nearly reach Costin's hands, but he heard the ice beneath him weakening.

Someone grabbed his ankle, yanking him back.

"Wait!" he screamed, holding out his hands to Costin, who had leveraged himself onto his belly but could not get the rest of his body out of the water. He reached for Radu, but it was too late. Costin's eyes widened in terror, his face as white as the ice, as Radu was pulled away.

"Wait, wait, we have to help him!" Radu tried to scramble

to his feet, but another hand took hold of his other ankle and slammed him down. His chin bounced against the ice, teeth biting into his tongue and drawing blood. Then he was thrown onto the bank of the river, with Lada slapping his face.

"What were you thinking?" she screamed.

"We have to help him!"

"No!"

"He will drown! Let me go!"

She picked him up by his collar, shaking him. "You could have died!"

"He will die!"

"He is nothing! Your life is worth a hundred of his, you understand? Never, ever risk it again for someone else."

She was still shaking him, jarring his head, so he could not see the river, could not see whether or not Costin had made it. He could hear the other children shouting, but they sounded far away and indistinct over the pounding of his pulse. Radu finally looked at Lada, expecting to see fury, but instead she looked . . . unfamiliar. Her eyes were brimming with tears she would have mocked him for.

"Never do that again." She stood and pulled him up beside her. Bogdan took his other arm, and they dragged him away. Radu tried to look back, but Lada grabbed his neck and forced him to keep his gaze forward. He expected her to walk ahead of him on the long, cold trek home, or to yell at him. Instead, she stayed at his side, silent.

"He was fine," she finally said, after several minutes of listening to Radu sniffle. "He climbed out."

"He did?" Radu shivered with hope, trembling all over.

Lada pointed to the shield. "Sit." She made Bogdan pull Radu on it. She called Bogdan so many terms for an ass that Radu forgot Costin's face and fell over laughing. That night, she sat close to him while they ate supper in front of the fire, picking at him, fussing over him in her way.

When she thought he was sleeping, she crept into his room. Radu did not sleep much, always awake and worrying over something. But he lay as still as possible, keeping his breathing even, curious as to what she would do.

She sat beside his bed for a long while. Finally, she put a hand on his shoulder and whispered, "You are *mine*."

Radu had been thinking about the way Lada sounded when she told him that Costin had escaped the river. The tone of her voice, the lack of an edge. He was almost certain she had lied. He fell asleep, wrapped in the secure warmth of her next to him and nagged by guilt over how happy the day had made him.

Still made him.

7

THE SPRING AFTER SHE had nearly lost Radu to the icy
river, Lada lay on her back, staring at the leafy branches
overhead, boughs laced together so tightly everything was filtered through vibrant green. Their tutor droned on—Latin,
today—and Radu dutifully repeated everything. He was almost twelve years old, and she nearing thirteen. Something
about the passage of time and the addition of years to her
name filled her with dread. She was not enough. Not yet. All
this time and still she had so far to go.

But after seven years of study—seven years in this city, in
the castle—she could read, write, and speak Latin as well as
anyone. It was the language of contracts and letters and God,
formal and stiff in her mouth. Wallachian was considered a
low language. It was a spoken language, rarely written.

But oh, how lovely it tasted on the tongue.

"Ladislav," the tutor prompted. He was a young man,
clean-shaven because he did not own land and thus was not
allowed to grow facial hair. Lada found him insufferable, but

her father insisted she be educated alongside Radu. In fact, her father's exact words had been *It is a waste to educate the mewling worm, but at least we can include Lada, who has a brain worth shaping. Pity she's a girl.*

Smarter, stronger, bigger. She had never forgotten the reasons her father listed that she could not have hoped to beat him all those years ago. Her goal since then had been to earn his love, to show him that she could be all those things. It was a challenge she chased relentlessly. Because on the other side of that challenge—when she had achieved smarter, stronger, bigger—she was certain her father would look at her with more pride and love than he ever directed at her older brother, Mircea. He was twenty now, a grown man, and her father's heir. Mircea campaigned when battles called for it, soothed tension between boyar families, ate with her father, planned with her father, rode with her father. He was the right hand of Wallachia; it was his hand that was always pulling hair, pinching skin, finding little ways to hurt someone that no one else could see.

And someday he would be prince.

If he lived that long.

But before then, before it was too late, Lada *would* take Mircea's place in their father's heart. That day he had returned the knife to her and pronounced her the daughter of Wallachia had been the first time he had ever *truly* looked at her, and the memory of that was both a pleasure and an agony she had been nurturing ever since.

She repeated the last sentence her tutor had said in Latin, then said it in Hungarian and Turkish for good measure.

"Very good." The tutor shifted uncomfortably on the wooden stool he carried with him. "Though we would all be better served learning indoors."

Her last tutor had slapped her for demanding to go outside. She broke his nose. This tutor never did more than make gentle suggestions, which were summarily ignored.

"This is my country." Lada stood, stretching her arms over her head, stiff sleeves straining against her movements. She did not like staying in the castle to study. Every day she made them ride out from the walled inner city, past the smaller homes and then the hovels and then the filthy, seedy outskirts of life clinging to the capital, into the fresh, green countryside. The horses were left in fields brilliant with purple flowers, while she and Radu studied in the shade of dense, pale-barked trees.

"The country is not *yours*." Radu scraped a stick against the ground to write out his Latin verbs.

"Is this not Wallachia?"

Radu nodded. He had a smudge of dirt on his nose. It made her brother look small and ridiculous. It irritated Lada. He was always with her, an appendage to her life, and she never could decide how to feel about him. Sometimes, when a smile broke across his face like sun reflecting off a stream, or she saw him relax into sleep, she was filled with an unaccountable sort of ache. It terrified her.

"Sit up straight." She tugged on his chin and wiped his nose with her shirt so viciously that he cried out and tried to get away. She gripped his chin tighter. "This is Wallachia, and I am the daughter of Wallachia. Our father is the prince of Wallachia. This is *my* country."

Radu finally stopped struggling, glaring at her instead. Tears pooled in his big eyes. He was so pretty, this brother of hers. His was a face that made women stop in the lanes to coo at him. When he flashed his dimpled smile, the cook gave him extra servings of whatever he loved best. And when Lada saw him hurt, she wanted to protect him, which made her angry. He was weak, and protecting him felt like a weakness. Mircea certainly suffered no such weakness on her behalf.

She let go of Radu's chin and rubbed the back of her head. Last month Mircea had yanked her hair so hard he had left a bald spot, which only now was starting to fill in. *Girls should know their place*, he had hissed.

Lada lifted her face to a ray of sunshine fighting its way through the leaves. *This*. This *is my place*. Her father had given it to her, and Wallachia would always be theirs.

Radu kicked at his scribblings in the dirt. "Not everyone wants the country to be ours."

"Can we return to—" the tutor started, but Lada held up a hand, silencing him.

Dropping to a crouch, she picked up a round stone, one perfectly fitted to her palm. Balanced. Heavy. Spinning, she launched the stone through the air. A thud was followed by a sharp cry of anger, and then laughter. Bogdan stood from where he had been creeping along the ground, trying to sneak up on them.

"Try harder, Bogdan." Lada's sneer shifted into a smile. "Come sit. Radu is mangling Latin."

"Radu is doing very well." The tutor frowned at Bogdan. "And I am not employed to educate the son of a nursemaid."

Lada stared down at him with all the cold, imperious

command she was born to. "You are employed to do as you are told."

The tutor, who was very fond of his straight, unblemished nose, sighed wearily and continued the lesson.

———•———

"Now in Hungarian," Lada commanded Bogdan, her walk quick and assured down the hallway. Tirgoviste was set up like a great Byzantine city: castle in the middle, manors of the boyars circling it, dwellings of the artisans and performers who earned the patronage of the boyars circling that, and then, outside the massive stone walls, everyone else. Within the walls, homes were painted a dazzling array of reds and blues, yellows and greens. Riots of flowers and tinkling fountains competed for attention. But the stench of human waste lurked beneath everything, and the poor and sick masses seemed to creep ever closer to the inner city. Lada had even seen their shacks built against the wall itself.

Lada and Radu were not allowed to spend time in the outer rims of Tirgoviste. They were bundled and rushed through the streets whenever they left the city, catching only glimpses of ramshackle homes and suspicious, sunken eyes.

They lived in the castle, which, for all it tried, could not pretend at the splendor of Constantinople. It was dim, dark, narrow. The walls were thick, the windows slits, the hallways labyrinthine. The castle's construction proved the pools and gardens and brightly clothed bodies were lies. Tirgoviste was no glittering Byzantium. Even Byzantium was no longer Byzantium. Like everything else this close to the Ottoman Empire, Wallachia had become a stomping ground for stronger armies, a pathway smashed by armored feet again and again and again.

Lada put her hand against the wall, feeling the cold that never quite left the stones. The castle was both the goal and the trap. She had never felt safe here. She knew from the snapping tone and tense demeanor of her father that he felt constantly threatened, too. She longed to live somewhere else, in the countryside, in the mountains, somewhere defensive where they could see their enemies coming for miles. Somewhere her father could relax and have time to speak with her.

Two Janissaries walked past. They were elite Ottoman soldiers, taken as young boys from other countries in the name of taxes, trained and groomed to serve the sultan and his god. Their ceremonial caps, bronze with flowing white flaps, bobbed as they laughed and talked, perfectly at ease. Her father insisted the castle was a symbol of power, but he refused to see the true symbolism of Tirgoviste. It did not give them power—it gave others power over them. They were trapped here, prisoners to the demands of the powerful boyar families. Worse, despite her father's anointment to crusader by the pope, they were still a vassal state to the Ottoman Empire. Her father sacrificed money, lives, and his own honor to the Ottoman sultan, Murad, for the privilege of this throne.

Bogdan babbled on in the language of their Hungarian neighbors to the west, telling Lada about his day. She pushed into the grand hall, occasionally correcting his pronunciation. The two Janissaries were there, lounging against a wall. Lada spared them only a brief glare. They were like a rock in her slipper, constantly irritating.

Bulgaria and Serbia had similar arrangements with the

sultan, paying money and boys to the Ottoman Empire in return for stability, while Hungary and Transylvania fought to avoid being vassals. The tension between borders demanded Vlad's constant attention, forced him to leave for weeks on end, and gave him pains in his stomach that made him nasty and irritable.

Lada *hated* the Ottomans.

One of the Janissaries raised a thick eyebrow. Though he looked Bulgarian, maybe Serbian, he spoke Turkish. "Ugly thing, the girl. The prince will be lucky to find her a match. Or perhaps a nunnery with low standards."

Lada continued as though she had not heard, but Bogdan stopped. He bristled. The soldier noted his understanding and stepped toward them in interest. "You speak Turkish?"

Lada grabbed Bogdan's hand, answering with perfect pronunciation. "One must learn Turkish if one is to command the castle dogs."

The soldier laughed. "You would be right at home with them, little bitch."

Lada had her knife out before the soldier or his companion noticed. She was too short to reach the man's neck, so she satisfied herself with a vicious slash across his arm. He shouted in pain and surprise, jumping back and fumbling with his sword.

Lada gestured, and Bogdan threw himself at the soldier's legs, tripping him. Now that he was on the floor, his neck was an easy target. Lada pressed the knife beneath his chin, then looked up at the other soldier. He was a pale, lean man— almost a boy, really—with shrewd brown eyes. He had one hand on his sword, the long, curved blade favored by the Ottomans.

"Only a fool would attack the prince's daughter in her own home. Two soldiers against a harmless girl." Lada bared her teeth at him. "Very bad for treaties."

The lean soldier took his hand off his sword and stepped back, his smile a perfect match to his weapon. He bowed, sweeping out an arm in deference.

Bogdan jumped up from the floor, trembling with rage. Lada shook her head at him. She should have left him out of this. Lada had a sense for power—the fine threads that connected everyone around her, the way those threads could be pulled, tightened, wrapped around someone until they cut off the blood supply.

Or snapped entirely.

She had few threads at her disposal. She wanted all of them. Bogdan had almost none, and what threads he did have were his simply by virtue of his being a boy. People already respected him more than they did his mother the nurse. It made Lada's jaw ache, the ease with which life greeted Bogdan.

She jabbed her knife, poking the prone soldier once more for good measure, but not quite hard enough to break the skin. Then she stood straight, smoothing the front of her dress. "You are slaves," she said. "There is nothing you can do to hurt me."

The lean soldier's eyes narrowed thoughtfully as he looked over Lada's shoulder, where Bogdan loomed. She grabbed his arm and walked out of the room with him.

Bogdan was fuming. "We should tell your father."

"No!"

"Why? He should know how they disrespected you!"

"They are beneath our notice! They are less than the mud. You do not get angry at the mud for clinging to your shoe. You wipe it off and never look at it again."

"Your father should know."

Lada scowled. It was not that she feared punishment for her actions. What she feared was that her father would find out how the Janissaries viewed her and realize they were right. That she was a girl. That she was worth less than the castle dogs until the day she could be married off. She *had* to be the smartest, constantly surprising and delighting him. She was terrified that the day she stopped amusing him would be the day he remembered he had no use for a daughter.

"Will we be punished?" Bogdan's face, as familiar and beloved as her own, wrinkled in concern. He was growing like a spring shoot, so much taller now. As far back as she could remember he had been at her side. He was *hers*—her playmate, her confidant, her brother in spirit if not blood. Her husband. Where Radu was weak, Bogdan was steady, strong. She tugged one of his big ears. They stuck out from his head like handles on a jug, and were more precious to her than any of the fine things in the castle.

"The Janissaries have only what power we decide they do." She meant it as a reassurance, but her mind stuck on the curved sword that hung above her father's throne. A gift from the sultan to her father. A promise and a threat, like most things in Tirgoviste were.

The next morning Lada awoke late, eyes heavy with sleep and mind muddled by nightmares. There was a strange noise, a hiccuping sort of moan, coming from the other side of her bedroom door. Angry, she stomped out into the chambers that connected her room to Radu's, where their nurse slept.

The nurse had all her soft parts hidden as she held herself, rocking. She was the source of the noise. Radu patted her back, looking lost.

"What happened?" Lada asked, panic rising in her chest like a handful of bees.

"Bogdan." Radu held up his hands helplessly. "The Janissaries took him."

The bees turned into a swarm. Lada ran from the room, straight to her father's study, where she found him bent over maps and ledgers.

"Father!" It came out breathless, desperate. Small. All her efforts to force him to see her as something other than a little girl unraveled in that single word, but she could not stop herself. He would help. He would fix this. "The Janissaries have kidnapped Bogdan!"

Her father looked up, setting down his quill and wiping his fingers on a white handkerchief. It came away smudged with black, and he dropped it to the floor, discarded. His voice was measured. "The Janissaries told me they had some trouble with one of the castle *dogs*. An injury to a soldier. They requested we supply a replacement who had been taught Turkish. It is a fortunate turn of events for the son of a nursemaid, is it not?"

Lada felt her lower lip tremble. That feeling she got in her heart when her father looked at her—that frantic, desperate pride—twisted and soured. He knew what Bogdan was to her. He knew, and he let the Janissaries take her dearest friend anyway.

He did not care. And now he watched for her reaction, weighing her.

She clenched her shaking hands into fists. She nodded.

"See that the dogs behave themselves from now on." Her father's eyes cut straight through her, releasing the bees and leaving her echoing and empty inside. She curtsied, then walked stiffly out, collapsing against the wall and shoving her fists against her eyes to push the tears back inside.

This was her fault. She could have walked away from the Janissaries. Radu would have. But not her. She had to defy them, had to taunt them. And one of them—the thin one— had known just by looking at her the best way to hurt her.

All her tiny threads snapped and circled back around her heart, squeezing too tightly. This was her fault, but her father had betrayed her. He could have said no—should have said no, should have stopped it, should have shown the Janissaries that it was he, not them, who ruled Wallachia.

He had chosen not to.

Her mind stuck on the image of his discarded handker-chief. Dirtied and dropped, forgotten now that it was not pristine. Her father was wasteful. Her father was weak.

Bogdan deserved better.

She deserved better.

Wallachia deserved better.

She went back to the mountain in her mind, stood on

its peak, remembered the way the sun had embraced her. She would never toss aside her country the way her father had. She would protect it.

A small sob threatened to break free. What could she do? She had no power.

Yet, she vowed. She had no power *yet.*

8

RADU HAD ALWAYS HATED Bogdan, hated that he stole Lada's time and attention, hated the way he tugged on Radu's hair, or pulled his ear, or sneered when Radu scraped a knee and could not help crying.

Hated most of all that Bogdan ignored him the rest of the time.

And now Bogdan had stolen Radu's nurse, leaving a hollow shell behind. It was Bogdan's own fault he was gone. He had to ruin everything else on his way out, too.

Radu's rooms were a suffocating sepulchre to Bogdan. His nurse wept in her chair, sewing basket dormant beside her. Lada was worse, though. Normally when something did not go her way, she became a torrent of rage, a sweeping storm that flew in and overwhelmed everything, working itself out as quickly as it had descended.

With Bogdan's loss, however, Lada was silent. Staring. Calm.

It terrified Radu.

He tucked himself into a corner of the stables, a dark,

musty spot where only someone looking could find him. No one was ever looking for Radu. A spider crawled down his hand and he lifted it, gently placing the spider on a wood beam where it would be safe.

Two swaggering Janissaries led their sweating and quivering horses into the stables. Radu watched through narrowed eyes as they efficiently wiped down the horses, watered them, and got them fresh feed.

When Mircea returned from riding, he always jumped down, threw his reins at a servant, and walked off. Mircea whipped his horses, too, the angry furrows in their flanks marking them as his favorites. Once, Radu had been watching when no stableboy was present. Mircea simply got off his horse, a long gash on its leg seeping blood, and left.

Radu wanted to hate all Janissaries out of loyalty to Lada, but he liked the way they took care of their animals. He also liked their funny hats, and the way they always had someone. There was never a Janissary by himself.

The two men had been talking in low, comfortable voices the whole time. "Have you noticed the new animal in here?" one asked. His back was to Radu.

The other Janissary, a young man with pockmarked skin and dark eyes, shook his head.

"A shy creature. I should think he's very valuable, but I have yet to see anyone take him out for a ride. Pity."

"Oh, do you mean the pale one? Big eyes? Curly hair? Hides in a corner?"

Fear seized Radu. They knew he was here. What would they do to him?

"Yes, that one! Seems a sad little thing. Perhaps if he made friends with some of the other animals . . ." The Janissary straightened, and turned his head, smiling with kind eyes at Radu's hiding spot. "Would you like to help us with the horses?"

Radu did not move.

"This one is very gentle. See?" The Janissary nuzzled the horse's head with his own. The horse huffed right in his face, and both soldiers laughed. "Come on, come meet your stable-mate."

Radu shuffled forward, pressed against the stall doors, eyes darting to the entrance.

The Janissary held out a stiff-bristled brush. "Here now, make yourself useful. We have to bend over so far to reach the lower spots. Help save our poor aching backs."

The brush was heavy in Radu's hand. He reached out with it, hesitant, barely touching the horse. He had been trained to ride, but Mircea had been in charge, which meant Lada became wild and competitive and Radu got yelled at the whole time. He still had a mark on the back of his neck from where Mircea whipped him once. Mircea claimed he had been aiming for the horse.

The kind-eyed Janissary put his hand over Radu's, showing him how to stroke, how much pressure to use. "I take it you are not a stableboy."

Radu shook his head, keeping his eyes down.

"Oh, I know who our little creature is!" The pockmarked Janissary grinned, a gap-toothed smile. "Do they keep all the little princes in the stables? What odd customs Wallachia has! I trust you like eating oats?"

Radu knew he was being teased, but it felt kind. Playful. He ventured a smile. "I prefer cake."

Both Janissaries laughed, one patting him on the shoulder. Unlike when Mircea did it, it was simply a pat on the shoulder, and not a disguised blow.

Radu helped the soldiers with the rest of their chores, asking a few questions but mostly listening. When they were finished, they told him to meet them there earlier the next day to help exercise the horses. He practically skipped back to his rooms, breathless and flushed with happiness. Lada, thankfully, was nowhere to be found. His nurse was in her usual spot. Radu climbed onto her chair and snuggled into her side, putting his hand on the back of her neck. She sighed, not looking at him.

"Did you know," Radu said, as carefully as he had set the spider down, "that Janissaries are very prestigious in Ottoman society?"

His nurse frowned, and looked at him for the first time in days.

"They are educated and trained and even paid. Everyone admires them. I was talking to one today who told me his mother gave him to the Janissaries to save him from a life breaking himself to bits against the rocky soil. He said ..." Radu paused, his voice getting softer. "He said he was grateful. That it was the best thing that could have happened to him. He always has enough to eat, and he has plenty of friends, and money to spend when he wants to. He said he is smarter and stronger than he ever would have been. He says he prays every day, out of gratitude to and love for his mother."

The Janissary had not actually said any of that. But his nurse held Radu's hand so tightly it hurt. He did not move away. She nodded, wiping at her eyes. "Be a good boy, hand me my sewing basket."

Radu settled in and watched her trembling hands get surer with every stitch.

———◆———

The air was heavy and thick with humidity as Radu dragged a stick along the cobbled path behind the castle that led to the stables. He hummed happily to himself, but the humming was cut short when someone cuffed him on the back of his head.

"Where are you going?" Mircea asked.

Radu did not answer. Silence was the best tactic with Mircea.

Their father came sweeping along behind Mircea, and Radu shrank back even further. He had not spoken to his father in . . . he did not know how long. His father's black eyes passed over him as though he were not even there. Then Vlad blinked, and finally focused on his youngest son.

"Radu." He sounded vaguely questioning, as though reciting some fact he could not quite remember.

Behind him came several boyars, mostly from the Danesti family, their long-simmering rivals. Andrei was with them, skittering and withdrawn as he always was now. Dressed for riding, they all paused, staring at Radu.

Radu wished they were women. He had a much easier time with women. Men were harsh and hard and unmoving in the face of a quick, brilliant smile. Lada would know what to do. She would scowl and stick her nose in the air and dare any of them to think they were better than her. Radu stood straighter and pretended to be her.

"Can the boy ride?" one of the oldest Danesti boyars asked, his tone bored but with a slight challenge.

His father considered Radu, eyes hard. "Of course he can."

Radu hurried along in the wake of his father and brother. He worried that he was not invited and would be punished, but he worried even more about what would happen if he was expected to come and failed to comply.

His Janissary friends were in the back of the stable, waiting for him. Lazar, the one with the gap-toothed smile and easy laugh, took in the scene—and Radu's terrified expression—with a quick look. Radu had been riding with them nearly every day, and under their playful tutelage he had become comfortable, even skilled, in the saddle. He had also perhaps told them too much about his family. He hung his head as the horses that had been prepared for the riding party were brought out. There was not one for him, making it clear to everyone that he was not intended to be a part of this. Or a part of anything, for that matter.

As Radu watched his father mount, shame welling up and threatening to leak from his eyes, Lazar cleared his throat. "Your horse." He held out the reins and nodded respectfully, as though Radu were more than a forgotten boy.

Radu took the reins, grinning, but then closed his mouth quickly and imitated Lazar's detached formality. "Thank you." He mounted as smoothly as he could, sitting straight in the saddle and nudging his horse forward to be level with Mircea's. He clenched his fists around the leather straps so his fingers would not tremble. The party headed toward the forest, keeping together as they rode through an open field.

His father looked over and, as though once again surprised to see him existing, took in Radu's excellent form. Radu's chest swelled with pride to be here, riding with his father and his older brother, at the head of a group of boyars. Where he belonged. He lifted his chin higher and met his father's eyes, anticipating a smile.

"Do not embarrass me," his father said, tone flat, before urging his horse forward without another glance.

Radu's chest collapsed, all his pride and hope turning ugly and sour in his stomach. The rest of the ride was a sweaty and uncomfortable slog among trees buzzing with insects. He let his horse fall back, ending up near the rear of the group with the less important boyars, who grumbled and gossiped among themselves, oblivious to his presence.

Twice branches whipped Radu's face, leaving it stinging. But he did not cry out, and he did not break form. He listened to the conversations around him, and he noted when complaints were a bit too pointedly directed at the head of the group.

He embarrassed no one. He remained unnoticed and invisible.

It was, apparently, both the least and the most he could do for his father.

9

LADA COULD NOT BREATHE in the castle. A miasma of anxious fear hovered over everything. People gathered in dark corners, whispering. Her father threw banquet after banquet, trying to appease the boyars, who were growing increasingly open in their hostilities. Everywhere she went eyes followed her. Bogdan had been a sort of shield—always at her side, always obedient. Losing him would have been difficult enough, but she had also lost the love and worship she had nurtured for her father.

Now she could see how little her father actually cared for Wallachia. Everything he did was for himself, to protect his own power at whatever cost. The armor she imagined his love had given her had been stripped away, and without it, she was naked and vulnerable. Every day was precarious, every smile and interaction dangerous. One false move and perhaps she, too, would be discarded. Her father still favored her, and she suspected that, in his own way, he truly cared about her, but his love was as contemptible and flimsy as one of his endless string of false political promises.

She would be thirteen this summer. Her mother had married at thirteen.

Lada's mouth tasted like blood and iron all the time now. It tasted like defeat. As she walked through the corridors one evening on her way to the kitchens, a boyar knocked her out of his way without so much as an apology. It made her feel small and unimportant.

She *was* small and unimportant.

She hurried to the gardens behind the castle courtyard, dunked her head in a fountain, and swished water through her mouth to rinse everything away. Muffled screams caught her attention. She knew that sound well, as she was usually the one causing it. A fierce possessiveness welled in her chest and she stormed through the garden, closing in on Radu and his assailant.

Mircea had Radu by the back of his neck and was pushing him deeper and deeper into the unforgiving thorns of a dense rosebush. Mircea was strong and thick like their father, but his facial hair was still patchy. Sometimes Lada caught him standing over a reflecting pool and tugging on his sparse mustache like he could make the symbol of his status grow faster.

"What did you hear?" Mircea hissed, unaware of his audience. Radu screamed as Mircea pushed harder.

"Nothing, nothing," Radu insisted.

Lada silently unsheathed the knife she always wore under her sash and held it behind her back. "There you are." She scowled. "Father has been asking for you."

Mircea looked over, face open and pleasant as though he had not been caught torturing their brother. "Has he?"

"Something about the boyars." Lada lifted her free hand and waved it in disinterest. It was a good lie. There was always *something* about the boyars that needed attending to. She plucked a rose and held it to her face. She hated the way roses smelled, their sweetness too fragile. She wanted a garden of evergreens. A garden of stones. A garden of swords. She smiled conspiratorially at Mircea. "He seemed angry."

Mircea met her smile. "He is always angry."

"Perhaps his cap is too tight."

"Perhaps his breeches are too small."

"Perhaps," Lada said, noting that Mircea had relaxed his grip on Radu's neck and that Radu had the sense to stay perfectly still, "what is *inside* his breeches is too small."

Mircea let go of Radu, throwing his head back and roaring a laugh. He clapped his hand on Lada's shoulder, squeezing too hard. "Be careful, Sister. You have dirt inside that mouth."

He directed one vicious kick at Radu's prone backside, then hurried past them into the castle. There was meanness at Mircea's core. Lada had watched him torment the castle dogs for sport, causing pain for no reason. She did not understand it. Why do anything without purpose? She had no love whatsoever for him, but she had a healthy portion of fear.

"Come on." Lada yanked Radu free of the bush, his sleeves catching and tearing on the thorns. Based on his cries, his skin caught and tore as well. She pulled him along after her, out of the garden and through the gate into an abandoned stable, empty save for the overwhelming odor of rotting hay. Any extra horses they once had had been sold to cover their father's spiraling debts. Most of the main stable was occupied by Janissary horses, boyar horses, horses of their debtors.

"If Mircea finds father, he will know I lied." Lada sat on the floor, skirts bunching beneath her.

Radu wiped his nose on his sleeve. "Why did you help me?"

"Why do you always need help?" Exasperated, she directed him to sit next to her and examined his face. The cuts were shallow, nothing serious. She pulled a few thorns from his arms, not pausing at his whimpers. She was never kind or tender with Radu, but what she did was for his own good. He was too delicate for this world, and the sooner he changed, the easier life would be for him. "What was Mircea so angry about?"

Radu shifted, angling his face away from her. "Nothing."

She grabbed his chin and forced him to look at her. A stray beam of light hit his ears, and she felt Bogdan's loss and her loneliness like a pain in her stomach. Sighing, she put an arm around Radu and drew him closer. Would their father send Radu away, too? Would he let Mircea, the eldest and most favored, kill him?

The pale spring day was chilly, and her wet hair left her shivering. "You have to stay away from Mircea," she said. "He is meaner than Father's falcon, and far dumber."

Radu sniffled a laugh. "And far uglier."

"And far more likely to carry fleas."

They were quiet for a while, breathing together, when Radu spoke again. "I was hiding behind the drapes. I heard him speaking with a Danesti family boyar."

In the fifteen years before their father took the throne,

there had been ten princes, alternating between two families: the Basarab line, now out of contention with no heirs of age, and the Danesti line. The Danesti family was not happy with the Draculesti usurpers, first Lada and Radu's uncle Alexandru and now their father. And, as history proved, being prince was a very tenuous position in Wallachia.

"Why was he speaking with the Danestis?"

Radu squirmed, and Lada realized she was squeezing his shoulder so tightly she was hurting him. She let go, and he said, "There is talk of a boyar coalition. They mentioned Hunyadi."

Lada's skin prickled. Hunyadi was the military leader of Transylvania and Hungary, their constantly shifting border countries to the west. Where her father had sworn to fight the Ottomans, Hunyadi actually *did*. He had beaten the sultan on numerous occasions.

Lada could never decide what to think of Hunyadi. She sensed that he was a threat to her father's power, but she could not help seeing that Hunyadi was the man her father was supposed to be. She listened in when she could, stole her father's letters and annotated maps, and studied Hunyadi's strategies. He was fascinating. He fought like a rabid dog at unexpected times, and then disappeared to harass the enemy again later. Even with inferior numbers and forces, he usually wore the Ottomans down.

He was the Draculestis' ally, but he was also dangerous and did not look kindly on her father's double-dealing. "I thought the boyars supported Ottoman ties. They encouraged Father to seek their help."

"Most of the boyars are unhappy. They see how successful Hunyadi's campaigns against the sultan are. They want to ally only with him now. There is talk of a betrothal."

Lada stiffened. "Who?" she asked, though she knew the answer.

"Matthias, Hunyadi's son."

A sharp pain beneath her fingernails alerted Lada to the fact that she was scraping them against the rotting wood floor so hard that slivers were stabbing into her palm. She would be married to grant someone else an advantage. And when that alliance fell through, as all alliances did, she would be shuffled to the side. Left in a convent, abandoned and cut off.

An image of their mother, nearly forgotten since she had left them, crawled through Lada's mind. She recoiled from the memory of that woman. Powerless. Broken. An abandoned alliance had left her a prisoner in someone else's home, someone else's country.

Lada squeezed her hand shut around the splinters, warm drops of blood pooling in her palm, covering the scar of her playacting with Bogdan. There would be no happy marriage of equals for her, no one who would agree to let her rule. "I will *never* marry."

Radu pried her hand open and attempted to dig out some of the slivers. She let him. He was far gentler with her wounds than she had been with his.

"How do you know all this?" She considered him in wonder. She had assumed Radu spent his days dreaming. His big eyes had a way of looking pleasantly vacant, as though he were not even aware of conversations going on right in front of him. While Lada was fixated on tactics and Hunyadi, she had studiously ignored the intrigues of the boyars. She saw now that was an error.

"People forget I am listening. I am always listening."

"We should tell father about Mircea's plans."

Radu went perfectly still, head down. Lada did not have to see his expression to know how he looked. Terrified. "He will be angry. And Mircea will kill me. I am scared to die."

"Everyone dies sometime. And I will not let Mircea kill you. If anyone is going to kill you, it will be me. Understand?"

Radu nodded, snuggling into her shoulder. "Will you protect me?"

"Until the day I kill you." She jabbed a finger into his side, where he was most ticklish, and he squealed with pained laughter. The look he gave her was one she recognized—the same hungry, desperate look she used to give their father. Radu loved her, and he wanted her to feel the same for him. For the first time since he had been introduced into her life, placid and beautiful and worthless, she found Radu interesting. Perhaps even useful. And more than that, in Bogdan's absence, she felt like someone belonged to her again.

10

The scratches on Radu's face and arms from Mircea's garden attack had faded to thin red lines. He had lied to his nurse, told her that he tripped and fell into a bush. Reporting on Mircea never accomplished anything.

But this time . . . this time perhaps it would. Lada had told him to talk to their father. And he could.

He would.

Radu paced in their chambers. The information he had about Mircea conspiring with the boyars would hurt all Radu's enemies. Mircea, first and foremost. Oh, Radu would love to see him fall from grace. And the Danesti family were the main aggressors behind the coalition, so if they were punished or ostracized, it would hurt Andrei and Aron.

Of course, Andrei and Aron avoided him now, avoided nearly everyone. They were already outcasts in the court after their false crime and real punishment. But Radu still feared that someday they would trace it back to him. He had made his nurse arrange for the servant boy who had helped him to be sent with a family to Transylvania, lest the boy reveal

Radu's deception. He lied to himself that Emil was better off, but Radu knew it had been entirely selfish.

But beneath every other motivation—the desire to hurt Mircea, to punish the Danestis—was this: if Radu heroically revealed the plot, his father would finally see him. He would know that Radu was smart, that Radu was valuable. And Lada would be proud.

Lada entered their chambers, glaring at him. "Sit down. You make me dizzy."

He did not sit, too flushed with excitement. "I am going to tell Father about Mircea and the boyar coalition. He will be so proud of me!"

"He will be furious."

"Not with me!"

"Do you imagine him thanking you? Embracing you warmly, thrilled with the news that his own son is working against him? You are a fool."

All Radu's careful hopes were fleeing. He shook his head. "He will be glad to know! He will thank me!"

"We cannot always predict how our father will respond." She looked at the corner, where their nurse's basket of mending sat beneath her chair. The nurse used to darn Bogdan's socks, cursing him for wearing them out so quickly. She no longer had that task.

A dark realization seized Radu. "You are jealous. You want Father to see only you."

Lada laughed, a bitter sound. "I do not want Father to see me offering him a conspiracy to take away even more of his power. You are welcome to that." She stomped out of the room.

Radu found her later that day, standing on the narrow walled ledge that surrounded the tower. "Did you tell him?" she asked without looking at her brother.

Radu did not answer.

"Coward." But she angled her body so he could stand next to her. "We will think of some way to reveal the truth without entangling you in the mess. You do not want to draw Father's attention as being part of this."

"But how?"

"We need a little time. We have information, which means we have power. We must think of—" She stopped, narrowing her eyes at something in the distance.

A man rode down the main street, surrounded by soldiers. As the man got closer, Radu saw that he smiled, one hand uplifted in a gesture of friendship. His men, grim and hardened, with hands hovering near their swords, promised something else entirely. Several flags Radu did not recognize hung limply from poles carried at the group's rear. "Who is he?"

"Hunyadi," Lada said, the name dropping from her lips like a curse.

They watched from the tower and, though Radu knew he was supposed to hate Hunyadi, he found himself in awe. Hunyadi rode into another man's kingdom and the people he passed smiled and bowed. When Radu's father was on horseback, he rode hunched over and leaning forward. Whether to arrive faster or to make himself a smaller target, Radu did not know. Hunyadi sat straight in his saddle, shoulders back, chest presented to the world in defiance of assassins' arrows.

"We are too late," Lada said. "All your information is worthless now."

Radu's eyelids felt heavy with shame. He had never managed to be useful to his father, and now, because of his cowardice and delay, he had failed once again.

Lada turned toward the door. "Well, we may as well see what doom the Transylvanian terror brings with him."

Radu tripped over his own feet in his haste to keep up with Lada as she threw herself down the tower steps and into the great hall before Hunyadi arrived. She paused at the entrance and Radu slipped past her, finding a dim corner where he often stood unobserved. She elbowed him sharply in the side, and he made room for her.

A few minutes later, their father rushed in. His hat was askew, his mustache so recently curled Radu could still smell the oil. He sat down on his ornate throne, fixing his hat and breathing heavily.

He was sweating.

In that moment, Radu knew his father was no longer in control of Wallachia. Perhaps he never had been. The stinging taste of his father's perfumed oil was heavy on Radu's tongue as John Hunyadi strode confidently into the room.

"He is magnificent," Radu whispered.

"He is the end of us," Lada answered.

———◆———

When his father pulled him out of bed, Radu was certain he was dreaming. He dressed in a sleepy, candlelit haze, his father's murmured, anxious words washing over him. He knew it was a dream because his father had never been in his room before, had never helped him dress or asked if he would be warm enough. Radu was twelve, he was old enough to dress himself, but he let his father help.

He would not puncture this dream, not willingly.

It was not until they were outside in the sharp night air and Mircea arrived, leading horses, that panic set in. He and Lada were lifted onto saddles, though they could mount by themselves. Several Janissaries waited nearby, their horses huffing soft white clouds of breath.

"Where are we going?" Radu whispered. No one had told him to be silent, but a blanket of stealth and threat hung over them all and he did not want to disrupt it.

No one answered.

The horses moved forward, a cart loaded with supplies in the middle of the party and Janissaries surrounding them. Radu looked over his shoulder to see Mircea standing with a torch, watching them leave. Staying behind. Smiling.

Radu shivered. He had not been frightened until he saw the look of triumph on Mircea's face. Nothing that made his older brother look that happy could be good.

As his wariness abated, Radu dozed on and off in his saddle, startling awake several times when he nearly slid off. One of the times a hand steadied him, and he found Lazar next to him, holding the reins of Radu's horse and his own. Comforted, Radu snuggled deeper into his cloak and was lost to the lullaby of hooves and the whisper of leather.

They made camp well after the sun had risen. Their party was small. Several Janissaries, a few servants, a driver for the supply cart, Lada, and their father.

Radu rubbed his sore neck, then realized with a start that his nurse was not with them.

"Lada!" He tugged on her sleeve, interrupting her ferocious attempt to braid her hair. "They forgot Nurse!"

She glared at him, eyes red and tight with exhaustion. She watched the camp around them warily, tracking the movements of the soldiers. "She is not coming."

Radu swallowed hard against the painful lump in his throat. He had never been a day without his nurse. Here with his father, but not his nurse? He had the same sensation as when he had been out on the ice and felt it shifting beneath him, threatening to plunge him into frozen terror. "But how long will we be gone?"

Lada strode past him, ripping her bundle of possessions out of Lazar's arms. "That is *mine*," she snapped. "*Never* touch my things." She turned on her heel and stalked away, toward their father's tent.

Lazar made an exaggerated bow, then winked at Radu. "Charming girl, your sister."

Radu's mouth formed a smile for the first time all day. "You should see her when she has had enough sleep."

"Is she nicer?"

"Oh no, far worse."

Lazar's laugh made Radu feel lighter. Lazar motioned for him to follow, and he did, helping the Janissaries unload and set up their spare, efficient camp.

They traveled this way for more days than Radu thought to count. At first he worried about what his father would think of how he spent his time, but his father never so much as spoke to him or Lada. He wore his worry in the gloom of his brow, wrapped around him tighter than his cloak. He muttered, practicing some sort of speech, waving away anyone who got too close.

So Radu was free to ride with the Janissaries. He loved the constant jokes, the exaggerated stories, the calm and easy way they rode, as though they were not fleeing—which Radu suspected was the case, though no one would tell him—but rather on an adventure.

"Your sister rides like a man," one of the soldiers—a quiet Bulgarian with an old scar cutting across his chin—said one day as they passed through a rocky valley.

Radu shrugged. "They tried to teach her to ride like the ladies, but she refused."

"I could teach her to ride like a lady," the Bulgarian said, something in his tone different. A few of the other Janissaries laughed, and Radu shifted uncomfortably, certain he had missed something, but unsure what.

"Too young," Lazar said dismissively.

"Too ugly," another soldier added.

Radu glared, but he could not tell who had said it. He watched his sister ride tall and proud and alone. "She could beat any of you." The soldiers laughed, and he scowled. "I mean it. Any one of you."

"She is a *girl*," the Bulgarian said, as though that were the end of any discussion.

"Shhh." Lazar shook his head. "I think no one has told her this. We would not want her to hear it from us." He grinned at Radu, bringing him in on the joke, and Radu smiled, though it was not as easy as his smiles for the Janissaries usually were.

———

After that, Radu spent more time riding beside Lada. She pretended not to notice, but she held her shoulders a little more loosely when he was next to her. Her hands drifted frequently to a small leather pouch, tied around her neck and tucked under her collar. Radu wondered what was in it, but he knew better than to ask.

They were going south, through Bulgaria, studiously avoiding any cities as they picked their way across valleys and over steep terrain. Radu had gleaned enough to know that they were heading for the Ottoman capital of Edirne. The closer they got, the further into his cloak their father retreated. He spoke only when he had to, casting heavy, worried looks at Lada and Radu over the evening fire.

"I am sending them back," he said, several nights into the journey. "I do not want them with me. They slow us, and the boy is too weak to travel so far. He has always been delicate."

Radu did not realize whom his father meant until all the Janissaries turned toward him and Lada. What had they done wrong? Radu had kept his homesickness and his longing for his nurse to himself. Surely no one had noticed him crying silently the first two nights. He had ridden without complaint, helped set up and take down camp, done everything right!

He expected Lada to protest their father's rejection, but

she remained silent, staring at the fire. Their father looked anywhere but at them, his face a mask in the darkness.

Lazar rested a hand on Radu's shoulder. "Radu is doing very well. He rides like a seasoned soldier. Besides, we cannot spare a guard for them. The sultan's hospitality is beyond compare. You would not want to deprive your children of the opportunity to experience his generosity."

Radu's father sniffed and turned his face away, staring into the night. "Very well. It is all the same."

He retired to his tent, and for the rest of the trip he neither spoke to nor looked at them. Radu tried to ask Lada about it, but she, too, was silent and preoccupied.

When at last they came over the crest of a hill and saw Edirne laid out before them, Radu's heart seized with joy and wonder. The buildings were pale white stone, the roofs red. Streets lined with spring-green trees weaved through it all, leading to a building with a spire so high that Radu was surprised it did not scratch the blue of the sky. Several domes made up its roof, and another, shorter spire rose to greet the party, welcoming them.

Nearby was a large, imposing building, its outside striped red and white with alternating brick and stone, but Radu could not take his eyes off the spires that reached so confidently for heaven.

They had arrived.

11

1448: Edirne, Ottoman Empire

V LAD WALKED BEHIND SULTAN Murad, half stooped
from bowing so often. Lada watched with resigned wariness. Radu was at her side, clinging to her like a small child.
She had to pry his hand off her arm, where he was wrinkling the sleeve of her finest dress. He had acted as though
their journey here was playtime and befriended the soldiers.
The *enemy* soldiers. Radu was a fool. They had not journeyed
here, they had *fled*. Leaving the throne in the waiting hands of
Mircea.

Mircea, who had long curried favor with the boyars and
Hunyadi. Mircea, who promised to hold the prince title in
wait for his father's return.

Lada had no doubt her father would need an army to return, and not just against the boyars and Hunyadi.

For a few precious hours Lada had nurtured a dream that
perhaps she could find Bogdan here, but all hope had vanished. They had been welcomed with rooms prepared just for
them. Lush, perfumed, and pillowed prisons they had not

been permitted out of for the past two days. Vlad had paced so much, muttering and practicing speeches, that sweat soaked his silk undershirt. Radu had stared out the window, which was framed by metal twisted and shaped like vines. Lada had watched her father, his threads snapped. One left. One single thread that he desperately hoped to loop around the sultan and his mercurial support.

She tugged Radu's hand to make him walk faster so they could keep up with the party of adults. This was not the behavior Lada expected from Vlad Dracul. From her father. From a dragon. A dragon did not crawl on its belly in front of its enemies, begging for their help. A dragon did not vow to rid the world of infidels, and then invite them into its home. A dragon did not flee its land in the middle of the night like a criminal.

A dragon burned everything around herself until it was purified in ash.

The party came to a stop on a balcony overlooking a square paved in intricately swirled tiles of bright blue and yellow. Edirne was beautiful—ornate and stately, but with a dizzying elegance to everything. Lada distracted herself by imagining razing it to the ground.

"It is settled, then," the sultan said, not looking at her father while he spoke. His eyes were dark points beneath carefully shaped eyebrows that were turning silver with age. He was cradled in silks, an enormous turban towering above and around his head. He traced the line of his mustache down into his beard, fingers glinting with jeweled rings. "I will send you back with a Janissary guard and the full support of the

Ottoman throne. You will pay a yearly tribute of ten thousand gold ducats and five hundred Janissary recruits for the honor of our patronage, and you will ensure that our interests are protected along your Hungarian and Transylvanian borders."

Lada stopped listening as her father bowed and made promises and expressed his gratitude. The sultan left, leaving behind one of his advisors, Halil Pasha, to finalize the details of the agreement.

She no longer cared. For all its beauty, Edirne was alien and cold, the earth beneath her foreign and uncaring. Five times a day a voice somewhere near her window called out a song in a language she did not know, its inescapable notes stabbing into her. Radu became excited whenever the singing happened. Lada plugged her ears.

Wallachia was out there, somewhere. Her Wallachia. Though she despised her father for his weakness, at least it would get her home again.

Several soldiers dragged two bound men into the center of the square. Lada noticed a series of holes in the ground, the tiles surrounding them stained dark. The prisoners were laid on the ground next to the holes. A man dressed in flowing lavender robes with a brilliant red plumed turban entered the square. More soldiers, carrying two long, sharpened planks of wood, followed.

"Ah." Halil Pasha interrupted Vlad's continued praising of the sultan. Though her father was a prince and Halil Pasha merely the Ottoman equivalent of a noble, the other man acted as though Vlad should pay him deference. And Vlad did.

Halil Pasha swept a hand toward the courtyard. "Here is the head gardener."

Lada wondered if she had mistranslated. The man looked nothing like a gardener, and there were no plants in the empty square.

Halil Pasha kept his eyes on the courtyard. "As a further favor to you, our court will oversee the education of your children."

The blood drained from her father's face. "You are too generous. I could not accept such an offer."

"It is our pleasure to teach them."

Vlad looked at the square, where the two bound men had been stripped of their clothing. He met Lada's questioning eyes, and his own widened with an expression she had never before seen in them.

"Radu, then," he said, hurriedly. "The girl is due for a convent. She is far too willful and contrary to be taught, and anyway, education is wasted on women."

Normally such a statement would have enraged Lada, but she was unnerved by her father's face. Last year she had wandered out to the slaughterhouse, drawn by the noise of the pigs. She had expected them to scream only when being killed, but instead they began screaming, their eyes rolling back in terror, at the mere scent of their littermates' blood.

That was the expression flickering beneath her father's composed features, betrayed by the whites showing around his dark irises.

"Hmm." Halil Pasha stroked his thick beard thoughtfully. "We would hate for an unfortunate marriage to shift your allegiances westward. You have a history of forgetting your promises. Besides, the girl speaks perfect Turkish; I have noticed that she understands all our conversations. Time and attention has been put into her education. A great deal of *care*. Our children are our most precious possessions, are they not? The sultan wanted Radu, but I insist we educate both of them."

Her father swallowed roughly, eyes lingering on Lada's. Then he turned away and nodded.

"It is settled, then," Halil Pasha said. "We will keep Radu and Ladislav here with us so they will be safe while you re-member to serve our interests on the Wallachian throne."

Radu looked to Lada, trying to put together what he was hearing. Lada understood perfectly well what this man was saying. Their lives were valuable only insofar as their father did what he was told. And instead of just taking Radu, Halil Pasha had known what her father valued the most.

All those years working toward her father's love and ap-proval had led her here.

It had made her a prisoner.

The Ottomans held all the threads, and they had looped Vlad's around his own neck. Lada had known that her mar-riage, her future, was a tool for bargaining, but she had never considered that the very spark of life itself was something to be traded and bartered. And that her father would be so will-ing to do precisely that.

"Ah! They are ready. Your education starts now, young ones. Behold, the gardener, pruning treason."

They watched as the head gardener slit an opening into

each man and then, with practiced efficiency, inserted the long, thick wooden stakes. The men were lifted into the air, and the stakes planted into the holes in the ground. Lada saw how the men's own weight would slowly pull them down, forcing the stakes higher and higher along their spines until they finally exited through the throat.

She did not stop staring, but something behind her eyes shifted and changed the scene. She needed to see it differently. These men were not real. They did not matter. It was not real. Their screams were distracting. She was trying to think. She needed to focus on her threads. She clutched the pouch around her neck and stared at the men until they blurred into indistinct shapes. There. They were not real.

She felt Radu squeezing her hand, heard him gasping for breath through sobs. She saw the anguish written across their father's face. Whatever underhanded dealings he had antici-pated with this new treaty, he could no longer act. He had made the critical error of loving his children—or Lada, at least—enough that they could be used against him.

Love and life. Things that could be given or taken away in a heartbeat, all in the pursuit of power. She could not avoid her own spark of life. Love, however . . .

Lada let go of Radu's hand.

She took a step away from him and watched as the head gardener finished his work.

—————•—————

Lada hated herself for it, but she loved the food. Delicately spiced meats with cool, contrasting sauces, roasted vegetables, fresh fruits—every bite she enjoyed felt like treason. She should miss everything about Wallachia. She should hate everything about Edirne.

But oh, the sweetness of the fruit. Perhaps she had a bit of Eve in her after all.

The clothes, too, were infinitely preferable. A light entari robe was worn over flowing skirts and woven tunics. Everything was bright and soft, far less restrictive and binding than the fashions in Tirgoviste. Easier to move in. Easier to breathe in.

It should be harder to breathe here, with the air of her enemies surrounding her. Lada rebelled where she could, wearing her hair loose instead of elegantly wrapped as was the fashion, holding on to her shoes from Wallachia, and always keeping her precious tiny pouch around her neck and tucked against her heart.

Because food and clothing could never replace what she had left behind, and she would not forget.

She picked through a bowl of dates, sucking on them as noisily as she could to annoy their tutor. He was currently instructing them on the military structure of the empire. Which was better than religious instruction, but still odious.

"How are spahis different from Janissaries?" Radu's forehead wrinkled as he tried to sort through the information they were receiving.

The tutor looked bored. He always looked either bored or angry. It was the only thing Lada felt they had in common. "Spahis are local garrisons, citizens of the Ottoman Empire. They are not regular troops; they are called up when we have need of them. Local valis of small areas, or beys of larger cities, lead them as appointed by the sultan. Janissaries are a standing force, their only role to be soldiers."

"Slaves," Lada said.

"They are educated, paid, and the best-trained soldiers in the world."

"Slaves," Lada said again, her inflection never changing. Radu squirmed next to her, but she refused to look at him.

"Janissaries can rise to meteoric heights. We recognize and reward the exceptional. Some Janissaries even become beys. Like Iskander Bey, who ..." The tutor trailed off, blanching as though a bad taste were in his mouth.

Lada sat forward, finally intrigued. "Who is Iskander Bey?"

"A poor choice of example. I had forgotten about recent events. He was a favorite of the sultan, promoted to bey and given the territorial city of Kruje, in his homeland of Albania. He has ... not been cooperative since then. It is a deep betrayal and shameful to the highest degree."

Lada laughed. "So your sultan educated and trained him, and now he is using that knowledge to fight you? I think he is a perfect example."

Their tutor sat back in disgust, glaring at Lada, while Radu toyed nervously with his quill. "Let us move on. Repeat the five pillars of Islam."

"No. I like this other subject very much. I want to know more about Iskander Bey."

The tutor pulled out a wooden switch and tapped it menacingly against his leg. Lada's hands were purpled with bruises, yellow in the spots that had not yet been covered by fresh bruises. Doubtless they would be soon. She leaned back, stretching languorously.

"Perhaps we should visit the dungeons," the tutor growled.

"Perhaps we should." Lately the tutor had been taking Lada and Radu on frequent tours of the prisons and torture chambers in addition to viewings of public executions. It seemed that they spent more time in the damp, airless corridors of the prisons than they did in their own rooms.

Radu was constantly ill. His eyes were dark and sunken. He could barely eat, and he was plagued by nightmares.

Lada suffered no such effects. Occasionally she informed her tutors when a torture method appeared to be less effective than others. They ground their teeth and whispered that she had no soul.

She had a soul. At least, she was fairly certain she did. But she had learned that first day with the head gardener to see people as the sultan did. They were objects. They could be pushed and pulled and fed and starved and bled and killed in any variety of ways, depending on the type of power you wanted to exert or obtain. Sometimes an image—eyes in a dirty, ravaged face meeting hers with startling clarity, or a pair of feet, too small to belong to an adult, sticking out of a shadowed corner—struck her. Nagged at her. Pulled at the curtains she had drawn tightly over that part of her mind.

But she could dismiss those images. She *had* to dismiss them. Because if she did not care what they showed her, or how they hurt her, then these men, these ridiculous tutors, this obscene court, had only one way to control her: by killing her.

They were not able to do that just yet, or this tutor would have had his hands around her throat long ago.

"It is time to move on in our studies. Repeat the five pillars of Islam," the tutor demanded.

Lada yawned.

Radu spoke for her, giving a precise and perfect answer. Their Orthodox upbringing had consisted of attending services at the castle chapel every week. Lada had found the process of regular worship insufferable, but there was a time last spring that she found herself remembering it with longing.

Her father regularly donated to churches, trying to buy favor with God the same way he bought favor with boyars and sultans. As a result, they had been invited to spend a week at an island monastery located in the middle of Lake Snagov. When the boat pulled away from the mainland shore, Lada had felt a strange sense of release. Of peace. On the island there were only silent monks, far less intimidating than the patriarch and priests, who were elaborately robed in pomp and tradition. She had wandered alone, walking the entire coast of the island, feeling the water as a barrier between herself and the pressure of Tirgoviste. Her tiny room in the belly of the monastery was decorated with images of saints and Christ, watching impassively from gilt frames. She did not care about them, and they did not care about her, and she slept as deeply as she ever had.

Here, there was no peace, no separation from the world. Lada longed for it. Instead, she was forced to learn a religion as though it were equal to languages or history. It was agonizingly irritating. At least with Christianity they had been actively discouraged from reading the Bible on their own, study being the realm of the clergy. Her only responsibility had been to appear to be listening.

She refused to even give that impression here. The tutor nodded wearily at Radu's response before sitting up straight. A spark had returned to his eyes.

Lada pretended not to notice, but every nerve was on alert for whatever solution to her insolence he had stumbled upon.

"Ladislav gave the wrong answer." The tutor lifted his arm, fingers heavy with thick rings, and backhanded Radu sharply across his face. Radu's head snapped to the side and he fell out of his chair with a cry of shock and pain.

Lada would kill him. She would cut this man's hand from his body for striking her brother; she would—

She composed herself before the tutor looked at her, his chest heaving and his eyes bright. Waiting for her reaction. If she killed him, they would kill her, and no one would be here to protect stupid, fragile Radu. *Her* stupid, fragile Radu. And if she got angry, the tutor would know—they would all know—how to control her. The same way they had known to control her father. The same way the Janissaries had known to hurt her by taking Bogdan away.

She raised her eyebrows impassively.

"What are the five pillars of Islam?" he asked as Radu got back into his chair, tears in his eyes and a shocked expression on his face.

Lada smiled and shook her head.

The tutor hit Radu again.

Radu stayed on the ground, gasping out the answer, his

words garbled by a split and swiftly swelling lip, but Lada did not look away from the tutor's face. She kept a pleasant smile on her own, kept her hands loosely folded in her lap, kept control. Control was power. No one would make her lose it. And eventually the tutor would realize that she would let him hit Radu over, and over, and over.

And only then would Radu be safe.

12

RADU CURLED IN ON himself as he leaned against Lada's door. He cradled his hand, welts swelling along his palm. His lip was starting to heal, but only because the tutor had been focusing on his hands lately.

How could she do this?

How could she let him be beaten on her behalf?

She had always been his protector. Even when she was cruel, she never let anyone else hurt him. In spite of everything they had seen since coming to Edirne, Radu had never been truly scared or desolate because he knew—he *knew*—that Lada would keep him from any real harm.

He cried, because no one was here to see. The salt in his tears stung his split lip.

Did she know? Could she tell that he was interested in Islam, had become fascinated with it, had even started praying in secret? That had to be why. She did not let him be beaten for any other reason, but when the tutor asked about Islam she refused to answer, even though she knew it meant Radu would get hurt.

He wanted to tell her, *needed* to tell her, that he was sorry. That he would stop studying Islam. But . . . maybe he could explain how it made him feel, how the basics of the religion made so much more sense to him than the endless array of saints and icons they had in Tirgoviste. He had never really understood what he heard in church, the Latin so formal it created a barrier between himself and God. Everywhere in religion there had been barriers between Radu and God— Christ stood between them, the fall of man stood between them, his very soul stood between them.

God had always seemed like his own father—distant, unknowable, disapproving. Radu feared that, as always, nothing he did would ever be good enough to earn the love of an omnipotent and unknowable God.

Islam made sense to him, appealed to him with its generous simplicity. But if Lada wanted him to hate Islam, he would. If it meant getting his protector back, he would do anything.

He wiped away the remains of his tears, hiding his weakness. Then he pushed open her door.

Wearing only a long shirt, Lada was crouched by the hearth. Instead of stone, like the hearths in Tirgoviste, this one was framed by white tile with a repeating pattern of an eight-sided star. Although it was warm, Lada had stoked a bright fire. She was shoving her nightclothes into it. Next to her on the floor were blankets torn from her bed. They were stained red.

"Lada?" Radu stepped into the room, looking for her assailant, looking for her wound. "What happened?"

She turned to him, eyes wild and filled with tears. "Get out!" she screamed.

"But—"

"Get *out!*"

Reeling as though struck, Radu ran from the room, then out of their joint chamber. He did not stop running until he was free of the palace's sprawling labyrinth and weaving through the crowds of people on the streets.

He was lost.

He kept walking, turning in aimless circles, numb. The familiar call to prayer sounded, this time closer than Radu had ever heard it. He stopped in his tracks, finally looking up to see the towers and spires of a mosque. But his heart felt leaden, lower than the ground. He could not follow it up to the sky.

A soft hand came down on his shoulder, and he jumped, cringing.

A man—head wrapped in a simple white turban, robes of fine material but plainly made—crouched down so he was eye-level with Radu. His eyes widened for a moment as he took in Radu's beaten face, then they crinkled with a gentle smile. He could not be much older than Mircea, but kindness was written on his face in a way that made him seem wise. "Do you need help?"

Radu shook his head, then nodded, then shook his head again.

"Would you like to join me for prayer?"

Radu had never prayed before, not like this. He had seen his tutor do it, but it felt strange and intrusive to watch, so Radu usually looked away. But he had wanted to enter a mosque since they had arrived in Edirne.

"I do not know how," Radu said, face burning, eyes on the ground.

"We will put our rugs in the back. You can watch me." He guided Radu up the stairs. There was a fountain with clear water. The man stopped, washing his hands with particular movements. He smiled and nodded toward Radu's own hands. Self-conscious, Radu carefully imitated the man's actions.

When they were done, the man unstrapped a rug from his back. Radu panicked because he did not have one, but the man handed his own rug to Radu and took a worn rug from a stack in the back for himself. Eyes still on the floor, Radu followed him into a massive room where men were setting up in lines with practiced, calm efficiency.

The man led Radu to a corner, where he pointed for Radu to put down the rug. Radu copied the man's posture and knelt, nervous and regretting his decision to come. There was a wide variety of men in the room, old and young, wearing the finest clothes to patched and worn ones. But everyone belonged, everyone had a place. They would know he did not have a right to be here. Maybe they, too, would beat him.

And then the prayer started.

Radu watched in wonder as the men closed their eyes, following the same movements, praying together, their bodies and voices in perfect unison.

He had never seen anything so beautiful.

For once in his life, he did not want to observe. He wanted to be a part of it. Keeping one eye open to follow his friend's motions, Radu joined in. Before long he was lost to the rhythm of it, the peace of becoming one small part of a whole, the words he could only partly understand nonetheless making him *feel*, tugging his worn and bruised soul upward.

When the prayer was over, he looked up, up, up. The ceiling soared above him, interlocking, many-pointed stars drawing the eye inward until finally releasing the gaze into the open minaret. Toward heaven.

"Are you well?"

Radu looked at his friend, startled, then wiped his eyes. He smiled. "Yes. Thank you."

The man held out a hand, helping Radu to his feet. They returned the borrowed mat and then walked back out into the day.

"What is your name?" the man asked.

"Radu Dragwlya."

"I am Kumal Vali. Come, take a meal with me. You look as though you need someone to talk to."

Kumal led Radu through the streets to a section of tall, narrow stone homes. They were close enough to the palace to be important, but not so close to be part of the palace compound. Radu realized Vali was not the man's name but rather his title. Clearly he was someone valued, maybe even a friend of the sultan's.

A servant met them at the door, bowing and taking Kumal's rug. "My friend Radu will be joining us," Kumal said. They followed the servant to a room at the back of the house. Glass panes lined the walls, opening up to a modest but well-tended garden. There was a low table with cushions surrounding it. Kumal sat, gesturing for Radu to do the same.

Sitting across the table from Kumal, a stranger, Radu

suddenly wondered if this had been a terrible idea. No one knew where he was. Worse, he did not know if he was even allowed to leave the palace. And Kumal was an official. Would Radu be punished? Killed?

Kumal ripped off a piece of warm flatbread and passed it to Radu. He did not look up as he started talking. "I would like to know who has hurt you, and whether there is anything I can do to help."

Radu shook his head, standing. "I should go."

"Please stay. If you cannot speak of what has happened, then let us speak of other things. How did you like the prayer?"

Radu slowly sat back down, closing his eyes, trying to recapture how he had felt. "It was ... wonderful."

"Yes, I think so, too. I always look forward to being in the city and joining so many of my brothers in prayer."

"You do not live here?"

"No, I have an estate in the countryside. I am not often in Edirne, as my responsibilities at home keep me quite busy. I leave tonight, in fact."

Radu wilted. He had no right to expect more from Kumal, but the brief moments of hope he had had in his presence seemed like a cruel tease now.

"You are not Ottoman."

Radu shook his head. "I am from Wallachia."

Kumal frowned thoughtfully. "Yet you are not a Janissary."

"My father is Vlad Dracul, vaivode of Wallachia. He left my sister and me here for ... our education."

Understanding settled into Kumal's face, but where Radu

feared seeing anger or derision, there was only sympathy. "Ah, I see. It would appear your education has been less than kind."

Radu lifted a hand to his face, self-conscious.

Kumal took the hand, squeezing it, then putting it down so Radu would look at him. "Please do not judge my country by the cruelty of a few. Though there is one God and one Prophet, peace be upon him, not everyone interacts with him in the same way. There are varying levels of faith and practice, just as in everything in life. But you have a choice."

"I do not feel like I have any choices left to me."

Kumal nodded. "It may seem that way. But you always have a choice. You can choose to find comfort and solace in God. You can choose to be brave and compassionate. And you can choose to find beauty and happiness wherever they present themselves." He smiled. "I think you already know this, though. I hope you can hold on to that through the coming years, because you have much to offer the world, Radu."

A girl slipped onto a cushion across from Radu, her eyes bright and her mouth a perfect full-lipped circle. Her clothes were as pretty as she was, and a cheerful yellow scarf covered her hair. She smiled shyly at him, then took a piece of bread. "Is my brother lecturing you?"

Radu shook his head, looking down at his plate. "No."

"Good. He does so love to lecture. I am Nazira."

Kumal put a hand on her shoulder. "Nazira is my youngest sister."

"And his favorite."

"And my favorite." Kumal laughed; and then the servant returned, setting out a spread of roasted fowl, vegetables, and a cooling sauce. Kumal promised to take Radu back to the palace after the meal. Then he and Nazira traded stories, enveloping Radu in their laughter and shared history as though he were a natural part of it.

The warmth between them should have made Radu feel cold in comparison, but he stole a portion of it, tucking it away for the coming days when he knew he would need it.

13

LADA DID NOT KNOW how much longer she could get away with stealing bedsheets. Radu had complained that his bed was stripped of everything but a single blanket. She had to sit with her back against the door to guard against discovery as she ripped his sheet into manageable pieces to staunch the flow.

Her room was stifling. The smell of burning cloth had lingered through the month, and now the blood was back.

When her nurse had told her she would not have to worry about marriage until her monthly courses started, it had been a comfort. Until the morning Lada awoke covered in blood, in her enemy's house. She lived in terror of the day she was discovered. Servants were turned away from her chamber door with screaming fits or, when that failed, with her fists. No one could know.

But it was only a matter of time. The door to her and Radu's tiny joint rooms had no lock.

Still, Lada never cried.

Radu thought his crying was a secret, but every night she heard him through the thin wall that separated them. Sometimes she hated him for crying, and sometimes she hated him because she could not join him.

He looked happy only when he sneaked off to pray, an act that enraged Lada. She picked at him mercilessly for it, but he never acknowledged her anger. Finally, she resigned herself to sullen silence. If she ignored it, maybe he would stop.

The days passed in a desolate blur of lessons and *lessons*. Today, they were watching a highway robber being hung by a large metal hook inserted between his ribs. *Did you know,* her history tutor intoned in her mind, *that there is very little crime in the Ottoman state? Our highways are safer, our homes more secure than those in insignificant and tiny countries such as your own. Our people love their sultan.*

Lada should have conceded that there had been a great deal of crime in Tirgoviste and the surrounding towns. Instead, she remarked that perhaps the Ottomans' devotion was a result of their turbans being wrapped too tightly and strangling their brains.

When the robber had finished the long, agonizing process of dying, his body was taken down to be displayed on the highway with a sign proclaiming his crimes. Lada's feet hurt. She was tired of these lessons. There was nothing else to learn. The sultan controlled everything. If you crossed the sultan, you died. People obeyed not out of love but rather because punishment was swift, severe, and extremely public. It was effective justice. Admirable, even. The sultan cowered to no one, did not have to play games and bow to the whims of people beneath him, as her father so often had.

Radu looked as though he was going to lose his stomach again, so when they were excused Lada dragged him through the corridors and out into the streets. She had already explored as much of the palace grounds as they were allowed to. They passed the mosque, swirling minarets reaching up to pierce heaven itself. She wished they *would*—wished they would poke a hole through the sky and shower God's wrath on this whole city. Then they would see whose god was real.

But perhaps not. She was not in Wallachia. Even the god she had been raised with was absent here. Perhaps the sky would consume *her* in the wrath of the Ottoman god.

They passed a high wall surrounding a lush garden, trees drooping their heavy green boughs over as an invitation. Lada saw a fig tree laden with ripe fruit just out of reach. Her stomach growled. It was Ramadan, and she and Radu were expected to observe the fasting. Lada stole food and secreted it away whenever possible, but most days she went hungry from dawn until dusk. In the corner, where the wall met the side of a small building, a sprawling, ancient grapevine clung. She climbed it, hoisting herself onto the wall.

"We should go back," Radu whined, looking around. He rubbed his ribs anxiously, no doubt imagining a hook tearing through his muscles and organs. Radu had lost weight since they arrived, and not simply from the fasting. His cheekbones stood out starkly, making his eyes appear even larger.

"Fine. Wait there. By yourself."

He scrambled up after her, almost toppling over the wall in his haste. They crawled onto a branch, working their way down a tree until they could drop to the ground.

The smell was not right. The green scent was too pungent, the sweetness of some flower a shade off. The mosque loomed overhead, watching. But the serpentine paths bordered by trees and wild hedges that Lada wandered made the garden feel secret. She picked several figs, offering one to Radu. He refused, so she threw it at his head.

Biting into her fig, she trailed her fingers along the rough, waxy leaves of an untrimmed hedge and pretended she was in Wallachia.

Radu heard it first. "Listen," he whispered. "Someone is crying."

"And it is not you. What a wonder."

He glared at her, then strode forward with purpose. Hissing, Lada chased after him. For all Radu's fear that they were trespassing, he was a fool and would get them caught. She turned a corner and grabbed his vest, only to stop at the sight of a boy, perhaps twelve or thirteen, curled up on the edge of a reflecting pool, weeping.

"Are you hurt?" Radu asked.

The boy looked up, his black eyes framed with lashes so thick they caught his tears and held them. His hands were covered in marks, vicious and purple. His face, too, had been punished. A bruise was forming on one cheek.

Radu peeled off his vest and soaked it in the pool. He placed the wet cloth gently over the boy's hands to soothe the hurts. Lada had never let him do the same for her, and she had certainly never done it for him.

The boy watched, spine straight, considering them as he looked down his long, straight nose. His full lips were pursed against the pain. "My tutor," he said. "Father gave him permission to hit me for disobedience."

Radu dipped his hand in the water and brought it up to the boy's cheek. The boy seemed startled. He regarded Lada with expectant imperiousness, as though inviting her, too, to attend to him. She folded her arms and looked down her hooked nose at him. "If you are too weak to stand being hit and too stupid to avoid it, then you deserve more pain."

Anger flared the boy's nostrils. "Who are you?"

Lada leaned against a tree, plucked another fig, and took the biggest, messiest bite she could. "I am Lada Dragwlya, the daughter of Wallachia."

"You should be fasting."

She spat the pulpy skin at his feet, and took another bite.

He frowned thoughtfully. "I could have you killed for that."

Radu trembled, starting to bow.

"Oh, stand up, Radu." Lada grabbed his shirt and yanked him upright. "He is a stupid boy. If even the tutors are allowed to beat him, I doubt the head gardener is under his command. He is probably a pampered captive, like us." She felt no sympathy for the boy. He reminded her of what she was—powerless, young—and it made her angry.

The boy stood, stomping a foot. "I am no slave. This is my city!"

Lada snorted. "And I am the queen of Byzantium." She turned on her heel, pulling Radu along.

"I will see you again!" the boy called. It was not a question, but a command.

"I will burn your city to the ground," Lada called back over her shoulder. The boy's only response was a burst of surprised laughter. Lada was shocked when her lips answered with their first smile in weeks.

———◆———

Lada furiously scrubbed the blood from her nightclothes.

As she did, she cursed her mother, for making her a girl.

She cursed her father, for leaving her here.

And she cursed her own body, for leaving her so vulnerable.

She was so busy with a stream of cursing that she did not hear the door open.

"Oh," said the maid, a girl fragile and darting as a bird.

Lada looked up in horror. Evidence of her womanhood draped over her hands, the red an undeniable testament. She had been caught. An image of herself crawling and weeping swept through her mind. That was what a wife was. What a wife did.

And now this maid, this spy, knew she was old enough to be a wife.

With a scream, Lada jumped on the maid, hitting her around the head. The maid dropped to the floor, bracing against the blows and crying out. Lada did not stop. She hit and kicked and bit, all while screaming obscenities in every language available to her.

Arms pulled at her, a voice she knew pleading desperately, but she did not stop. She could not stop. This was the end of her last shred of freedom, all because of the prying eyes of a maid.

In the end, it took two palace guards to pull her off. Radu looked at her with the terror of a small prey animal startled from its den. Lada would not answer his questions. It did not matter. Nothing mattered anymore.

———◆———

Lada had been expecting punishment, so the invitation to join women for an afternoon meal came as a shock. She was escorted by a narrow-shouldered bald man to a section of the palace she had never visited.

Two women stood when she entered the elegant room. One was young, perhaps only a few years Lada's senior. She had her hair wrapped in a cheerful blue scarf, with a veil over the lower half of her face. Her eyes were big and projected a brilliant smile.

Lada flinched as the woman rushed forward, but she only took her hands and squeezed them.

She spoke Turkish. "You must be Ladislav. You poor dear. Come, sit. I am Halima. This is Mara."

Lada allowed herself to be pulled toward the cushions around a table, taking in the other woman, who sat straight-backed and corseted, her structured dress in contrast to Halima's flowing layers of silk. This woman's hair was dark brown, elaborately curled and formally twisted in the style of the Serbian courts.

"Why am I here?" Lada asked, tone as blunt as she could manage in her confusion.

"Because no one knew what else to do with you." Mara's tone was cold, her eyes narrowed. "When they discovered why you beat that poor child, the men refused to acknowledge the topic further. We were asked to speak with you about your feminine issues."

"Did you not understand what was happening?" Halima leaned forward, eyes crinkling in sympathy. "You must have been so frightened! I knew to expect my monthly courses, and still I nearly fainted at the blood! But here you are, with only your brother. You must meet with us, let us teach you and help you." She clapped her hands together in delight. "It will be fun!"

Lada remained where she was, standing stiffly by the table. "I want nothing you can offer."

"Oh, but you must have questions! Do not be afraid. You cannot embarrass us. We are wives, after all."

"That is exactly the fate I am trying to avoid," Lada muttered.

"Then you are a fool," Mara answered.

"Oh, be kind, Mara! She does not understand. It is a wonderful thing, being a wife! Murad is so attentive, and we are taken care of better than we could ever hope for." There was no hint of furtiveness or secrecy in Halima's tone. Her statement was as honest as her big, stupid eyes.

"You are married to Murad?" Lada asked, the sultan's name foul on her tongue.

"We both are." Halima smiled brightly. Lada looked in horror toward Mara.

Mara's smile was the bitter winter to Halima's brilliant spring. "Yes. We are both his wives, among other wives and many concubines."

Lada recoiled. "That is an abomination."

"If I recall correctly," Mara said, "your father has another son, from a mistress."

Lada did not answer, but her face was confirmation. They never spoke of the other Vlad, but Lada knew he existed.

Halima gestured eagerly, as though she could pluck the thoughts from Lada's mind and smooth them out into more pleasant shapes. "That is how it is done here. Men are allowed to have more than one wife, if they can provide for them. And the sultan has a tradition of keeping a harem. We are all loved and cared for. It is such a privilege to be a wife!"

Mara took a sip of tea from a delicate teacup, unlike any Lada had seen. When she spoke, she spoke in Hungarian. "Halima is an idiot."

Halima tilted her head to the side. "What?"

Mara continued. "She is a child. She fancies herself a princess in a tale. Murad choosing her as a wife from among the harem was the biggest thing a girl like Halima could ever accomplish. I do not know whether to strangle her or to do everything in my power to keep her in her glittering fantasy."

Lada answered in Hungarian, intrigued by Mara's honesty. "What about you?"

"I am here for the same reason you are. My marriage to Murad was the seal of a truce with my father and Serbia. My presence here keeps Serbia free."

Lada scoffed. "But Serbia is not free."

Mara raised a single eyebrow. "What do you think freedom is?"

"The right to rule yourself! Not to be beholden to a foreign nation for safety."

"Every country is beholden to other nations for safety. That is what treaties and borders are."

"But this is different!"

"How so?"

"You! You should not be forced into a marriage! It is not fair."

Halima coughed deliberately, her lips turned down. "Perhaps we could speak in a language everyone understands? So no one's feelings are hurt by being left out?"

Mara continued without acknowledging her fellow wife. "Hmm. And what do you think would have happened to me if I had stayed in Serbia? I would have been married to another man not of my choosing. I despise my husband and this entire empire, but at least here I have accomplished something. Halima's marriage to Murad keeps her safe and taken care of. My marriage to Murad keeps all of Serbia safe and taken care of. It is not fair, no. But it is more important than fairness. Do you love Wallachia?"

Lada scowled at the trap of the question. She knew where it would lead, but she had to answer truthfully. "Yes."

"Just as I love Serbia. I serve my country and my family by being exiled. We must all do what we can, Ladislav. This was my contribution."

Halima cleared her throat prettily. "Are we ready to speak in Turkish now? I thought of some advice I would like to give Ladislav!"

Lada picked her way through the meal, observing the two varieties of wife before her. She could never be like Halima, grateful and naive. But could she be like Mara—resigned to a fate she did not choose, in defense of her country?

Halima kept up a chirping discourse, talking of nothing of substance with such dreamlike joy Lada almost understood Mara's protectiveness of her. There was something comforting about the mindlessness of it all. And Lada enjoyed Mara's wry, biting comments, often delivered in a language Halima did not understand. Maybe Lada would ask to meet with them again. It would be nice to have someone to talk to besides Radu and their hated tutors.

Halima was in the middle of a lengthy story. "... and Emine, she is my dear friend, you know she joined the harem on her own! It was quite the scandal. She left her family and walked right in! Of course they had to take her then, her family would not have her back, and so—"

"What?" Lada interrupted, confused. "Simply because she entered the harem?"

"Oh yes! That is why we met you here. If you enter the harem building, you are technically the property of the sultan! It has to be that way, you know. To protect the bloodline."

Mara noted Lada's look of horror with a bleak smile. When she had finished eating, she primly wiped her mouth. She spoke in Hungarian again. "It is good for you to be with us. Try to be like this beautiful idiot. The sooner you stop fighting, the easier your life will be. This is what your purpose is."

Lada stood so abruptly she nearly fell backward. "No."

She turned and fled from Mara's heavy, knowing gaze, feeling the weight of it on her shoulders for long after.

14

THE MAN WAS FAT.

Tiny purple veins painted his face, webbing out from around his nose. His eyes were watery, his jaw weak, his fingers strained around too-tight rings.

He trembled with age, illness, or nerves. Lada trembled with rage.

Radu silently prayed to whichever god was listening that she would not get them both killed. He had no idea what set her off on that poor maid, but she had drawn official attention as being a problem. Now they stood in one of the opulent courtrooms of the palace. There was more silk and gold in this single room than in the whole caste at Tirgoviste. Various dignitaries stood nearby, murmuring among themselves, waiting their turn to speak with Halil Pasha, the horrible man who had made Radu and Lada watch their first impalings. Normally Radu would have seized this opportunity to listen in and get a feel for the court, but he was too sick with fear and could look only at Lada. If only Kumal were here, if only he lived in the capital. Radu knew he would help them.

But they had no friends, no allies. No help.

Lada did not look around the room. She stared directly ahead at Halil Pasha, who was finishing the contract that would betroth her to the Ottoman next to her.

"Your father will be pleased," Halil Pasha said, giving Lada a thin-lipped smile. "It is a great honor to the Draculesti line for you to marry here."

Radu's would-be brother-in-law signed his name, the ink scratching out along the paper in blotchy lines like the veins on his face.

Lada spoke with a quiet, clear voice, and the room hushed in surprise. No one expected a girl to speak. She was probably not allowed to. Radu knew Lada would not care either way. "On our wedding night," she said, "I will cut out your tongue and swallow it. Then both tongues that spoke our marriage vows will belong to me, and I will be wed only to myself. You will most likely choke to death on your own blood, which will be unfortunate, but I will be both husband and wife and therefore not a widow to be pitied."

Lada's intended dropped the quill. A single spot of ink bled onto the marble floor. Halil Pasha stared at her, his thin smile transformed into an expression of dangerous consideration.

Radu stumbled toward them, trying desperately to think of a way to ease this situation. Then someone laughed, puncturing the silence of the room. Radu turned, surprised to find the weeping boy from the garden standing near the door beside a gaunt, bespectacled man.

Radu had looked for the boy whenever they went out or were near a court function. In the two months since, he had never seen him again, but it did not stop his eyes from hoping to find a friend.

Now, however, Radu had no hope left to give.

The boy whispered something to his companion, whose brows came down around his glasses. He murmured something back, but the boy shook his head, watching Lada with merriment dancing across his face. She stared coolly back.

Radu wondered whether Lada or himself would be killed first. Would it be worse to watch it happen to Lada and know what was coming, or to . . . no, it would be worse to be second. He hoped they killed him first. Perhaps that was ungenerous, but this was all Lada's fault.

The gaunt man motioned to two soldiers who wore cylindrical brass hats with a long flap of white cloth to show their rank as Janissaries. Radu always looked closely at Janissaries, hoping to find Lazar, but this city determinedly refused him friends. Then the man and the boy from the garden turned and left. Radu's eyes followed them until they disappeared.

Lada's intended looked like one of the fish they had kept in the fountains circling the castle at Tirgoviste. Mouth open, then closed, then open. He shrugged at Halil Pasha, clearing his throat. "Perhaps the sultan— Perhaps another arrangement could be— I would never question the sultan's judgment, but—"

He was flustered, a bit outraged, but it was apparent from the faces around them that no one took Lada's threat seriously.

Radu knew she had meant every word.

The soldiers appeared at her side. "She is to come with us."

Lada leveled a flat stare at her intended. He began to smile—a dismissive, smug smile—but something about the intensity of her gaze froze it halfway, so he looked imbecilic. The way his eyes widened showed that, at last, he realized her threat had not been idle.

He took a small step back.

Lada followed the soldiers out of the room without even glancing at Radu. Halil Pasha watched them leave, and something in his gaze told Radu that he knew more about what was going on than they did. And he was not pleased.

"Wait!" Radu ran to catch up. He held out his hands in supplication. "Please, she did not mean any harm. She was teasing. In Wallachia, it is customary for ... betrothed couples to ... threaten each other. As a sign of affection. When our parents were betrothed, our mother told our father she would disembowel him and wear his intestines around her neck as jewelry."

The two soldiers stared at Radu, believing every ridiculous lie coming out of his mouth. Lada stifled a laugh. How could she be so calm?

Stop it, he begged her every night. *Stop making them angry. Stop making them hurt us. It is your fault. You will get us both killed.*

Finally, she had snapped at him, *No one will kill you.*

But if they kill you, I will be alone. And I will want to die.

He did not want to die at all, but he definitely did not want to die second. Radu met his sister's eyes, sending her all his heartbroken betrayal. She could not even pretend to be civil to save their lives.

She spoke in Wallachian, voice calm and unconcerned about her armed escort to what was likely her death. "Halil Pasha is the reason I am a prisoner here. I will not let him take any more of my freedom. I cannot accept that a political marriage is my fate. It would mean I was set aside and forgotten, and I would rather die than be forgotten."

"I would never let that happen," Radu said, but he did not know if he meant he would never let her die, or he would never let her be forgotten.

He wished he had more options than those two.

"We have orders to take her to the south wing," one of the Janissaries said. "You can come along if you would like."

Radu snapped his attention back to the soldiers, giving them a smile as brilliant as the summer sunshine. He walked next to them, asking what region they were from, getting them to talk to him. Very soon he knew their names, their various duties, and what they hoped to eat for supper that night. Their hands never drifted toward the swords at their side, and his chatter remained light, friendly, focused on keeping them calm so they would not provoke his sister into doing another stupid thing.

Lada walked behind them, thankfully silent.

The soldiers instructed them to wait on a gilded bench outside two massive copper doors. Then they left.

Radu sank onto the bench, wiping his hands over his eyes in relief. "If they are leaving us here, you might live after all."

"How do you do that?"

"Do what?"

"Make people talk to you. Is it because you are a boy?"

Radu knew she envied him his ability to persuade people to trust him. She looked sharp, contrary, and sly. Hers was the face of a fox raiding the livestock. Radu's was the face of an angel. But it hurt Radu that she thought it was a trick. Did anyone ever truly like him, or was she right? Did his face and tongue merely fool them into thinking they did?

Radu gazed at the gilded ceiling in exasperation. "People respond to kindness, Lada. They trust a smile more than a promise that you will leave them choking on their own blood."

Lada snorted. "Yes, but my promise is more sincere than your smiles."

She was right, of course. It had been a lifetime since his smile felt like anything more than a desperate and false ploy. He sniffed, trying to keep the mood light, keep his sister calm. "But no one knows that."

"Someday they will, Radu. Someday they will."

They both startled as the door beside them opened. The gaunt man swept into the hall, his robes a bland brown, oddly austere for the court. Even his turban looked functional rather than ornate. He considered them both with a penetrating stare magnified by his spectacles. Radu had never seen any like them. The glass pieces were perfectly cut and polished, balanced on the bridge of the man's nose by a thin length of metal that connected the two pieces and fitted to his face.

"You may go in," he said, gesturing to the door behind him, then leaving.

Radu and Lada entered. These apartments were to their sparsely furnished rooms what Edirne was to Tirgoviste. The ceiling soared overhead, painted in bold, clear blues with gold script swirling around the edges. Chandeliers hung down, glowing even during the day. The windows, taller than Radu, were peaked at the top and framed by scrolling metal lattices. Silk in blues, reds, and purples—the colors of wealth—draped everything. The floor beneath them shined so clearly that Radu could see his face in it. A fountain of water bubbled in the middle of the room, and the walls were lined with low cushioned benches. Sitting near the fountain on one of a dozen lush pillows was the boy.

He clapped delightedly and stood. "Here you are!"

"*Where* are we?" Lada asked.

"In my chambers!"

"And who are you, to earn such esteem from the devil?"

Radu elbowed her. The boy's smile turned wicked. "Why, I am the son of the devil himself. Mehmed the Second, son of Murad."

"God's wounds," Radu gasped, clutching at his stomach. He swept into a deep bow. He had hoped to see the boy again, had thought of him often since their meeting, imagining what friends they would be. And now this. Lada had threatened him, had insulted his father, and would doubtless continue to do both. Radu's fear was replaced with weary resignation. Lada would be the death of him, and that death would be swift and soon.

"I had you brought here." Mehmed waved an arm dismissively. Radu peered up through his lashes, where he could see another massive room behind this one and several doors.

"Yes, congratulations," Lada said. She had not moved since finding out they were in the chambers of the sultan's son. There was no indication of respect, no deference in her wide-legged stance. "But *why* are we here?"

"Because I hate Halil Pasha, and I hate my cousin."

Lada shook her head in exasperation. "And who is your cousin?"

Radu flinched at her tone. He straightened. No point in continuing to bow if Lada was going to get them both killed.

"Why, your beloved, of course! The man whose tongue you are going to cut out and devour." Mehmed collapsed back onto a velvet pillow as large as a horse, overcome with laughter. "I thought he would piss himself, he was so humiliated! By a *girl!* Oh, he is a loathsome, foul man. I have never been so delighted as I was today."

"I thought Lada would be punished." Radu took a hopeful step forward.

Mehmed shook his head, putting his feet up on another pillow. "No. I requested that she—and you, too, I suppose—be brought to me. I am being sent back to Amasya to govern. I suspect it is more to get me away from here, because my father has no use for me, and my mentor, Molla Gurani—he is the one who sent you in—does not get along with Halil Pasha."

Lada tapped her foot impatiently. Radu pinched her, and she slapped his hand away.

Mehmed snapped his fingers. "Yes! The reason you are here. I have requested that you come with me to Amasya as my companions."

Lada sat on a pillow nearest the door and sighed. "So I *am* being punished."

"She does not mean that!" Radu glared at her, then looked

at Mehmed, trying not to betray himself with the obvious-
ness of the hope writing itself all over his face. Away from
here! Away from the tutors and the head gardener! And with
Mehmed, the boy from the garden, who maybe would be his
friend, after all. He wanted to know Mehmed with a painful,
yearning desperation. Even now, aware of who he actually was.

Mehmed smiled. "I think she does mean it. But I do not
mind. I find your sister very amusing."

Radu sat on a pillow near Mehmed, back straight and
hands folded carefully in front of him. "Tread carefully, in
that case. She very much hates to amuse."

Lada threw a pillow at Radu's head with vicious accuracy.
Mehmed watched it all, his face a picture of joy. Radu did not
know what to make of this new development, but he dared
to nurture that seed of hope sprouting inside him. The smile
that met Mehmed's did not, for once, feel false.

15

Amasya, Ottoman Empire

ANOTHER CITY, ANOTHER TUTOR. Lada's life seemed an endless parade of droning men pushing information between her ears. It could be worse, though. It could be an endless parade of droning women. Halima painting the world in cheerful tones while Mara loomed over her, insisting she accept her fate. Embroidery in place of history, courtliness in place of languages. But at least if she was learning embroidery with Halima, she would have needles to stab out Molla Gurani's eyes.

Molla Gurani, Mehmed's lifeless teacher, either did not realize or did not care that Lada spent much of her time idly dreaming of smashing his spectacles into his face. She suspected that if he did know, it would not change his expression one bit. He was a man without passions. This meant he did not beat Lada for disobedience. Thankfully, he also did not beat Radu on her behalf. Her relief was tempered by the knowledge that they would find something else to hurt her with. They always did.

During their first lesson, as Radu had feverishly scrambled to keep up and Mehmed had recited whole sections of the Koran, Lada spoke only in Wallachian. Molla Gurani had merely gazed at her, impassive behind those hated lenses, and informed her that his sole duty was to educate Mehmed.

And, he had added in a disinterested tone, *I do not think women capable of much learning. It is to do with the shape of their heads.*

Lada excelled after that. She memorized more sections of the Koran than either of the boys, and intoned them in a mocking imitation of Molla Gurani. She completed every theorem and practice of mathematic and algebraic problems. She knew the history of the Ottoman state and Mehmed's line of descent as well as Mehmed himself. Mehmed was nearly thirteen, born between Lada and Radu. He was a third son, his mother a slave concubine, and his father favored the eldest two sons, which subjected Mehmed to gossip and shame. It was dreary knowledge, and Lada worked hard not to relate to or pity Mehmed.

But above all, more than any other subject, she devoured lessons on past battles, historical alliances, and border disputes.

For a while she had feared that Molla Gurani had meant to trick her into studiousness with his challenge, but he remained as impassive as ever, showing no pleasure in her attentiveness, never rising to her baiting. It did, however, greatly chagrin Mehmed whenever she surpassed him. That became her new goal.

Every day she waited for a beating, for some new horror to be visited on her and Radu, for the real reason they had been brought to Amasya to be revealed. The suspense made her quiet and sullen. Radu, meanwhile, gained back some of the weight he had lost. Lada no longer heard him crying at night. She hated seeing him grow comfortable. It would make whatever *lesson* was coming for them that much worse.

After all, Mehmed was the son of Murad. He was not their friend. He was their captor.

After their main studies, Molla Gurani always spoke with Mehmed about nothing but the Prophet and the destiny of the Ottomans to overthrow Byzantium and Constantinople once and for all. Lada soured at the notion that a mysterious god hovered above everyone, singling out a sultan to spread the Muslim religion to the world. She had never seen such a god, nor any evidence of him. The Ottomans were successful because they were organized, because they were wealthy, and because they were *many*.

Most afternoons, tired of studying and drained from being constantly on guard against whatever new devilry the sultan had planned for them, Lada wandered away, leaving Radu to nod and agree and fetch things like a puppy for his masters. Amasya was no Wallachia, but it was closer to it than Edirne had been. The city was built into the rocky hills, with a ponderous green river curving lazily along its base. Many of the buildings, including the keep where Lada and Radu stayed, were built into the side of the mountain itself. Behind the keep, growing up the hill in tangled, dense orchards, were apple trees.

Lada amused herself by lying on her back, throwing a knife straight up to try to snag an apple. Sometimes she did.

Sometimes the knife came back down and nearly stabbed her. She was equally entertained by both outcomes. The mere fact that she was allowed to have a knife again was evidence of how invisible, how unimportant she had become.

Even the crispest apples tasted mealy and bitter to her in Amasya.

The orchard was where she lay one day in early autumn, as the light turned low and golden, so heavy around her she imagined she could taste it. It would taste nothing like the apples of her captivity. It would taste like home. Home.

She lifted the pouch around her neck free of her top, pressed it to her nose, and pretended she could still smell the evergreen sprig and the flower, now so old and dry it had crumbled to almost nothing. She had moved them to the pouch the night they fled Wallachia, and carried it with her ever since.

A couple of Janissaries passed nearby, unaware of her presence. They were joking, and though they talked in Turkish, one of them still carried the shape of Wallachian vowels on his tongue. Lada got up, then darted from tree to tree, following the soldiers to their barracks, a cluster of low stone buildings grouped around a dirt courtyard. Harsh laughter accompanied the ring of swords clashing. Lada peered from behind a wall, watching.

She was grabbed roughly by the shoulders and pushed forward into the open. "A spy!" called out an uneven voice, still clinging to the last remnants of youth. "Or a thief!"

To Lada's horror, at least a dozen Janissaries turned to see what the matter was. Open curiosity on their faces, they formed a loose semicircle around her.

"That is no spy," said a short, barrel-chested boy with a single thick eyebrow over both eyes. "The little zealot keeps her as a concubine."

"Not very pretty for a whore." The soldier behind her tugged on a strand of her hair. She ducked under his arm, grabbing his wrist and twisting it behind his back to pin him. It was a trick she had learned under the harsh tutelage of Mircea and perfected by practicing on Bogdan and Radu. The soldier shouted angrily and tried to pull away, so she twisted harder, pushing up against the joint. He yelped in pain.

"You are prettier than I." She put more pressure on his arm. "Perhaps you could offer yourself as whore instead."

"Help me!" he gasped. Lada looked up, defiance in her set jaw, to find the other Janissaries grinning in delight. The single-browed soldier, who could not have been more than eighteen or nineteen, laughed and walked forward, patting his trapped comrade on the head condescendingly.

"Poor Ivan. Is the little girl picking on you?" He wrapped his arm around Ivan's neck. Lada released him, and the other soldier twisted, taking Ivan to the ground and sitting on his back. Ivan kicked out angrily, but to no avail.

"You have met Ivan. I am Nicolae. And you are Wallachian!"

Lada nodded, realizing it had been Nicolae's voice she had heard her home's tones in. "Ladislav Dragwlya."

Lada felt a pang at saying her name out loud. They had not been allowed to write their father, nor had they received any letters from him. She did not know if he knew where they were, that they had left Edirne.

She did not know if he would care.

Radu still worried about their nurse. She had lost her son and now her charges to this wretched empire. Lada wondered if she had found other work. She hoped so. She did not bother hoping that her father would think to take care of the woman who had raised his children. But she never said these things to Radu. It would do him no good to dwell on their nurse.

And Lada did not like the discomfort of remembering the woman who had always been so kind to her for so little thanks. If she ever got back to Wallachia, she would remedy that.

"The daughter of the Dragon?" Nicolae laughed, but it sounded good-natured, rather than mocking. "No wonder poor Ivan was no match for you. What brings you here, little dragon?"

"Not whoring." She kicked Ivan's prone backside.

"I would be terrified to take a dragon into my bed. Even the little zealot must feel the same."

"Molla Gurani is your zealot? I think he is made of parchment, not flesh."

Nicolae laughed, shaking his head. "No, 'the little zealot' is our name for Mehmed." The other soldiers nodded, giving each other wry smiles.

Though she knew from experience that Janissaries were far from decorous, she was surprised to hear such open mockery of the son of their sultan. She tucked it away as information she hoped to be able to use someday. "I am here with my brother. We are Mehmed's companions, studying with him."

"You must be dreadfully bored, then. Come on." Nicolae

stood up, dragging Ivan along with him. "You can watch me teach Ivan to respect scholars."

———◆———

As another infinite afternoon dragged on, Lada stared out the window, straining for a breeze to cool her skin. Mehmed rarely interacted with her now except to glare when she bested him in their studies. She often caught him staring intently at her, as though willing her to accomplish some mysterious task. She always met his gaze with her own unflinching one.

Radu followed Mehmed like a lapdog. Even now he sat on the floor by Mehmed's feet, poring over the same texts Mehmed had studied a hundred times.

"You see, there." Mehmed pointed at a passage. "The Prophet, peace be upon him, speaks of the man who will conquer Constantinople and what a wonderful leader he will be." Mehmed's eyes went faraway and soft.

"But there have been attempts," Radu said.

"Yes. Even my father tried. But now he is tired from fighting his brothers' challenges to the throne, from spending his reign merely maintaining what we already have. He loves to talk and philosophize, but he fails to see the calling of duty his faith has given him. My elder brothers might answer the call, but they are less than devout. The Prophet, peace be upon him, mandated that we should not have a state but an empire. We should be so much greater than we are, and my father refuses to—"

Lada let the door slam behind her. She was quivering with rage from listening to them talk yet again about the glories of the Ottomans, and their destiny to spread across the world. The Ottomans had already seeped like a poison into her own world, pulling her away from everything she loved. How much farther would they go? She stormed through the keep and into the small armory. It was abandoned, the barracks holding most of the actual weapons, but there were a few items left that she made free use of.

"Are you well?"

She spun, surprised to find Mehmed standing in the doorway. "What are you doing here?"

"You seemed unhappy when you left."

Lada laughed, as bitter as the skin of the Amasya apples. "I seem unhappy? Pardon me if I do not delight in listening to you extol the virtues of your glorious empire and what a favor you will be doing to spread it by the sword."

Mehmed's narrow eyebrows, finely shaped like his father's, drew low over his eyes. "You have seen my country. Where are the poor, suffering, and starving in the streets? Where is the crime? Radu told me that you cannot go into the streets of Tirgoviste at night for fear of thieves and murderers. Yet one can walk in Edirne without assault."

"Yes, but——"

"And our roads are safe for trade, which means our people have what they need to buy and sell, to live on what they have been given. They are free from hunger and poverty."

"But you oppress those who do not believe in your god!"

Mehmed shook his head in anger. "We do not act as your precious Christians do, slaughtering other Christians for believing the wrong way. Yes, we ask for payment. That is the price of safety. But we allow all people under our rule to believe what they will, so long as they do not disturb the peace."

"I am here as evidence of the *peace* your father instills, the freedom he grants others. My father is free to rule his people, so long as he rules them the way the sultan sees fit! And if not, his children suffer the consequences."

"Do you know what kind of man your father is?"

Lada turned away from Mehmed, hiding the shame that colored her cheeks. "The kind of man who promises the pope to fight infidels, and then makes peace with them. The kind of man who leaves his children under a sword to return to a false throne. Yes, I know what kind of man he is. He is the kind of man your father loves to deal with. They are both of them devils."

"We keep your country safe!"

Lada whipped around, crossing the room and hissing in Mehmed's face, "I would sooner see my country burn than see it improved under Ottoman rule. Not everywhere needs to be remade in your image. If we were not so busy constantly defending our borders and being trespassed by other nations' armies, we would be able to care for our own!"

Mehmed stepped back, puzzled. "Then you do not hate me on your father's behalf?"

Lada's shoulders dropped, weariness tugging them low. "My father is weak. Wallachia deserves better."

"Perhaps *you* deserve better than Wallachia."

"No." Lada felt the fire rekindling in her chest, burning away her fear and exhaustion. She had been away from her land too long. Sometimes she wondered if she remembered it rightly. But here, now, she knew she could never truly leave it behind. It pulsed in her veins, beating through her. "I love Wallachia. It belongs to me, and I belong to it. It is *my* country, and it should always be mine, and I hate any king or sultan or god or prophet that proclaims anyone else has any right to it."

"Please do not say that about the Prophet, peace be upon him." Mehmed's voice was soft. Not commanding—requesting. "Why do you refuse to listen to what Molla Gurani teaches us?"

Lada looked at the wall of practice swords. Though Mehmed scoffed at the amount of time she spent watching the Janissaries, she spent every spare hour observing their practice sessions and drills. After a couple of weeks, Nicolae had even let her join in, correcting her form, laughing at her mistakes, but increasingly admiring her ferocity and determination to win.

Do you know of a Bogdan of Wallachia? she had asked as soon as she dared. The words stung as they left her mouth, cutting her up with the hope they contained.

My brother's name is Bogdan, he had answered.

So is my cousin's! said a Bulgar.

And my father's! answered a Serb.

Nicolae had smiled an apology, and Lada had swallowed the pain that saying Bogdan's name had caused. And then she had fought.

Now, ignoring Mehmed, she selected a blunted sword, curved like the one that hung over her father's throne. Even the sight of it fed the fire in her chest. She hefted it, tested the balance. She liked being angry before fighting with Nicolae. Anger carved away everything else inside—doubt, fear, embarrassment—leaving room for nothing else. She never felt more powerful than when she was angry with a sword in her hands.

"Stop," Mehmed said, joining her at the wall. "You have not answered my question."

"You may worship your prophet, but he is not mine and never will be. Belief is weakness." She would not cave to Islam as Radu had. But neither did she cherish the Orthodoxy she had grown up with. Religion was a means to an end. She had seen it wielded as a weapon. If she needed to use it, she would, but she would never allow herself to be used by it.

Mehmed grabbed her arm, spinning her around to face him. "You are wrong, Lada. Belief is not weakness. Faith is the greatest strength we can have."

"Can faith take me back to Wallachia?"

"Faith can show you there are more important things."

Lada scoffed. "If you want someone to listen to your inane ramblings, go find Radu. I have other things to do."

She pulled the door open, but Mehmed ran forward and shoved it closed. "We are not done speaking!"

Lada's blood turned to ice. "Would you command me to stay? And if I refuse? Will you have me beaten? Whipped? All that and more I have faced in your father's courts. I did not bow before your god or your sultan then, and I will not now. Why did you bring me here, Mehmed? I will not be ruled."

Mehmed's face fell. He lowered his hand, and the line of his back—so straight—curved. "I have never wanted to be your master. I *have* servants. And teachers, and guards, and a father who despises me. I want you . . . to be my friend."

This was not the answer Lada had expected. She grasped for a response. "Why would you want that?"

"Because." Mehmed looked at the ground. "Because you do not tell me what you think I want to hear."

"I would more likely go out of my way to tell you something you do not want to hear."

Mehmed's dark eyes flashed up to meet hers, something deep and hungry in them. He grinned. It was an off-center smile, pulling back his full lips and reshaping his face from arrogance to mischief. "Which is precisely why I like you."

Lada huffed, exasperated. "Very well. What exactly does a friend do?"

"I have never had one. I was hoping you would know."

"Then you are even stupider than you look. Radu is the one who makes friends. I am the one who makes people want to whip me."

"I recall you giving me advice that helped me avoid being whipped. That seems a good foundation for friendship." He held out a hand.

Lada considered it. What threads would be woven from this arrangement? She had given her heart to a friend once before, and losing Bogdan had nearly broken her. But Mehmed was no nursemaid's son. "Your father would object to our friendship. He showed us no kindness in Edirne."

"I do not care what my father thinks. If you have not noticed, no one cares what I do here. Amasya is ignored. As am I. I am free to do as I wish."

"You are fortunate."

"But am I fortunate enough to call you friend?"

"Oh, very well." Some of the tightness left Lada as she at last realized that the punishment she had been waiting for all this time was not coming. They were not free of Murad, but they were far from his eye. For now, that was enough.

"Good. In the spirit of friendship, I must tell you that I am bitterly jealous of the time you spend in the Janissaries' company. I want you to stop training with them."

"And, in the spirit of friendship, I must tell you that I do not care in the slightest about your petty jealousies. I am late for my training." She hooked her foot behind Mehmed's ankle, then slammed her shoulder into his, tripping him and throwing him to the ground.

He sputtered in outrage. "I am the son of the sultan!"

She pulled the door open, slicing her sword through the air in front of his throat. "No, Mehmed, you are my friend. And I am a terrible friend."

His laughter made her steps—always purposeful and aggressive—seem almost light.

16

AUTUMN REFUSED TO COOL down. The stone walls of the fortress trapped the sun's brutal rays, holding the heat. Radu imagined the shimmering air was an oven; soon he would be cooked alive. Molla Gurani, who always seemed more than human, now neared godlike status: He did not even so much as sweat as he walked back and forth in front of them, reading aloud from a book about the life of the Prophet, peace be upon him.

But it was blasphemous to think of anything as being like god except God himself. Radu closed his eyes and expunged the thought, trying to bring his mind back in line with his tutor, with God, with what he loved learning.

When it was not so damnably hot.

Mehmed fell off his stool, collapsing to the floor. Radu rushed to his side, along with Molla Gurani. "Are you unwell?" their tutor asked, hands against Mehmed's cheek and forehead.

Mehmed's eyes fluttered open. "We must continue my studies."

"No." Molla Gurani straightened, helping Mehmed to his feet. "You are overcome with the heat. We should guard against further illness. I insist you go to your bed and remain there the rest of the day."

Mehmed nodded weakly. "Very well."

"I will call for a guard to help you."

"No, no. Radu can take me." Mehmed held out an arm; Radu draped it over his shoulders and put an arm around Mehmed's waist.

Molla Gurani watched them go, concern pinching the skin around his glasses. When they were in the hallway, Radu turned in the direction of Mehmed's chambers, two doors down. He walked as slowly as he could, shouldering most of Mehmed's weight as the other boy leaned against him. When they were nearly to the door, Mehmed looked behind them. And then pulled away from Radu so quickly that Radu stumbled from the absence of his weight.

Mehmed's eyes turned up in delight. "Run," he said, sprinting down the hall.

Radu ran after him, finally catching up as Mehmed burst through a side door leading to a balcony that overlooked the wilting garden. "What are you doing?" he demanded, frantically searching Mehmed's face for signs of madness. "You need to rest!"

Mehmed laughed, shaking his head. "No, I need to get out of this horrible, hot prison."

Radu gasped. "You lied to Molla Gurani!"

Shame colored Mehmed's face. "I did. But if I had asked to be excused, he would have been so disappointed in me. I will study all night to make up for it. You can study with me.

But right now it is too hot, and my brain is melting, and we have to get out of here."

He climbed onto the stone railing, then in a breathless leap, threw himself onto a nearby tree. Grinning at Radu, he clambered down.

Radu looked over his shoulder at his responsibilities. He did not want to misbehave, or draw attention, or do anything that would bring punishment down on his head.

But it was simply too hot for worry.

He copied Mehmed's movements, surprising himself with the ease of his own descent. Lada always made him feel weak and clumsy, but Mehmed expected him to keep up, which made it easy to do so.

They ran, hunched over and low to the ground, stifling laughter as they went. Not far from them was a spot where a tree had grown over the wall. Radu knelt, boosting Mehmed up to grab a branch. Mehmed scrambled on top of the wall and reached back down to help Radu climb. They both jumped to the ground on the other side, where it was noticeably cooler, the heavy stone of the mountain and the crowding trees doing their part to defeat the sun.

They had escaped only a short distance when they heard a soft thunk, followed by a string of cursing.

In Wallachian.

"Lada," Radu whispered.

Mehmed put a finger to his lips, and they crept forward with exaggerated stealth. Lada stood in the middle of a small clearing, her back to them, a quiver of arrows next to her. She had marked out targets on a tree some distance away, ambitious even for a practiced bowman. She pulled back the bowstring, then released it. The arrow flew wide of the tree, landing two arm lengths away.

She stomped her foot, berating herself in meaner, more foul terms than any Radu had ever heard. Mehmed could not understand what she was saying, could not hear the hatred and recrimination Lada spat out on her own head. Radu could, though, and he wondered when his sister had decided that nothing less than perfection was acceptable. He stood, wanting to go to her, to hug her, to tell her that it was okay. She still had time to learn, and she was good at so many other things. He wanted her to stop saying those horrible things, to stop thinking them.

Mehmed had other ideas. He crept forward, then grabbed the quiver and, whooping loudly, ran.

Lada spun, murder in her eyes.

Radu ran, too.

He passed Mehmed, motivated by knowledge of what awaited them if Lada caught them. The two boys sprinted headlong through the trees, dodging low branches and leaping over logs, Lada close on their heels.

Radu burst out of the trees and skidded to a halt. He threw out an arm to stop Mehmed. They were on the edge of a drop, a deep green pool a body's length beneath them flanked by sheer rock on one side and tumbled boulders on the other. A slender creek sang down the boulders, feeding the pool. Everything was still and quiet, the only sound their labored breathing.

Lada caught up to them, fists raised, momentum set to carry her straight into them.

"Stop!" Radu said. "There's a drop into a pool!"

With a shout of triumph, she shoved both boys over the side and into the water.

Radu spluttered to the surface, immediately looking for Mehmed. The pool was not deep—his feet had touched the bottom—and he was terrified that Mehmed might have hit his head or broken his neck, or suffered some other grievous injury.

Instead, Mehmed floated on his back, arms behind his head as he laughed. "Why, thank you, Lada. This is quite the miracle on a day like today."

With a growl, she jumped, landing between them with a great splash. After she had satisfied herself by shoving their heads underwater again and again despite their fighting to get away, she swam to a submerged boulder and sat on it. She looked content, her head tipped back to feel the sun on her water-cooled face. The self-hating, cursing demon of the trees seemed forgotten entirely. Radu had done that. A flush of pride warmed him against the icy water.

"I did not know this was here," Mehmed said. "I think no one does. Though there is a story . . ."

"Tell us!" Radu splashed water at him.

Mehmed slipped into a deeper voice, speaking slowly, relishing the tale. "Once, long, long ago, there lived a great king who had a single daughter. Her name was Shirin, and her beauty was legend."

Lada made a sound like a horse. Radu glared at her.

"Shirin lived on the other side of this mountain. One day, she traveled with her maids to this side, for the apples were said to be sweeter, fed by a clear, cold stream of unparalleled purity. A young man, Ferhat, from a humble family saw her and immediately knew he would never love another. He presented Shirin with the bushel of apples he had been collecting for himself, and as their hands touched he knew she felt the same."

Lada yawned dramatically.

"But she was a princess, and he was no one. Still, he traveled to the other side of the mountain to ask for her hand in marriage. Her father, aghast, but seeing his daughter's preference, presented Ferhat with an impossible task: if Ferhat brought the stream of pure water to the king's side of the mountain, he could marry Shirin. Ferhat tried many things. He carved irrigation channels, but the water turned sluggish and muddy as soon as it left its source. He carried the water in giant vessels, but it spilled or dried up before he could complete the journey. Finally, desperate to be nearer Shirin, he began to dig. He cut deeper and deeper into the mountain, guiding the stream along with him, traveling through the darkness, knowing her light shone on the other side.

"But this did not sit well with the king. He heard of Ferhat's progress and knew that if Ferhat succeeded, he would have to live with the shame of giving up his prized daughter. Since he could not go back on his word, the king sent a servant to spread the tale that Shirin had died. Ferhat, stumbling from the mountain after countless hours in the dark, was met with the news that the light he dug toward had been extinguished forever.

"Overcome with despair, he fled back into his tunnel and beat his head against the end of it until he died. Shirin, heartbroken and betrayed by her father, disappeared. They say she wandered into the mountain in search of Ferhat and was never seen again. Together, they form the heart of the mountain, still beating, pouring forth a spring as pure as their love forever."

"That is beautiful," Radu said, swishing his hands reverently through the water, as though it carried the legacy of the lovers, buoying them up.

"That is absurd," Lada said. "They both died for nothing."

Mehmed frowned. "They died for love!"

"They wasted their lives."

"It was not a waste." Radu smiled, tentative and shy. "I would tunnel through the mountain for both of you."

Lada laughed. "Then you are a fool, too, because you cannot marry either of us."

Her words stung after his sincere offering, and Radu was reminded why he no longer trusted her. "I did not mean that!"

Mehmed put a hand on his shoulder, his smile healing the hurt of Lada's mocking. "I know what you meant. This pool is as old and as pure as that story, I think."

"It will be ours, then." Radu beamed.

"Our secret," Mehmed agreed.

Radu ducked under the water, his whole body smiling and infused with the warmth of a prayer of gratitude for the grace of a beautiful, safe secret and someone he loved to share it with.

17

LADA AWOKE WITH A hand over her mouth. She punched twice in rapid succession, aiming for the kidneys. Her assailant rolled away. "Lada! Stop!"

She sat up in bed, squinting in the dark. "Mehmed?"

He groaned in pained assent.

"What are you doing in my room?"

"We are sneaking out."

She detected another figure in the darkness. Radu. Exasperated, Lada flopped back, rolling onto her stomach. But it was no use. The spike of alarm that had awoken her robbed the remains of sleep, and she knew it would be hours chasing them before she found her way back. Besides, she was . . . curious.

"Fine." She threw aside the blankets and grabbed a tunic to yank over her nightclothes. She pulled a cloak on over everything, then gestured impatiently for Mehmed and Radu to lead on.

Instead of leaving through the door, though, they climbed

on top of her bed and squeezed out the narrow window. The fortress at Amasya was old, squatting low and heavy on the ground. A wall ran the length of it, oftentimes nearly swallowed by trees and rocks. Some nicer flourishes had been added: a few balconies, a mismatched tower, and the wing where Lada and Radu lived. The fortress had also recently been repainted white with stripes of blue, and the tower painted in swirling lines.

Lada avoided most of it, preferring to spend her time with the Janissaries or in the trees on the mountain. Mehmed rarely left. When the three of them did sneak away, it was during the day to the hidden pool, but it was too cold for swimming during the day now, much less in the middle of the night.

They moved along the tree line, skirting the edge of the woods, running a course parallel to the river below. When they were a good distance from the fortress, the path began to climb. The terrain was rocky and covered with low, scrubby bushes, and navigating in the dark was difficult work.

"Where are you idiots taking me?"

"Patience, Lada," Mehmed said.

"I am going to start sleeping with a knife."

"If you had had a knife, you would have killed me!"

"Yes, exactly. And then I could have gone back to sleep."

Radu snorted. "Nothing like cuddling a corpse to give you sweet dreams."

Mehmed pointed ahead of them, to shapes looming in the dark. Lada thought they were more massive boulders in the mountainside, but as she edged around them, she saw they were carefully shaped and carved into the mountain. Ferhat's tunnel to Shirin! Elation overtook her, the taste of cold, clear water and the sound of beating hearts rushing over her.

Then she realized what was really before her.

Tombs.

"Whose are they?" she asked, to cover her strange and embarrassing disappointment. She ran her hand along the outside of one. There was something carved, so faint she could barely feel it.

"Pontus kings who ruled here more than a thousand years ago."

"What were their names?"

"No one remembers."

She placed a hand flat on the cool limestone of one of the tomb covers. No one remembered the kings' names, but they were still here, overlooking their land.

Mehmed spread his cloak out and lay on his back, gesturing for Lada and Radu to join him. Radu immediately lay to Mehmed's right. Lada stayed where she was. "Come on," Mehmed said, "I did not bring you here to show you the tombs. We can look at them sometime when it is light."

Sighing loudly enough for him to hear, Lada dragged her feet and lay down on Mehmed's left side, annoyed with him for asking and herself for obeying.

And then everything else was swallowed by the enormity of the sky above her. The dark curve of the atmosphere was littered with light, stars spilling across her vision, overwhelming and beautiful. Vertigo briefly claimed Lada as she stared upward, and she felt as though she were falling into the sky, toward the stars. Then she saw a brilliant flash of light, trailed with fire. Radu gasped. Another star fell, burning brilliantly in the dark before disappearing.

Mehmed whispered, as though afraid to break the spell, "Molla Gurani said this would happen tonight."

"How did he know?" Radu asked.

"It happens on a cycle of years. He has books that note its occurrence. Tonight he is up in the tower recording our falling stars for the future to study."

"Why do you like him so much?" Lada asked, the wonder of the night above her stealing the sting from her question.

Mehmed was quiet for a long time before answering. "That day you found me in the garden? Molla Gurani is the tutor who struck me."

"You should have had him killed," Lada said.

Mehmed laughed softly. "It sounds odd, but I am glad he hit me. Before him, no one, no tutor, no nurse ever stood up to me. They let me rage and rant, allowed me to be a terror. The more I pushed, the more they looked the other way. My father never saw me, my mother could not be bothered to take so much as a meal with me. No one cared who I was or what I became."

Lada tried to shift away from the thing poking into her heart and making her so uncomfortable, but there were no rocks beneath her.

"And then Molla Gurani came. That first day, when he hit me, I could not believe it. I wanted to kill him. But what he said the next day changed me forever. He told me I was born for greatness, placed in this world by the hand of God, and he would never let me forget or abandon that trust." Mehmed shrugged, his shoulder pressing against Lada's. "Molla Gurani cared who I was and who I would become. I have tried ever since to live up to that."

Lada swallowed hard against the painful lump that had built in her throat. She could not blame Mehmed for latching on to a man who *saw* him, who demanded more of him and helped him attain it. It was a lonely, cold thing to live without expectations.

She unwrapped her hand from where it clutched the pouch at her heart and cleared her throat. "He is still the most boring man alive."

Mehmed laughed, while Radu remained far away and silent.

The streaks of light continued, sometimes coming so fast Lada could not keep track of them. Mehmed held up his hands, palms out, to either Draculesti beside him. Radu took one hand. Lada did not move, but when Mehmed lowered his hand to hers, she did not pull away.

Radu lifted his free hand as though he would catch an especially bright star. "It is so sad they have to die."

Lada's eyes watered from being held open so long, and a tear fell from the corner of her eye into her hair. Here, tonight, with Mehmed and Radu, felt like a dream she was terrified to let slip away. But the stars were real, and she would not miss the passing of a single one. "If they were not burning, we would never know they were there."

"I am glad we are here," Mehmed said.

Lada opened her mouth to agree, and then bit her tongue in horror. She was not glad. She could not be glad. Being glad would be the greatest betrayal of herself and her home she could ever commit. *The sooner you stop fighting*, Mara said in her head, *the easier life will be.*

It was getting easier to be here. She could not live with that.

"I want to go home," she said, sitting up, pulling her hand away from Mehmed's. It was cold where the air hit the skin that had been sealed against his.

"Can we stay a while longer? Then we will walk back."

"No! I want to go home. To Wallachia."

Mehmed sat up slowly, looking at the ground. Radu stayed where he was, perfectly still. "Why do you want to go back?" Mehmed asked.

Lada let out a strangled laugh. How had she felt so close to him just now, when he could ask her a question like that? He knew nothing about her. "Because I belong there. You said yourself no one cares what you do. So send me back."

He stood, turning his back on her. "I cannot."

"You can! Has your father ever once inquired after us? Has anyone? No one remembers we exist! That is how un-important we are." How unimportant Wallachia was. Even as leverage they were forgotten.

"My father would be angry."

"He would not care. And if he did, what of it? He will not send you to the head gardener. He has already banished you here. What more can he do?"

"Enough! I said I cannot do it."

"Cannot or will not?" Lada stood, head pounding. She did not want this, did not want to feel things or care about

Mehmed. "Are you so desperate for friends you would keep us captive?"

"I do not need you! I do not need anyone!"

"Then prove yourself and send me home!"

Mehmed closed the distance between them, his face so close she could see his eyes in the darkness. "I have no power! Is that what you want to hear, Lada? I could not so much as requisition a horse and supplies for you, much less get you safely to Wallachia. No one cares what I do here, because I can do nothing. If you want to get away from me so badly, do it yourself." Mehmed turned and stalked into the night.

"What is wrong with you?" Radu sounded on the verge of tears. "Why do you have to destroy everything good we have here?"

"Because," Lada said, voice flat with the sudden wave of exhaustion pulling her heavily to the ground. "We have nothing. Can you not see that?"

"We have Mehmed!"

Lada looked up. The stars were static, still and cold in the night, all the fire gone from the sky. "It is not enough," she said.

18

RADU SAT BEHIND LADA, brushing her hair, tearing it into submission. Lada hissed at him.

"Hold still," Radu said, ignoring her slap at his hands. They sat as close to the fireplace as they could, a thick rug beneath them doing little to muffle the deep cold from the mountain beneath the keep.

The door to their joint chambers burst open. Mehmed rushed in, face pale and eyes wide. Radu was thrilled— Mehmed had not visited them much this winter, not since Lada's cruelty that night on the mountain. Lada studied alone now. Though Radu attended lessons with Mehmed, a formality had descended. Radu hated the distance between them and he hated Lada for putting it there.

But Radu's elation fell away as he realized something was wrong. He dropped the brush and rushed to Mehmed's side. After guiding Mehmed to a cushion, Radu filled a cup with water and handed it to him. "What happened? What is it?"

"My brothers," Mehmed said, staring vacantly into the

cup. "My older brothers are both dead. They have been for months. No one told me."

"Oh, Mehmed, I am sorry." Radu put an arm around Mehmed's shoulder and drew him close. Mehmed stiffened, then relaxed against Radu's side. Radu could have warmed the room with the happiness burning inside him at this closeness after so many chilly weeks.

"Did you even know your brothers?" Lada leaned back, toying with her now-smooth hair.

Mehmed shook his head, dazed. "No, not really. Their mothers were important wives. They were raised to inherit the throne." Mehmed's mother was a concubine, a slave. Mehmed spoke of her infrequently, but when he did Radu listened with envy. He missed his nurse, and he missed the idea of a mother.

Lada sat up straight, suddenly interested. "And now?"

"Now they are dead. And my father has finally made peace with Hunyadi. He is tired, and his heart is heavy, and he wants nothing more than to retire to his estate in Anatolia and spend the rest of his days talking and dreaming and drinking with his philosophers." Mehmed held out the sheaf of parchment he clutched in one hand. Lada stood and took it, scanning its contents. Mehmed rested his head on Radu's shoulder. Radu stayed as still as he possibly could, even when his muscles begged for him to shift, scared that the tiniest movement would scare Mehmed away like a bird.

Lada stumbled down onto the nearest cushion, rereading the missive. "He has abdicated. To you. He gives you the title of sultan under the banner of new peace."

The floor rushed out from under Radu. His ears buzzed

with wind in the still room. Mehmed—his Mehmed—had been given the throne of the Ottoman state. One of the greatest powers in the world, draped over his shoulders like a rich, heavenly cloth. What would it mean for Radu and Lada? Would they be allowed to stay with Mehmed?

Would it mean Mehmed could send them back to Wallachia?

Because . . . Radu was not certain he wanted that.

"I was third in line. I was never supposed to inherit. And I am too young. I am twelve!" Mehmed's hand trembled, spilling water.

Radu took the cup from him gently, setting it on a table, then took Mehmed's hands in his. "What are you going to do?"

"There is nothing I can do."

Lada stood. She dropped the parchment on the floor and stomped on it. Radu was scared, but Lada was angry. "There is something you can do. You can stop sitting here, trembling and fearful. You can stand up like a leader, put on your finest clothes, and ride into Edirne like the sultan you are."

Mehmed looked up at her with tears in his eyes. "You do not understand. The courts—they will never accept me. I was never supposed to be sultan. They will devour me. I have no allies, no one on my side."

Lada smiled viciously, put on her most mocking voice. "So now you would prove me correct. I thought you had your faith as your greatest strength."

Mehmed's face hardened. "My faith *is* my strength."

"Then you have your god on your side. What is a court full of sycophants and rivals against that? Wrap yourself in the armor of your faith. Take your throne."

Mehmed pushed away Radu's hands and stood, shoulders back, spine straight. He looked down his nose at Lada. Beneath the skinny body, behind the face just beginning to shift into a man's, Radu saw a glimmer of what Mehmed could become. He shivered.

"I will *be* sultan," Mehmed growled. "When I take the throne, I will be the hand of God on Earth. I will fulfill the destiny laid out by Muhammad the Prophet, peace be upon him, and you will know that he was right." He slumped, the fire gone out of his voice. "But I need more time. I want to do more than merely occupy the throne. I want to *command* it."

"How can they expect you to lead?" Radu asked. He hurried on, afraid of insulting Mehmed. "You *will* be a great leader. This is right, the hand of God in giving you the throne." As soon as Radu said it, he knew it was true. He had seen what Mehmed was, what he could become. Mehmed was smart and true, clever and strong. When they prayed together, Radu felt it more deeply than when he prayed alone, as though Mehmed's very soul was stronger than everyone's around him.

Lada tapped her chin. "I think we can help. Your father is abdicating because of the peace with Hunyadi, yes?"

Mehmed nodded, frowning curiously. Radu flopped back. He put his hands over his face and groaned. He knew his sister too well. No help from her would be a good thing.

"Very well, Sultan Mehmed. We go to claim your throne." Lada's face twisted into a smile that a wolf would envy. "And, since your father only felt safe enough to abdicate because of peace? When we get there, we start a war."

19

John Hunyadi, vaivode of Transylvania,

I am writing on behalf of our shared interest in defeating the infidel Turks and protecting the Christian sanctity of Transylvania, Wallachia, and Constantinople itself. You will know me as the daughter of Vlad Dracul, vaivode of Wallachia. These past years I have been held in the Ottoman courts as ransom to secure my father's loyalty.

During my time here, I have become privy to many secrets. I desire the overthrow of the plague of Islam upon the earth, and you can help achieve it. Murad has this very day given up the sultanate, handing the throne to his young son, Mehmed. Mehmed is impetuous and untried, a zealot, fixated on taking Constantinople. He has neither the respect of his soldiers nor control of his people. Strike now. Strike hard. Secure our borders, push the infidels back, squeeze their filth from the lands of all Christendom.

I will do what I can to foment dissension and rebellion within Mehmed's own borders. I trust you to be an Athleta Christi beyond them. Rally the forces for a crusade such as the world has never seen.

I look forward to the day when I am released from this den of vipers and can join you in protecting Wallachia, Transylvania, and blessed Constantinople.

Ladislav Dragwlya, Daughter of the Dragon

Lada slammed her knee into Nicolae's stomach, narrowly missing his groin. His deflection threw him off-balance. She pressed her advantage, hitting him with her wooden practice sword until he dropped his own sword and stumbled back. To keep the fight challenging, she threw her sword down as well.

She hated being back in Edirne, hated the way it made her feel caged, hated even more that she had briefly imagined she was free in Amasya. Freedom in these lands was a lie, a glittering fantasy to lull her into sleepiness, into acceptance, into forgetfulness.

She was not free here and never would be.

She had not seen Halima or Mara and did not know if they were even still in the capital, or if Murad had taken his wives with him. She hoped for Halima's sake that he had, and for Mara's sake that he had not.

But she had no desire to see either of them, or ponder the questions they had raised.

For now, she and Radu were stuck waiting. Mehmed had laughed, delighted, at Lada's statements in her letter to Hunyadi. Radu had laughed as well, while giving his sister terrified looks behind Mehmed's back. He understood the truth behind each and every one of her words.

But until they found out if Hunyadi would take the bait, if a war would threaten the empire and lure Murad back from his early retirement, Mehmed was sultan. In the two weeks since they had come to Edirne with its new sultan, Lada had not seen him once. He had been snatched away by the courts, pulled under in a too-familiar poison current of enemies and allies. More of the former than the latter. No one was happy with the young new leader.

Lada had been certain he would wilt under the pressure, but in spite of his machinations to lure his father back, Mehmed had risen to the occasion. He bent to no man and met every challenge in the open, eager to learn.

But all doors to him were closed now. Lada missed him sometimes, and she hated him for that. She had been right to push him away. Trusting him would only hurt her in the end.

She swung her fist at Nicolae's head. He raised an arm to block the blow, and she delivered a killing stab with her wooden dagger.

Nicolae laughed, staggering dramatically to the ground. "Dead, again, at the hands of the ugliest girl in creation." He stuck out his tongue, face contorted in a grimace.

Lada kicked him in the stomach. "I am no girl. Who is next?"

The other Janissaries, gathered in a loose circle around Lada and Nicolae, shuffled their feet and avoided eye contact. Nicolae pushed himself up on an elbow. "Really? Cowards!"

"I still have bruises from the last time."

"I cannot sit without pain."

"She fights dirty."

Ivan did not even respond, having never forgiven Lada for besting him when they were introduced. He refused to fight her and rarely acknowledged her presence.

Lada laughed, showing all her sharp teeth. "Because when you are on the battlefield, honor will mean so much. You will die with a blade between your ribs, secure in the knowledge that you fought with manners." She picked up her dull practice sword, abandoned on the edge of the circle, and swung it through the air, sweeping it across the line of the Janissaries' collective throats.

"I would rather die in this ring at your hand than on the field in the name of the little zealot," Nicolae said. The other Janissaries grumbled in assent. They had become more and more vocal in their complaints about Mehmed, about their work, about their pay. Lada did not fail to notice that their grievances were aired without regard for who could hear, indicating little fear of reprisal or reprimand.

"What is going on here?" A short man with piercing dark eyes, one ear a mangled, scarred stub, strode into the practice ring. The Janissaries snapped to attention.

"We were practicing, sir." Nicolae stared straight ahead, as though if he did not look at Lada, the commander would not notice her.

She met the man's gaze without batting an eye. "I train with these Janissaries."

"Since when?"

"For months now. I traveled with them from Amasya."

"We are not so lax in Edirne as they are in the outer regions. You will remove yourself." He turned, effectively dismissing her.

"No."

He cocked his head. "No?"

"No. I am doing no harm, and your men can certainly use the challenge."

The man turned toward Nicolae. "Show this girl that she has no place on a field with Janissaries."

Nicolae grimaced, rubbing the back of his neck. "Do I have to, Ilyas?"

"Did it sound like a request?"

"But I just fought with her. Make someone else go."

Disbelief coloring his face, Ilyas gestured at one of the other Janissaries. He was a Wallachian, so Lada automatically liked him. With a beleaguered sigh, Matei stepped forward, picking up a practice sword. Lada had not fought him yet. The Edirne Janissaries always hung back, confused and wary, while the Amasya Janissaries were used to her.

Matei had decent form, his precise movements backed by a compact, powerful body. Lada had him disarmed and on the ground in six moves. The next Janissary took four. The third Janissary was more difficult, and it was a full minute before he, too, was beaten.

"Enough!" Ilyas took up a sword and strode into the center of the practice ring.

Lada attacked first—she always attacked first. He anticipated it, blocking her strike with bone-jarring force. He seemed to know what she would do before she did it, reading her as easily as Radu read people's emotions.

After several of her failed attacks, Ilyas caught the edge of Lada's sword, ripping it from her hands. Instead of backing away, she screamed and spun herself into him, past his sword, a dagger pulled from her wrist sheath at his neck.

He slammed his head into hers, knocking her to the ground.

The bright blue sky spun above her. Ilyas leaned into her view, holding out a hand. She took it, and he pulled her up.

She refused to sway on principle, though her head complained bitterly.

Ilyas regarded her. "Carry on." He walked away.

"I lost," Lada said, hand against her head.

"No," Nicolae answered, draping an arm across her shoulders. "I am pretty sure that means you won."

"Lada!"

She turned, scowling, to find Radu running toward her. He was gasping and breathless. She crouched into a fighting stance, looking behind him for the threat, ready to kill whatever was chasing him. Instead, he grabbed her by the shoulders. His eyes shone with panic or excitement or both.

"Hunyadi. The pope. They have declared a crusade. They are already marching."

Lada blinked. Even as she wrote to Hunyadi, she doubted anyone would listen to her. They must have already been poised on the brink of attack, waiting for an opening. And now they were taking it. She threw her head back and laughed, a barking, strangled sound like that made by the stray hounds that slunk through the streets of Tirgoviste. "Hunyadi! A crusade!"

Matei shouted a command, and the Janissaries left, instantly falling into formation as they headed to the barracks for more information. Radu had not let go of Lada's shoulders, his grip crushing. Lada looked at his face, the tightness and fear there.

"What? This is what we wanted. What Mehmed wanted. It will force Murad to take the throne again."

Radu shook his head. "No, there is more. Father ... he sent troops. Mircea leads a contingent of Wallachians."

For one brief, glorious moment, Lada's heart swelled with pride for her father. He had finally found his spine, had come down in defense of his own people, against—

Against the country that held their very lives as collateral. "He has sacrificed us," Radu whispered.

Lada squeezed the pommel of her practice sword until her fingers cramped. Mara's talk of duty to one's country was meaningless if one's country cared nothing for its duty to you. "He sacrificed us years ago. But I will be damned if I let him kill us." She dropped her sword and grabbed Radu's wrist, pulling him along behind her as she rushed to the main wings of the palace. Her head ached, a bump already growing where Ilyas had struck her, but she did not have time to indulge the pain.

"Mehmed will not let them kill us. He is the sultan now." Radu sounded as though he was trying to convince himself.

Lada hissed, nearly laughing at the irony. "We engineered this whole situation to get his father to be sultan again. Mehmed may not have a say for long. We are running. Right now. We can slip out during the confusion of troop movements."

"With what supplies? With what money? Even if we make it out of the city, we have no way of getting back to Wallachia."

Lada skidded to a stop in front of the door to their small apartments within the palace. Mehmed paced there, hands behind his back, forehead creased in worry. With him was a contingent of guards, and Halil Pasha, the main advisor he had inherited from his father. The man responsible for

Lada's stay as captive. If Halil Pasha was here, Mehmed must have lost the argument to protect Lada and Radu. Her fingers twitched toward her wrist sheaths, where she had not removed the daggers.

Mehmed looked up, his expression unchanging. Lada lifted her chin in defiance. If she and Radu were to be punished for their father's actions, she would not let it happen without a fight. The first man to touch Radu would die.

"There you are!" Mehmed hurried forward, waving for Lada and Radu to join him. "You are excused, Halil Pasha." Then the guards were not here for Lada and Radu. Lada did not relax her posture.

The older man narrowed his eyes. "We still have much to discuss."

"I said you are excused!"

Lada noted with interest the look of derision that crossed Halil Pasha's face, and the petulant tone to Mehmed's voice. It was not the tone of someone in power.

She met Halil Pasha's shrewd eyes. As he walked away, she could practically see the threads trailing from him, snagging on everything he passed. Mehmed was sultan, but he was not in power.

They were escorted to Mehmed's new chambers, which were even more opulent and dizzying than his previous ones. He instructed his guards to remain outside, then slammed the doors shut and threw himself onto a pillow.

"He will not come."

"What?" Lada walked the borders of the room, tracing the gold patterns painted onto the walls.

"My father. He has refused to come lead the armies. He says that I am sultan now, and it is my job. I will do it if I must, the best I can. But I am not ready to face Hunyadi!"

Radu spoke up, voice high and fast with the relief that they were still safe. For now. "Lada could tell you about Hunyadi's tactics. She studied him."

Lada's eyes cut at Radu like a knife. "Yes, and I can tell you that he and his forces have the blessing of God and the fervor of a renewed crusade. That he uses wagons as mobile barricades, that he is organized and swift and brutal. That they have been waiting for this opportunity to unify them for years, and they will descend on your holdings like a swarm of locusts. And I can tell you that your Janissaries— the soldiers you need to obey you without question—call you names behind your back and complain of poor wages and treatment. I can only imagine you are equally popular with the spahis." Spahis had even more to lose under an unsuccessful sultan. They had land and wealth, prestige and influence. All the Janissaries had were their lives and their salaries.

Mehmed threw his hands up in despair. "I know I am not ready to face Hunyadi! That was never the plan. I need my father!"

His voice broke at the end of the sentence, and Lada realized with a pang that he had been thrown to the wolves just as she and Radu had. His father had abandoned him, sacrificed him, as assuredly as their own had. If this war did not devour him, men like Halil Pasha would.

Lada sighed, sitting down near Mehmed and leaning back

to look at the grandeur of the ceiling's carved geometrics. "Your father says you are the sultan."

Mehmed clicked his tongue in annoyance. "Yes, that is the problem."

"That is the solution. If you are the sultan, he must obey your command to come and lead your armies. And if you are not the sultan, he must come back and lead his armies."

A slow smile spread across Mehmed's face. "Lada, I think I love you."

She slammed her fist into his shoulder, and he slouched away, looking at her in outrage. "How dare you strike me!"

"I dare perfectly well. Now go write your missive. The crusade is not waiting, and neither should you."

While Mehmed went to gather his writing tools, Radu stood in the middle of the room, wringing his hands. "What about our father? What should we say?"

"We say nothing. We do nothing. You do not poke a sleeping bear to ask what it will do when you wake it up."

"I think I have an idea, though. To keep us safe."

Lada let out a dismissive puff of air between her lips. "I keep us safe. Remember what I told you in the stables when Mircea was torturing you?"

A smile finally broke through Radu's concern. It lit his face with a beauty to rival the ceiling. "You would not let anyone else kill me."

"That honor is mine and mine alone."

Radu finally relaxed, sitting back on a pillow and flinging his arms wide. He was still such a child in so many ways, and Lada wanted to keep him that way.

Or force him to leave it behind forever.

She never could decide which, and it nagged at her.

Only when Radu was no longer looking did Lada let her smile fade into a calculating frown. She had to keep them safe from Murad's wrath. She had to turn Mehmed's rule to their advantage, but she did not know how.

20

"WHERE ARE YOU GOING?" Radu asked, though he knew the answer.

Lada finished tugging on her boots. She wore trousers beneath her skirts, the skirts ill-fitting and put on almost as an afterthought. "To train."

"Even with all the Janissaries gone to fight?"

"There are a few left."

Radu scowled. "You are such good friends with the Janissaries. I never see you." He tried to keep the pleading out of his voice, but he was lonely. Mehmed was always busy, and Radu dreaded ever becoming the nuisance he had been viewed as by Lada and Bogdan growing up. When Mehmed wanted him, he was there without question or delay. But if Mehmed did not call for him, Radu drifted, listless.

Lada did not respond, and Radu could not resist digging at her. "Do you remember when we came here?"

"Of course I remember. It has only been a few weeks. Are you stupid?"

"No, I mean the first time we came here. With Father."

She got quiet, then. They never spoke of their father, not to each other nor to anyone else. Tension pulled around Lada's eyes that Radu felt, too, as though merely by invoking their father's memory someone would realize that his contract with the Ottomans was broken and Lada's and Radu's lives were the price.

"You were angry with me the whole time."

"I am always angry with you, Radu. Say what you mean."

"You were angry with me because I befriended the enemy. Riding with the Janissaries, talking with them. I simply find it . . . amusing that now they are your dearest companions."

A flurry of emotion descended on Lada's face. Guilt, Radu suspected, though the rage that followed was more familiar. She finally settled on derision. "I do not have to answer to *you*. Go crawl on your belly in front of their god. At least I have a sword in my hands."

The door slammed behind her, punctuating her exit. Radu sighed and rubbed his face, wondering what he had hoped to accomplish by needling his sister. Did he want her to stop training with the Janissaries? Or did he want her to admit that she had accepted this as their home? Because if she admitted it, then he finally could, too.

The unfairness pricked at him—that she could hate them and enjoy them at the same time. If anyone deserved to be friends with the Janissaries, it was him. He had never found Lazar again and wondered about his fate, wishing he were here to joke with and to help Radu find a place he belonged, as he had so long ago in the stables.

His soul sputtering like a candle at the end of its wick, Radu went in search of Molla Gurani. The tutor was in his chambers, studying. He weighed Radu with his eyes and stood. "Let us walk."

Lada loved to make comments about how dull Molla Gurani was, claiming he was the bastard son of a shepherd who had become too amorous with the sheep. She used to repeat his lessons at night in a bleating monotone until Radu begged her to stop, worried her version would replace the real lessons in his mind.

Radu found Molla Gurani deeply comforting, his ascetic demeanor restful and safe. When they were standing in front of a fountain, Radu blurted out what he could not admit to Lada. He had come so close, had even thought that if he presented it as a secret plan to save their lives she might agree. But he was alone in this, as always. "I want to convert."

Molla Gurani simply blinked and nodded, as though Radu had commented on the weather.

"No one can know. I mean, would that be acceptable? If it was just between God and me?"

"A true conversion is always only between a man and God."

Radu wiped his brow, relieved. If Lada found out that he had made it official, he worried it would break what remained of their bond. Whatever else she was, Lada was his family, his childhood, his past. They had to stay together.

A man walked past them, his robes formal but unfamiliar. He was slender with a pronounced belly, like his middle was a bulb anchoring slender branches. His face was devoid of hair.

Not clean-shaven, but hairless. Molla Gurani inclined his head, and the two men exchanged a greeting. The hairless man looked toward Radu as though expecting an introduction.

"Radu is one of my students. Radu, this is the chief eunuch," Molla Gurani said.

Radu knew it was a title of some sort, but he did not know what level of respect he was supposed to show. Embarrassed, he asked, "What is a eunuch?"

For the first time he could recall, Molla Gurani looked ill at ease.

The chief eunuch smiled, though, and gestured for Radu to join him. "Walk with me and I will tell you."

⋇

Radu stood neck-deep in the water, then bent his knees to leave only his nose and eyes above the surface. The steam rising all around him obscured the patterns of blue and white tile, everything a dizzying blur of heat and color. In Wallachia, they had only bathed during the summer when they stayed on the banks of the Arges. The rest of the time they washed with cloths and basins. Baths were a luxury of the Ottomans he savored.

Lada enjoyed no such comforts. Though the palace bath had certain hours set aside for women, Lada refused to use them. There was a permanent private bath for women, but it was in the harem complex. Lada, of course, could not and would not set foot there. Radu had heard tales of women who entered the harem as a method of divorcing their husbands. The chief eunuch had more stories than anyone in the whole city, and Radu loved hearing them.

But no matter. Lada could spend her free time with the soldiers and their crude jokes and their worse smell. Radu spent his studying the scriptures and the teachings of the Prophet. The feeling he found in holy words was one he could only compare to the long afternoons he had spent with his nurse, sitting by the fire, safe and separate from the rest of the world. He could not quite describe it, and hid it as well as he could from Lada, but when he listened to the call to prayer it felt like home inside his heart.

He wanted to ponder this more, and to practice the words of conversion he said so many times in his heart but never aloud, so he was glad for the solitude of the baths today. He always went at odd times to avoid a crowd. He had begun sprouting hair in new places, his legs aching every night with the stretching pull of time finally claiming his childhood. Besides, there was the curious effect the warm water had on his developing manhood, which he quite enjoyed and preferred to experience alone.

Poor eunuchs. Though the chief eunuch said being castrated and sold was the only future his parents had been able to offer him, Radu did not think it was very kind. The chief eunuch was powerful, yes, in charge of the entire harem and privy to the inner workings of the empire, but what a sacrifice!

Radu closed his eyes, let his arms float, felt all the tension swirl away from him.

Then someone grabbed his ankles and dragged him under the water.

He kicked out, terrified and frantic, remembering the times Mircea would hold his head beneath the fountain until his vision went dark and his lungs nearly burst for want of air.

A horrible thought clawed through Radu's panic. Had Mircea been killed in battle and sent his spirit to drag Radu down with him?

As his scream bubbled out around him, Radu's foot connected with a shoulder and he twisted free. He surfaced, spluttering.

Mehmed popped up next to him, water streaming down his face, white teeth shining. No ghost. Mehmed teasing, not Mircea tormenting. Mehmed's laughter echoed around them, filling the room until they were completely cocooned by it.

Radu felt as though he were breathing in Mehmed's laughter, warm and heavy as it filled his lungs and settled on his skin. "You scared me." His tongue was thick and clumsy in his mouth. He had not seen Mehmed for days, had not seen him alone for weeks.

"Yes, that was apparent." Mehmed's lips twisted into a playful grin. "You looked like you were about to fall asleep. I was worried you would drown."

"Well, thank you for preventing my drowning by pulling me under the water in an attempt to drown me."

Mehmed bowed with a dramatic flourish. He was giddy, cheeks flushed brighter than the heat could account for. The war had not been going well, even with Mehmed's father reluctantly taking the lead.

"Do you have good news?" Radu's chest twisted tight with bands of hope. It was a strange sensation, and one he did not know what to do with. Did he hope Mehmed's forces were winning? Was that traitorous, knowing that his own brother led troops in the conflict? Did the Ottomans winning make it more or less likely that Radu and Lada would be killed for their father's betrayal? And then, seeing the relief shining in Mehmed's black eyes, Radu knew what he hoped for: He hoped for the best for his friend. Regardless of what that meant for himself.

Mehmed threw his arms in the air, splashing them both. The gesture was childlike in its joyful abandon. Ever since they had returned to Edirne, with its politics and demands and war, Mehmed had held himself as unyielding and straight as a stake. Radu laughed to see him relax back into himself.

"My father has triumphed at Varna. The crusade is defeated. Hunyadi fled like a dog, and the Hungarian king's head travels here now on the end of my father's spear!"

Radu smiled as best he could, but his mind worried away at what this meant and how it would affect him.

Mehmed's expression turned thoughtful. "Your father was not there."

Feigning a casual, joking tone that could not be further from how he actually felt, Radu put a hand to his chest. "My father, the coward? Miss a battle where he has tepidly supported both sides? I am shocked."

"I have no word on Mircea's fate."

"His fate is nothing to me." Radu's pretense of disinterest was betrayed by the bitterness that curdled his words.

Mehmed put a hand on his shoulder, the weight of it there both a comfort and a strange thrill. It made Radu feel *real* in a way he often struggled to. "It will work itself out," Mehmed said. "There will be a new treaty. And my father wishes me to remain on the throne. I . . . think I am ready. I know that was not our plan, but the last few weeks have changed my mind. I want this. I think I can be the sultan."

His voice raised at the end, a hint of a question lingering there.

"I think," Radu said, putting his own hand on Mehmed's shoulder, "you will be the greatest sultan your people have ever seen."

"Lada does not believe in me." Mehmed's mouth twisted wryly. "She believes in no one but herself."

Radu shook his head, so aware of the space between them, the water connecting their bodies. He felt secure and happy and closer to Mehmed in this moment than he had ever felt to anyone. "I believe in you enough for both of us." Radu knew Mehmed could do this. And he would be at Mehmed's side, helping him. Lada would, too, even if she pretended at hating life in Edirne. The world and their future opened up before him like the soaring ceiling of the mosque. Upward.

Mehmed nodded solemnly. "And you do not have to worry about your father. As long as I am on the throne, you are under my protection. I will make sure no one hurts you."

Radu closed his eyes in relief. Finally, someone cared enough to keep him safe. Someone who actually had the power to do so. It was a very different reassurance than Lada's promise that no one would kill him but her. Blinking away the emotion that had pooled in the corners of his eyes, Radu nodded. "But . . . perhaps you could make certain that no one lets my father know we are safe."

Mehmed's eyebrows lifted quizzically.

"He does not deserve to be reassured. Let him think he

has killed us. Let him be poisoned with whatever guilt he has the capacity to feel."

"That is fitting. Though I am glad for your father's weakness. Without it, I would have been denied your friendship. And Lada's."

Radu beamed. "I am glad, too."

He had only a split second to register the shift in Mehmed's expression from sincere to mischievous before Mehmed's ankle hooked around Radu's own and Mehmed pushed his head beneath the surface.

Radu rose, coughing, as Mehmed cut through the water away from him, laughter trailing in his wake. As he gave chase, the steam, so thick it looked like a living creature, parted briefly to reveal a man sitting, unnoticed, in the corner of the baths.

Watching them.

The steam once again hid the man just as Radu was able to place his face. Halil Pasha. Mehmed's laughter rang through the room, disembodied as it bounced from wall to ceiling and back again, sounding like a warning bell.

21

A ND HUNYADI FLED," Lada said, riding beside Nicolae. "Like a rabbit before a hawk."

She nodded thoughtfully. "With the Hungarian king dead, everything is in turmoil. Hunyadi might even have an avenue to the throne."

"You think he wants to rule Hungary?"

Lada snorted. "No, he wants to defend Europe out of pure love for the cause of Christ. Of course he wants to rule." She leaned back in her saddle, closing her eyes against the sun. It was a relief to have the Janissaries back. While they had been out fighting, she had worried she would lose her mind with idleness. She had never known what outcome to hope for, either. A win for the Ottomans? A triumph for Hunyadi and hated Mircea?

It did not matter now, as everything was decided. And due to several key deaths, Ilyas had been promoted to lead a larger group, including the Janissary troops who had accompanied Mehmed from Amasya. All together there were several thousand Janissary troops spread throughout the empire, with only a couple hundred regularly stationed in Amasya with Mehmed. It was a nice promotion for Ilyas, but she knew he was destined for bigger things.

"I wish I had been there," Lada said.

Nicolae laughed darkly. "I wish I had not. But if you had been there, little dragon, whose side would you have fought for?"

"My own."

"And which side is that?"

Their father had killed Lada and Radu twice over—first by leaving them here, and next by breaking the treaty that protected their lives. She would not fight for him. And certainly not for Mircea, contemptible worm. Hunyadi she would kill on sight.

No. She rolled her head around on her shoulders, stiff neck straining against jacket collar. It was not Hunyadi's fault her father left Wallachia weak enough that Hunyadi had found a foothold there and forced her father to turn to the sultan.

Mehmed, then? He was her ally in a world straining at its bit, bristling for her death. A laugh, a flash of his dark eyes, a tug on her hair. He was her friend.

He was also ruler of the country holding her captive.

She finally fixed her hooded black eyes on Nicolae. "My *own* side."

She tethered her horse while the Janissaries—Ilyas's men and a few other groups—drilled their horses, practicing formations. Lada was never invited to participate in those, as her participation served no purpose. Weapons training and sparring were individual skills, but hundreds of men moving and reacting as one was something she had no part in. She settled against the roots of a tree at the edge of the open space, in the shade and facing away from the troops.

". . . seems fair enough," said a man walking close by.

"I like him more than the last commander we had. He was a Bulgar. I cannot stand Bulgars."

"I am a Bulgar, you cur."

"And I cannot stand you, either."

They laughed, then the first spoke again. "Are they really leaving the brat on the throne?"

Lada tried to see who was speaking, but the tree blocked her view. Her first impulse was to stand and defend Mehmed. But what would she say? That Mehmed was her friend? She doubted they would accept that as evidence of his leadership qualities.

"As far as I hear, yes. Murad has returned to his retirement."

"Barely on the throne and we have already fought one crusade. How many more are we to fight to defend him?"

"They do not pay us enough to shoulder the burden of the brat."

"They simply do not pay us enough. Last week Ismael openly spoke of protesting in front of the sultan's own bodyguards."

"What do they say?"

"They say nothing. They also do not prevent anyone from saying it. If we could get a few higher-ranking officials on our side, we would be able . . ."

AND I DARKEN

They drifted away, and Lada lost the last of their gossip. Their complaints were not unfamiliar, though they sounded more widespread and accepted than she had thought they were. The Janissaries were a privileged class, educated and paid, but they were still slaves. She wondered how much actual force was behind their words, and how much was empty complaints.

Nicolae rejoined her some time later. They rode out behind the corps, done for the day. He let his horse slow, putting more distance between them and the rest.

When he spoke, he lacked his usual jesting tone. "I have been here since I was seven years old. I have trained alongside brothers from every nation under the shadow of the Ottomans. We fight, we bleed, we die for a country that is not ours, commanded in a tongue our mothers never spoke to us, instructed in a religion that allows us to be enslaved because we were not born to it." He paused, their horses' hooves meting out a discordant rhythm. "And yet my life is better than it would have been at home. I am educated and better trained than anyone we fight. I have enough to eat and clothes on my back, opportunities to advance. Until I am broken against the walls of a city that should be my ally, or die on the end of a sword held by a cousin I never knew. We are the most valuable force of this empire, and we exist here *because* we are not actually part of the empire. Most days I think I owe my life to the Ottomans. On the field at Varna, I realized I do not want to *give* my life for them. But in my heart, I am a soldier, and I wish to do nothing else." He shook his head, a heavy sigh punctuated by his hands lifted into the air, palms up. "I would like to be as certain as you are, Lada, who my side is."

She looked at his palms, open, waiting to receive. "In your heart, where you know you are a soldier, tell me: What language beats there?"

Nicolae's eyes fell, his face going soft and far away. "Wallachian."

She reached out and put her hand on his, resting it there, palm to palm. "We are on the same side."

He wrapped his fingers around hers, then opened his eyes and smiled wryly. "We had best not tell anyone else, then, seeing as how we are deep in enemy territory."

Lada pulled back her hand and took the reins. "For now." She kicked her horse to a gallop, past the soldiers, hair whipping around her face as she raced toward home. *Toward Edirne,* she corrected herself, silently cursing her traitor mind. Maybe she was not so certain whose side she was on after all.

In spite of Ilyas's allowances, the leaders in Edirne were stricter than they had been in Amasya, and too often Lada had been prevented from training with Nicolae's men. She stomped into her chambers, startled to find Radu deep in conversation with Molla Gurani, whom she had not seen these last three months since leaving Amasya.

Her brother looked up, guilt painting itself across his face like the sun disappearing behind a cloud.

"Lada! I thought you would be with the Janissaries."

"Are we being forced to endure his lessons again?" She

scowled. In their time here, with the war and Mehmed's constant duties as sultan, she and Radu had not yet received regular tutelage. While she wanted to resume the history, logic, and strategy lessons, she had not missed Molla Gurani's insufferable dronings on Islam.

Molla Gurani's eyebrows lifted slowly, heavy with the weight of his disdain. "I am here at your brother's request. You are welcome to be elsewhere."

"What is he talking about?" Lada snapped, lapsing into Wallachian for privacy.

Radu shrugged, head tilted to one side as though he were trapping something between his ear and shoulder. "Know your enemy?"

Caught off guard, Lada barked out a sharp laugh. "You will have to know this enemy enough for both of us." She bowed mockingly toward the teacher and went into her own small room. While this freed her from Molla Gurani's fetid-water voice, it left her with nothing to do and no refuge.

She flopped onto her bed and boredom made her eyes heavy with sleep. She dreamed of Amasya, swimming in the pool with Radu and Mehmed, stars swirling and burning around them. When she awoke, it was with Mehmed's name heavy on her tongue, his absence in her life a palpable pain.

She hurried out of their rooms before Radu could ask where she was going, before she had to admit to him—and herself—how much she longed for a few private moments with Mehmed as her friend, not as the sultan.

In the halls of the palace, she felt invisible. There were

so few women here. In Tirgoviste women had been far more present, less separated from the regular courts. She wondered, sometimes, what her life would have been like had her mother not fled. Would she have had an ally? A friend? Would her mother have stopped her father from leaving them here?

Probably not. Her mother had not been strong enough to stay with them, much less keep them safe.

Perhaps, though, she would feel stronger walking down these halls with another woman at her side. Halima laughing, or Mara glowering. Maybe they did have something to teach her, after all. Men here either looked right past her as though she did not exist, or looked so hard that she knew they were not seeing *her* at all. It made her long for a weapon in her hand, for a crown instead of snarled braids, for a beard, even. For anything that would make them see her for what and who she was.

Or perhaps, looking at her and seeing nothing, they understood perfectly well who she was already.

She was not certain the guards would allow her to see Mehmed. She had never come without an invitation. If she was turned away, she did not know what she would do. But after only a few heartbeats of waiting, the guards let her through.

Mehmed looked up from his desk, eyes lighting as he stood. Lada felt the tension and terror of anonymity drain from her body.

She mattered to Mehmed.

"To what do I owe the honor?" he asked, sweeping his arm back in an exaggerated bow.

"Do not make me knock your turban off." She pushed past him and sat in his seat, examining the papers so he would not notice how grateful, how glad to be in his presence she was. He did not need anyone else nourishing his ego; Radu did that enough for the entire Draculesti line. Lada lifted several pages, all notes and ledgers and maps. Detailed lists of troops and supplies, Janissary forces, horses, wagons, weapons. Ledgers of various accounts. Maps of . . . Constantinople.

She tapped a finger on one. "You have been busy."

He leaned over her, tracing the edge of the map reverentially. "I am the sultan, Lada."

"I have noticed."

He grinned, the expression wiping away the regal years he tried to force onto his face by distant scowls. "My father has returned to his retirement. I did not think I was ready, but the throne is mine regardless. And I will be worthy of it."

Lada shrugged, shifting away from the intensity of Mehmed's pose, his body radiating energy so near hers. It was only because she had not been around him much these last three months that his presence affected her so. Or maybe it was because she could not help noticing he was growing taller, more handsome, more . . . No. She needed to focus on something else. *Anything* else. "Constantinople? This soon?"

He walked away from her, began pacing. "We have a five-year peace treaty with Hungary and Hunyadi. My borders are as peaceful as they ever were. This is why I am here. This is why I was born."

"Your father started out his rule trying the same thing, and it brought him nothing but trouble."

A line formed between Mehmed's fine brows. "He had too many fronts. His brothers trying to claim what was his, trying to steal land. He had to attend to problems at home."

"And your advisors support you?"

His scowl deepened. "Not all of them, no. But I am sultan. They must follow me."

"A sultan who summoned his father to fight his first battle."

Mehmed's face erupted into a storm. "That was your idea! If you—"

Lada heard the noise before she registered that anything was wrong. An instinct honed by all those days in the forest with Bogdan hunting her, a body trained with focus provided by desperation and loneliness. A sudden sense of wrongness she could have ignored.

She threw herself forward and tackled Mehmed as a dagger flew past where his chest had been. It cut her shoulder before clanging sharply against the wall and falling to the ground. Lada and Mehmed hit the floor hard, with Mehmed letting out a breathless groan. Lada rolled forward, picking the dagger up, then turned and threw it as soon as she spied a moving target.

The man dodged a fatal blow, the dagger glancing off his side. His face was wrapped in black cloth, features hidden; his clothes were plain.

Their assailant pulled out another dagger, crouching defensively and stalking to the side, trying to find a better angle on Mehmed. Lada kicked her friend toward the desk. "Get behind it!" she shouted.

The man passed his dagger from hand to hand, movements lazy and unhurried as Mehmed scrambled behind the desk and shouted for his guards.

The assassin did not seem concerned.

His eyes crinkled in a smile as he looked at Lada. He pointed the dagger at her, then looked toward Mehmed. Lada launched herself forward, barreling into him with all the momentum she could build. He was strong, lean and lithe, but she was solid and lower to the ground. She hit him squarely in his middle, the air leaving his lungs in a rush as she took him to the ground. His grip on the dagger loosened, and it skittered away, out of both of their reach.

The assassin was stunned, but he would recover fast. Lada punched him in the face, again and again, but her angle was off and she could not use as much strength as she hoped to. He grabbed her wrists, pulling her to the side. Her face was forced close to his, his hands too strong to break free from. She slammed her forehead into his nose, then bit into his cheek where his head wrap had come loose.

He cried out and released her wrists. Rolling away, she found the dagger and spun around as he stumbled to his feet. He dodged her first lunge, moved with her in a dance she had practiced many times in the ring with Nicolae. A dance they both knew the same moves to. Even bloodied and dazed, he was more than a match for her.

And still no help had come.

Her training was failing her, the jabs and the lunges

anticipated, killing blows knocked aside. One of these times he would catch her wrist and get the dagger, and then he would kill her and Mehmed.

Despair welled up in her. A look of triumph shaped the assassin's eyes into omens of death. He knew everything she would do. He only had to outlast her. She was a girl, and a child. He was stronger, and faster, and . . .

With a scream of rage, Lada abandoned her learned moves, her careful training. She flew at him like a wild boar, all fury and animal instinct. He did not know where to block because her blows made no sense, her movements had no grace. She slashed at his face, and when he grabbed her wrists, she bit his hand, clenching her jaw, teeth clamping onto bone. She kept her teeth in him as he shook her, slamming the dagger into his side again and again, following him as he fell away from her, trying to break free. She stayed on top, stabbing, not caring where she hit, not going for a careful, efficient blow. An animal scream, muffled by his hand, continued from her throat.

"Lada!"

Shaking and panting, she blinked her eyes clear of the haze that had descended. Her jaw would not unlock, the muscles so tight she wondered if she would have this man's hand in her mouth forever. Finally, with pain shooting through her whole face, she managed to part her teeth enough for his hand to fall free. It was then that she tasted the blood that filled her mouth, then that she realized she was on the floor, on top of the man.

On top of the body.

She staggered to her feet, then fell back down, crawling away from the ruined body.

Mehmed placed a hand on her face and turned it toward his own. "Are you hurt?"

She shook her head, then nodded, then shook it again. She did not know if she was hurt. Everything was trembling, everything was numb. She looked down at her hands, covered in blood, and could not feel them.

"Lada. Lada. *Lada.*"

She snapped her eyes back to Mehmed. He was the only thing in the room that she could focus on, the only thing that made sense.

"My guards never came."

She knew that was important, knew she had known it was important, before . . . this. Before the blood. So much blood.

"Do you think they are dead?" Mehmed took a step toward the door. He should not go out there. She knew he should not, tried to figure out why.

Everything snapped back into place. "Stop! We need to leave. Another way. The guards are either dead or they were collaborators."

Mehmed shook his head. "They are Janissaries. They would never—"

"He was a Janissary."

"What?"

Her teeth trembling, Lada peeled back the man's mask. She did not recognize him, and found herself deeply grateful for that. But she still knew what he was, if not who. "The way he fought. I have sparred with dozens of versions of him. He trained as a Janissary. We need to get out of here, now, and we need to hide until we know who to trust."

Mehmed was shaking as much as she was. "Who can I trust?" he whispered.

Lada held out her hand. He took it.

22

UNDER OTHER CIRCUMSTANCES, the look of utter bewilderment on Lada's face would have delighted Radu. She was always so certain of herself that the image of her standing in the middle of the room, stiff, arms wrapped protectively around herself as her eyes darted everywhere, should have been one he treasured.

But she was covered in blood, and Mehmed's jaw trembled when he was not talking, and both of them looked the way Radu always felt on the inside.

He could not feel that way right now. They needed him.

"We have to go somewhere else," Radu said. "It is well enough known that we are Mehmed's friends. If there are more assassins, and they search for him, they may look here."

Lada shook her head, eyes pleading. "I could not think of anywhere else to go."

If, as Mehmed and Lada suspected, a group of Janissaries were behind the attempt, the palace was not safe. They had no way of knowing who had set it up, whether it was the soldiers themselves, or whether they were acting under orders from someone else. What if they ran to an advisor or a pasha for help, and ended up in the clutches of the very person who had ordered Mehmed's death?

No, they needed somewhere secure. Somewhere secret. Somewhere no one else here could go, but that they could get to quickly. Because they could not simply run. Mehmed was the sultan, and if they ran now, he would lose everything.

Where could a sultan go to hide?

Radu snapped his fingers. "The harem!"

Lada's look of horror intensified.

Mehmed frowned. "But they might look there, too."

"Your mother is there, yes?"

Mehmed nodded. "We do not speak much, though."

Harem politics were as complicated as court politics, if not more so. Though the harem was a community unto itself, the women could exert incredible influence on the most powerful man in the empire, making them a political force to be reckoned with. The most powerful woman in the harem— and, therefore, in the empire—was the mother of the sultan. Radu had never met her, but the chief eunuch had remarked on her intelligence.

"Your mother stands to lose the most if you are killed, so she will protect you," Radu said. "And the guards there are eunuchs, not Janissaries. We will be safe, and you can begin investigating."

Mehmed clasped his shoulder. "Yes! Yes. Thank you, Radu."

"No!" Lada shook her head, eyes still wild. "I cannot go

in there! If a woman enters the harem complex, she belongs to the sultan!"

Mehmed peered out the window they had climbed through, to make sure their path was clear. "I would not hold you to that, Lada, and—"

"It would not matter! Everyone would know, I would be labeled your concubine, and—"

Radu took her hand, which still hung in the air pointing accusingly at Mehmed, and squeezed it in his own. "And you would be unmarriageable? What a tragedy. I know how dearly you treasured the hope of marrying some minor Ottoman noble, dear sister."

She finally met his eyes, hers still feverish and frenzied. "But I would be his."

"I think our Mehmed is smart enough to know he could never claim you. Right?"

Radu's tone was light, and he turned to Mehmed with a playful smile. Perhaps it was the dimness of the room, or the stress of the night, but Mehmed's face was clouded with ... disappointment? Hurt? Then a tight, false smile took its place, and he nodded. Radu's own chest felt equally tight with anxiety and fear and a twisting, bitter sense of jealousy.

He pushed it down. Assassins were after them. Lada had killed a man. They needed to move. He said a prayer in his heart, then went first, climbing slowly down the palace's carved stone exterior to the ground. Mehmed followed, and then Lada. Radu led the way, creeping through the gardens, keeping to the deepest shadows.

"How do you know the way to the harem so well?"

Mehmed said. "I think you are more familiar with the path than I am."

Radu flushed, feeling defensive, but there was no accusation in Mehmed's voice. "I know the chief eunuch. He has an amazing collection of maps, and I visit him sometimes. Did you know he was born in Transylvania?"

Mehmed's tone was strained but amused. "I did, in fact, know that about the third most powerful man in my government."

"Oh. Right." Even when Radu had the best idea for keeping them safe, everyone always knew more than he did. He stopped outside the guard gate, a side entrance to the vast harem complex. A guard stood posted, his white turban a bright spot in the dark night. On his first trip, Radu had tried to see a difference in the eunuchs as opposed to uncastrated men, but other than their voices not being as deep as a man's nor as high as a woman's, he was not able to tell who was a eunuch and who was not.

The guard, whom Radu had met before, cocked his head curiously at Radu before noticing Mehmed behind him. He bowed low to the ground, then stood at attention.

Mehmed did not acknowledge him as he walked straight past. Radu nodded, and the man's eyes followed them. Without knocking, Mehmed entered the outer apartments of the chief eunuch.

Though it was late, they had not been in the room more than a minute before the chief eunuch joined them. He was an older man, nearing forty, skin wrinkled and features indistinct, as though his face had never decided quite who it wanted to be. He bowed to Mehmed, then straightened with a smile for Radu. He took in Lada's bloodstained appearance with a mere flick of his gaze. "How can I serve you, My Sultan?"

"I need a conference with the valide sultan. Also lodging for the night."

"Of course. Whose company would you like?"

It took a moment for Radu to follow the easy way in which the chief eunuch asked the question. And then another moment to process what it meant. His face grew heated with embarrassment, and also curiosity. Was this— Did Mehmed come here regularly? Was he already enjoying the benefits of being sultan? How many concubines could he have amassed after so short a time? Did he have a wife already? Islam had rules about how many wives a man could have, but exceptions were made for sultans.

And what was it like, being with him? Did they love him? Did they wait every day, hoping to see him?

Radu glanced at Lada to see if she was wondering the same things. Her eyes were fixed determinedly on the far wall, a scowl set on her face. They had cleaned the blood from around her mouth and off her hands, but there were traces of it still. She looked wild and angry, nothing like a concubine. At least, not how Radu imagined them to look.

Radu pictured concubines like his nurse, matronly and soft and always sewing or fussing. He knew that was not their purpose, but whenever he tried to imagine *that*, everything got hazy and confused.

Mehmed's voice was strained. "None tonight. I am here on business. Prepare a room for my companions as well. Lada will need a bath."

"Shall I have the servants escort her to her new room?"

"No!" Mehmed's voice came out a shout, making the chief eunuch startle. "No. She is here as a guest, not as a . . . resident. House us in the guard wing."

"And no one can know that we are here," Radu said, unsure if he was allowed to speak, but worried that Mehmed was too distracted.

Mehmed gave him a brief, grateful glance. "Yes. My business is with the valide sultan alone, and no one—not even my guards, should they inquire—is to know that we are here."

The chief eunuch nodded, then bowed again and left the room to make preparations. As soon as he was gone, Mehmed's shoulders slumped. He put a hand over his eyes, head hanging low. Lada had found a bit of dried blood on her hand and was furiously rubbing it against her skirts, trying to get it clean. The fact that her skirts were stained with blood did not seem to occur to her. Radu stood between her and Mehmed, not knowing what either needed, suspecting they both needed the same thing.

He went to Mehmed instead of his sister, and put his arm around the sultan's shoulders. Mehmed leaned gratefully against him. Radu looked up at Lada and held out his free arm. She considered it, eyes heavy with exhaustion and something that looked suspiciously like sorrow. Before she could move, the chief eunuch returned. Mehmed straightened and stepped away from Radu, and Lada resumed staring at the wall.

"Follow me," the chief eunuch said, and Radu once again found himself in the back, the pool of light from the eunuch's lamp not quite reaching him.

23

MEHMED'S MOTHER MOVED WITH a sensuous grace that terrified Lada.

Lada could not seem to get comfortable, no matter where she sat in the opulently perfumed and padded room. The valide sultan occupied too much space here, with her silks and her veil and her dripping jewelry, with her careful face and her calculating smile and the way she lay across several pillows with as much precision as any Janissary sword.

If Halima and Mara were different seasons, Huma was nature itself.

"Sit down." Her voice was kind, but a narrowing of her eyes indicated that she would brook no argument. Mehmed ceased pacing and sat across from her. He seemed as out of sorts as Lada. He had never known his mother, not in any real sense, and now came to her from a place of weakness. It was not ideal.

Lada remembered the sensation of the dagger meeting the resistance of flesh, the unyielding bone that made it turn course, always seeking more, deeper, deeper. . . .

Not ideal. None of this was ideal. She had bathed, her hair still wet, but her hands felt sticky and her mouth would not surrender the memory of the bright, metallic taste of blood.

Radu, however, seemed fascinated, even delighted by the valide sultan. He sat near her, a rapt, worshipful look on his face. As though sensing the weight of his admiration, the valide sultan turned to him. Her lips, so much like Mehmed's, parted in a way that was almost like their nurse's smile. A way her lips had not moved for Mehmed.

"You were very clever, to bring him here. Radu, is it?" She sat up, leaning forward and putting her finger under his chin to lift his face. "Beautiful," she murmured. Her gaze flicked toward Lada, whose spine stiffened and jaw jutted out defiantly. She knew how she would compare. The valide sultan's smile shifted into something less maternal, but Lada did not know what it was.

"Valide Sultan," Lada said, scowling over the show they were being forced to endure, "we need to—"

"You may call me Huma. Both of you." She turned back to Mehmed, settling back down and resting her lovely cheek on her palm. "And you may call me Mother." A small laugh, like coins being dropped into a well, escaped her lips.

"We do not have time—"

Huma held up a hand heavy with gold, cutting off Mehmed. "We do not have time to panic, or to display weakness. We have all the time in the world to allow you to engage in your much-deserved holiday as you take full advantage of the pleasures of your harem. Indeed, were the new sultan to spend an entire week of debauchery and riotous celebration with his women, no one could blame him. Or interrupt him. Or access him. And no one could discover how tenuous his power truly was and how close he came to being murdered before he could rule."

"But the assassin—"

"Did not exist. It never happened. No one would ever attempt to take the life of the sultan, because to admit an attempt happened and nearly succeeded is to admit that it is possible to imagine an Ottoman empire without you at its head." Her darkly lined eyes narrowed. "Do you understand? You are not hiding here. You are reveling. You are enjoying your power."

Mehmed nodded, one slight dip of his head.

Huma's face returned to its cheerful, lovely mask. "I have already sent the chief eunuch notice to inform the pashas and viziers of your activities. Word will spread. We have all the time we need."

It was a good lie. And in order to be a good lie, it had to be believable. Lada did not want to think about why it would be so easily believed, how much time Mehmed had already spent here, whether there was precedence. She did not want to think about any of this.

It made her weak, this avoidance of reality. And still she recoiled when her mind tried to settle on it.

Huma stood, a rustling of silks and a cloud of sweetness trailing in her wake. But there was an undertone to it, a sharp scent that made Lada's eyes water and her head swim. "Now go to your rooms. Servants will be by to see to you shortly."

Mehmed opened his mouth as if to argue. Huma raised

a single perfect brow. "Let your mother take care of this, my precious son." The soft and comforting words were spoken in a tone that pierced like a needle.

Feigning a look of indifference, Mehmed walked past her, followed by Radu. Lada stood to leave as well, but Huma's arm shot out, blocking her way. "Take a meal with me."

"I would rather return to my room."

Huma traced a finger down the line of her own hip, stroking the material of her dress lazily. "It was not a request."

Lada took a step forward, but Huma seized her wrist. Huma laughed, and in her laugh Lada heard all the secrets she had never been privy to. "Ladislav Dragwlya, daughter of Vlad, who sent forces, including his own son, to fight at Varna, thus invalidating his treaty with the Ottomans and leaving his children's lives utterly forfeit. Ladislav, whom no one in the world other than her beautiful brother and a powerless sultan care about. Little Lada, who is in my house under my protection, *sit down.*"

Lada remembered the feeling of skin and tendons clamped between her teeth, the resistance of flesh meeting the determination of her jaw. For one brief, dizzy moment, she considered attacking Huma, savaging her the same way she had Mehmed's attacker.

Instead, she sat.

"Good girl." Huma clapped her hands and a trio of delicate flowers in girl form came in, setting food and drink in front of them, then gliding silently away. Lada watched the girls, and as she watched them, she wondered, *Are they Mehmed's? Has he been here? Has he picked these flowers?*

Huma's pointy red tongue flicked out, running along her

teeth as she considered the meal in front of them. Lada was reminded of a snake, which confused her. Women were the garden, and men were the snakes. Her nurse had explained how men and women came together in the marriage bed to her when she was very young, around the same time her religious tutors had taught her the story of Adam and Eve. The two had mixed together in her head, until it was men and their snakes that had persuaded Eve to lose her beautiful, perfect garden.

No garden could survive the introduction of a snake. Everything would be lost, would then belong to the snake forever.

Lada knew more now, of course, from the rude talk and graphic stories of the Janissaries. They had only served to further her conviction that her interpretation had been correct all along.

But here was Huma, and she was no garden. She was a serpent. "Murad liked his girls very young. I spent several years eating almost nothing so that I could stay small and undeveloped." She picked up a leg of chicken, roasted and covered with cracked flakes of pepper. Her eyes rolled back as she bit into it, a soft, satisfied hum slipping through her lips. "I thought I would die of want before I ever managed to conceive an heir. But then precious Mehmed took up in my womb, and I could eat again."

Lada took some flatbread, tearing it into small pieces as she watched Huma luxuriate over her food. Several more times the little flowers brought food, refilled Huma's wine, even wiped her mouth clean.

"You are fascinated with the girls," Huma said. Lada

snapped her attention back to the older woman. She had assumed Huma was so absorbed in her consumption of food that Lada had let her mind and gaze wander.

"Why do they veil their faces? Does your god hate even the sight of women?"

Huma laughed. "You misunderstand. Women should veil their bodies, yes. But veiling the face is a symbol of status. Only women who are so well provided for they can afford not to do menial labor may wear a veil. These girls have earned their veils. It is a mark of privilege."

"Privilege? They are slaves!"

Huma laughed. "So am I, dearest. I was sold as a very young girl, brought to the harem as a servant as well."

Lada scowled. "You should have fought them. You should have escaped."

"To where? I was angry, for many years. And frightened. But there are many ways to be powerful. There is power in stillness. There is power in watching, waiting, saying the right thing at the right time to the right person. There is power in being a woman—oh yes, power in these bodies you gaze upon with derision." Huma ran one hand down her ample breasts, over her stomach, and rested it on her hip. "When you have something someone else wants, there is always an element of power."

"But it can be taken from you." Lada had seen enough of men and the world to know that a woman's body was not an object of power.

"Or it can be given in exchange for more important things. These girls, my servants, understand that. The smart ones, anyhow. They will spend years climbing, trying to get in a position where they have some measure of control. The ones who are clever will do better than the ones who are merely beautiful."

Her gaze was so pointed, Lada felt herself blush. She dropped the pieces of ripped flatbread onto the plate in front of her. She felt awkward, ungainly, and uglier than she had ever considered herself before. It had not bothered her, most of her life, knowing that she was not beautiful, would never gain admiration for her looks alone. But Huma used her face as a weapon and a tool in a way Lada never could. Lada had never realized that simply by being attractive, she might have gained more threads of power.

Lada lifted her chin defiantly. "I can be strong without giving anything up. I saved Mehmed."

Huma picked up a date and sucked on it. "Mmm. Yes, you did. And that was well done. But you did not think you were the only woman who has ever killed to protect him, did you?"

Lada frowned in confusion, then immediately regretted it. Huma seemed to be pulling information from everything. She was dragging her long fingers through Lada's very soul, merely by watching her face.

Huma lay back on her pillows, lifting a hand to her forehead, her sleeve falling down to reveal the long, pale curve of her arm. "It was such a tragedy when Mehmed's eldest brother fell ill and died so suddenly. To be struck down in his prime! And then Mehmed's second brother and his two sons, murdered by unknown assailants. Oh, what sadness. Only one son left of an age to inherit should Murad fall in battle!" Her expression of mock sorrow shifted to something darker, angrier. "Or, should he decide to *retire* and simply throw his one remaining heir to the wolves. Murad has jeopardized everything I worked for."

Lada's mind spun. "But you cannot leave the harem! How could you have done all this?"

"Did you notice the men who work here?"

Lada shook her head.

"Exactly as it is supposed to be. My precious eunuchs, they make everyone so deeply uncomfortable. Men cannot stand to look upon them, tormented with imagining what they must have endured to become what they are. The eunuchs are slaves, just as I am, but they, too, have sacrificed. They have had something precious and irreplaceable taken from them, and in doing so, have created a place of power for themselves. They are everywhere in this country, in every important household; they are clerks, they are guards, they are *mine*." Huma sat up, her movement so sudden and violent compared with her lazy, sensual motions that Lada jerked back.

"You see this"—Huma gestured to the room, the building, and finally to herself—"as a prison. But you are wrong. This is my court. This is my throne. This is my kingdom. The cost was my freedom and my body." Her fine eyebrows raised, mouth playful, eyes hard. "So the question becomes, Daughter of the Dragon, what will you sacrifice? What will you let be taken away so that you, too, can have power?"

This was so different from what Mara had presented to Lada. Not an offering of oneself for the benefit of a bigger cause, but the offering of a portion of oneself for the pursuit of personal gain. "I—nothing, I—I," she stammered.

"Would you sacrifice my son?"

"What? No! I protected him, I—"

"Would you sacrifice what you think your life should be for what it *could* be, were you to rule at my son's side?" Huma paused, then laughed at Lada's tortured expression. "So that is not your design. Very well. You may go now. But I want you to think on what must be sacrificed to secure a future where no one can touch you. I want you to think of Mehmed, and his future." She waved a hand dismissively, and Lada fled.

24

A LL THE FEAR THAT had felt so overwhelming in the darkness seemed tempered the next day, as the brilliant sun illuminated a palace going about business as usual.

Huma had instructed Radu and Lada to act as if nothing had changed, but to draw no attention to themselves.

Radu took a deep, shaking breath, then slid along the wall toward Mehmed's rooms. Returning to the scene of the assassination attempt was probably a bad idea. If there were soldiers in the hall, he would turn and run. Pretend to be lost. Pray they were not the ones who let this happen, since Mehmed did not know who had been on duty, and they could not very well ask.

But Radu wanted to be brave. Maybe Lada and Mehmed, in their terror, had missed something. If he went in, if he searched the . . .

Even thinking the words *the body* made him recoil. But he would. Huma wanted to pretend it had never happened. Radu wanted to know why it had. If he found some vital clue, he might be the one to rescue Mehmed this time. Radu might have gotten Mehmed to safety, but Lada was the one who had actually saved him.

That bothered him more than it should. And made him reckless.

However, when he turned the corner, the cavernous hall outside Mehmed's rooms echoed with the absence of life.

Was the body still inside? Had no one discovered it? Huma had notified everyone that Mehmed was reveling in the harem. Perhaps no one had been in Mehmed's rooms since. Sick with dread and a morbid curiosity, Radu slipped through the doors, past Mehmed's waiting chamber toward his study. He held his breath, then stepped inside.

No blood on the gleaming tile floor. No discarded dagger. No lifeless assassin.

Someone had cleaned up after all. There was nothing to suggest the violence this room had held.

But no—that was wrong. A rug, one of Radu's favorites, cheerfully blue and yellow, was gone. The only evidence was the absence of things that should have been there: the body, the blood, the rug, and Mehmed.

Radu walked to the desk, reverently placing his hands on various objects. An inkwell. A map of Constantinople with notes scrawled across it in Mehmed's compact, aggressive script. Several booklets of religious thought that Radu had been hoping to borrow. A heavy, leather-bound tome detailing the life of Alexander the Great.

The whisper of an outer door sent Radu into a panic. He threw himself behind a pillar, just as the door to the study opened.

The intruder's steps were quiet but assured. Radu heard

items being shuffled, then the crackle of a stiff sheet of parchment resisting being rolled. The intruder left as quickly as he had entered. After a few seconds to calm his racing heart, Radu left his hiding place and returned to the desk. Everything was there.

Except the map of Constantinople with Mehmed's careful notes.

Without giving himself time to think better of it, Radu raced out of the rooms. He saw a hint of movement around a far corner and ran after it. He turned the same corner and saw the figure—a boy, perhaps sixteen, wearing the plain clothes of a servant, walking with submissive but purposeful posture. It was exactly how Radu would move if he needed to get somewhere without being noticed.

And so he copied the boy's posture, always keeping him in his line of sight, but staying far enough back not to be noticed. He followed the thief out of the palace grounds, to the nearest street, where opulent, majestic homes bullied the cobblestones for space. The thief joined several people filing in and out of the gates of the first estate. Radu grabbed a basket lying on the stones near the entrance and tucked it under his arm, grateful that he was wearing simple clothes today instead of one of the nicer outfits Mehmed had gifted him with.

The thief entered the home through a side door. He knew where he was going. Radu followed, winding his way through a busy kitchen, nearly losing sight of his prey. They went through a back hallway and then up a narrow flight of hidden stairs for the servants' use. The walls were close, the steps uneven, the air damp with confinement. In the gloom, Radu only just saw a door swing shut, as he was about to climb another flight of stairs. He pushed through the door into another world. Light spilled with reckless abandon through a wide, high-ceilinged hallway. Thick woven rugs lined the floor, with tile gleaming in the gaps. Statuary and pottery kept the turquoise-hued walls company, reassuring each other of their glorious beauty. Highly polished metal mirrors hung at regular intervals, giving the impression of hallways beyond this one.

All the doors were shut, and there was no sign of the thief.

Radu nearly backed into the stairwell when he noticed that one of the heavy wooden doors was slightly ajar. He crept toward it. If anyone caught him, he would have no excuse for his presence.

"... cleaned up, as you predicted," said a voice Radu did not recognize but suspected was the servant's.

"The little swine," a deeper, older voice growled. There was a rough sound of parchment being flattened, then a few seconds of heavy silence. Radu glanced nervously down the hallway, but he was still in the clear.

"Arrogant devil," the older man said, followed by some choice curses. "He thinks he can defeat the walls of the city? That it is his divine calling? May God save us from servants such as these."

There was a swish of parchment, the scratching of a quill. Sweat trickled down Radu's back. Taking a deep breath, he put his eye to the cracked door. The room was revealed in a single line, and Radu shifted to expand his view. There, the back of the servant. And at a desk, pouring wax onto a folded letter to seal it, the man.

Halil Pasha.

Halil Pasha pressed a ring into the wax, then handed the letter to the servant. "See that this is delivered."

Radu darted from his perch near the door, back to the stairwell. His breath came in shallow, desperate gasps. He crept into the shadows clinging to the bottom of the next flight of stairs, waiting.

The door opened, and with a terrified rush, Radu launched himself forward against the servant. The boy grabbed at Radu's shirt, but his fingers found no claim as he fell backward down the narrow stairs, head slamming into the wall as his feet went over and his body thudded before coming to a stop, jammed at an awkward angle.

Radu waited one breath, two breaths, three interminable breaths that filled his lungs with fear instead of air, and then, when the servant did not move or cry out for help, he rushed to his side. The letter was not in his hands, it was all for nothing, Radu had murdered him and now—

The boy's chest moved and a low groan escaped his lips. Radu prayed his relief to the heavens, then felt in the servant's clothes for . . . yes! The letter! He tucked it into his own shirt, then hurried down the stairs, nearly falling over his own feet. Taking a few precious seconds at the bottom, he slowed and entered the kitchen calmly. Every limb screamed at him to run, but he walked at a measured pace, a pleasantly blank look on his face, before he finally emerged into the sunlight of the yard, and then escaped through the gate. Only when he had turned back to the palace grounds did he allow himself to run.

A flash of dark hair and a familiar, aggressive walk caught

his eye. Gasping with relief, he changed direction, plowing into Lada and nearly knocking her over.

"What is wrong with you?" she said, grabbing his shoulders to steady them both.

"I have just come from ... someone was in Mehmed's rooms, and they stole ... there is a letter here!" He waved it in front of Lada's face. Scowling in exasperation, she snatched it from him and stalked away. He followed her, checking over his shoulder.

"Stop it," she snapped. "You might as well be waving a flag that says 'I am guilty!'"

He tried to copy her walk, forced himself to stare straight ahead. When they arrived at the harem, a eunuch let them in and they returned to Lada's room. It was sparsely furnished with a plain bed and a simple chair, the chamber pot tucked into the corner and a small washbasin on a low table.

"My room is nicer," Radu said, nerves bubbling over.

"Of course it is." Lada sat on the bed and dropped the letter beside her. "Huma loves you. Everyone loves you."

Radu itched to find out what was in the letter, to tell Lada how well he had done. It would be important. It had to be. But ... what if it was nothing? What if he had attacked a servant over a letter to a distant relative? Halil Pasha had said nothing of the assassination attempt. The servant could have been picking something up Halil Pasha was meant to have.

Terrified to be wrong, terrified to be right, Radu delayed. "What were you doing out?"

"I visited Nicolae. He has heard nothing of an attempt

on Mehmed's life. Ilyas continues to lead his men as though everything is normal."

"But we were supposed to keep it—"

Lada lifted a hand to silence him. "Nicolae will not spread the news. We can trust him. Though he was surprised at the attempt, he seemed less surprised at my theory it was a Janissary. Dissatisfaction spreads through the men like a disease. Nicolae even heard talk of hating Mehmed from several chorbaji—" She huffed in exasperation at Radu's confused look. "Chorbaji are the Janissaries' commanders. I have heard talk among ranking Janissaries, but for chorbaji to be speaking up, things must be serious. But Nicolae does not know who is responsible."

Radu held up the letter, his hand trembling. "Maybe this has answers."

Lada cracked the seal and opened the letter. The ink was so fresh Radu could smell it. His eyes went immediately to the signature.

"Halil Pasha." Lada spat his name like a curse. She did not even elbow Radu away as he leaned against her to scan the letter. "He is writing to Constantinople. Reassuring them that Mehmed will never lead the Ottoman troops against them."

"But he cannot promise that! Mehmed is determined to . . ." Radu stopped.

Lada met his eyes, her own heavy with knowledge. "He *can* promise that. Mehmed cannot lead Ottoman troops against them if he is dead."

Radu stood up. "We have to tell someone! Halil Pasha will be arrested, and—"

"And who will arrest him? The sultan's Janissaries? They hate Mehmed. We do not know which of them—or how many, or how high up—knew of the attempt. And who would believe us? This says nothing of killing Mehmed, or having already tried to. It is flimsy evidence against a powerful man."

"We have to do something!"

Lada scowled. "If only Murad had come back like he was supposed to, none of this would be happening!"

"Mehmed will not give up the throne. He wants it now. There has to be another way to help him."

Lada folded the letter, tapping it absently against her leg. "What would you sacrifice for power?"

"What?"

She looked up at him, brows furrowed, an expression of intense thought on her face. "For power, Halil Pasha would kill Mehmed. For power, the Janissaries would abandon their duty to the throne. Everyone is willing to sacrifice Mehmed. We must figure out how to do it first."

Radu backed up, aghast. "We have to protect him! I will not let you sacrifice him!" He turned to leave. Lada grabbed his arm but he shook her off, turning the door handle. Lada knocked him to the ground, her knee digging into his back.

"Shut up and listen to me! Something must be sacrificed. That something is Mehmed. We sacrifice Mehmed's throne now, so that he lives to take it later. If he stays, he will die. We keep him safe until he is older. Smarter. Stronger. When he will come to the throne not as a powerless child but as his precious hand of God on Earth."

"Do not mock him!"

"We will lose everything, Radu." Lada's voice was ragged, and Radu felt a sudden fear that if he could see her face, she would be crying. That terrified him more than anything, the idea of Lada breaking down. The man she had killed, the attack, they were foreign to him. He had not seen them or felt them in any real way. But Lada crying meant the end of his world. If Lada could not be strong, how could he ever hope to be?

She continued. "Mehmed is our only protection. Do you think I want to see him powerless? Without Mehmed in charge, we face execution for our father's crimes."

"So we help him! We figure out how to beat Halil Pasha!"

"We would be gambling with Mehmed's life. The next assassination attempt will not fail." She leaned heavily on top of him, easing her knee off his back. "Our lives were forfeit the moment Father brought us here. I cannot . . ." She paused, and her voice got softer. She tangled her fingers in one of his curls, tugging like she used to when they were small, but with no force. "I *will* not risk Mehmed's life on the chance that it will work out in our favor."

"It does not matter. Mehmed will never give up the throne." If Lada had seen him that day in the baths—seen his joy and his determination—she would understand. Mehmed was the sultan now, with as much passion as he had for everything he set his sights on. Lada moved, her back against the door. Radu joined her, shoulder to shoulder. "If we ask him to abdicate, if we tell him he cannot stay sultan, he will never forgive us. We will lose his friendship and his trust."

"Then we arrange for the throne to be taken from him.

It is that, or his death. The throne and his pride, or his life, Radu."

Radu thought of his friend, thought of the fire in his heart that was burning ever brighter as he worked to claim his destiny. He thought of it all being taken away in the most humiliating way possible.

He thought of Mehmed's spark being taken from the world forever.

He leaned his head against the heavy wood of the door. It would break Mehmed. But it would save him. "How do we do it?"

Lada rested her hand where a sword would be sheathed if she were practicing with the Janissaries. "I think I have an idea."

———◆———

"You want me to *what*?" Huma asked. Laughter teased her voice, but there was violence behind her eyes.

"Get the Janissaries to revolt."

"Why would I do that? It would destabilize the whole city."

"Exactly." Lada sat perfectly still and spoke calmly. Radu knew it was taking great effort—he could tell by the way one of Lada's feet, not quite hidden beneath her skirts, bounced up and down. "They are already primed for revolt. If you can bribe someone high enough up to ignite it, the soldiers will follow. When Mehmed comes to you for advice on how to handle it, tell him to raise their pay."

Huma frowned. "I know the Janissary commander,

Kazanci Dogan. He would do it. But it is a dangerous precedent. That money comes out of taxes we take from very wealthy, important people. They will not be happy about Mehmed caving to the demands of the Janissaries, rather than ruling them."

"If enough unhappy viziers, pashas, beys, and valis demand Murad come back to the throne, even he will have to listen."

Huma's elegant hand cut through the air between them. "No. I will figure out another way. I do not want Murad back. There is only unrest because the Janissaries have another option. If Murad were dead, they would have to accept Mehmed." She stood, pacing. "With Murad dead, I could be declared regent until Mehmed is older. I would have to get support. I think I could have Kazanci Dogan behind me, but Halil Pasha . . ." She sat down heavily, all grace gone out of her movements. "No. He would never support me. If anything happened to Murad, Halil Pasha would arrange to be declared regent. And once he has the throne, we will all be dead."

Lada pointed emphatically. "We need Murad. If he does not come back, Mehmed will die."

"No! With time, everyone will see that he will make a good sultan."

Radu handed her the letter, which felt far heavier than the parchment could account for. "We do not have time."

As Huma scanned it, her mouth drew down at both corners. Lines appeared between her eyes. "Constantinople. That damnable city."

"It is the heart of everything," Lada said. "The Janissaries do not want to fight there, and they fear Mehmed will lead them against its walls. Halil Pasha is obviously in contact with Constantinople, and the city itself is seeking Mehmed's death. And Mehmed will make no secret of his goals, so it is impossible to persuade his enemies that his life should be spared."

Huma's voice came out in a whisper. "There must be another way. I have worked so long and so hard to get here."

"This is not about you," Lada snapped.

Huma's face hardened. Radu leaned forward, desperate. He had to persuade her. "A dethroned son is of more value to you than a dead one. We keep him safe now so that when he comes back to the throne, he can truly rule. With you as the most powerful valide sultan the empire has ever seen."

For a few eternal moments, Huma stayed exactly as she was. And then the stone left her face. Her eyelids were heavy with resignation. "Very well. I will set this in motion. Get out."

Relief engulfed Radu. He and Lada stood to leave.

Huma's tone resumed its normal lingering, teasing state. "You two are very good friends to my son."

Radu beamed. They had made the right choice. But then Huma continued: "And very, very bad ones. Pray he never finds out what you have done today."

———————

Two weeks later, Lada and Radu rode beside Mehmed in the carriage, past the smoldering remains of buildings burned in the revolt. Out of Edirne. Toward Amasya.

As one, they stared at the passing countryside, carried away from all of Mehmed's dreams.

Murad was back on the throne. Radu and Lada had not seen him or even mentioned his name, each too terrified to even whisper about what he might do if he remembered what he owed their father. All they had to do now was disappear into anonymity and hope no one realized that they should be dead.

And so Radu and Lada sat next to their one friend. Radu was relieved to be free of pressure. At least they were returning to Amasya. They had been happy there. Maybe they could be again.

But they were both silent in the shared secret of their escape, the truth that Mehmed could never know. Their secret was deeper and darker than the pool in the woods. Lada took her brother's hand and squeezed it, a grip as painful as their new bond.

They had betrayed Mehmed.

25

1451: Amasya, Ottoman Empire

LADA SCREAMED, HER VOICE ripped away by the wind to trail behind her. She pushed her horse harder. Her quarry was close, nearly within reach, but they were fast approaching the trees and she would lose him once they got there. That could not happen.

One last burst of speed and she drew to within a hand's length of the other horse. She threw her leg over the saddle, balancing on the side. With a battle cry, she launched herself from her horse and slammed into Radu.

He shouted in surprise, and she scrambled for a handhold. With her hand wrapped in his cloak for leverage, she threw her upper body over the saddle and grabbed the reins. Thrown off-balance, the horse veered wildly to the side, skidding to a stop so sudden both Lada and Radu tumbled to the ground.

"What is wrong with you?" Radu shouted, shoving her away. She rolled onto her back, the brilliant blue sky spinning above her.

She laughed.

"Have you lost what little wits you had to begin with? You could have killed us both!"

Still gasping with laughter, Lada patted Radu on the cheek, the force of it making a light slapping sound. "But I won."

"You—" He jabbed a bruising finger against her arm. "You—" Finally, getting his breathing under control, Radu shook his head and smiled. "You cheated."

"There is no such thing as cheating. There is only winning or losing. I won."

"And if we had both died?"

"As long as you died first, I still would have counted it as winning."

With an exhalation that might have been a laugh, Radu hurried to his horse, who stood nearby, eyes still wide with fright. He talked to it in low, soothing tones, stroking its long velvet nose. Lada looked around for her own steed. It was also nearby, under cover of the trees, peering out at them.

Probably hiding from her, smart beast.

Radu calmed and gathered both horses, and then held out a hand to Lada. She experienced her usual jolt of surprise and jealousy at finding his hand was larger than hers. She came to his chin, if she stood on the balls of her feet. Somewhere in the last two years, her baby brother had become a man. He had grown fast and straight and strong, the cherubic round-ness of his cheeks slowly fading to reveal cheekbones and a jaw of stone. With no baby features to balance his large eyes, they were striking, a dark sweep of lashes framing them beneath thick brows. He wore his long, lazy curls tied at the base of his neck.

"Ugh," she muttered, tugging his hair. "You are so pretty. Like a delicate butterfly beneath my boot."

"Ugh," he replied, pulling one of her own curls, which were thick and coarse. "You are so mad. Like a rabid hound that needs to be put down."

Their ride back to the keep was leisurely, meandering along the banks of the river. As they passed through the city, various storekeepers and merchants waved happily to Radu, who paused to inquire about sick children, hoped for crops, and various other mundanities that made the space behind Lada's eyes go soft and blank with boredom. No one said hello to or even acknowledged Lada.

Without Radu, she would have gone mad living here. In the two years since they left Edirne, some of the distance between them had closed. They shared blood and secrets enough to know that without each other, they had no one.

It was something.

Mehmed was the third part of their bond. He considered them his truest friends and only allies. The guilt of knowing better made Lada softer, broke down the anger she had kept up for so long.

They were safe here. That was also something.

The last six months, though, had been the dullest she had ever known. With another war against Hunyadi, everyone who mattered was gone. Even Mehmed had been called up.

Someone shouted her name, making her startle and pull her horse to a quick stop. She turned to find Nicolae riding toward her, his familiar grin quick and easy despite the large gash that ran from the center of his forehead to the bridge of his nose and onto his left cheek.

"Lada! Did you miss me?"

She frowned, tapping her chin. "Have you been gone? I had not noticed."

"You cried yourself to sleep every day."

"I luxuriated in the blessed quiet that you left in your wake."

He clapped a hand on her shoulder, still beaming, and she finally allowed herself a smile in return. In truth, she was overjoyed.

"Tell me everything. Including how that happened." She nodded toward his scar.

"This? Alas, my beautiful face. Is it not tragic?"

"You should be grateful. For the first time in your life you have two eyebrows instead of one."

Nicolae threw his head back, laughter roaring through the square. "My little dragon, always finding the bright side of life. Come. We drink."

Radu caught up to them, pulling his horse alongside Nicolae's. His eyes scanned the street, body tense as he stood with his feet in the stirrups as though by standing tall he could make what he wished for materialize. "Is everyone returning?"

Lada and Nicolae met one another's eyes with a knowing look. She feigned annoyance, but in truth she desperately wanted to ride through town to catch the very first glimpse of Mehmed. Where was he? Was he safe? Had he been wounded like Nicolae?

Nicolae tried to pat Radu on the head, but he could no longer reach high enough. "Mehmed stopped in Edirne. I do not know when your master will return, young pup. Tell me, Lada, have you been able to house-train him while Mehmed was away?"

"Alas, all attempts have failed. He wets his mat nightly with both piss and tears."

"Always so nice to have you safely returned, Nicolae," Radu said, his tone as dry as the crops beneath the unseasonably warm autumn sun. He waved and rode away, leaving Lada and Nicolae to their own devices. He would not admit it, but he left to avoid what they were going to do next, and so he could hide the fact that he was preparing to observe Ramadan. As though Lada did not know.

Lada and Nicolae settled in the back of a small shop the Janissaries frequented because, with a little extra coin, the owner conveniently forgot the prohibition against alcohol. Lada waited through several stories, including the disgraceful flight of Hunyadi, before finally broaching the only subject she wanted to hear about.

"How did Mehmed do?" She feigned innocent curiosity. They had spent so much of their time the last two years studying tactics, examining old battles, gathering what information they could of the various threats to the Ottoman Empire. After his humiliating ejection from the throne, Mehmed had been determined to never fall short again.

And after her betrayal of Mehmed and her own father's betrayal of her, Lada had done everything she could to help him.

"The little zealot surprised us all." Nicolae raised his drink, his cheek distorted by the livid scar when he smiled. "Those of us in the right flank under his command suffered the fewest casualties. He knew his part, and he played it well. Better even than our father the sultan."

Lada hid her traitorous smile behind her heavy mug. "Careful, Nicolae. That sounded almost like praise."

"I will be damned if I ever call *him* father, but your Mehmed may yet make a decent sultan. Until he bleeds us all out against the walls of Constantinople."

Relieved and buoyed by news of Mehmed's triumph, Lada relaxed into her seat, enjoying Nicolae's tales of the campaign and exaggerated stories of mayhem, gore, and personal hero-ics. They were joined by several other Janissaries who were not devout and loved to imbibe, each settling into the dim space. Soon the room was packed shoulder to shoulder, everyone silly with drink and post-travel lethargy.

"But you still have not told me how you finally got two eyebrows," she said, after a comic reenactment of Nicolae's struggles to pull his sword out of a Hungarian soldier's stub-born ribs before a screaming Transylvanian reached him.

"Oh, that. I ran afoul of the camp seamstress." Nicolae gestured to his groin. "She always has to adjust the standard uniform to account for my massive manhood, and she finally tired of all the extra material required. Her shears are very sharp."

The room roared with laughter. Lada rolled her eyes, glad it was dim enough to hide her blush of discomfort. Though she usually avoided this talk with the men, worrying what it might encourage, she had missed them too much to let them exclude her from their bawdy jokes. She sniffed derisively. "More likely she mistook your manhood for one of her delicate needles."

She got a louder laugh than Nicolae had, along with several slaps on her shoulders. She leaned back, stretching out and taking up space the way the men around her did, and grinned at her friend.

"I could show it to you, if you like." Nicolae held his arms out wide. "Are you prone to fainting?"

"My eyesight is quite poor. We would need some sort of lens for me to be able to see something so small."

Several soldiers banged on the table, and one fell off his chair, either from drunkenness or laughing so hard. Ivan, who had disliked Lada since the day she bested him when she first met Nicolae, leaned forward. "But some things are not so small in here." He reached out and grabbed Lada's left breast, squeezing painfully.

Before she could react, Nicolae spun Ivan away, slammed his head against the table, and threw him to the ground. Grinding Ivan's face into the hard-packed dirt floor, Nicolae growled, "Lada is one of us. And we do not treat our own that way. Understand?"

Ivan groaned his assent. Nicolae sat down again, easy smile back in place, but a weighted silence had poisoned the atmosphere. This had never happened to Lada before, but she suspected she had Nicolae to thank for that. How long had he been deflecting things like this? How much had been said when she could not hear it? Nicolae's defense had proved the exact opposite of his claim that she was one of them. She felt it, like a curdled meal threatening to come back up out of her stomach: the knowledge that she could never be their equal. She would always be separate.

Ivan's glare as he pushed himself off the floor promised a future of violence.

She met his stare with an unflinching one of her own.

26

RADU WAITED, BREATHLESS WITH excitement as he watched the caravan approach the keep. There was a fine carriage in the center, with twenty Janissaries and a couple of mounted eunuchs, which Radu thought odd. However, the presence of the eunuchs was explained when the carriage opened to reveal a different member of the sultan's family than the one Radu was desperate to be reunited with.

Huma stepped out, distaste written across her features as she took in Amasya clinging to the river beneath them. The sight of her after two years—knowing what their last meeting had been about—filled Radu with fear.

"Radu! Look how you have grown." She held out her arms and Radu took her hands in his, unsure of how to greet her.

"You look well."

She laughed, the sound low and itching, like a breath full of smoke. "Appearances are deceiving. He is not with me, so you can stop watching over my shoulder."

Radu gave a false smile. "What brings you to Amasya, if

not returning with Mehmed?" He wanted nothing more than to ask her when Mehmed would be returning, what the delay was. But he felt it important to appear calm.

"I am here on family matters."

"But . . . Mehmed is still in Edirne? What family matters do you have here without him?"

Huma watched his face for a few heartbeats and then laughed again. "You really do not know much about my son's life, do you? Sweet boy." She patted his cheek, her hand dry and soft. "Come, take me inside. We will catch up. Call for your charming sister so we can reunite our happy band."

"She will be with the Janissaries. Since they returned, I have hardly seen her."

Huma made an interested sound in the back of her throat but said nothing. After she was settled in one of the keep's nicest apartments, Radu went to find Lada. He could have sent for her, but he did not want to stay in Huma's company alone. The secret between Lada and himself felt like a burden but still a bond. With Huma here, it felt like a threat.

The Janissaries who had arrived with Huma were unloading gear. "Can you show us the barracks?" one asked.

"I am going there now. You can follow." He turned to gesture to the soldier, then froze, trying to place how he knew him. The man's face was round, with full lips over gapped teeth; it promised a heaviness that was at odds with his long limbs and slim build. He looked much younger than Radu had remembered, now that Radu was nearly as tall as him. "Lazar!"

Lazar smiled, puzzled. "Do we know each other?"

"I have looked for you ever since we got here! I cannot believe this!" Radu grasped Lazar's shoulders, and finally Lazar's face erupted in the warm, open smile Radu had found such comfort in a lifetime ago.

"The little boy from the stables! Can it be?"

"What are you doing here?"

"I have been reassigned to Ilyas's men. We all have."

"I am so glad! It is a joy to see you. It truly is." Radu could not take his eyes off Lazar's face, could not believe this friend lost to him so long ago was back. It softened some of the sting of his disappointed hopes for Mehmed's return.

"My presence does not usually elicit such joy. I will make a point of disappearing from your life for years only to surprise you again more often." Lazar put an arm around Radu's shoulders, and they walked to the barracks together.

Lazar was quickly drawn away by logistical duties, but with a promise that they would be seeing much of each other. Humming with happiness, Radu found Lada. His mood fell as he remembered why he was there.

"Huma is here," he said without preamble.

Lada flinched, putting away the sword she had been sharpening. "Mehmed?"

"No. She wants to see us."

"I do not wish to see her."

"Lada," Radu said, and Lada hung her head, resigned. She had to know, as he did, that Huma could always have whatever she wanted of them.

When Radu and Lada entered the sitting room, Huma had her hands buried in a large piece of carefully embroidered cloth. She looked up, smiling brightly. "Lada, dear girl. Do you have any thread?"

Radu did not understand the humorless, near-hysterical laugh that burst out of Lada's mouth. "No," she said, shaking her head. "I have no threads. Not a single one."

Huma raised an eyebrow at Lada's outburst, then swept her eyes up and down Lada as though she were a crumb on the floor. "I see you have not given up your pursuit of becoming a man."

"I have no desire to be a man," Lada snapped, coming back to herself.

"And yet you wear trousers and train with the Janissaries."

"Yes, when otherwise I could be sitting in this room with you, invisible, sewing and growing old. How strange I should choose something else."

Huma tsked. "There is great power in being a woman. You are ruining your chances. There is much I could do with you, if you chose to let me."

Lada turned to leave, but Huma cleared her throat, patting the space beside her. Scowling, Lada slouched against the wall, watching with hooded eyes.

"What did you want to talk about, Huma?" Radu asked. The longer she was here without telling them the reason, the more nervous he became. Why was Mehmed not back yet? Had something happened in Edirne? Was Huma here to tell them their plot had been discovered and Mehmed hated them?

Radu clutched his hands together, knuckles white.

Huma ignored him, picking at colored strands that trailed from her embroidery. "Tell me, have you ever heard of Theodora of Byzantium?"

Lada leaned her head back, raising her eyes in exasperation. "Does she sew, too?"

"Actually, she was a prostitute."

Radu sat on a bench near Huma, confused but intrigued. This did not sound like the beginning of a way to tell them that Mehmed wanted them dead for taking the throne from him.

"She lived nearly a thousand years ago in Byzantium, when Byzantium was still Byzantium and not a single, sad city clinging to life behind its walls. Her father trained bears, and her mother was an actress." Huma said the word *actress* with a knowing smirk that implied all the other duties an actress would have had. "Theodora followed in her footsteps, becoming quite accomplished at everything she did. There are some interesting stories about her early life. But I will skip those, as they are not polite for mixed company." She glanced at Radu, who looked away, trying not to blush. Why she would think those stories fine to share with Lada but not him, he did not know.

"Why are you telling us this?" Lada said, her voice flat.

"I am doing you a favor. Be gracious. Theodora, after many years, ended up accepting Christianity and living an honest but simple life of spinning wool near the palace. That is where she met Justinian. *Emperor* Justinian. Perhaps it was her cleverness that attracted him, her humble roots, her . . . experience. Regardless, he fell in love with her. He threw out the laws that prevented him from marrying an actress, and she was crowned empress. Not empress consort, mind you. Full empress, full partner with her husband. Imagine." Huma paused, her gaze going far away and soft. Then, she returned to herself. "She went from entertaining men on stage and behind it, to ruling all of Byzantium. She crushed a rebellion when her husband would have run, she improved laws for all women under her rule, and she helped build the most beautiful cathedral in all the world—the Sancta Sophia. It stands in Constantinople to this day as a testament to what Theodora and her husband accomplished together." Huma leaned forward. "She never picked up a sword, but thirty thousand traitors died under her command. She was a prostitute, bowing to any man with enough coin, then a woman who never again bowed to anyone. And do you think she did that wearing trousers?"

"She still needed a man," Lada said, her eyes slits.

Huma showed her teeth in a predatory approximation of a smile. "You understand the story perfectly." She coughed, a dry, rattling sound, and it was a while before she could speak again.

"Can I get you anything?" Radu asked.

She waved him away. "I understand your position, better than you know," she said to Lada. "But you are holding Mehmed back. Make a decision, Lada. If you do not wish to marry my son, release him."

Lada stood straight, sputtering. "I have no hold on Mehmed!"

Radu, too, could not believe what he was hearing. "There has never been talk of marriage, to anyone!" He looked to Lada for confirmation. It was the three of them—together—and had always been. There was no love between Lada and Mehmed that Radu and Mehmed did not also share. No, he would have seen it. And Radu and Mehmed shared the bond of a brotherhood of faith, which surely drew them closer than any bond Mehmed shared with Lada.

Huma shook her head. "Mehmed wanted to return to Amasya immediately. I persuaded him to stay in Edirne to create connections, build a foundation of strength. Little has changed since he left. I have nothing, not the esteem of my husband"—she spat the word like a fig gone rotten—"and not the promise of a son who will ever be able to keep the throne I have secured for him. He should be capitalizing on his success against Hunyadi, not yearning to return to this forsaken place. But he has been so content with his dear, *faithful* friends here that he has not been paying attention to the things that matter. So I tell you again: let him be free of your hold."

A chill flowed from Lada's mouth, her cold fury palpable. "You will have to excuse my confusion. Freedom is not something with which I am well acquainted."

"This is foolish." Radu held out his hands and tried to sound lighthearted. "Mehmed has spent all this time studying, preparing to rule. And we would never hold him back from that. You know that we would do—*have done*—anything to protect Mehmed."

"Oh yes, I know. But he does not know, does he? And if I ever suspect you two are getting in my way, I will not hesitate to remove you."

Radu's blood went cold. Huma could have them killed, doubtless. But worse, still: she could tell Mehmed the truth of how he had lost the throne. They would lose him forever. Radu could not imagine a life without him.

No, that was not the problem. The problem was that he could perfectly imagine a life without Mehmed. He had lived it all the years of his childhood, and he never wished to go back to that cold and lonely state, even if Lada was forced along with him.

Huma stood, letting her embroidery drop to the ground. "I have other business to attend to. Do not forget what we have spoken of." As she left, she stepped on the cloth as though the hundreds of hours of work that had gone into the stitches were nothing.

27

Two weeks after Huma's painful visit and quick return to the capital, a full month after the Janissaries returned but Mehmed did not, Lada once again made excuses for why she could not join Nicolae's contingent for practice. Everything was different now. Before, she had striven to prove herself the fastest, the cleverest, the most ruthless. But after Ivan's lewd attack and Nicolae's protective response, she had seen that none of it mattered. She would never be the best Janissary, because she would never be a Janissary. She could never be powerful on her own, because she would always be a woman.

She had thought the return of the soldiers would signal an end to the directionless melancholy that had plagued her during Mehmed's six-month absence, but it only sharpened it. Even Radu was distracted and cranky, worried that Mehmed would never return, worried about what Huma would say to keep him away.

The sun beat brutally overhead as Lada stripped down

to her underclothes. She had taken to wearing long tunics, tied with a sash, with loose breeches underneath. Huma disapproved, but if it scandalized anyone in the fortress or the village, no one bothered—or dared—to say so. She had also had new leather cuffs made to wear on either wrist, a hidden knife in both. These she unbuckled and laid on her clothes, alongside her boots. Finally, she undid the white scarf that bound her tangled and knotted hair, and lifted it from her neck. She held the scarf out, looking at it. Wondering if she always chose white because it looked like a Janissary cap.

But nothing would ever look enough like one.

With a sigh, she slipped into the hidden pool, nestled among rocks and hidden by trees. The water was a deep green, and so cold it took her breath away and left her toes numb.

It was still their glorious secret, a place that felt truly theirs. When they got back to Amasya, Mehmed had been so sad, so frustrated. He had not wanted to lose the throne. So Lada and Radu had bent all their attentions to distracting him. They made a game of how often they could evade Mehmed's guards and retreat to the pool. It had been an escape they had all needed. But with Mehmed gone, Radu had not wanted to come here. Lada, too, had not been here since, dreading the quiet and the solitude.

Until today. Everywhere she went, no matter how many people surrounded her, she knew now she was alone. She may as well be alone in a place that was beautiful.

Closing her eyes, she floated on her back and let herself hang, only her face above the water, the sunlight brilliant and hot in contrast to the cold water. Her breasts floated up beneath her clinging undershirt, which she found both amusing and oddly disturbing. While she had not grown much in stature, becoming thicker and more solid instead of taller, her breasts had become soft, full things. She had been forced to adjust her knife-throwing and her archery—always her weakest skill—to account for the unwieldy changes. And now here they were, bobbing gently in the water, unavoidable.

There was something claustrophobic about breasts.

Her nipples, too, seemed animated with a will of their own. Sometimes they were flat and small; other times they puckered and stuck out. She suspected it was the cold now, but on a few other occasions it had happened. Her nurse could have explained it to her.

Or Huma. Though she would cut off her breasts before asking Huma for advice about her body.

Sometimes she wondered what it would be like to have a mother. Would she have guided Lada through her traumatic first bleeding, reassured her that no, she was not dying? Helped her hide the evidence for longer than she had been able to?

No. Her mother would have crawled away in terror or made the nurse do it.

Lada let her face go underneath the water. A mother. A nurse. Even a friend. Perhaps if she had more women in her life, she would not feel so outraged at the physical and social demands of being one.

She thought of needlework. Of the weight of layers of dresses and the pinching of shoes. Of downcast eyes and well-timed smiles. Of her mother. Of Huma, Halima, and Mara. All the ways to be a wife, all the ways to be a woman.

No, more women in her life would change nothing.

And she could still learn to shoot a bow better, breasts be damned. She put her hands on either breast and squeezed until they hurt, trying to figure out what Ivan had wanted. What could possibly be the allure of the fleshy mounds? And then she screamed, as a body half landed on her, pushing her underwater. Choking, she clawed her way to the surface.

Only to find Mehmed's smiling face inches from her own.

Her anger at being startled was washed away, carried in rivulets down her face and hair. He looked different. He had aged in the months he had been away. While the changes that growing had carved into Radu's face made her brother more beautiful, the changes in Mehmed's made him look harder. Distant. Less like the crying boy she had met at the fountain, and more like what she felt a sultan should be.

But now, so close to her, the hard planes of his face softened into familiarity as he flashed the smile that had not changed since he was a boy. His lips were soft and full and welcoming, but his eyes were sly.

It was his lips she found herself unable to look away from.

"Did you miss me?" he teased.

Sincerity betrayed her, tumbling out of her mouth in a whisper before she could rein it in. "I did."

He put his hands on her waist, as he had done so many times last summer, pulling her under, pushing her, playing. But this time he left his hands there. They were warm through the thin material of her underclothes. His voice was husky, lower than it had been. "I missed you, too."

He pulled her closer, and Lada warred within herself. Her inclination was to push him away, to cut him with a clever, sharp remark, to find something, *anything* to do with her hands, her worthless hands that floated uselessly at her sides.

Huma's words echoed in her head. *Set him free.* Did she truly hold him that way?

Did she want to?

As though heeding her desperation but heedless of the confusion and fear ringing through her like the clash of blades, her hands lifted and grabbed the back of Mehmed's head, tangling in his wet hair. And then her lips, from which nothing but poison had ever dropped, found his and were baptized with sweet fire, reborn into something new and wild. His mouth answered hers, lips parting, his teeth catching hers, her tongue meeting his.

It felt like fighting.

It felt like falling.

It felt like dying.

"Mehmed?" Radu called, his voice muffled and indistinct, as if Lada's head were still underwater. She and Mehmed paused their mouth-to-mouth combat, and Lada realized her legs were wrapped around his waist, his hands around the backs of her thighs, their chests pressed together.

She pushed him away, dropping beneath the water and swimming to the other side just as Radu appeared from the trees and jumped into the pool between them. He burst up, water raining from his hair, droplets of sunshine glittering in it. His laughter matched, ringing with joy. Mehmed's laughter was not quite so genuine. His gaze burned into Lada's. His eyebrows formed a question or a promise—she could not tell which.

"Mehmed is back!" Radu shouted.

"I think she noticed," Mehmed said.

"Lada." Radu swam over and pushed her shoulder playfully. "The pool is not *that* cold. Why are you trembling?"

Lada tore her eyes away from Mehmed's. "No reason."

28

Radu laughed, breathless, and dropped his wooden practice sword. "I am finished."

Lazar's lazy smile belied the perspiration beading on his forehead and upper lip. "You have gotten quite good." He adjusted his long white cap, a few strands of dark hair peeking out.

Lazar was one of the happiest parts of Radu's life, second only to getting Mehmed back the month before. Although at Mehmed's suggestion Radu had been training with the Janissaries for a couple of years now, having a familiar face among them made it enjoyable rather than a chore. Lazar always volunteered when Radu visited the barracks looking for a training partner. Quick with a sword and quicker with a laugh, Lazar was the same bright spot he had been in Tirgoviste. Their ten-year age gap seemed so much smaller than it had when Radu was a boy.

Lazar set his sword next to Radu's. "Very soon you may even best your sister."

Radu leaned against the wall, shaking his head. "Do not let her hear you say that, or she will spend even more time training than she already does. I never see her as it is."

Lazar raised a black eyebrow. "And that is a bad thing?"

"She is my family."

"Yes, you poor thing."

Radu laughed, reaching for a bucket of water. He scooped some into his mouth, then put a wet hand to the back of his neck. Lazar leaned over, shoulder brushing Radu's, and took the bucket. He pulled off his cap and upended the whole thing over his head.

Radu jumped away, but his side still got soaked. "Wasteful cur!"

Lazar's smile turned his face from boyish to wicked. He held the bucket behind his back. "Come and get it, then."

There was something in his voice that gave Radu pause, made a strange buzzing void come between his heart and his ribs. But then he heard his name being called. He turned to find Mehmed at the far wall of the small practice enclosure.

"Mehmed!" Radu called, beaming. It still delighted him to see Mehmed after such a long absence. His face was always surprising, like a question Radu had yet to find the answer to.

Mehmed gestured animatedly, his hands too excited to be still. "Tonight at supper we host a dervish, who has traveled here by way of India. Wait until you see his feet! And his face—he is truly a holy man. Get cleaned up and come to my rooms."

Radu nodded, Mehmed's excitement contagious. Ever since Molla Gurani's death the previous year, Mehmed sought more and more outliers in the faith: dervishes who took vows of poverty and wandered the earth, scholars who studied to better understand the words of the Prophet, even teachers deemed heretical. He was never content with a simple, unquestioning practice of Islam. It was one of the things Radu loved about him. Studying and learning at his side had always been an adventure.

Bidding Mehmed a temporary farewell, Radu returned to Lazar, his steps buoyed with anticipation. Lazar's eyes narrowed, his lips twisted in a back-market imitation of a real smile. "Watch yourself, little brother."

Radu paused in picking up the weapons they had left scattered around the yard. "What do you mean?"

"There are some things it is not acceptable to want, but there are ways around it, and those who will look the other way. And then there are some things that it is impossible to want. Even the mere act of wanting, if noticed by the wrong people, can get you killed." He gave a heavy, meaningful look at the spot where Mehmed had been. "Be more careful."

Radu's throat constricted, his heart racing so he thought he might die of it. What had Lazar seen? What did he suspect? Could he tell simply by watching Radu that something was very wrong with him, when even Radu did not understand what it was? All he knew was that there was some light, some pull, some *fire* that Mehmed carried, and Radu only felt truly alive when he was nearby.

Was that wrong?

Lazar put his long fingers on the back of Radu's neck, let them linger for a few impossibly long seconds, the time beating past in the terrified pulse of Radu's blood. "Let me know if you ever want to . . . talk."

Radu watched him walk away, soaked tunic clinging to his broad shoulders, and knew he would never, ever seek Lazar out again. Because whatever this secret was, whatever this question Radu now knew he did *not* understand, whatever this aching, secret hollow inside of him meant, an answer felt far more terrifying than any question could ever be.

———◆———

Two days later, the conversation with Lazar still felt like sand against sunburned skin, a prickling discomfort when Radu least expected it. He sat in a garden tucked into a far corner of the keep, hidden in the cool, dim shade of a tree overburdened with weeping branches. Maybe he would ask Mehmed to have Lazar sent to another part of the country. He knew Mehmed would. But what if Mehmed asked why? How would he answer? He had told Mehmed how happy he was to be reunited with his old Janissary protector.

He should stop worrying. Mehmed was his friend. His dearest friend, his only friend. Perhaps Lazar had never had a friend like Mehmed. He could not possibly understand how Radu felt. It was foolishness for Lazar to imply there was something wrong, something dangerous with loving Mehmed more than anyone. Mehmed was the heir to the throne! They should *all* feel that way about him.

Mehmed had brought him safety and hope, helped nourish the seed of God planted by Kumal's kindness when Radu needed it most. Of course Radu valued Mehmed above all others. He even loved him more than he loved Lada, which filled him with guilt. But Lada had let him be hurt on her behalf, all that time ago, by their first Ottoman tutor. Radu had never forgotten the way she sat back, impassive, as he was beaten for her failure to respond. Mehmed would never have let that happen.

His love for Mehmed made perfect sense.

Why, then, did Lazar's look still make him feel strange and wrong?

He was distracted by the sound of feet stomping gracelessly along the gravel path. Well hidden, he peered through the curtain of leaves. Lada was prowling up and down, turning in one direction before jerking herself back in the other, as though her body were engaged in an argument that neither side was winning. After a few minutes of furious indecision, during which an entire generation of flowers was mercilessly decapitated, Lada went suddenly and shockingly still. Not her usual type of watchful stillness, but a dreamy, placid cessation of movement. Her limbs, normally so rigid, looked almost soft as she lifted a hand and traced her lips, eyes closed.

Radu held his breath, watching, wondering what was going on in his sister's head. It had been a long time since he wished he could understand what she was thinking. Most of the time he knew and wished he did not. But in this moment she was transformed from his determined, brutal sister, into . . .

A girl.

That was it. Lada looked like a *girl*.

He exhaled sharply, holding back a wondering laugh. In a flash, his sister turned from a girl back into a predator. Her eyes found the source of the noise, and a dagger flashed in either hand.

"Who is there?" she demanded, feet spread, stance low and balanced.

"Please do not kill me." Radu pushed aside two curtains of branches, holding his hands out in mock supplication.

"Were you spying on me?" Her voice was shrill, panicked, as though she had been caught at something devious.

But no—that was not it. Radu had caught her doing terrible things during their childhood. Once he found her in the stables, choking Vlad Danesti, an insufferable son of rival boyars. When Radu shouted in surprise, Lada had merely looked up and calmly informed him that Vlad had told her she was worth less than the bastard son of their father. She was punishing him, and wondered how long she would have to choke him until he fainted.

Interrupted, she released the red-faced, coughing boy, who ran away sobbing and never played with them again. But thinking about the focused, thoughtful look on Lada's face, Radu had occasionally wondered whether, if he had not happened upon the scene, she would have continued to see how long it took for the boy to die.

Comparing her unruffled reaction then with her rage now, Radu's curiosity grew tenfold. He hid it with a placating look of combined fear and confusion. "I did not know you were here until you shouted," he said. Big eyes, round mouth, palms up. It was an expression that had gotten him out of trouble too many times to count. His eyes were so large anyhow, when he widened them like this, no one believed him capable of guile.

Stealing food from the kitchens, being caught eavesdropping, forgetting Janissary protocol: the big eyes and confused apology worked for everything.

Lada should have known better than to fall for it, but her shoulders relaxed and she tucked the knives away. "What are you doing skulking around?"

He held the branches for her. She hesitated, then climbed under the tree with him. It was snug, but they both fit, backs curled against the trunk. The air was cooler, damp with the smell of young green things and old wizened growth. "It is nice here," he said.

Lada nodded, her mouth grim with the concession. "It feels . . . secret. Safe." She spoke in Wallachian as she toyed with the small leather pouch she always wore around her neck. Radu had heard her speak their language with Nicolae, but after she let him be beaten by their first Ottoman tutor all those years ago, he almost always refused to speak it with her. They spoke only other tongues to each other. Hearing the language of their shared childhood now was a strange and startling intimacy.

"I have never been to these gardens," she said.

Radu tapped the dagger strapped to her wrist, trying to keep the gesture light to avoid puncturing this precarious and precious moment that had descended between them. "Well, it is good you came prepared, because the gardens are frequently populated by assassins and thieves."

Lada elbowed him sharply in the ribs. From her, it was almost like a hug. They had grown closer in the months of Mehmed's absence. Now, wrapped in leaves and the language of their childhood, Radu wondered at how they had let so much space expand between them, and whether it was possible that they were finally closing it.

A voice drifted along the path.

"Mehmed," Radu whispered.

Lada glared in exasperation, switching to Turkish, their moment gone. "Of course it is Mehmed. But where is he going? He told me he had a council today about province taxes."

Radu frowned. "He told me he was meeting with the Janissary leaders to go over budgets."

They waited, two pairs of eyes peering out, searching for the object of their desire. He walked past in the company of a man Radu did not know. But he recognized the clothes, the white robes and the shaved head. A eunuch. Mehmed laughed as he drew even with the tree, and for a breath Radu thought he had spied them and was amused at the strangeness of their hiding spot. But he continued on with the eunuch, the comfortable match of their paces and the ease of space between them speaking of familiarity.

When the two men passed out of the garden, Lada lunged out from under the tree and followed. Radu ran to catch up with her. He had never been through the gate at the far side of the gardens. Lada paused, peering carefully over, then opened the gate. A path wound along the back of the fortress, still walled in but narrow and unusually private.

They turned a corner and Lada stopped so abruptly that Radu ran into her. Ahead of them was a building, one Radu had never seen before. Judging from Lada's expression, he assumed she was equally surprised by its existence. The walls around it were high and crawling with ivy, but the two heavy entrance gates were thrown open. Through them they saw a section of sumptuous garden, vibrant to the point of garishness, trees dripping fruit and flowers painting every surface in a riot of color.

Radu felt a flare of resentment that Mehmed had kept the most beautiful part of the grounds from them, until he realized that waiting in the garden were several women. They mirrored the flowers, petaled and swirling with color, beautiful with the same temporary vibrancy. And one of them, standing in the center, held an infant.

In the time it took Radu to process that it was Mehmed who walked confidently forward and took the baby, Mehmed who laughed and held the infant up as though it were a piglet at a market, Mehmed who placed a wondering kiss on its forehead, the gates swung closed and sealed them off from the bright dream within. Radu could not say whether the gates actually made a deep clanging sound, or if he merely felt it inside.

"Did you know?" Lada's voice came from far away, from underwater, from a cavern the depths of which would never see the light.

"No."

It was an age before Radu realized the sun was setting and he was alone, still standing, staring at the gate and the mystery of the Mehmed he had seen inside. The Mehmed who had left him behind.

That night, Radu and Lada sat alone in Mehmed's chambers, waiting far past the normal time when he usually met them for a late meal. Neither spoke nor looked at the other. Radu was cloaked in a suffocating blanket of misery and hurt. How could Mehmed have done this? How could he be a *father*?

Radu was hurt because Mehmed had not told him of this development. That was why. That was the reason for this horrible, clawing feeling.

Lazar's knowing smile.

The door opened, and Radu cried out with relief. Mehmed was here, he would explain, it would make sense, and things would go back to how they had been. Radu would know how to feel again.

Lada, too, stood, leaning forward. Her face was a mask.

Mehmed's face, however, was like the desert during a windstorm. Everything in his features was ripped away to one raw expression of rage. He threw a heavy piece of parchment onto the floor in front of them.

Lada picked it up. She frowned, etching her own trails of rage. "What is this? Are you mocking me?"

Mehmed shook his head. "I assure you, I am as surprised as anyone." He held a hand up and out toward her, as though calming a spooked horse. Radu looked from one to the other. There was something off there, something new. Something he had missed while lost in his own swirl of confusion. What was it? What had happened?

Panicked, Radu tried to snatch the parchment from Lada, but her grip held tight.

A smile twisted Mehmed's lips as his words came out in the same manner. "From my father. Apparently, I have been invited to my own wedding."

29

Edirne, Ottoman Empire

THERE WAS GOLD EVERYWHERE.

Gold on fingers fat and thin, gold in noses long and stubby, gold in ears and on foreheads and necks and wrists, gold on arms, gold on ankles. The most gold on a pair of delicate ankles peeking out from beneath silk trimmed with gold threads, weak ankles that could never carry their owner in a fight or keep up in a race.

Sitti Hatun, Mehmed's bride, had detestable ankles.

They were two days into the monthlong wedding celebrations, and already Lada had a headache from the perfume, the rich food, and the incessant music. She wanted to use the harpist's instrument as a bow and fire arrows of burning incense into the beating gold hearts of everyone here.

She had not had even a moment to speak with Mehmed, had not been alone with him once since the pool, since the kiss, since everything became tangled and confusing. And Mehmed smiled and laughed and sat with his slender-ankled bride, his achingly beautiful bride, leaving a charred hollow where he had ignited something deep inside Lada.

A young man, as curved and gleaming as a Janissary sword, stood on a dais nearby, reciting poetry. His voice was a river, pulling her along, slipping her under the current and spinning her until his tales of valor and love and triumph felt like they were drowning her lungs so she could not breathe.

She grabbed a goblet from a meek-eyed servant and drank the sour wine as quickly as she could, trying to wash away the taste of the poet's passion. It surprised her that Mehmed would have wine served at his wedding, when he refused to drink on religious principle. But she was very, very glad to have it.

On the other side of the cavernous room, beneath a shimmering drape of silk, propped up on velvet pillows, Mehmed and his bride reclined. Everyone pulsed out from them in streams. The beating heart of the empire, fed by the love and adoration of the vessels in the room.

Lada would rather bleed out than pretend to be happy for him.

"Lada!" Radu's face was as bright as the lamps overhead. "May I have this dance? We should talk."

"I would sooner let the head gardener take me for a walk in the courtyard," she snapped.

Radu's face fell. "But I had something I wanted to ask you about."

A young woman passed deliberately close, looking up at Radu through her eyelashes and smiling so demurely it was almost obscene. Lada realized she had seen Radu dance with nearly every woman present. He had never pursued anyone in Amasya, but there had not been any opportunity. She felt the wine slosh sickeningly in her empty stomach.

If Radu wanted advice on courting Ottoman women, he should know better than to come to her. "I am sure you can manage perfectly well on your own," she said, sneering.

Radu looked hurt, but then his jaw set and he walked away. Frustrated with him, frustrated with herself, Lada turned to flee and found herself face to face with Huma. Her lips were stained a deep red that matched the cloth she was draped in. She looked like a glittering wound.

"Walk with me," Huma said, holding out a hand.

Scowling, Lada let Huma take her elbow and lead her to the far edge of the room, a corner not quite blazing with light from the dangling chandeliers. So many burned so brightly that the ceiling was obscured by a haze of smoke, the patterns there shifting and blurring.

Or perhaps Lada had finally had too much to drink.

"You seem troubled, little one."

Lada laughed bitterly, picking at her clothes. She had been dressed by servants every day this week. Though she had tried to insist that she wear the same style of clothes as the Janissaries, she had been provided with draped dresses and silk shoes. Tonight her dress was a red so deep it looked nearly black, cut lower than she cared for, with a white sash. Her hair had been tamed and pulled back into a series of braids and curls that trailed down her back. She wore her boots, at least.

Huma traced a finger along Lada's collarbone. "You ought to have a necklace here, to draw attention." She pointed at Lada's breasts.

Lada would shoot an incense arrow at Huma first.

But looking at the older woman's face, Lada realized

Huma was not pleased to be here, either. Lada had assumed Huma would be thrilled—in her element as the mother of the groom, preening and parading her new power. She had not wanted Lada to marry Mehmed, and here he was, married to another.

Instead, Huma surveyed the room with narrowed eyes.

"I have not offered my congratulations," Lada said.

Huma huffed, waving a hand sharply. "Let us not pretend. I was not consulted on any of this. It is a political alliance chosen by Murad to secure the eastern borders. An odd move if he was planning to abdicate the throne again soon, now that Mehmed is older."

Lada looked at the room through new eyes. None of Mehmed's teachers were here, none of his favorite holy men. No one he had worked with during his brief time as sultan. And yet Kazanci Dogan, who had been the head of the revolt, *was* here. Surely Mehmed would not have invited him. The veins of power were not, as she had thought, radiating out from the beating heart of the newlyweds. They were radiating out from . . . Murad.

"But I thought with the marriage, and Mehmed having an heir . . ."

Huma laughed darkly. "A baby with a concubine is hardly a guarantee. And a marriage to a Turkmen tribe we are already allied with? This is a move of strengthening, not building. Not expanding or creating power and connections for Mehmed. This strengthens Murad and gives no benefit to Mehmed. The baby and this bride mean nothing. They change nothing."

Something in Lada's chest loosened, made it easier for her to breathe in the cloying atmosphere.

Huma looked at where Sitti Hatun's father was talking with inebriated passion to several pashas who stared over his shoulder at where they would rather be.

"Did you know Murad welcomed a son two months ago?" Huma asked. "Such a blessing to have produced yet another boy." In the pause, Lada heard a horrible grinding noise she suspected came from Huma's teeth. "And such timing, staging a marriage so soon after, so that everyone can learn of the new heir from Murad himself. Who is to say that, with the heavy encouragement of his trusted Halil Pasha, Murad has not decided to wait out another decade or two in favor of a more pliable heir?"

"None of this is for Mehmed." Lada leaned heavily against the wall, seeing the celebration for what it was. She knew she ought to feel sick, worried for Mehmed, angry on his behalf, but all she could feel was overwhelming relief. This world, this glittering poem of power that contained no words for her . . . none of it was his. Did he know?

"No. Murad is reminding us all that he is strong and virile and going nowhere. That Mehmed belongs to him and—" Huma was cut off by a fit of coughing, something rattling deep inside her. It was the same cough she had had when she visited them in Amasya, but grown much worse.

Huma wiped her face with a cloth pulled from her sleeve. A layer of powder came off, revealing dark circles beneath her eyes and hollows where her cheeks had once been full. Her lips pulled back over her teeth, all sensual fullness stretched back to grim hatred. "Everything I have built, all that I have worked toward, is being ripped from me. I cannot bear it. I took everything I could from him, and still he took more." Her eyes tracked Murad as though she were sighting prey too far off to kill.

And, in that moment, Huma was no longer threatening to Lada. She was her sister. Murad had taken both of them, forced them into a country and a life neither had wanted. "We will kill him," Lada whispered.

"I have tried."

"I could do it."

Huma tilted her head, considering, then sighed. "No. I do not doubt you could get a knife into the chasm between his ribs, but you could not get out alive. That is not a real victory for you. Stay with Mehmed, help him. He is our best hope. We must protect our investment." She put a dry, cold hand on Lada's cheek, her face almost tender. "Marry him, too, if you wish. I was wrong to warn you away. Carve out a life for yourself however you can. No one will do it for you."

She nodded toward a group of turbaned and caped young men standing in a cluster near Mehmed's enclosure. Radu stood in the center, laughing, sharply outlined even amid the incense haze. "Your brother, though. People will pluck out their own hearts to create a place for him. He will never have to get his hands dirty."

She held her hands beside Lada's and smiled. "But hands painted red are hands that do what needs to be done." She straightened, letting the mask of playful sensuality fall back onto her face, though it did not fit as well as it had the last time Lada saw her. Then, in a whisper of crimson, she drifted away.

———•———

Mehmed was inaccessible as the weeks dragged on. They were now four weeks into the wedding and Lada did not know how they had not all died of excessive enjoyment. Even Radu would have been an acceptable distraction at this point, but he was always at the center of gatherings or simply gone. She did not know where he disappeared to. Probably celebrations of the celebration, where even more glittering people would fawn over him and his clever, beautiful mouth.

Huma's words had stuck with her. Mehmed's position was as precarious as it had ever been, if not more so. And Lada could not forget what had happened the last time they were in Edirne. She still awoke with the taste of blood in her mouth sometimes, the memory of bone beneath teeth, her hand curled around a dagger that was not there anymore.

Nicolae, recently off duty, sighed as he walked with her. The barracks were dark, and they stopped to lean against a wall. Floral perfume hung heavily in the night, but at least out here Lada could breathe. She liked the dark better than all the forced, false light of the wedding nonsense.

Nicolae took off his white Janissary cap and rubbed his sweat-slick hair. "I understand why you are concerned about Mehmed's safety, and I agree. But there is a difference between the last time Mehmed was here and now."

"And what is that?"

"Before, he was under the guard of the old Janissary corps.

They had been stationed in the city forever. They have their own politics, their own allegiances, none of which were to him, leaving him vulnerable. This time, he is under our guard. We have been with him for years. And he is no longer an insufferable zealot, a brat we cannot respect and care nothing for. We have fought under him, and we will fight *for* him. You will not find a traitor in our ranks. You know that, Lada." He clapped her on the shoulder. "Let Mehmed worry about pleasing his pretty bride. Let us worry about keeping him safe."

"And what am I to worry about?"

"Nothing! Get some sleep, little dragon. That is an order." He walked into the barracks, joining his fellow soldiers, and leaving Lada alone with her worries. They were poor company, nagging and tugging, pulling her hair and whispering in her ear.

Mehmed dead. Mehmed in love. Mehmed forgetting she existed. Everyone forgetting she existed. Continuing to exist in a world that cared not one whit whether or not she did. Continuing to exist in a world where she would never be kissed again.

Caring whether or not she was ever kissed again, damnable Mehmed and his lips and his tongue and everything that came from them!

She needed a job, something real, something she could focus on and channel her energies into. Nicolae did not think Mehmed was in danger, because he did not see how Mehmed could be a threat to anyone. Murad was back, the country was stable, everyone was happy. But as long as Mehmed was alive, there was the promise of him coming to the throne. Who would be threatened most by that?

Halil Pasha.

Halil Pasha! Lada latched onto him as a new goal. He had always been a menace, had probably even been behind the first assassination attempt. Surely he was still a danger to Mehmed. Lada would follow him, shadow him, see any threat before it even approached Mehmed. Energized by her newfound purpose, she had no time to waste. She stopped at the harem building, lit up like a bonfire against the night, and asked the eunuch guarding the gate to speak with Huma. Lada had not seen her at the day's celebrations, and this late many guests would already be home and in bed.

The eunuch frowned, considering her. "Huma is not well."

"She will want to see me."

He shook his head, pale skin gleaming dully in the light spilling out of the windows. "She cannot see anyone. I can take her a message."

Lada deflated, already delayed. But no. She did not need Huma's permission or guidance. "Can you tell me where Halil Pasha lives?"

With a passive look that spoke of years of training to show no emotion at any request, the eunuch gave her directions to Halil Pasha's grand estate.

Lada seeped like a shadow out of the palace grounds and into the nearest quarter, where the wealthiest and most powerful pashas and viziers lived. Halil Pasha's home was massive, a towering testament to his influence and to his regard within Murad's reign. Avoiding the gate, Lada found a narrow alley between Halil Pasha's wall and the next compound where she had enough leverage to climb the rocks and boost herself into Halil Pasha's grounds. Dropping down, she crouched in stillness, the flagstones beneath her still smelling of sun-warmed dust.

A bright mess of voices drifted from the back of the building. Sliding along the wall, she came around a corner to find a courtyard. Lamps were strung like beads, dangling over a gathering still going strong despite the hour. It was smaller than the wedding feasts and dances, obviously a more intimate affair. Lada had no idea what to do with it. It was a waste of her time. She looked toward the main house, which would probably be nearly empty.

Going back to the side of the building, she found a small door, with piles of vegetable skins and refuse in baskets haphazardly placed near it. Inside was a narrow hallway, the end leading to an overtaxed and exhausted kitchen, still limping along late into the night. To her right was a narrow set of stairs. She took those to the next floor, where she opened a door. This hallway was broad with high ceilings and thick carpets. Lada strode along it, not knowing what she was looking for but desperate to find something.

Low laughter warned her a second too late that she was not alone. She stopped as two men, one facing her and the other looking away, came out of a room.

She locked eyes with Radu.

His face froze in horror, then smoothed into a smile as he put his hand on his companion's back and pointed at something in the opposite direction of Lada. "Have you ever noticed this portrait of the pasha? It looks as though it were painted by an elephant. A very old, sick elephant."

The other man laughed, not turning around, and Radu

directed a pained and panicked look at Lada, jerking his head toward the servant staircase.

She was through it before Radu and his friend reached the painting, then outside and off Halil Pasha's grounds before humiliation finally came crashing down around her. She had found nothing. Worse, she had been caught. By *Radu*. What was he doing there? Why did he act as though he knew the house? As though he belonged there?

She returned to the palace. Instead of going to her own room, she went to Radu's, where she paced like a caged animal. Alternate rounds of fury and embarrassment warred within her, suspicions rising and then summarily dismissed. Finally, when she thought she would go mad, Radu came back. He closed the door behind himself and then leaned against it, rubbing his head wearily. Lada opened her mouth to berate him, but he beat her.

"What were you *thinking*, Lada?"

"What do you mean, what was I thinking? I was thinking that Halil Pasha threatened Mehmed once before, and he may very well do it again!"

"Yes! But what were you trying to accomplish sneaking around his home at night?"

"I—I thought, if I could catch him before . . . if I could discover something, so we would know . . ." She stopped. She did not know what she had hoped to accomplish. She had simply wanted to act, wanted to *do*. Wanted to do something other than stand in a room full of glittering strangers, watching Mehmed with another woman.

"Did you take note of Halil Pasha's inner circle?" Radu

raised his eyebrows, began pacing around her. "Who was at the gathering, who talked to whom, who lingered in conversation with Halil?"

Lada scoffed. "I could never have seen that much and remained hidden."

"No, you certainly could not. You would need an invitation. You would need to have befriended all the pashazadas, especially Halil Pasha's son Salih. You would need to be liked and trusted well enough to be welcomed into the rivers of influence that flow around Halil Pasha."

"So you are his friend now, are you? Have you forgotten what he tried to do?"

Radu threw up his hands, then sat heavily on his bed. "He has never spoken to me. I doubt he even realizes who I am. But because of his son, I am welcome in his home. I am invited to his gatherings. I can drift around Halil, I can listen, I can watch, I can trade false secrets for real ones, I can keep my finger on the pulse of life in that wretched man's plans. You were skulking in his hallway like a thief while I was sitting in his personal study like the adored friend I am to his oft-forgotten middle son."

"But you never said anything."

"I tried to. You would not let me."

It was true. Lada had been so absorbed in her misery, so jealous of how happy Radu seemed, that she had pushed him away that night he wanted to dance and talk to her. But that had been four weeks ago. And how could she have known he would be up to something like this? "You— It does not seem like you. I never thought you could do something like this."

Radu stiffened. "You may have been the one who stopped the dagger last time, but *I* am the one who will know before the dagger ever comes close to Mehmed."

Lada shook her head in numb disbelief. Radu had come to the same conclusion she had—Halil Pasha was still a threat to Mehmed—and instead of running around in the dark, climbing walls, prowling aimlessly through a house, he had figured out a way to protect Mehmed. A way that Lada, for all her training and ferocity, could never accomplish. No wonder he had not involved her in his plans.

"What can I do?" she whispered.

Radu's voice was strained with exhaustion. "Stay out of my way."

Lada stumbled to the door, ignoring Radu's hastily called-out apology. She crossed the thankfully empty hallways to her own room, locked the door behind herself, and curled up on her bed.

She wanted to dream of Wallachia.

She failed at even that.

30

RADU LOVED DANCING.
The beat, the music, feeling it from his head to his toes as he twirled around the room in perfect synchronization with the other dancers. There was something achingly right about moving together, guided by sound, everyone part of something bigger, giving up individuality to create something beautiful. He did not have to think or feel or be anything other than movement. It was almost like prayer.

As one song blended into another, he danced with nearly every woman in the court. A flattering word, a charming smile, an assurance that they were his most graceful partner. And, of course, when handing them back to their husbands, an acknowledgment of what superior taste and fortune that man had to be deserving of the most stunning jewel in the room.

It was so easy to be liked, and so pleasant.

And so *useful*, too, he thought as he smiled and accepted an invitation from Halil Pasha's son Salih to join him for a private supper.

Distractions were many and easy to come by. Most of the time Radu was able to reduce his desperation to talk to Mehmed, to be near him, to be reassured that he would still be part of Mehmed's new life as a husband and a father. If he had enough to do, he could turn his thoughts of Mehmed from the loudest bleating trumpet to the softest whispering flute.

A woman with a full mouth and a face that shone as soft and sweet as the moon smiled at Radu from across the room. She was young, and though he did not recognize her, there was something familiar about her. He crossed to her, bowing.

"You do not remember me," she said.

"I should be flogged for forgetting such a face."

She laughed. "Your words are as sweet as honey, and as lacking in substance. I am Nazira, Kumal's sister."

Radu straightened, looking around in excitement. "Is Kumal here?"

"No, he hates the capital. I am here with my uncle, and only for tonight. I wanted to see this." She gestured to the room, the glittering decadence.

"Ah." Disappointment tugged Radu's spirits down. He had long wanted to thank Kumal for his kindness during such a terrible time, for teaching him to pray when he had nothing else. Bowing again, he held out his hand. "Would you like to dance?"

She nodded, and they joined the dancers. Radu kept Mehmed's enclosure in view, watching from the corner of his eye, wondering if Mehmed saw him and wished he could join the revelries instead of sitting.

Nazira danced prettily, and at the end she thanked him

with a secret smile. Radu saw that she danced with no one else after, instead staying close to a wizened old woman.

He was about to join Salih and several of the sons of prominent pashas when he noticed the one spot of stillness in the enormous room: Lada, slumped against a wall near a towering pair of gilded doors. Beneath her dress Radu saw that she wore not her favorite Janissary boots but a pair of beautifully embroidered slippers.

She did not look like she was secretly hoping to kill someone. She did not look like she was hoping for anything. She looked like Radu had felt when he saw Mehmed's son.

A knife of pity stabbed into his side. He had tried to soften his words that night a week ago when she had nearly ruined everything by being caught spying, but she had fled before he could make her feel better. And part of him, a compact, dark lump of meanness buried deep in his chest, had been glad. Let *her* feel useless. Let her feel like a failure. Let her see that he could do things she never could.

Seeing her now, though, engulfed him in a rush of empathy. He crossed the room, exchanging greetings and promises to dance later, until he reached her. "Lada?"

She blinked, eyes slowly focusing on him. "What," she said, her tone flat and lacking any inflection.

"Would you like to dance?"

Her forehead shifted, expression sharpening with a hint of the old Lada. "Do you hate me that much?"

He laughed. "It could be fun."

"Yes, I love humiliating myself in front of hundreds of strangers."

"You cannot be worse than Nebi Pasha's wife. She has all the grace of a pregnant sow."

Lada snorted. "Yes, and I have all the grace of a speared and dying boar."

"Even a speared and dying boar can still kill a man."

This, finally, teased a smile, though she quickly bit it back.

"Come on. Remember how we used to dance when we were little?"

"I remember wrestling you to the ground and pushing your face into the hearth's ashes."

"Exactly! And remember all the time you spent training with the Janissaries?"

"Yes, training to fight."

"Fighting is just like dancing! Only I end up with marginally fewer bruises." Radu held out his hand and, to his surprise and delight, she took it.

Lada was, in truth, an oddly graceful dancer. While there was nothing beautiful about her movements, there was a flow and power to them that was arresting to watch. Her sense of her own body moving through space was instinctive, well honed after so many years of training to fight. And if her expression looked as though she were plotting to murder her partner, well, Radu was used to that.

He had missed it, actually.

Moving in a circle with other dancers, they passed Nebi Pasha's wife. Radu levied a significant glance at her, then raised his eyebrows at Lada, who let out a loud bark of laughter, not quite muffled by the music. He barely managed to stifle his own laugh as they finished the dance.

She leaned her head against his shoulder, still laughing. "You were right! She does move like a pregnant sow."

Radu nodded solemnly. "There is a veritable farm's worth of dance partners here, and I have spun in circles with all of them."

"Tell me what kind of animal Huma is."

"A cat with weak hips, too proud to give up mousing."

She snickered, keeping her face hidden in his shoulder. "And Halil Pasha's wife?"

"An ill-tempered goose with flapping flat feet."

"What of Mehmed's dear bride? What animal is she?"

"Yes," a low voice interrupted. "What *is* my bride?"

Lada jerked, jumping away from Radu. They both stared at the floor rather than meet Mehmed's eyes. This was the first time Radu had been close to him at any of the celebrations. Mehmed was always separated by a draped cloth or by a ring of dignitaries, always at the side of Sitti Hatun.

"We must offer our congratulations on your wedding," Radu said.

"Stop."

Radu looked up, surprised by Mehmed's sharp tone.

"Please, not you, too. I cannot stand any more of this—" He waved his hand to encompass the room and everyone in it. "Do not tell me this nightmare has stolen my only two friends as well."

Lada said nothing, looking at Mehmed with eyes that burned darker than the coal braziers.

Radu chanced a small smile. "Perhaps she is a songbird?"

Mehmed snorted in derision. "Clearly you have not heard

her voice if you think that. No, my precious bride is like a cornered mouse, trembling and squeaking and utterly worthless."

Perhaps the meanness in Radu's chest had not been extinguished, after all, because he swelled with joy hearing this. "She is lovely, though," he offered, whether to combat his own pettiness or in hopes that Mehmed would contradict him, he did not know.

"She is a waste of air." Mehmed rolled his head from side to side, stretching, an angry energy to his movements. "I want to dance."

Radu looked to the raised dais where Mehmed's bride still sat, forlorn. It looked as though she had been crying. "I do not think Sitti Hatun wants to—"

"Not with *her*," Mehmed snapped. He held out his hand to Lada. Radu stared, noticing after a few seconds that Lada was doing the same. Only she did not look at Mehmed's proffered hand with confusion. She looked at it with rage.

"Now?" Her voice trembled with the force of keeping it quiet. "*Now* you want to dance? *Now* you want to speak with me?" The coals in her eyes had burst into flames. Radu took a knowing step back, but rather than striking, Lada turned on her heel and ran from the room.

"What did I do?" Mehmed asked, brows knit together.

Radu rubbed the back of his neck. He was not certain why Lada had reacted so strongly, but he had not had an opportunity to talk with Mehmed, and he would not waste it. "We . . . saw you. Before we came here. At the harem."

Mehmed's expression revealed nothing.

"With . . . your child."

Mehmed's eyes fell shut, and he released a heavy breath. "Ah. Yes. My son." He put a hand on Radu's shoulder. All the greetings, all the dancing, all the friendly touches that pass from one person to another in conversation felt like a dream. Mehmed's touch was like waking up. "It is strange, is it not?"

Radu lit up with relief. Mehmed understood how it felt when they were together! It was normal, it was shared, they could—

"I still forget that I am a father."

A tiny exhalation escaped Radu's lips, carrying with it all of his false relief. "Yes. That is strange."

"I look at the baby and he feels so foreign, like sleeping in a bed not my own." Mehmed's hand dropped from Radu's shoulder, and he lifted both palms up. "Still, as my father would say, it is my *duty*."

"Like Sitti Hatun."

"Yes, like Sitti Hatun. I will be happy when this is finally over, and we can go home and get back to how things were before."

Radu nodded. That was what he wanted, too. That was the aching, the need, the wanting inside him. How things were before.

With a brief nod, Mehmed strode away, his expression distracted. Radu watched him, always aware of where Mehmed was in the room like he was of the sun in the sky. So when Mehmed slipped out a side door as everyone's attention was focused on a poet beginning a recitation, only Radu saw.

He knew Mehmed should not be alone. Not ever. By the time Radu got through the door, he caught only a flash of

Mehmed's purple cloak as his friend turned a corner. Radu had not been invited, and Mehmed probably needed a moment alone if he was sneaking off. So he followed, quiet and at a distance. He was so intent on not losing sight of Mehmed and remaining invisible that he did not realize where Mehmed was going until he peered around a corner and saw him pounding on Lada's door.

"Open it!"

"Take yourself to the devil!"

"We need to talk!"

"I need nothing from you!"

Mehmed put his head against the door and took a deep breath. When he spoke again, his voice was softer. Radu had to strain to hear it, as Lada no doubt had to do on the other side of the heavy wood door. "I did not know about the baby until I returned, after I met you at the pool. And then I did not know how to tell you. I still do not, I have no idea how to feel about it. It is . . . a duty. It is the same as sitting through endless councils, hearing the complaints of pashas and the petty disputes of Janissaries and spahis."

Mehmed paused, as though listening to something, then shook his head. "She is detestable. And the harem, I— It is not real, Lada. I visit, and they flit about like phantoms, like paintings. None of them are real to me." He paused again, placing a hand flat against the door. "You are the only real thing in my life."

Radu gasped with the sheer physical pain the words sent through him. But the sound of his agony was covered by that of the door opening. Mehmed reached in and pulled Lada out to him, and then his mouth was on hers and his hands were in her hair and he was holding her so tightly, so tightly, and they stumbled back into Lada's room and closed the door.

Radu tripped forward, feet dragging, until he stood outside the room. He wanted to be inside it. He wanted to be the only real thing to Mehmed, just as Mehmed was the only real thing to him.

He wanted—

No, please, *no*.

Yes.

He wanted Mehmed to look at him the way he had looked at Lada.

He wanted Mehmed to kiss him the way he had kissed Lada.

He wanted to be Lada.

No, he did not. He wanted to be *himself*, and he wanted Mehmed to love him for being himself. His question, the question of Mehmed, was finally answered, piercing him and leaving him shaking, silent, on the floor.

He did not want this answer.

31

Though Mehmed had to leave far too soon lest his absence be discovered, Lada could still feel the memory of his hands and lips.

She did not know what it meant or what they had set in motion. But Huma had been right, after all. Because the way Mehmed looked at Lada as he left made her feel as powerful as she ever had.

They would see each other again at a late-evening party. Until then, the men were attending a bathhouse, and the women were meeting for a more intimate meal.

Lada had not planned on going, but her room was too tight, just as her skin was too tight. She had to do something lest she burst. The last place she wanted to be was around Nicolae and the Janissaries, and Radu was not in his chambers. So she found the gathering, slipping in with her secret wrapped around her as securely as armor.

When she saw Sitti Hatun at the head of the table—tiny and perfect, and perfectly miserable—Lada nearly laughed. Her rival was diminished, unworthy of even scorn.

Lada saw a familiar face and took a cushion beside Mara. Mara frowned thoughtfully, and then she smiled.

"Ladislav. You have grown."

This afternoon alone, Lada felt she had grown by leagues. She carefully tucked the corners of her mouth back down around her memories. "Yes. You look well. Where is Halima?" Looking around, Lada did not find her. The room's doors were attended by eunuchs, with most of Murad's wives and concubines present.

A twist in her stomach demanded Lada remember that it was very likely at least a few of the women here were Mehmed's.

No. She refused to think about it. If they were here, they were like Sitti Hatun: duties, forced upon him. Not a choice, not a desire. Not like her.

Mara smiled, though it was mirthless. "Did you not hear? Halima had a child not two months ago. She is still in confinement."

Lada could not help the gasp that escaped her. "Murad's new son is Halima's?"

"Oh yes. She was violently ill all nine months of carrying him, and then nearly died giving birth. He is the ugliest infant I have ever laid eyes on. He never stops crying. Halima has never been happier."

Lada snorted a brief laugh. "Poor happy Halima. And you? Are you happy?"

Mara took a sip of wine. Most of the women around them had none, but she made no secret of drinking it. "Serbia is peaceful. My husband neither requests nor demands my presence. I am quite well. You are, too."

Lada blushed, looking down and toying with her plate. Did she wear Mehmed's touch on her skin so obviously that others could see it? "What do you mean?"

"You are not the same miserable, terrified creature you were when last we met. You have stopped fighting."

Mara's words struck deep, and Lada struggled to disagree. But it was true. Lada let her eyes rest on the empty space around Sitti Hatun, the way all the women around them talked to her without saying anything. Even surrounded, Sitti Hatun was alone. She had been bartered by her father. Lada quickly tamped down a brief swell of pity. That was what fathers did. It was up to daughters to figure out survival by any means possible.

She turned back to Mara and spoke the truth. "I stopped knowing what to fight against."

Mara lifted her glass. "May you find some measure of happiness in your surrender." She drank deeply. "May we all."

———◆———

Tortoises with large candles melting onto their backs made a circuit through the garden. Pools of light crept slowly along to illuminate different groups of people, like snatches of conversations overheard in passing. The flowers surrounding them, black in the night, would suddenly bloom into brilliant color before slipping back into silhouette.

As one of the tortoises labored past her, Lada felt as though she were rising from the darkness, a burning brand. She burned far more brightly inside, though, knowing Mehmed was nearby. She had partaken of too much wine at dinner, troubled by Mara's questioning. She did not want questions tonight. She wanted something simple. Something physical. Something real.

A song began, the singer telling the tale of Ferhat and Shirin.

Standing alone, motionless as a mountain, Lada let the candle tease her location. She kept her eyes fixed on the spot where she could feel Mehmed watching her, even if she could no longer see him. Then, a smile pulling her lips at the memory of feeling his, she stepped into the shadows, backing deeper into the garden's secret corners where the tortoises had not yet made their leisurely trek.

Even the music was muted by the dark, drifting in snatches, twisted and distorted by the wind into mere rumors of a tune. She felt alone. It was no longer a feeling of desperation, but rather one of anticipation. Mehmed would leave the pavilion he shared with Sitti Hatun and find her. She knew it down to her toes. It was foolish and reckless, and that made it better. Lada wanted no careful thoughts of the future. Tonight, the future was only as long as it took him to follow her.

She found a sheltered spot under a tree with branches arching overhead to create a roof, and tucked herself against its trunk, relishing the feel of the bark against her skin. As much as she used her body as a tool, she had never truly appreciated skin before.

"Lada," Mehmed called, his voice a rough whisper carried on the heavy night air and trailed by the scent of broken flowers.

She could see him, backlit by the distant garden party. He

turned one way, then the other, searching. A giddy thrill went through her, seeing him desperate to find her.

The memory of the last few weeks was as sharp on her tongue as the taste of him, and so she said nothing. Let him wait, let him search, let him be alone. She would go to him when she *chose* to, just as earlier in her bedroom she had let him touch her only where she allowed.

But his head turned in her direction, and he walked forward, steps tentative, posture searching. He reached out and found her face without fail.

"How did you know where I was?" she asked, disappointed and thrilled in equal measure.

Mehmed's laugh was a silent exhalation. "This is the best area of the garden tactically. Your back is protected, but you have an open view of everything going on, while remaining hidden. Of course you are here."

Lada's scowl at being predictable was erased as Mehmed's mouth met hers with greedy intensity. He pushed his body against hers, pressing her back into the tree. She grabbed his shoulders and spun him around, pinning him there. He smiled against her mouth, and she bit his bottom lip, hard enough that he startled. He twisted his fingers in her hair, pulling her in tighter, his mouth leaving hers and finding her neck. Everywhere he touched burned with feverish heat, aching and tender. He put his hands around her wrists, then paused. "What are these?" he murmured against her neck, feeling at the leather braces beneath her sleeves.

Her heartbeat was almost as loud as her breathing, and she closed her eyes to hold her breath and focus on—

There was a noise behind her. She smashed a hand over Mehmed's mouth, muffling his own heavy breathing. Turning so her back was pressed against him, she squinted out into the night.

A shadowy figure crept toward them. He wore no Janissary cap. A predatory angle to his body eliminated his being a servant. Servants walked with submissive, downturned lines. This man prowled with hands held at the ready. An errant ray of light flashed like a beacon off something metal in one of those hands.

Lada slipped both daggers free of their sheaths. The hunter was directly in front of them, leaning forward in an attempt to see into the deeper darkness beneath the tree.

Lada leaped out, one arm blocking the hand that held a weapon, her other dagger finding its goal with a wet whisper of success. The hunter was still for one eternal moment, then, with an agonized scream escaping his lips into the night, he crumpled to the ground. Lada stood over him as his life pulsed frantically from his neck. Two twitches, and then nothing, where once a man had been.

It was only when Lada realized she could see well enough to notice the deep red of her target's blood that she looked up. An enterprising tortoise had finally made its way to the depths of the garden. She was illuminated—dagger winking playfully, hand covered in blood, Mehmed standing behind her.

"Lada?" he asked. His eyes were fixed on the body.

But the rest of the garden party, including Murad himself, stared in horror right at her.

32

"ARE YOU CERTAIN YOU feel well?" Salih leaned forward intently. His eyes, which turned down at either corner and made him appear perpetually mournful, wrinkled in concern. He was eighteen, only a couple of years older than Radu, kind and anxious and always eager to be in Radu's company.

Radu nodded, unable to shake off his daze.

Mehmed's lips.

Mehmed's hands.

Mehmed's heart.

Tangled up in Lada, not in him. Lada, who could not love someone else if her life depended on it. Lada, who had taken all their father's attention, who had preferred Bogdan over her own brother. Lada, who had abandoned Radu to beatings and lonesomeness his whole life. Lada, who was cold and vicious and loyal only to herself.

Lada, who was not even beautiful.

"Am I not handsome?" Radu blurted out, the words spilling like tears from his mouth.

Salih's eyebrows raised, making his expression almost comical with its mix of sorrow and surprise. "You—you are."

"Am I not deserving of love?"

The surprise in Salih's face shifted to something raw and terrified. "You are."

Radu dropped his head. What did he know of love? This was not a love that he had heard of, this was not a love sung about by poets, celebrated in stories. This was something ... else, something he had no words for. And who could he speak to? Who could tell him how to love another man?

Or how to stop?

Trembling, Salih's stubby fingers alighted on his shoulder. "Radu, I—"

A servant knocked on the doorframe, interrupting them. Radu looked up, wearily, to see the thin, greasy boy he had paid yesterday. Yesterday, when he still cared about intrigue. When he still viewed himself as Mehmed's protector.

Yesterday, before the world ended.

"Salih, there is someone to see you." The servant bowed, waiting.

Salih's face creased in consternation. "I am sorry, I—"

"Go," Radu said, eyes on the floor. Their plates of food, his barely touched, sat cold and abandoned. "I will wait for you in your father's study. He has a book on the Prophet, peace be upon him, that I wanted to look at."

"I will hurry."

As soon as Salih had left the room, Radu dragged himself down the hall, steps as heavy and leaden as the beating of his heart. He did not feel daring or clever. His efforts here would be for naught, just as his love for Mehmed. Just as his life.

He did not bother closing the door behind him. He slowly pulled out the chair at the elaborate wood desk, the top of which was inlaid with patterns of lighter wood and whorls of pearl. What did he think he would find, anyhow? None of it mattered. He really should look for a book on the Prophet, peace be upon him. God was the only thing left to Radu. The only thing he could not lose.

The only thing Lada could not take from him.

He pushed to stand up, knee jerking awkwardly beneath the desk, slamming against it. A curse stopped halfway from his lips. Something had shifted. He got down on the floor and looked up at the bottom of the desk. A false panel, jarred loose by his knee, hinted at something within.

Radu eased it free and pulled out a thick sheaf of parchments. They were written in Latin, dense script neatly marching down each page. He scanned as quickly as he could, his despair forgotten. Most of the top letter was about a man named Orhan, a claim, an allowance. It meant nothing to Radu, but he tucked the information away. He flipped through the pages, stopping with a shock at the end of a short missive. It was signed on behalf of Constantine XI.

The emperor of Constantinople.

Footsteps from down the hall set him panicking. He shoved the letters back into the hidden compartment, then slid the panel into place. It failed to line up exactly, but he was out of time. He threw himself across the room and stood in front of one of the book displays, trying to hide his guilty countenance.

The heavy door swung shut, and he did not dare turn around. If he never turned around, he would never have to see that he had been discovered.

A hand came onto his shoulder, not heavy and violent, but gentle.

"Radu," Salih said, his voice as tentative as his touch.

Radu turned around with a shaking breath and a falsely bright smile painted on his face. Salih was standing close, too close, only one of those trembling breaths away.

Before Radu could form a question, his mouth was covered by Salih's.

Radu tensed, shocked and confused by this attack. Salih's hands gripped his waist, pulling him closer, mouth desperate and hungry against his own. Finally, Radu's panic-soaked brain processed what was happening. He lifted his own hands, unsure what to do with them. He put them on Salih's shoulders and pushed him back.

Salih met his eyes with a desperation Radu felt to his core. The desire there was raw and so obvious it hurt.

This was what Lazar had seen when Radu looked at Mehmed. A wave of humiliation and despair washed over him. Everyone had to know. If Radu was this obvious, surely Mehmed knew how he felt, knew what he was, even before Radu had.

Lada must know, too.

Rage flared up, eating away at his humiliation. He narrowed his eyes, refocusing on Salih in front of him. Sad, lonely Salih. Salih, who wanted him.

He brought his lips to Salih's with a ferocity that bruised his mouth against Salih's teeth. Salih opened his lips with a gasp as Radu grabbed the back of his head, sliding his fingers beneath Salih's turban to knot them in his hair. Salih pawed at Radu's tunic, tugging on the sash around his waist. He pulled Radu's tunic up, and ran his hand from Radu's stomach to his chest.

Radu did not know if this was desire or anger or disgust, or some combination of the three. He hated Salih for wanting him, hated himself for liking it, hated Mehmed and most of all Lada.

He kissed Salih harder.

The handle to the door clicked, and Salih jumped away from Radu, terror on his face. Radu turned to the shelf behind him and pulled out a book at random, opening to the middle. An illuminated page in artful Arabic script, the edges leafed with gold, blurred in front of him.

"Salih?" a deep voice lined with disapproval asked. "What are you doing in here?"

Radu glanced back to see Halil Pasha. The older man was out of breath and sweating. He glanced once toward the desk reflexively, then looked back at his son.

"We were looking for a book," Salih said.

Halil Pasha finally noticed Radu. He took in everything, realization moving slowly across his face as his lip curled in disgust. Radu's out-of-place tunic. Salih's raw and red mouth. Radu felt as dirty as he ever had, the evidence of his manipulation of Salih written all over both of them.

"This is my private study," Halil Pasha growled.

"I know! I am sorry. I thought— You were at the garden reception. Is it over so early?"

Halil Pasha waved a hand dismissively, but his tone was strained. "There was a murder. Some whore of Mehmed's killed one of the guests."

Radu dropped the book. Halil Pasha glared at him, but

Radu could not react how he was supposed to. There could be no other woman there who would kill someone. No one but Lada.

"Wait. I know you." Halil Pasha's eyes narrowed as he finally looked at Radu's face instead of merely registering his guilt. "You have grown. You were Mehmed's friend, when he was sultan." The realization finished clicking into place. "Your sister. I remember her now."

Radu swallowed. "I must go. My apologies for interrupting your night." Radu dipped his head, not looking at Salih, and fled.

He went to Lada's room first, but it was empty. The vast hallways of the palace were empty as well, ominous with their lack of activity. Radu turned a corner, heading for Mehmed's chambers, when he nearly ran into Lazar.

He grabbed the soldier's arm. "Where is Lada? What happened?"

Lazar frowned. "She is in a lot of trouble. You should stay out of it."

"Where?"

He sighed. "Come with me."

They hurried down the hallways until they reached one of the rooms that, two days before, had been overflowing with food and drink and light.

Now, it held a trial.

Lada stood, straight and solid in defiance, in one corner. Murad, surrounded by several guards, stood at the other end of the room, nodding as an enraged man dressed in Italian finery screamed and gesticulated in Lada's direction.

Mehmed stood in the center, watching his father with a mixture of veiled fear and simmering rage. To anyone who did not know him, it would have appeared he was merely bored. But Radu knew every expression, every change of his face.

Radu's stomach turned, and he crossed his arms over his chest, as though he could keep his heart from eating itself with bitterness and loathing. Lazar put a hand on his shoulder. "We should go," he whispered. "This is a dangerous time to draw attention to yourself."

"Not yet." Radu slid along the wall, disappearing into the milling crowds of whispering people. It looked as though most of the wedding party was here, waiting to see how the evening's unexpected excitement would play out.

Lada was alone. The hem of her skirts was stained a rusty dark brown. One of her hands, too, bore the proof of her guilt. She made no attempt to hide it or rub the dried blood away. Instead, she stared steadily out at the room, looking as though she would like to continue the work of killing as soon as possible.

In her place, Radu knew he would have been a sobbing waste of a man. And he had seen her, the first time she had killed, how hollow and shaken she had been. He could see a hint of the same displacement in the way her eyes focused on nothing, but, as with Mehmed, no one who did not know her would realize how upset she was.

Radu knew her. He understood.

He still hated her.

"Enough." Murad waved his hand to cut off the increasingly loud discourse of the Italian. "Mehmed, tell me what happened."

He spoke through gritted teeth. "I do not know, Father."

"Why were you in that part of the garden?"

"I needed to breathe. Sitti Hatun's perfume turns my stomach."

There was a ripple through the crowd as various people reacted to Mehmed's cruelty toward his bride. Murad's eyebrows descended lower. "And why was *she* in that part of the garden?"

Mehmed's lips twitched tighter and he raised his eyebrows in a challenge. There was a sudden intake of breath as everyone in the room came to the same conclusion.

Murad's face purpled with rage. He stalked across the room to stand in front of Lada. Several inches taller, he loomed over her. She did not move. "What *were* you doing that deep in the garden?"

Radu wondered why Murad would direct his anger toward Lada and not Mehmed, when it was his son who was embarrassing him.

Radu bitterly wanted the truth, even as he desperately wished for something else. Lada, however, said simply, "Following Mehmed."

"And why would you do that?"

"To protect him."

"At his own wedding party? What harm did you think could befall him?"

She finally changed her stony expression, raising a single

eyebrow in disgust. "A knife in the dark. The exact harm I prevented."

"We found no knife on the man you killed."

Mehmed spoke. "Several people got to the body before the Janissary guards did. Anyone could have removed the weapon."

Murad turned toward Mehmed. "Did the man attack you?"

"He was looking for me."

"And no one could have been looking for you at your own party with anything other than murderous intentions?"

"I am not that popular," Mehmed answered, his voice dry.

Murad's face turned a deeper shade. He jabbed a finger toward Lada. "Why did you kill that man?"

"I saw him stalking Mehmed. I saw a glint of metal in the darkness. I acted without hesitation to protect Mehmed, just as I have done before."

Murad tilted his head. "What do you mean?"

Radu cringed at her error, and saw Lada blanch. The attempt on Mehmed's life during his time as sultan was secret. She could not claim it now. She shook her head, stammered, "I—I mean, just as I have been trained to."

"*Trained* to?"

"I am a Jani—" She stopped, as shocked by what she was about to say as everyone else was. All the training in the world would not make her a Janissary. And it left her without a clear reason for taking it upon herself to kill a man.

"You are not a Janissary. Who are you?"

Lada looked at Murad with cold fury, her voice trembling with pain. "You do not remember?"

Radu leaned heavily against the wall, a bitter laugh trapped in his throat. The man who had stolen them, the man they had lived in terror of all these years, the man who had destroyed their lives *did not even remember them*. The secret to their survival, then, revealed: not Mehmed, not the grace of God, but rather an oversight by a man who could not be bothered to keep track of them.

"I know who she is." The crowd parted to let Halil Pasha through. He looked around, and Radu knew whom he was searching for. He shifted and Lazar casually stepped in front of him, blocking him from Halil Pasha's view. "She is Ladislav Dragwlya, daughter of Vlad, the treacherous vaivode of Wallachia. The treaty breaker. Was it not part of the terms of his princedom that he maintain loyalties to you? In exchange for the lives of his children?"

Mehmed stepped forward. "That is not at issue here! We are talking of the attempt on my—"

Halil Pasha waved a dismissive hand and continued talking. "How many times now has Wallachia gone against our interests? Should we not take this opportunity to remind Vlad of the consequences of disloyalty?"

A cold clarity fell on Radu like the first frost of autumn. Just as it signaled the coming winter, he could see what was happening. Halil Pasha did not want further inquiries into the incident in the garden. He was distracting Murad by bringing up a larger issue, that of their father's betrayal. And in doing so, he was eliminating the girl who had twice disrupted what Radu suspected were Halil Pasha's own attempts at ensuring Mehmed never ruled.

Lada was going to die tonight.

Murad was examining her with narrowed eyes, the Field of Blackbirds where they had fought rising again in his memory. Now, no doubt, that memory was filled with the Wallachian soldiers who had defied him—and here was Lada, representing the whole country.

Radu took a step nearer the door. He had gifts from Mehmed and others, things that could be sold. He had a horse and traveling clothes. He could slip into the night and disappear. He looked at Mehmed, who was looking at Lada.

Only ever looking at Lada.

Bitterness so heavy he could taste it welled within Radu, and he turned to leave. But as he did, he caught a glimpse of Lada. Instead of seeing the girl Mehmed had chosen, instead of seeing the girl who had failed him time and again by never being what he needed her to be, he saw the same expression she wore that day so long ago when she crawled out on the ice to rescue him. At the time, he had thought it was anger. He saw now that it was terror, and defiance in the face of her own all-consuming fear.

He hung his head. She had ventured onto the ice for him to spite death. And he knew she would do it again without hesitation.

"How could I have forgotten about you?" Murad asked Lada. His voice balanced on a sword's edge between venom and amusement.

Radu stepped forward, breaking free of Lazar's grip, with a laugh as though this were all an amusing game between friends. It was just in time, as everyone looked at him and missed the snarl that deformed Lada's face and betrayed her increasingly murderous anger.

With a flourish, Radu bowed deeply. "My Sultan, jewel of Anatolia, vessel of power, chosen and most beloved of God, it is an honor! I can assure you that *we* have never once forgotten about *you*." He straightened, a benevolent smile lighting his face. "Indeed, if it is not impertinent, I have adopted the Janissary tradition and think of you as Father. For years I have wanted this opportunity to thank you."

Murad's eyebrows lifted beneath his turban. "Thank me?"

"For saving us. For educating us, bringing us out of the dark, and, most important, for bringing us to God."

"What are you talking about?" Halil Pasha snapped.

"My sister and I converted to Islam years ago. It has been the greatest source of light and joy in my life, and I would have been left in the darkness without the generosity of our father, the sultan. I speak for both of us, of course."

Lada's face turned a deep, angry red. Radu smiled at her, twitching his eyes narrower for a split second. If she messed this up, they would both die.

Murad turned to Lada, and for a breathlessly terrifying second she did nothing. Then, every muscle strained, she bowed her head in acknowledgment.

"But what of their father?" Halil Pasha's voice sounded like that of a child stamping its feet in rage.

Radu grinned. "You have not communicated with him since his betrayal three years ago?"

Murad shook his head, expression still wary.

This time, Radu let his laugh ring through the room, showering his delight on everyone listening. "Then he will have assumed us dead this whole time! What a just punishment for the slithering infidel. I hope every day has been agony and every night a torment! Will you tell him now that we are alive, happy and settled in our home? Imagine how his heart will swell. And then you could inform him of our conversion, cutting his joyful heart right out." Radu clapped his hands together gleefully. "I am sorry. I overstep. Of course it is up to Your Magnificence to decide how to deal with that man. I am simply so grateful to finally have an opportunity to thank you myself for all you have given us. Your grace and benevolence have shaped my entire life." He bowed again, even deeper, then looked up reverently.

Murad was smiling. And Mehmed looked relieved and grateful as he met Radu's eye. Radu dared not look at Lada and draw anyone's attention back to her. He needed them to focus on him, on his grand performance.

But it was an easy one to act. Because, while he hated Murad, he did consider this home. And he *had* converted, with Molla Gurani as his witness. Islam had given him a home, given him a place to belong, given him peace when nothing else had.

Well, almost nothing else. He looked away from Mehmed. He still had God.

Murad's smile was thoughtful, not cruel. "I will not forget you again."

"It is the deepest honor imaginable to be remembered by you." Radu bowed yet again as Murad walked past him. Murad placed a hand on top of his head, then exited the room. Radu straightened, meeting Halil Pasha's calculating gaze.

"It would appear," Halil Pasha said, so quietly only Radu

could hear, "that the sultan has entirely forgotten the matter of your sister murdering a guest at the party."

Radu smiled knowingly, as though he and Halil Pasha shared the same concerns. He knew only a few things about Halil Pasha, and he would bring them all into play. "Perhaps it is for the best that no one looks closely into what happened."

The other man's voice grew wary. "What do you mean?"

"Simply that it is a wedding. A celebration. We should move past this unfortunate incident, pray for the poor man's soul, and anticipate the day when Mehmed once again returns to the countryside, far away and forgotten."

With a grunt of what could have been assent, Halil Pasha swept from the room, followed by the remaining attendees, who were now certain that nothing of interest would happen. If any of them were concerned over the lack of resolution regarding the matter of the murdered man, no one mentioned it.

Lada called Radu's name, brows furrowed, hands reaching out toward him. Mehmed looked toward Radu, waiting for him to join them and discuss what had happened.

Radu turned and left.

33

LADA PUT ON HER boots with a sigh of relief. Their tenure here had been interminable. After last week's debacle, she had kept a low profile. Mehmed was constantly surrounded by guards. Perhaps Murad had not entirely forgotten that someone had tried to kill Mehmed.

If that was, in fact, what had happened.

Lada had been certain she had seen the flash of a weapon, but no one could identify the man, and the guest list had been conveniently misplaced. It was part of the reason the matter had been dropped. No one would claim the murdered man, which pointed to the fact that he should not have been there, whatever his purpose.

But it remained that she had killed him before being sure that he was, in fact, after Mehmed.

She frowned, tying a sash around her tunic. If the man was innocent, she was sorry, but she knew she would make the same choice again. What did that say about her?

Leaving the rest of her things for servants to pack, she

crossed the hall to Radu's room. He had kept the opposite of a low profile, suddenly becoming even more a darling of the court. Lada had not been able to so much as speak to him all week. No longer did he keep company with second sons and minor officials. At last night's feast, he had spent most of the night at Murad's side, paraded around like a long-lost son. Meanwhile Lada had stood in the corner, and Mehmed had remained banished in his silken prison with wilting Sitti Hatun.

Lada pounded on Radu's door. He opened it, still in his bedclothes.

"Hurry up! We leave in an hour. Back to Amasya at last." She pushed past him and sat on his rumpled bed. "I will be so happy to have this nightmare behind us."

Radu looked at her with an intensity she was unaccustomed to. Usually he smiled or said something funny to deflect her bad moods. But now he stared expectantly and unkindly.

Lada shifted on the bed, scowling. "You are the one who has been avoiding me. I *was* going to thank you. It was very well handled with Murad. But how dare you say I have converted to Islam! I could have killed you." It was the most she could bring herself to say, because in truth she knew she would have been dead without Radu's brilliant intervention. She could muster some gratitude, but more than that she was annoyed, angry, even jealous. Radu was in his element among these people, while Lada could not be further from hers.

Radu's expression remained the same. Lada stood, throwing her hands in the air. "What do you want?"

"I know," he said.

"What do you know?"

"About you and Mehmed." He said Mehmed's name as he always had, like a prayer. But this time it was laced with despair and longing. Lada turned her head defensively, picking up a candle from its stand and playing with the flame.

"What do you think you know?"

"You do not deserve him."

Slamming down the candle, Lada spun on Radu. "Perhaps he does not deserve me! I asked for none of this! How can you judge me for finding some measure of happiness in—" She stopped, searching her brother's face. It was there, as plain as the stars in a cloudless night sky. Perhaps it had always been there. She sat back on the bed, all fight and fire extinguished.

She had heard rumors of this type of thing. Jokes and bawdy stories from Nicolae and the Janissaries about men who loved other men in the manner of a woman. It had never made sense to Lada, but then, she had never loved anyone the way she knew her brother loved Mehmed.

Had *always* loved him.

With knife-sharp clarity, her own feelings of powerlessness and loneliness since being taken from Wallachia rose within her breast. How, then, must it feel to want a some*one* as much as she wanted a some*thing*, and to know that someone would never want you?

"I am sorry," she said, unmoving and emotionless because she did not know how to express what she understood.

Radu's anguish was palpable, choking her from across the room. "You do not love him."

Lada shook her head. She did not know what she had with Mehmed, only that it buffered her against despair. She would not give that up. "I care about him."

"You care about how he makes you feel. You cannot love him."

Radu was quivering, fists clenched, consumed with his feelings. This love would break him. Unless Lada broke him now. It would not be the first time she had allowed him to be beaten down in order to protect him.

She spoke with all the bitterness of the truth, each word a lash against Radu's heart. "He will never love you. He will never look at you the way he looks at me. You cannot have this, Radu."

They locked eyes, neither moving. Finally Radu slumped to the floor, long legs folded up to his chest, hands over his face. "You have no love to give him, and I have no love he will accept. What are we supposed to do?"

Lada leaned forward, a hand outstretched. Then she curled it into a fist. She could not comfort him, could not fix this. He would need to be stronger. That was the only solution. "Get up. Stop pitying yourself. We are leaving, and things will go back to how they were before."

"We can never go back." Radu looked up at her with empty eyes, and the truth of his words rang through her like a bell. It was true. There was no going back from Radu's feelings, no going back from what Lada had let happen between her and Mehmed. Perhaps this had all been a mistake.

"Get dressed!" she snapped, overwhelmed and angry.

"No." A cold distance settled over his face as his square jaw tightened.

"We will not wait for you."

"I am not coming."

Exasperated, Lada began pulling clothes at random from the large armoire. "You are worthless. What will you do? Stay here?"

"Yes." He stood—straight, taller than her—then stepped close enough so that she had to bend her neck back to look him in the eyes. He stared down at her, and the little brother she had dragged through life was now entirely gone. "You have both been so busy learning tactics and studying battles, you have failed to see the truth of where thrones are won and lost. It is in the gossip, the words and letters passed in dark corners, the shadow alliances and the secret payments. You think I am worthless? I can do things you could never dream of."

Lada stumbled back. His words hit the precise tender spot she had been avoiding touching. "But—we have to stay together. We are all we have against this empire."

Radu opened his door, looking above her head. "Your mistake is in assuming we both view them as an enemy."

Rage and disgust spat from her lips. "You cannot mean that. We are Wallachian."

"*You* are Wallachian. I am home. Get out."

Lada could think of nothing else to say. She wanted to hit him, to pin him to the ground until he relented like when they were children. But this was not the child she had known. She did not know this man. She had lost Radu somewhere along the way, and she did not know how to get him back.

She walked numbly past him, the door nearly slamming into her as he shut it.

Dazed, she found herself astride a horse an hour later.

Mehmed, eschewing his grand carriage, rode beside her. He looked relaxed and happy, as though a weight had been removed from his shoulders.

It was not until they had entered the countryside that he looked around, puzzled. "Where is your brother?"

Lada thought how it would break Radu's heart to know it had taken this long for his absence to be noticed by the person he valued most in the world.

Lada thought how Radu had broken her own heart.

"I have no brother," she said, urging her horse into a gallop and leaving the party behind.

———

Amasya fit like a pair of boots she had outgrown. The contours hit at the wrong places, and it left her pinched, skin rubbed raw. Everything that had been comforting there, safe, was gone.

"Careful!" Nicolae shouted as Lada slammed her wooden practice sword into the side of one of the newly appointed Janissaries, a Serb her own age. But so much younger. She hated him for his youth, for his happy, easy laugh. She hated all of them. She spun and hit the boy again. He cried out and dropped his sword, backing away.

"Easy now." Nicolae held up his hands. Lada threw her sword at him. He laughed, catching it. "I thought we agreed you would save the beatings for Ivan?"

The rest of the soldiers laughed. Ivan glowered, viciously kicking the Janissary he was sparring with in the corner.

Ignoring them all, Lada stomped out. She had been practicing more with the Janissaries, throwing herself into their routine, but it ended. It always ended. Every night they went to the barracks, and she went to her empty room.

Mehmed went to wherever Mehmed went when he was not with her, and he was never with her long enough to make everything feel better.

And Radu was nowhere.

She scaled the stone wall surrounding the fortress and dropped to the ground, then headed straight up the mountainside into the trees. That still felt the most like home to her, the heavy scent of pine needles underfoot, sun-warmed dirt, cool shadows. She breathed in deeply, then choked on a sudden fear: What if this was nothing like what home smelled like? What if this had replaced her memories of her own land?

She stumbled to sit beneath a tree, hugging her knees to her chest, clutching the pouch around her neck. She was terrified to open it and find only dust, with no trace of a scent. Or, worse, a scent she did not recognize.

Maybe Radu was right. Maybe Amasya was home now, and she needed to accept that.

She heard the footfall a second before the sharp blow to the side of her head. Her vision spun as she sprawled on the ground, face pressed against a sharp rock and the rough, pungent needles. A kick to her stomach froze her breath, a creaking noise escaping her mouth. She panicked, begging her lungs to work as bright points of light swam lazily in her vision.

She reached for her wrist sheath, and a boot came down, pinning her hand to the ground. "I know your tricks, little whore."

Her sluggish, aching head recognized the voice. She gasped, grateful her stomach muscles were working again. "Ivan?" He was a dark blot against the sun, standing over her. He dropped to his knees, straddling her, pinning her legs beneath his and holding both her wrists above her head. His face was so close to hers she could see the pocked scars covering his cheeks, the dark roots of hair beneath his skin.

"You think you are special? You are nothing." He spat in her face, the warm, sticky saliva dripping down her temple and into her hair. "You are a whore, and whores are good for only one thing. You should know your place." Backhanding her across the face, he grabbed both her wrists in one of his enormous hands, then reached down to his trousers.

Lada tried twisting away, but his weight pinned her legs. Disbelief warred with the disorientation of the blows to her head. She could not be here. This could not be happening. *Ivan* could not be beating her.

"You will never be one of us," he said, putting his face right above hers so she could look nowhere else as he wrenched her tunic up and grabbed for her underclothes.

She slammed her head into his nose. In his momentary distraction, she pushed up, knocking him off-balance enough to free one leg. She brought it between his, and he howled in pain, rolling off her. He pushed himself to his feet, and Lada jumped on his back, fastening her legs around his waist and wrapping her arm around his throat. She grabbed her own wrist, pulling the arm tighter. Ivan staggered backward, slamming her into a tree, but she held tight. He clawed at her arm, trying to get a good enough grip to yank it away. She slammed her heel down into his stomach and groin, three sharp jabs.

Finally, he stumbled forward, falling to his knees.

"I am not one of you," Lada said, her mouth right next to his ear. "I am *better*."

Ivan pitched forward and Lada went with him, never relaxing her arm though her muscles screamed for release. Long after he stopped moving, she stayed there. And then she stood and walked away.

This was the third man she had killed.

This time, her hands were clean.

She found Mehmed in her room, waiting for her. Walking past him, she pulled off her tunic and dropped it into the hearth. The low-burning flames picked at it, a slow devouring as the cloth turned black and caught fire. "There is a body in the woods behind the fortress," she said, watching the tunic contaminated by Ivan's hands turn to ash.

"What?" Mehmed's hands hovered in midair, on either side of Lada's hips.

She turned to face him, carrying the fire in her eyes as a burning shield against everything she saw. "Also, I want to lead my own contingent of Janissaries."

34

RADU HAD NEVER IMAGINED how deeply lonely being well liked would be.

At tonight's feast, he sat only three people down from Murad. A position of honor, one that made him highly visible—and desirable—to all the attending pashas, their pashazada sons, visiting valis, local spahi leaders jockeying for position against rival Janissary leaders, even several powerful beys. People who were, by virtue of their birth, all more important than he was.

But he was here, and they were not, and they all wanted to know why.

Radu smiled, eyes wide and guileless, looking as though he were innocently delighted with everything before him. Halil Pasha sat immediately to his left, though, and it was hard to be aware of anything else.

Halfway through the course of roasted game birds with a delicate, creamy sauce, Halil spoke. "You have not been to visit my son Salih since your dear friend Mehmed left last month."

Radu swallowed the piece of meat threatening to choke him. There were so many traps in that sentence, so many things to avoid or spin in the right direction. He had no doubt that Halil Pasha viewed him with suspicion, and Halil Pasha was the deadliest man in Edirne. Radu shrugged, offering an embarrassed and pitying smile. "I found that Salih and I do not ... share the same interests."

Halil Pasha's eyes hardened knowingly as he glanced in Salih's direction. He was at the far end of the table, barely visible. At every event they had attended together, he had tried to catch Radu's eye, and he had sent him several invitations to visit, but Radu felt it kinder to do this than to let him think there could be something real between them.

"Yes, Salih's interests are rather peculiar." Halil Pasha resumed eating, then, his voice as casual as a knife in the dark, asked, "And what of your friend Mehmed? Do you hear much from him?"

Radu sighed, letting guilt play across his face as he looked over in Murad's direction. "My comportment with Mehmed does not reflect well on my character. It is a source of shame for me."

Halil Pasha leaned closer. "Oh?"

"When he left, he accused me of using his friendship to get closer to his father, and ... I fear he was not wrong. I am grateful for the kindness Mehmed showed me, but I never agreed with his tolerance for radical views on Islam, nor his misguided militaristic ideas. Though," Radu said, tilting his head thoughtfully, "he has softened considerably on those. I think his time in the country has much improved his temperament. But our sultan is a scholar and a philosopher of the highest order, and it has long been my dream to be near enough to absorb some small portion of his wisdom."

Halil Pasha made a thoughtful noise in the back of his throat, though he frowned as he digested Radu's words. Radu went back to his meal as if the information he had just given Halil Pasha was not carefully constructed and entirely false.

From across the table, a conversation grew more heated, loud enough for Radu to pick up a few words. One, *Skanderberg*, kept being repeated. "Who is this Skanderberg they speak of?" Radu asked, leaning close to Halil Pasha.

"Have you not heard? He was once a favorite of Murad, though back then he was Iskander Bey. An Albanian Janissary who rose through the ranks until Murad made him bey of Kruje. And Skanderberg repaid Murad's generosity by betraying him and claiming that section of Albania as his own. Twice now we have made attempts to reclaim it and been repulsed." He paused to give Radu a poisonous smile. "Favorites can fall far."

Murad shifted in his chair, face deepening to red. If Radu could hear the talk of Skanderberg, surely Murad could. It had to be a source of tremendous embarrassment for him.

Seeing an opportunity to insinuate himself further into Murad's good graces, Radu stood.

All eyes turned to him, but he bowed toward Murad. "If it pleases you, my father, I have written a poem about the glory of your rule."

It was one of the many weapons in his arsenal, one he had hoped to keep sheathed for a while longer. But Murad was primed for a strike. The sultan beamed, gesturing for Radu to stand on a platform in the corner of the room.

Radu had practiced the poem so often he could recite it in his sleep. He had stolen shiny bits from famous Arabic poems, gathering them like a raven to line his own nest. The language was dense and flowery, hyperbolic in the extreme. Murad listened, enraptured, as his reign was likened to the ocean and his posterity a mighty river.

While Radu performed the many long stanzas, he watched as the meal was finished and men began to move around the room. While Murad sat, untouchable, nearly everyone of any importance eventually followed the pull to Halil Pasha to pay their respects. He sat in the center of a vast web of influence.

Radu smiled and spoke in brighter tones to cover the despair he felt watching his enemy, the spider, and wondering how he ever thought he could hope to defeat him.

———— •=• ————

Lately, prayer brought Radu little comfort. Even joining five times a day at the dizzyingly beautiful mosque, surrounded by his brothers, Radu felt alone. Heart heavy and head hanging, he trudged out onto the steps of the mosque, evening already eating away the blue of the sky. If he lost his faith, what was left to him?

"Radu?"

He looked up to find a man staring at him, arms open, face wide with wonder. "Can this be the lost little boy I prayed with so long ago?"

Recognition dawned on Radu, warming him like the sun. "Kumal?"

With a laugh, the older man threw his arms around Radu, drawing him into an embrace. It was the first sincere physical affection Radu had had since that horrible night with Salih. Something in his chest broke free, and he hugged Kumal too tightly, clinging to him.

Kumal's voice was as tender as his touch on Radu's back. "Are you still lost, then?"

"I think I am."

"Come, let us take a meal." Keeping an arm around Radu's shoulder, Kumal shepherded him as he had when Radu was so much younger. They found an inn serving supper. Plates of spiced meat, steaming with fragrant warmth, were set before them.

"Where have you been?" Radu asked. "I have not seen you in the courts."

"I do not visit often. There is too much to do in my vali, and I have always preferred filling my duties there to spending time here."

Radu nodded. He had seen much of the striving of valis and beys, local rulers abandoning or neglecting their duties in hopes of being given even more.

Kumal's beatific smile lit up their dim corner. "And I have just returned from umrah in Mecca."

Radu leaned forward, drawn by the brilliance of Kumal's smile. "You made the pilgrimage to Mecca? And for umrah, not hajj. So you have been before!" The hajj, traveling to the birthplace of the Prophet at Mecca, was one of the five pillars of Islam. Along with prayer, fasting during Ramadan, giving charity to the poor, and declaring that there is no God but God, it made up the simplest base of being Muslim. It was the one that Radu knew the least about and doubted he would ever be able to fulfill. But here, in front of him, was the man who had helped him truly find himself in Islam, who had filled the hajj and returned to worship further. "I do not know enough about the umrah. Tell me everything."

Kumal described the long journey, exhaustion and excitement warring with each other. The city of Mecca where the Prophet, peace be upon him, had walked, and where pilgrims participated in the circling of the Kaaba. It was the most sacred site in the world, the place that all prayers were physically directed toward. And Kumal had been there! During the umrah, he performed further rituals to honor Ibrahim, his wife Hajar, and their son, Isma'il.

By the time Kumal had finished speaking, Radu was once again overcome with weariness. "Perhaps that is what I need. Maybe if I went to Mecca, if I saw it . . ."

Kumal smiled kindly. "Someday you will go, and your life will be blessed for it. But it will not fix you—all your troubles will still be here, waiting. First you should strive to find peace where you are, and then you can make the pilgrimage to celebrate that peace."

Radu shook his head. "I do not know where peace can be found in this city."

"That is your problem, then. Peace is not to be found in this city, or any city. Not even Mecca. Peace is to be found here." He pointed to Radu's heart.

Radu put a hand over his chest, feeling the beat of his life beneath it. The pulse that thrummed for so long to the name of Mehmed. "I think my heart is the problem."

Kumal paid for their meal, then stood. "I want you to visit my vali. Perhaps we can help your heart there."

———•———

Radu found a eunuch waiting in his chambers with a message from Huma, demanding he visit her. The eunuch stood, silent and impassive, and Radu suspected that being too tired was an excuse neither Huma nor the eunuch would accept. So he followed the other man into the harem.

Huma's chambers were no longer the luxurious rooms she had occupied before. They were in a side wing and had narrow windows and scarcely space for two. Radu sat on a cushioned bench against the wall. Huma, her skin tinged a sickly yellow, sat on a higher chair across from him, their knees nearly touching.

"Are you well?" Radu asked.

"I want you to kill Halil Pasha."

Radu choked on his surprise. "You want me to *what?*"

Huma shifted in her seat, eyes narrowing in direct contradiction to her innocent smile. "I know how you feel about my son."

Radu resisted the urge to turn away or to tense his body defensively. He had no doubt Huma could divine meaning from the slightest movement. "He is my friend."

"Do not lie to me. You love him like a flower loves the sun."

"I do not know what—"

She sliced her hand through the air, cutting off his pro-test. "These things happen. It is not without precedent. Did you know that some sultans have had harems with male members?"

Too late Radu realized his eyes had betrayed everything.

Huma settled back in her chair, self-satisfied. "I can help you. You do not have to despair that your love is impossible."

Radu shook his head, protests on his lips warring with the dark hope she had introduced. *Could* he have more with Mehmed?

Huma took a sip of water from a plain white ceramic cup, eyeing it with disdain. "I will help you," she said, not looking up, "when Halil Pasha is dead."

35

NEWS OF LADA'S TEST had spread throughout the city. Spectators lined the far edge of the field, sitting in the shadows of the looming trees on chairs brought by servants, or on the ground if they had no servants, which was most of them.

"This is ridiculous." Lada folded her arms tightly in front of her armored chest. She wore mail beneath a tunic; the heavy links rippled down her body. She had left her head bare, though the men behind her all wore Janissary caps.

Mehmed smiled, waving at the gathered crowds. He spoke to her out of the side of his mouth. "Please do not make this worse than it must be. You know I am not the ultimate authority. If Ilyas decided to go to my father about this, my hands would be bound. That Ilyas even agreed to give you a trial of merit speaks volumes of your reputation among the local garrisons."

Lada gazed across the broad field to where she could see Ilyas Bey, the leader of Mehmed's personal garrison. He had been a good addition to their forces here and had given her permission to train with the Janissaries. She respected him, admired him even.

But apparently he questioned whether she could *command* men. He had allowed her to pick a regiment of twenty to skirmish with his own twenty-man team. Each side had dull swords and blunted arrows with cloth-wrapped tips covered in flour to prove that they hit their marks. However, Ilyas's side had a light cavalry, mounted to represent the challenge Janissaries were often up against.

She caught laughter drifting her way from the spectators as Mehmed walked to join them, signaling the start of the skirmish. Ilyas remained where he was, immobile, waiting for Lada to make the first move.

"It is time," she said.

Nicolae threw up his arms in disgust. "This is insane, Lada! I will not put my reputation on the line for this."

"You promised!" she screamed, grabbing his shoulder.

He jerked free, throwing his sword to the ground. He walked back toward the fortress. Half of her men followed him, swallowed by the dappled shadows of the trees.

"Cowards!" She picked up Nicolae's sword and threw it after them. "Dogs! Crawl on your bellies after your own vomit!"

Breathing hard, she turned to the rest of the men, who shuffled in place, looking over their shoulders. "Shields up," she said, mouth a grim line. They formed, shoulder to shoulder, shields held in front of them as they marched slowly forward. A smattering of arrows hit, bouncing to the ground. The crowd laughed, jeering.

Ilyas shook his head, lifting an arm halfheartedly to command his men forward to slaughter.

He was interrupted by a rain of arrows from behind the spectators, thunking against the sides of nearly all the horses. Before Ilyas had time to process what had happened or remove the men who were out of play, another volley hit, striking him in the chest, taking out the remaining horses, and leaving only a handful of men. While they debated whether or not to fire over the spectators' heads toward the hidden assailants, Lada's forces dropped their shields to reveal their own bows, firing at the "survivors" until none were left unmarked.

The spectators were no longer laughing.

Ilyas walked forward, meeting Lada in the middle of the field, face impassive but something like pride shaping his eyes. His mustache twitched over his lips. "That was . . . surprising. You played on our expectations."

Nicolae strode out from the cover of the trees, grinning. He turned and gave a sweeping bow to the spectators. "Many thanks for your help!"

"We were not planning on the crowd." Lada nodded toward them.

"And yet you still managed to use them as a shield. Admirable. And also questionable. What if I had no qualms about firing into innocent bystanders?"

Lada shrugged. "That would be on your shoulders, not mine. Besides, I know you, Ilyas. You are a man of honor."

He laughed. "And you?"

"Not a man."

Mehmed reached them, beaming. "That was brilliant!"

With a nod, Ilyas frowned. "But now to the larger question: You can command these men. But they know you. They trust you. Do you really think that a garrison would willingly follow you in battle if they did not? Or a group of ajami cadets, fresh from training? I say this not to insult you, but to question the practicality of giving you a command. I fear it would be setting you up to fail, and embarrass the Janissaries."

"I agree." Lada smiled tightly at Mehmed's surprise at her cooperation. "Give me charge of a frontier group of Janissaries. Let me pick them by hand—men who will not question my orders, who are not afraid to follow a woman. Let me train them how I see fit to be Mehmed's personal guards. Twice now I have seen Mehmed's life threatened. It would be advantageous to have a group that thinks differently and functions outside of normal Janissary movements. We will see things no one else does. And if people dismiss my soldiers because they are led by a woman, well"—she gestured to the men cleaning flour off their horses—"I can use that to my advantage."

Ilyas's eyes narrowed with the weight of her proposition. He had to agree. Lada deserved this. She *needed* it. Finally, when she thought she would have to pull out her sword and hit Ilyas upside the head with it to get him to speak, he nodded.

"Very well. You can have your pick of Janissaries. Take as long as you need to gather them. You will report to me quarterly, but you can house and train your men wherever and however you see fit."

Shaking his head and laughing in disbelief over what he had agreed to, Ilyas turned and rejoined his men.

"You never smile at me like that," Mehmed said, watching Lada.

She turned to him, putting a hand to her mouth, which had betrayed her by bursting with her happiness. Over Mehmed's shoulder, she noticed the crowd of observers included several delicate flowers from the harem, complete with eunuch guards. When she lowered her hand, she took the smile with it. Raising an eyebrow, she said, "You never earn it."

He put a hand over his heart, staggering two steps as though wounded. Then he straightened, and his gaze became heavy with promise. "Come to my rooms."

She leaned toward him, closer than was appropriate, fully aware of the weight of the stares on them from everyone on the field. Including women who knew Mehmed in a way she had yet to. "I have work to do."

Turning, she lifted a hand and motioned for her men to follow her. Nicolae fell into step at her side. "We did it," she whispered, the smile creeping back onto her face.

"You did it." He elbowed her armored side. "Where do we start?"

"I want Wallachians. *Only* Wallachians."

Nicolae raised his eyebrows. "And why would that be?"

"If Ilyas asks, explain it is so that I can give commands in a language attackers will not understand."

"And if *I* ask?"

"Because I do not trust men who fail to remember they were not born to this."

Nicolae looked over his shoulder to where Mehmed was watching them walk away. His voice was as easy as a summer breeze, but it carried a hint of wildfire smoke. "And what of the man who was born to all of it?"

Lada did not look back. Because part of her did trust Mehmed, more than anyone. Part of her wanted to abandon Nicolae and meet Mehmed in his rooms. To take him as a lover instead of existing in this between state that was agonizing for both of them. To accept an easy life of being his.

And part of her wanted to stab him for that.

"I have no answer," she said, speaking the truth.

36

RADU FLED THE CITY.
It was half a day's travel to Kumal's home, and the farther Radu got from Edirne, the easier it was to breathe. But he knew Kumal had been right when he had said going somewhere else was not the solution. When Radu returned to Edirne, everything would be waiting for him. Any peace he found would be a dream, ephemeral and temporary.

Still, riding through the rolling fields and past groups of clean, organized cottages, it was easy to pretend that Huma had not offered him the impossible, that he would not have to figure out a way to kill Halil Pasha, that Lada had not broken his heart once again, that Mehmed would never be his the way Radu wanted him to be.

Or, even more painful to think about, that there was a chance that someday Mehmed *might* be his.

Though Radu had not sent word ahead in his haste to get away from Edirne, Kumal was waiting at the gate to his land. He greeted Radu as a brother, kissing his cheeks and leading the horse as Radu walked beside him, stretching his weary legs.

Kumal's home was beautiful, built around a center court-yard with a fountain. While everything in Edirne competed for the eye, demanding attention, Kumal's home was simple and clean. Wood paneled the walls, woven rugs lined the tiled floors, and only in the long gathering room was there orna-mental decoration: along the tops of the walls, gold Arabic script of a verse from the Koran.

It was time for prayer. Kumal laid out two mats, and they prayed together. Radu stayed on his knees afterward, trying to hold on to the feeling.

"I have a few matters to attend to," Kumal said. "Feel free to explore. We will meet back for the evening meal after it gets dark." With a friendly squeeze of Radu's shoulder, Kumal left.

Radu wandered through the one-story house, respecting closed doors. He sat for a while in the courtyard, enjoying the lingering low rays of the afternoon sun bouncing off the whitewashed stone walls. Then he strolled behind the house to the gardens. They were as carefully tended as everything else, but unlike the rest of the house, they were elaborate. High, trimmed hedges formed a maze, with plots of brightly bursting flowers greeting the spring. In the center, towering over everything, was a large tree.

Radu followed the twists of the hedge, trying to find his way to the tree. There was a rustling sound, and then two girls burst onto the path in front of him, laughing and holding on to each other. Their hair was messy, their eyes shining.

"Oh!" Nazira laughed. She straightened, letting go of her companion. The other girl took a step away, looking at the ground, quickly tucking her hair back into the wrap it had fallen out of. "Hello! There was—" Nazira was out of breath, a smile stretching apart her round lips. "There was a bee. We were running from it."

"Were you stung?"

"Yes! Repeatedly! It was wonderful!" Nazira said, then she held her lips shut before bursting into a peal of laughter. Her companion elbowed her sharply in the side, then, bowing her head, walked quickly away.

Radu had not remembered her being quite this strange, but her happiness was contagious.

"That was my maid, Fatima." Nazira leaned to look past Radu and watch the other girl leave. "Come, I will show you more of the garden." She took Radu's arm and guided him around, chattering happily. They found a bench in the very center of the courtyard, in front of the tree. A swing hung from two branches, its wood seat too small for an adult.

Radu realized with a start that he had no idea if Kumal was married or had children. He asked Nazira as much.

Her sweet mouth turning down, she shook her head and stood to put a hand on the rope of the swing. "He did. His son, Ibrahim, loved this swing. He died four years ago. He was only three. And then the next year his wife, Ine, died in childbirth. A little girl. We only got to keep her for three days before she followed her mother."

Radu closed his eyes against the pain of sympathy. Kumal

had lost so much. But three years past had been when they first met. "When he found me in Edirne . . ."

"We were there to pay respects to Ine's family."

"So he was deep in mourning." And still Kumal had found the time to show compassion and kindness to a lost little boy. "Your brother is a good man."

"The best I have ever known."

They sat in companionable silence, observing Kumal's loss, before winding their way back to the house. Nazira had a manner of teasing that made Radu feel bigger than he actually was, unlike Lada's teasing, which made him feel smaller.

The meal was the best he had eaten in ages. The food was plain, but there were no politics, no fear, no lies or pretending at being something he was not to secure an advantage.

"I am glad you have come, Radu," Nazira said, her voice uncharacteristically solemn. "It is good for someone to be here to show my poor brother what clothes are supposed to look like. I try to help him all the time, but it is not enough."

Kumal raised his eyes to the ceiling. "Save me from such a helpful sister."

"I would gladly take her from you," Radu said, then blushed as he realized how that sentiment might be misconstrued. "I mean, as a sister. She is much preferable to my own. Not once has she wrestled me to the ground, twisted my arm, or beaten me in a contest of strength."

Nazira waved her hand. "Oh, we save all contests of strength for *after* supper."

But mentioning Lada had removed Radu from the

moment, and he now participated in dinner as an observer, the dessert fruit on his plate turned bittersweet.

After they had eaten, Fatima appeared in the doorway. Nazira excused herself, and Kumal and Radu retired to his sitting room.

"I see now why you never come to Edirne."

Kumal smiled. "I am very happy here. Though I worry about Nazira. She is getting older. I should make more of an effort to find a match for her, but she expresses no interest and I, selfishly, wish to keep her here with me for as long as I can. Still, I know it will be better for her to be happily married and have a family of her own. If I were to die, my estate would pass back to the empire, and she would be left with nothing. And yet she insists she never wants to leave."

Radu nodded. "I do not blame her. If I could have your counsel forever, I would never want to leave."

"What counsel would you ask?"

Radu sighed, thinking of all that weighed on him and how paralyzed he felt. "What do you do when faced with a problem that has no good solution?"

Kumal frowned. "What do you mean?"

"I mean, in some situations, there is no easy choice. What, then, is the right choice? Commit evil for a good end, or avoid evil, knowing that you have allowed a worse end to come to pass?" Radu did not even know which evil he was referring to. Killing Halil Pasha, certainly. Lying and deceiving in his position in the capital in an effort to help Mehmed. Even the way he felt about and thought of Mehmed, which did not *feel* evil, but he suspected it was because no one spoke of it, and Huma acted as though it gave her power over him.

"I think your life has gotten complicated."

Radu dropped his head, covering his eyes with his hands. "I do not know what to do."

"I am in charge of many people in my vilayet. Sometimes, a decision I make will impact someone in a negative way. Perhaps one farmer wants more access to water, but giving him that would deny three other families the water they need for their crops. I am denying the first man the opportunity to expand his crops and make more money, but I am saving the other three families from starving. Some years I have had to increase taxes to lay up stores against the winter, which is a burden for my people. But it means we will have enough to sustain us through a bleak period. I have had to take fathers from their families for committing crimes—denying a family of their provider, but keeping the rest of my people safe." He sighed. "It is never easy. I try to build for the best future I can, where the greatest number of people will be affected in the best ways. Sometimes I have to make hard choices, but I try to do so with a prayer and the welfare of my people always in my heart. I have made mistakes, but I try to use regret as motivation to be more thoughtful, to consider things more carefully, and to be kinder and more generous in all my dealings."

Radu thanked him, though he was still left in the dark as to his own problems. Should he pursue good for himself, or good for others? What if Halil Pasha thought he was doing good by preventing Mehmed from taking the throne? Mehmed's idea of the future was in direct opposition of, say, the citizens of Constantinople's idea of a good future. Whose had more value? Whose was right?

And could he ever be generous enough to wish his sister happiness with the man they both loved?

———◆———

Radu's time at Kumal's home was too short, but after a few blessed days of peaceful respite, he was no closer to solving any of his problems. Edirne beckoned him back.

With a promise to visit soon, he returned to the city to find that Murad, still pleased with his poem, had waxed generous and given Radu command of a small group of frontier Janissaries. Bemused, Radu went to the barracks to meet with his men. He was a good rider, excellent with a bow and arrow, and skilled enough with a sword, but he had never aspired to commanding men. He thought it odd that Murad would think a poem qualified Radu—so young—to lead soldiers.

A familiar figure greeted him.

"Lazar," Radu said. He still did not know how to feel about the other man, knowing that Lazar knew the deepest secret of his heart.

Lazar saluted Radu with brisk formality, then bowed, popping back up with an infectious grin. "I knew I was right to stay in Edirne. I have requested to be assigned to your frontier group."

"I have no idea what I am doing," Radu admitted.

"That is why I am here." Lazar introduced him to the fifty men at his command, and Radu's fears about the other man disappeared. Lazar dropped the familiarity he normally held with Radu, speaking in crisp, commanding tones and showing the proper amount of deference when addressing

Radu. Radu stood straight, nodding seriously, trying to commit names to memory.

After the tour was done and the men were dispersed, Lazar walked with Radu out into the larger Janissary headquarters on his way back to the palace. "You will do well. I can take care of day-to-day organization and training. These positions are more ceremonial than anything, but you are liked. The men are happy to have you."

Radu nodded. "I am glad."

Lazar leaned in closer as they walked. "I am happy to have you, as well."

Radu cleared his throat, wondering if there was more meaning there, when a sweep of a cape around a corner ahead of them caught his eye. He sped up, turning in time to see Halil Pasha clasp hands with another man before they entered a room together.

"Who was that with Halil Pasha?" he asked Lazar.

"Kazanci Dogan, the commander of all the Janissary corps. You will meet him at some point, I am certain."

"Is Halil Pasha here often?"

Lazar shrugged. "I have seen him on occasion." He paused, eyes narrowing thoughtfully. "Would you like me to keep track of how often he visits?"

"Yes. And of anyone else Kazanci Dogan meets with outside of the Janissaries."

Lazar put a fist to his chest, then left.

Radu walked back to the palace, deep in thought. Halil had strings of his web everywhere. Viziers, pashas, beys, both major branches of the military, with the native spahi leaders and their regional forces, and the Janissaries with Kazanci Dogan. And at the center, fat and lethal, sat the spider Halil Pasha.

If they killed him, as Huma wanted, the web would remain. All these lines of power, tugged together, aligned against Mehmed. And who knew if another, more dangerous spider, would take Halil Pasha's place?

No. Huma was wrong. First, they needed to destroy the web. Then the spider would be powerless.

37

Lada and Nicolae lay on their stomachs, peering over the ledge at the city laid out beneath them. Wood homes stretched above the river, jostling for space as they lined its banks, growing straight up from the water. Amasya was a fairly recent addition to the Ottoman Empire, its long, storied history evident in the Roman tombs casting shade on Lada's legs. The last time she was up here, she had been with Mehmed and Radu, staring up at the sky and dreaming of stars.

Now, she looked down and plotted flames.

"We could use the river," Nicolae mused, speaking Wallachian as required by Lada. "Travel down it by boat in the middle of the night, setting fire to the homes. That would keep the locals busy, and many of the soldiers."

"Who is in charge of the spahi forces here?"

Behind her Petru, a young Wallachian only recently released from training, spat in derision. "Spahi! Lazy, fat pigs. Why should we worry about them?"

Lada had picked him because he had been pulled from Wallachia at a relatively late age—he was already fourteen by the time he came to the Ottomans. But he was arrogant and thickheaded, with a mean streak that reminded her of her older brother Mircea. Sometimes it made her like him more.

Most of the time it made her want to pitch him off the cliffs.

"And who told you the spahis were lazy, fat pigs? Have you fought them?"

"Why would I fight them? We are on the same side."

Lada and Nicolae shared a glance. Perhaps Petru would need to be released from her regiment. "Are the spahis forbidden from growing beards?"

Petru scoffed. "No."

"And yet you are permitted only a mustache."

"If he can ever manage that," said Matei, a wiry man with a perpetually hungry look whom Lada had recruited from his corps in Edirne. Petru threw a rock at him. All together Lada had ten men, varying in age from eighteen to mid-twenties. There were few Wallachians to choose from, the Ottomans preferring other nationalities as making smarter and better soldiers.

Fools. Lada squinted, looking for which houses could be blown up with the stores of Janissary gunpowder to most effectively block the roads to the keep. "And are the spahis forbidden to marry and have children?"

"No."

"Another thing our Petru could never manage," Nicolae said cheerfully.

Lada waited for the laughter to die down. "And are the spahis slaves, stolen from their homelands and brought here to serve another man's master and another man's god?"

She was met with silence. "The spahis resent our growing power. They resent our organization, our skill in battle, our position closest to the sultan and the sultan's heirs. Do not ever think you are on their side, because they are not on yours. They fight to gain land, prestige, and wealth. We fight because it is the only thing given to us."

She waited for a few moments, then continued. "Who organizes a city's defenses?"

"The spahi in charge." Petru sounded focused as he crawled next to her to look over the city.

Lada traced the line of the river as though it were a serpent. "Cut off the head in your first strike, and the body is powerless before you."

Matei continued sharpening a dagger on a whetstone where he sat on a fallen tomb marker. "Much as I would enjoy cutting off the heads of a few spahis, I am not certain I have time to set fire to the city tonight."

"Planning imaginary destruction is my favorite training game, though." Nicolae stretched long, rolling onto his back. "It is so very restful."

Lada pushed herself up, dusting off her tunic and adjusting the white cap she now wore. "Is Ilyas Bey on duty?"

Stefan, a quiet man whose face was a cloudless sky—devoid of emotion and impossible to read—nodded. He spoke little, but Lada had found he had a mind like an ant colony, constantly bringing in bits of information to feed itself.

She nodded in return. "Good. Time to assassinate Mehmed."

Nicolae groaned. "That is so much less restful." But the other men were already packing up, anticipation lighting their faces. As they wound their way down the mountainside toward the fortress, they made their plans. Stefan ran ahead to spy whether Mehmed was outside or inside. He could usually determine it solely by the presence of guards in certain areas.

If Mehmed was outside, they would launch a sneak assault over the wall, firing arrows as fast as possible. If he was inside, Matei and three others would get as close as possible, hoping no one noticed that they were not on duty, while Nicolae scouted for Mehmed's location and signaled from a turret where he was. That would leave Lada, Petru, and four other soldiers light and strong enough to climb the outer walls of the fortress.

They needed only one person to get close enough. One shot, one dagger, one chance was all it would take to kill the heir.

Stefan met them at a gnarled pine that grew sideways out of the rocks. Lada always chose this as the meeting spot, though it made her heart hurt with long-distant and time-poisoned memories of happiness.

Stefan's face was, as always, unreadable. But there was something defensive in his stance that put Lada's teeth on edge. She knew what he would say before he spoke, and she also knew that he knew it would upset her, which was almost as bad.

"Janissary presence at the gates to the harem, two eunuchs on duty at the doors."

Her men let out a collective breath, whether in relief or frustration she did not know. Nicolae's voice was deliberately bright. "Well, that signals the end of today's game. We cannot very well launch an assault on the harem."

"And why not?" Lada's jaw ached. She focused on that concrete, specific pain. Since she began training her men, she had seen little of Mehmed. And, when he did see her, it was always dark corners, stolen kisses, desperate hands.

"Because . . . ," Nicolae said, dangling the word on a line as though he hoped Lada were a fish that would swallow it and prevent him from having to explain. She did not bite. "Because," he said, sighing, "the walls are too high, the windows too barred, the doors too guarded. We have strategized this before, Lada, and the conclusion is always wait until he leaves. We cannot get in."

"*You* cannot get in," Lada said. "Stefan, did you recognize the guards on duty?"

He shook his head.

"Good. Then they will not recognize you. I need skirts, an entari, and a veil."

Petru's mouth hung open, making him look like the fish Nicolae had hoped to catch. "Skirts? But why?"

Lada motioned for them to follow. "Because a tremendous amount of weaponry can be hidden in skirts, and because Stefan is about to drop off a gift from the sultan."

Nicolae caught up to her as she made her way swiftly toward the outer building she had been given for her garrison.

It was another impediment to Mehmed meeting her—she lived in the makeshift barracks with her men. She was never alone. Because if she was alone, then there was no barrier, no impediment, nothing stopping them from . . .

He was in the harem.

"Lada," Nicolae's voice was low enough that the others could not hear him. "Is this really a good idea? I think we should wait. We can catch him coming out. We have plans for that."

"And they are good plans, which mean they are obvious plans, which means Ilyas may have already anticipated them. This is a better plan."

He grabbed her arm. "Lada, stop."

She wheeled on him, fury blazing, making her feel taller and stronger. "Do not tell me what to do."

He lifted his hands in the air. "I merely wonder if the harem is the best place for you to be."

The concern in his expression made her want to tear out her hair. And then strangle him with it. She sneered, "Do you think I do not know what happens in there? Are you worried for my tender sensibilities?"

"No! I would never think any of you tender, I promise." He grinned, scar puckering. "But I wonder about . . . your reputation. Women who go into the harem do not come out. It is a permanent position."

She batted the suggestion out of the air with a wave of her hand. She knew he was trying to say something bigger, and she would not acknowledge it. "I am not going in as a woman. I am going in as an assassin. So we have nothing to fear."

A few minutes later she was covered from head to toe in leftover finery from Mehmed's wedding. She had never worn half the clothes prepared for her, but an industrious servant packed them all to be sent back with her. Other than the wrinkled garments that would have had any maidservant beaten, she looked like a woman. And, veiled, she looked nothing like herself.

It was decided that only Stefan should accompany her. Any more guards would look suspicious. So, without fanfare, he brought Lada to the gate of the harem and handed her to the closest eunuch.

"A gift from Mehmed's mother," he said.

The eunuch nodded, uninterested, and led Lada straight past the two Janissary guards and into the harem.

She jumped in spite of herself as the door clanged shut. It sounded so formal, so final. Her heart was racing and her breathing shallow and unmeasured as she followed the eunuch down several twisting hallways, trying to memorize them. Everything was bright and clean. Elaborately patterned and gleaming tile beckoned them farther inside.

The eunuch opened a door to a small waiting chamber. "Someone will be with you within the hour to determine your placement and get you situated." He left her there without another word, closing the door behind him.

He did not lock it.

Not that it would have mattered if he had, but the principle of it made Lada burn with rage. It was only about the door, she told herself. About the eunuch's utter inability to see a woman as a potential threat.

She took out one of her daggers and stabbed it into the sofa. Tugging it along the length of the sofa, she created a jagged gash. Then she sheathed her dagger and fixed her veil. She stepped out into the hallway. She was perfectly capable of carrying out this mission without letting the fact that she was inside Mehmed's harem distract her.

Her only guess was to go farther in, so she picked up a large vase with a fragrant bouquet, holding it carefully in front of herself as though she had a purpose. Carrying a bunch of flowers around seemed like a rational occupation in this gilded birdcage.

After passing several closed doors and turning down three separate hallways, Lada was hit with a wave of despair. Mehmed would probably finish with his *business* here and leave before she ever found him, and then what would she tell her men?

The sound of a baby crying tugged at her ears. She swerved, following the shrill donkey-like braying until she came to a room with its carved wooden doors thrown open.

She slipped inside and immediately moved to the left, where a delicately painted screen stood in front of a large, open window. She managed to slide between the screen and the wall, the sound of her movements masked by the screaming infant.

Mehmed's laugh rang through the room, falling on Lada's shoulders like a blow.

"Am I holding him wrong? He does not like me."

"Of course he likes you!" The woman's voice was sticky sweet. Lada could feel it settling in her ears and knew that no amount of scrubbing would rid her of its residue. "He is strong, see?"

"My little Beyazit. Be strong while I am gone. I will be back soon."

Mehmed's words effused tenderness, and Lada wished for any other scenario. She had thought the worst that would happen would be finding him with another woman, but this . . .

She did not know how to be angry over this.

But still she managed.

"How long will you be gone?" the woman asked.

"However long it takes to defeat Skanderberg. Will you need anything?"

"No, no, we are very well taken care of. Be safe."

"Goodbye, my boy!"

Lada noted with some mean satisfaction that Mehmed's tone speaking to his concubine was the same he used when addressing any servant. But he clearly felt something for the child. And the concubine had given him that.

The baby's cries left the room. Lada heard someone stand. She stepped out from behind the screen, still holding the vase.

Mehmed barely glanced at her as he walked straight for the doorway. She threw the vase to the right of his head. He ducked as it shattered against the wall, water and flowers scattered among the sharp shards of glazed pottery.

He looked at her, face red with fury. "What in the name of—"

She ripped off her veil. For a moment his anger stayed frozen in place, then dissolved into a smile. He laughed, shaking his head. "What are you *doing* here, Lada?"

She closed the door. Hope lit his eyes, and he moved forward.

She twisted out of his reach. "I could have killed you."

"By all means, kill me." His smile was anything but concerned as he reached for her. It had been days since they had stolen a private moment.

Not here, she thought. *Anywhere but here.* "Skanderberg?" she asked, changing the direction of their interaction. Iskander Bey had been one of Murad's favorite Janissaries, and now he was one of Lada's favorites. He had been a thorn in the empire's side for years, using what he had learned from them to keep them at bay.

Lada had studied every account of his fights with the same devotion Mehmed gave to Islam.

Mehmed's expression closed off. "Yes, my father has declared a new campaign. I will ride with him and command a flank in the siege."

Lada's chest welled with excitement. She could prove herself, her men, and . . . she could *go,* finally see somewhere else, even if it was not home. "When do we leave?"

Mehmed did not meet her eyes. He leaned down and picked up several of the flowers, carefully avoiding the sharp edges of the broken vase. "I leave this afternoon."

Lada hurried to the door. "We can be ready within the hour, I—"

Mehmed grabbed her arm, pulling her back. "You are not coming."

"I— What? We are ready. My men are ready. My force is small in number, but we can scout, and I will—"

"You are staying here!"

Lada peeled off his hand and took a step back. "Why?"

He was suddenly fascinated by the bruised flowers in his hand. "I need to leave someone I trust in charge of the city."

"Anyone can do that! Nothing of value will be left here!"

Mehmed's gaze was heavy when it finally found her. "Nothing of value?"

Understanding hit Lada. She ripped the flowers from his hand and threw them to the ground. "I will not stay behind to watch your brat! I am no nursemaid!"

Mehmed blinked rapidly, then shook his head. "Lada, I was not talking about my son. Do you think he is the only thing here I value?"

"Then what?"

"You! I will not take you into battle! You have no idea what the conditions are like, no idea how many ways there are to die."

"I can handle myself."

"But what about me? What would I do if something happened to you? I have to keep you safe!"

She pushed his chest, sending him stumbling, vase shards crunching beneath his boots. "I am not something to be kept! Next you will tell me you want to keep me behind walls, keep me in padded, perfumed rooms, keep me *here*. I am not your concubine, Mehmed!"

"That is not what I am asking!" He threw his hands up, pacing in a circle. "You are precious to me. What is so wrong with wanting to take care of you?"

"If I needed or wanted to be taken care of, I would be no better than the women in here! I am nothing like them."

"No, you are not! I love *you*, Lada." He closed his eyes and lowered his voice, trying to regain control. "Please allow me to love you. You are the most important person in my life. You and your brother are the only people who truly know me."

Lada flinched, and Mehmed's eyebrows raised as he noticed her reaction. He did not understand why, though. Lada had not told him about her last fight with Radu, nor that she had heard nothing from him since they parted. Mehmed remained blind to the true depths of Radu's love—and to how much Lada missed her brother.

"Please," Mehmed said. "I have already lost Radu to my father. He rarely writes, and when he does it is as though he addresses a stranger. I cannot afford to lose you, too."

"You cannot lose something you do not own. Take me with you."

With a frustrated growl, he tore the veil from her hair and threw it to the ground. "You look ridiculous. Armor suits you far more than silk."

Lada put a hand to his cheek. His skin was soft and hot, always hot, as though he burned brighter than a normal person. Her voice came out a low purr, so like Huma's she startled herself. "Take me with you, and I will wear armor the whole time." She pulled his face down, kissing him, letting the fire he burned with ignite something inside her.

He grabbed her waist, pressing against her, matching her fierceness. She pushed her hip against his groin, where she could feel a hardness already formed. It terrified her, and also thrilled her that she had the power to make that happen. He groaned into her mouth, the kiss becoming deeper and more frantic.

"Lada," he said, kissing her throat, her ear, her hair. "Lada, Lada."

"Take me with you," she whispered in his ear.

He buried his face in her hair, arms holding her so tightly she knew she had won. Then he shook his head. "No."

With a scream, she pushed him away. He fell, his shoes soaked from the vase's water. She pulled out a dagger, leaned down, and cut off his sash. Crumpling the silk in her fist, she stared down at him. "You need me safe? Who will keep *you* safe? I have killed you again under your guard's very noses."

He had the audacity to lie back on the floor and laugh. "Lada, no one in the world would ever be as devoted or ingenious in the pursuit of killing me as you are time and again." He held out his arms, black eyes imploring. "Come, spend these few hours with me. I miss you."

She leaned forward, just out of his reach. "You should become accustomed to that sensation."

The way out was easier than the way in, the opposite of how a harem usually functioned for the women who crossed the threshold. As she left, she passed a startled Ilyas. She threw Mehmed's sash at his feet. "We killed him again. You lose. Try to bring him back alive from Albania."

Her own cruel words to Mehmed stung her as she nodded to a waiting Stefan, indicating their latest game had been a success. If Mehmed died, they would have parted with him declaring his love and her answering with cruelty. He would never know how she felt—that he tormented her, that he was a bright star in the black nighttime of her life.

It would be exactly what he deserved, to die without knowing, because he left her behind.

And she would never forgive herself.

38

1451: Kruje, Albania

Radu supposed that, with his new armor and weaponry, plus a personal servant, a tent, supplies, and a gorgeous horse, he was wealthier than he had ever been after years of owning nothing. He simply would have preferred this new-found prosperity to be the result of something other than marching to war at Murad's side.

He knew, too, that somewhere among the tens of thousands of men around him, Mehmed moved toward the same goal.

Remaining in Edirne would have been lonely with the pashas, pashazadas, Janissaries, and various friends he had made all gone for the siege of Skanderberg's Albanian holdings. He would have had far too much time to think when denied his daily scheming, spying, and socializing. He would have thought of nothing but Mehmed.

This was not a preferable scenario. He found himself scanning the endless sea of faces constantly—wondering, yearning, hoping for simply a glimpse of his friend.

But Murad's and Mehmed's forces were on different ends of the procession, separating Radu and Mehmed by a full day's march. The sheer logistics of moving this many men and this much equipment was staggering. Supply wagons and trains of animals trailed the soldiers, as did several hundred women who traveled with the men and offered various . . . services.

Murad had looked pleased when Radu blanched at an offer to take advantage of the women. "You are truly a devout son of God."

Radu had not known whether to laugh or cry over this praise.

Three days from their target city, Kruje, Radu had ridden ahead with Lazar and the scouts under his command. The rolling, soft green landscape had begun to show signs of civilization. Radu pulled his horse to a stop, patting her long, black neck while he waited for Lazar to catch up.

"What happened here? Is this where they fought before?" Radu looked out across vast, undulating farmland charred beyond use.

Lazar shook his head. "God's wounds. Skanderberg's welcoming gift. We will find no supplies from here to the city."

"He burned his own land?" Radu could scarcely take in the enormity of the destroyed crops. It was prime growing season, meaning Skanderberg would have had to destroy an entire season's worth of crops, leaving his people with nothing come harvesttime.

"Probably poisoned the wells and ponds for good measure."

"But what about his people? What will they do when the siege is over?"

Lazar shrugged. "Not our concern." He rode back toward the main body of the soldiers to report on their findings. Radu guided his horse forward at a slow walk, taking in the ravaged countryside. It would certainly make their work more difficult. They had accounted for taking livestock and supplies to supplement their stores. This would make things tighter and more difficult, splintering their men to guard the now-crucial supply trains. It also raised the cost of the siege to even more astronomical heights.

But it was the image of a stone foundation, charred wood walls drawing the crude blackened outlines of what had once been a home, that stayed with Radu for the remainder of his travels. Their forces would not have burned civilians' homes down. And, after they took the city, they would have allowed everyone in Skanderberg's domain to continue to live as they had before, to worship as they had before, giving them security and prosperity.

Radu wondered how much Skanderberg was willing to sacrifice and destroy in the name of protecting his people.

By the time they reached the walls of Kruje, Radu was already saddle- and soul-weary. Setting up and organizing camp took nearly a week. They were within sight of the city but out of cannon's reach. Radu's men pitched tent on the outer circle of Murad's vast pavilion, which was tucked into the center of the camp, buffered by tens of thousands of people around it. The Ottomans now had a larger population than any city within several days' march, including Kruje.

Radu commanded a frontier force. Their role was to harass and harry lines, not set up for siege. He helped direct where he could, stayed out of the way where he could not, and watched with a mixture of pride and dread as their superior force settled in to besiege the traitor Skanderberg.

And, five times a day, Radu set out his mat and prayed, sending extra hope toward God that the siege would be over quickly.

———◆———

Radu walked the perimeters of the camp. It had been three weeks since they arrived, with little to show for it. They had sent scouting parties to find the city's water source and cut it off, to no avail. They had tried to bribe the commander of the city and been rebuffed. The walls loomed, constant and mocking.

"It is a siege," Lazar would say, shrugging his shoulders. "The game is waiting."

Radu did not care for the game. His men had been used lightly so far, only escorting one supply train and doing guard duty two nights every seven. He had been frightened to be part of a siege, but now he was bored. All the waiting was liable to make a man mad.

He sighed, walking far enough from the camp that the fires did not impede his ability to see in the dark. He could have stayed in his tent, but if his men were out here, he would be, too. It was only fair.

Nearby, Yazid, a young Janissary, whispered as he walked. "What hangs at a man's thigh and wants to poke the hole that it has often poked before?"

Someone groaned in annoyance. Lazar hissed for Yazid to shut up. Radu blushed, grateful for being unseen. He already had a reputation for being too delicate about these matters, and wondered what the men said behind his back.

An odd clicking noise drew his attention. He squinted through the darkness.

"Get down!" Lazar slammed into him, bearing him to the ground. Something passed over them, more the rumor of a sound than anything.

Radu crawled out from under Lazar, dazed and in shock. If it had not been for Lazar, he would be dead. His impulse, strongest and first, was to run. He was not made for this. If Lada were here, she would have . . .

No. He was in charge. He would lead his men.

"To me!" he shouted. "Crossbows! Shields up, form a line!"

He held his shield in front of him, tense and cringing as he waited for a bolt to claim him. Lazar stood next to him, his shield pressed to Radu's. With a speed that made him proud, Radu's men joined them. As one, they moved forward, steady and sure, toward where their unseen assailants still fired at them.

They met no one.

Skanderberg's men had already disappeared into the darkness, whatever purpose they had been after thwarted. Radu's forces warily broke their line, ears and eyes on high alert.

"A key," Yazid muttered as he broke a crossbow bolt off from where it had lodged in his shield. "The answer was a key. Though I suppose *a bolt* would have been a good line, too."

Lazar stayed next to Radu, but he drew no comfort.

Everyone else seemed so calm, resigned to the familiar reality of battle. Radu was cold from the sweat that had instantly drenched him, his racing heart still frantic. He had always known they would be attacked, but it had been theoretical. He had not *known* it as he did now.

He walked, newly aware of every part of his body as though he were naked. He felt himself once again too small, too weak, like the boy terrified of Mircea's unpredictable bursts of violence. Only now he had no castle to hide in, no curtains to stand behind.

And he was responsible for so many more lives than his own.

39

THREE MONTHS AFTER THE rest of the Janissaries left, Lada's men finally had something to look forward to. They were expecting a shipment of gunpowder. Normally they would have had nothing to do with it. But with all the other Janissaries on the siege at Kruje, it was up to them to decide how to use it. The responsible decision would be to put it in storage and wait for the return of Ilyas. He would, no doubt, have specific people in mind to train on gunpowder uses and strategies.

But Ilyas was not here.

And with Radu far away excelling at politics and not a single letter from Mehmed, Lada wanted to burn things.

She was waiting at the gate to the keep when the wagon rolled to a stop in front of her. A woman climbed down, brows hunched low and matching her posture. "Where is the commander?"

"I am the commander."

Though her back would never straighten again, the

woman's eyebrows did. "You." Her gaze took in Lada's uniform, but it lingered like a question on Lada's chest.

Lada resisted the urge to fold her arms over her breasts. "Yes."

"You are not what I expected."

With a shrug, Lada said, "I could say the same."

The woman smiled, revealing several missing teeth. "We are at war. Again. My husband and sons are always called up by our spahi leader to serve. We have unique skills."

"We?"

"I know as much about gunpowder as any man."

"And yet you are left behind." Lada scowled, moving forward to look at the barrels in the wagon. "Does that make you angry?"

"Of course it makes me angry. It leaves me to do the work of my husband and our three sons all by myself."

"No, I mean you have as much place fighting as they do. They should not leave you behind like you are worthless."

"Bah. We shoulder a burden for the empire, just as the men do. Who else could keep everything running while soldiers tromp about having pissing contests?"

Lada laughed in spite of herself. "You would not say that in front of me if I were a man."

"I transport gunpowder and teach fools how to avoid killing themselves with it. I say whatever I want in front of whomever I want."

Nicolae tripped up to them, nearly dancing in his excitement. "What should we blow up first?" His eyes were bright enough to light gunpowder without a flame.

The woman sighed. "My name is Tohin. Might as well begin introductions, because it looks like I will be spending more time than normal keeping your fools from killing themselves."

"Tohin, I am glad to have you." Lada was surprised to feel how sincerely she meant it.

Tohin reminded Lada of her nurse, if Lada's nurse had had fingertips burned to thick calluses and had been expert in the use of gunpowder for combat. There was a quality there, a directness bordering on blunt hostility, that brought to mind the way her nurse would mutter to herself when she thought no one could hear. There was also a gleam of approval in Tohin's eyes as she watched Lada command her men that made Lada think of sitting by the fireplace, having her hair brushed.

If only this woman came with a Bogdan, too.

Or a Radu.

After several days training with tiny amounts of gunpowder—how to pack it, how to set a fuse so that there was time to get away before it blew, how to care for it—Lada's men were ready for a real lesson. They hiked up the side of the mountain and down into a narrow canyon, away from any homesteads. Each man carried a portion of gunpowder, and they took turns lugging a tremendously heavy small cannon. It was work slicked with sweat and punctuated with cursing.

Lada imagined she was climbing to Mehmed's side to fight next to him. And then she imagined she would be aiming the cannon at his heart instead.

She did not know which scenario made her feel better.

Finally at their destination, they set down the cannon. "I like crossbows more," Petru said, sulking as he massaged his hands.

Tohin slapped the back of his head. "Think bigger, little idiot."

The scenario was simple. An army would be coming at them through the canyon. They had to fire as many rounds of cannon shot as they could to disrupt the imaginary soldiers.

Lada knew the impact of the cannon would be more psychological than anything. Artillery light enough to be easily transported would not do much more damage than Petru's beloved crossbow, but the noise and newness of the cannon could be used as an intimidation tactic to break lines and trigger a retreat.

Still, it was an awful lot of work for relatively little reward. She stood back as Matei and Stefan adjusted the angle of the cannon with Tohin's guidance. The walls of the canyon were narrow and steep, with minimal cover. If an army was coming down it, there would be nowhere for them to go but forward—into them—or back, only to try again.

Lada looked along the top of the canyon on either side, noting the heavy rocks jutting out. What if there was nowhere to go at all?

"Stop," Lada said. "I can take out an entire army with two explosions."

Tohin let out an exasperated breath. "You soldiers always overestimate the damage. There is not enough gunpowder, and you would be killed if you stayed close enough to light it under an approaching army."

"Not under." The sun dazzled Lada's eyes as it shone down on her through a break in the rocks above. "Over."

———◆———

Tohin and Lada sat together on the jumble of rocks that had come down, blocking the entire bottom of the canyon.

In an actual battle, it would have been much more difficult. The timing would have to be perfect. They would need to wait long enough for the opposing army to be fully into the canyon. Stealth would be paramount—a single shot taking out either of the soldiers who were left to light the charges would ruin the whole thing.

But it had worked. Using the gunpowder to trigger an avalanche on two ends of the valley blocked the way forward and the way back. With steep sides and no cover, a force as scant as Lada's could have killed hundreds of trapped men, picking them off one by one.

"You have a very good mind," Tohin said. The rest of Lada's Janissaries were already starting the long, backbreaking process of lugging the cannon they had never bothered using over the mountain and to the fortress on the other side.

"The conditions would have to be specific for that to be effective."

"Still. Using the land around yourself as a weapon—that does not occur to most people. You heard that little idiot, the one with a head thicker than this rock. All he could think of was a weapon he could hold in his hand."

"And yet, for all my brilliance, I am fighting imaginary foes in a canyon behind a fortress no one would ever try to storm."

"Would you rather be on the field at Kruje? Throwing men at a wall that does not budge? Watching them die of rotting sickness?"

Lada felt a twinge of panic. They had had almost no word from the siege. She assumed that meant things were going well. "There is sickness?"

"A camp that large? There is always sickness."

"Have you heard from them?"

Tohin nodded. "My husband and one of my sons have written. There has been no progress. And disease is ravaging camp much faster than they expected it to."

"What about—" Lada stopped herself. She could not stop picturing Mehmed, lying on a cot, wasting away and sinking into himself. All this time she had imagined him with a sword in his hand, commanding men, accomplishing great things and never once wanting—or needing—her by his side. But disease was not a foe she had anticipated.

Lada cleared her throat, trying to ease the tightness that had taken root there. "What other news?"

"Nothing. They will push at the wall until it breaks or winter comes, and then they will return home. Whether they win or lose, the result is the same. The men come home, and I have less work to do but more mouths to feed."

"Why do they bother? What difference does Kruje make? Does it really hold so much value for the empire that it is worth this risk?" Lada stood, pacing. She let the fear she felt for Mehmed act as a fuse to light her anger. "Damnable fools!"

"It is not about Kruje," Tohin said.

"Of course not. It is about Murad's pride! He cannot stand that his protégé betrayed him, and so he risks Mehmed—"

Lada paused, taking a deep breath. "He risks thousands of men to take revenge against one."

"It is not about Skanderberg, either." Tohin raised a hand, cutting off the argument brimming on Lada's tongue. "Yes, he wants to make an example of Skanderberg, punish him. But what do you think would happen in the other border cities if Murad did not address this?"

"They would return to their rightful rulers! He overreaches. He has no business there."

"And what if he allowed Kruje to leave? If he allowed all the vassal states their freedom, if he withdrew to the borders of the Ottoman Empire as they were before we began eating into Europe, what then?"

"I do not understand the question."

"Where would it stop? Should we leave *all* the cities, go back to the deserts in the east? Roam on horses?"

"Of course not."

"So we stay here. You would allow us the first territories of our conquest—how generous of you. Do you think Hunyadi would be satisfied? Do you think Byzantium would thank us and happily live on their sliver of land? Do you think the pope would stop calling for crusades?"

"I do not think—"

"When do borders ever stay as they are? Our own people were driven from the east, fleeing from destruction. They saw cities and walls, and they wanted that. So they took them. If they had not taken them, they would have died. And someone else would have come and taken the cities instead."

"So defend what is yours! Why must it turn to conquest?"

"Kruje is ours. Skanderberg is ours. If we were not pushing, fighting, claiming what is ours and challenging what is not yet ours, others would be doing it to us. It is the way of the world. You can be the aggressor, you can fight against crusaders on their own land, or you can stay at home and wait for them to come to you. And they *would* come. They would come with fire, with disease, with swords and blood and death. Weakness is an irresistible lure."

Lada remembered Hunyadi riding into her father's capital as though he owned it. Her father was weak, and because he was weak—because he tried only to maintain what he had and avoid a fight—Wallachia suffered.

Tohin continued. "Murad takes war to other countries so that here, in the empire, we can carry on with the business of living. We expand, because if we did not, we would die. It is Murad's responsibility to see that we live."

Lada stared at the ruined canyon. "The price of living seems to always be death."

Tohin stood, joints popping audibly. "And that is why you become a dealer of death. You feed death as many people as you can to keep it full and content so its eye stays off you."

A dealer of death. Lada carried the phrase back to the fortress on her tongue, rolling it around. Borders and aggression, sieges and sickness. Dealers of death.

She prayed that Mehmed would not be one of those fed to death to keep it away from the heart of the Ottoman Empire.

40

No one was more surprised to see the shaft of an arrow appear in the middle of Yazid's torso than he was.

He looked up at Radu, a half smile on his face as though the arrow were the end of the joke he had been in the middle of telling. And then he fell off his horse, tangling under the wheels of the supply wagon behind them.

"Ambush!" Lazar shouted.

Radu should have shouted that. But he kept looking at the space on the back of the horse where Yazid had just been. Now there was nothing.

An arrow flew by, so close to his face that he felt the sting of its wind. Two more came in quick succession, though these were flaming and not meant for him. They found their larger target in the wood and canvas of the wagon.

Shouts up and down the twenty-wagon train sounded, letting Radu know the whole thing was under attack. The trees were close, pressing in like giant fingers ready to pull them all into the depths of the forest. To smother them in murky green and muffled birdsong until everything was quiet again.

There was a lot of screaming.

Water drenched Radu. Someone had thrown a bucket at the wagon and soaked Radu more than the wood. A flash of movement in the trees caught Radu's attention, and he threw himself from his horse, shouting as he drew his sword and ran for the enemy.

There was an arm, a scream, a flash of an eye showing white all around the iris, and then—

And then there was a body at his feet, his sword red with a terrible knowledge. Radu threw his head back in a howl of triumph. All he saw among the trees were men running, away from him, away from the wagon train. They had won.

He had won.

No one had been there to protect him, not this time, and he had—

He looked down.

The enemy—the terrible threat that he had single-handedly ended—was a boy. His wrists were knobby, his elbows sharp points. His eyes, wide and wondering with death, were orbs in a gaunt face that told of hunger and desperation. And so very, very few years.

Radu dropped to his knees and reached out. His hand hovered over the hole he had made that tore this boy from life. He had shot arrows at enemies before, had probably killed before, but never like this. Never with a face right there to fall still and cold with the question of *why*.

"Radu?"

A hand came down on his shoulder. "Radu, are you hurt?"

Radu twitched away with a shudder. "I will scout ahead." He stumbled back to his horse, galloping beyond the train, beyond the line, beyond the last scouts kneeling on the ground around one of their dead. When he had left them all behind, he gasped for air but could not find it.

For the first time ever, his life had been in danger and no one had been there to save him. He had saved himself.

But no one had saved that boy in the forest, and Radu cried for him, wishing that someone had.

Radu threw down his maps, rubbing his face wearily. "We could burn down the trees."

"Which trees?" Lazar leaned back, stretching his long legs and smiling with lazy amusement. He spent more time in Radu's tent than his own as the siege dragged interminably and the lines between ranks broke down. Five months they had been here. Five months.

"All of them. All the trees from here to Italy. All the trees everywhere. Any tree that could hide Skanderberg and his damnable men along any route our supply trains travel."

"Did you hear? The Venetians have announced they will no longer sell us supplies."

Radu sighed, the thick pole in the middle of his tent supporting his weight as he leaned against it. "Well, that solves the problem of how to guard the wagons, at the very least. If we have no supplies, Skanderberg's men cannot attack and steal them."

"Winter is nearly here. We will freeze before we starve, if that is any comfort."

Radu stood. "You are late to visit the women of the camp." Lazar spent much of his free time with the prostitutes that accompanied the soldiers. At first Radu had pretended not to notice, but now, as with everything else, he no longer cared.

"I like to make them miss me sometimes, too. I am generous with my love. I have enough for *everyone*." He climbed onto Radu's cot, lying back with a look that pretended at innocence. He was getting bolder, deliberately teasing when they were alone, and Radu did not know how to handle it. He cared about Lazar, valued his friendship and counsel, but . . .

He was in no mood to try to answer the question. Rather than facing Lazar, he walked out into the night. Smoke hung heavy on the air. Radu breathed it in, made it a part of himself. He was certain the smoke had lodged permanently in his nose, and he would never be able to smell anything else.

The careful rows they had laid out five months ago had decayed into a rambling warren of tents, muddy quagmires, and trash heaps. Radu avoided the worst parts, skirting campfires where men gathered, eyes permanently narrowed and fists clenched.

Kumal's tent grew from the midst of the camp like a diseased mushroom. Radu ducked inside, nodding at the grim-faced servants. The air was too close, a subtle, sour odor of sickness inescapable. He could, it turned out, smell something other than smoke.

He made his way quietly to Kumal's cot, then sat on the rug next to it. Kumal's face was sunken, his eyelids pulled so thin over his eyes that Radu could see each delicate vein beneath the skin. Too many in the camp were sick, with disease running rampant after so long in such close quarters. At least Kumal had the dignity of dying in privacy.

Kumal raised a hot, dry hand, and Radu took it in his own.

"How are you today, my friend?"

Kumal's lips cracked as he parted them in a smile. "I am well," he rasped.

Radu answered the smile as well as he could manage. "Do you need anything? Water?"

Kumal shook his head. "I need a promise."

Radu clucked his tongue. "I am sorry, the supply wagon carrying promises was waylaid by Skanderberg last week. We are entirely out of them."

Kumal's chest rattled with a laugh. "I am serious. I need a promise from you."

"Anything."

"Take care of Nazira."

Radu blinked and looked up at the draping cloth of the tent ceiling, now stained black with smoke, soiled and ruined like everything else here. "She will be very upset with you when we return and she finds out you were trying to get rid of her."

Kumal's grip tightened with more strength than Radu thought he had left.

"I promise," Radu said. "I will take care of her."

Kumal sighed in relief, his body deflating under the blanket until it looked as though a grown man could not possibly be beneath it. Radu stayed with him for another hour, but they did not speak again.

When Radu left, he wandered. Lost in thought, he drew closer and closer to the edge of camp. He stood outside the last straggling tents, staring toward the dark line of the wall. That damnable wall.

Three times they had directly assaulted it, only to be repulsed.

They had never managed to find the water source for the city.

They had even tried to bribe the city leaders again, to no avail.

There was a loud rumbling sound, and the ground beneath his feet shuddered. A plume of dust rose against the sky, blotting out the stars. Men shouted, but there was none of the typical clash of metal and scream of horses that signaled a surprise attack from a raiding force. This was something new, something bad.

Radu ran forward, drawing his sword. He stumbled in the dark, raising an arm to his mouth to avoid inhaling the dirt that drifted in the air like the grave coming to collect them all.

On his left, another man joined him. "No, no, no!" the man screamed.

Radu tripped and fell hard to the cold ground, nearly impaling himself on his sword. Because he knew that voice. And he knew the hand that reached out to pull him up.

"Come on, we have to help! The tunnels collapsed!"

In the dark, Mehmed did not know him. But Radu would

know him anywhere. He took the hand, held it as though it were his anchor to this world. And then it was gone and Mehmed disappeared into the night ahead of him.

Radu hesitated. If he went back to camp now, Mehmed would never know. They would not speak. Radu could slip back into the blood-tinged monotony of his days. But that was a lie. Because even when Mehmed was not in his life, he was the missing sun at the center of everything. Radu still revolved around Mehmed, even when he was gone.

Radu ran forward, catching up to Mehmed, who had stopped on the edge of a sunken line in the ground. It led from where they stood to within a few arm spans of the wall.

Mehmed dropped to his knees, hanging his head in despair. A couple of men moved up and down the line, calling frantically, but it was obvious that anyone who had been inside the tunnel would not be coming out.

Radu knelt beside Mehmed, putting a hand on his shoulder. Mehmed looked up in surprise, but whatever he was about to say died on his lips as he squinted at Radu. Without a word, he threw himself forward. He wrapped his arms around Radu's torso and buried his face in his shoulder. The earth shifted again beneath Radu, or inside Radu, the rumbling and collapsing groan of all his promises to himself falling away.

Mehmed.

His Mehmed.

He put a hand to the back of Mehmed's neck, holding him.

"I failed," Mehmed said. "They are all dead, and I failed."

Radu shook his head, cheek brushing the top of Mehmed's head. "We have all failed. This is not your fault."

"This was my plan, though. My idea to save the siege."

"No one can save it. Do not hold yourself responsible for your father's folly. Learn from it."

Mehmed nodded into his shoulder, then pulled back. He grasped Radu's shoulders too tightly, as though he was afraid Radu might drift away. How could he? Mehmed was his sun. He would always return.

"How are you here?"

"I came with your father. I have been here the whole time."

Shock and hurt played across Mehmed's face. He did not look well, drawn and pale even in the darkness. Either he had been sick, or he was getting sick. Radu wanted to run his fingers down Mehmed's cheeks, to touch him, to fix him.

"Why have you not found me before?" Mehmed asked.

"I . . ." *Because I am in love with you. Because I cannot be around you for fear you will finally see what is written across my heart. Because the pain of you is one I cannot bear.* "I could not, not without betraying my true purposes to your father's inner circle. They must think I am indifferent to you."

"I do not understand."

"I am spying for you, Mehmed. Learning how everything in the city works, tracing the lines of bribes, corruption, conspiracy. So that when you take the throne again, I can give you what you did not have before. Allies. Information. Plans."

Mehmed dropped his hands. "This is why you left?"

Radu nodded, shivering against the bitter cold left in the absence of Mehmed's touch.

"You left to help me. Not because you hate me."

Radu's voice trembled with how much he wanted Mehmed to hear, to understand, in the next sentence: "I could never hate you."

Mehmed drew him close, pressing their foreheads together. Mehmed's was feverishly hot. "You broke my heart for missing you, Radu."

Eyes closed, Radu drew a shaking breath. "Mine, too."

"You are my best, my truest friend. Will you return with me? Come home!"

Radu nearly said yes—could not have said no—when Mehmed continued: "Lada needs you, too."

Radu dropped his head, pressing it harder against Mehmed's, then straightened, pulling away. "How is my sister?"

"She breathes fire and pisses vinegar."

"So, the same."

Mehmed laughed darkly. "The same. I fear she will never forgive me for leaving her behind, but this is no place for a woman."

"Lada is no woman."

"Be that as it may, I could not bring her into so much danger. But you! I could have had you by my side this whole time."

Radu sat back onto his heels, putting more distance between them. He did not know whether to rejoice that Mehmed would have brought him over Lada, or to despair that Lada was too precious to risk, while Radu would have been welcomed. Everything that Radu had been through, all the things he had done while here. He could never go back to what he was before. He had lost too much. But Mehmed could not see that.

"I have to stay with your father." Radu stood, his knees nearly betraying him by sending him back down to the ground, to Mehmed. He locked them in place, standing as tall and straight as the impregnable city behind them. "Otherwise . . ." Otherwise he would be unable to repair the vicious rubble this night had made of the walls around his heart. "Otherwise all my work will be for naught, and I intend to be the more useful Dragwlya for you." He forced a smile and a light tone. "Lada is already two assassination attempts ahead of me. I have some catching up to do."

Mehmed stood. "You say you have to do these things. But what do you *want* to do?"

Radu stretched his fingers, reaching toward Mehmed, touching just the hem of his tunic. Behind Mehmed, he saw a group of Janissaries running toward them.

Radu smiled his best, most innocent smile. The smile without guile, the smile that said, *Tell me your secrets, no harm will come,* the smile that said, *There is nothing more to me than what you see, trust me, trust me.* "What I want does not matter. What matters is preparing the way for you to be the sultan we both know you can be. You will be the hand of God on Earth, and I will do whatever I can to see that come to pass."

———

Radu walked back to camp alone, wondering if maybe he did understand Skanderberg, after all. Because there was nothing he would not sacrifice for Mehmed.

Including himself.

Lazar stood, alarmed, when Radu entered the tent. Radu had not expected to see him again tonight.

"What happened? You look as though you have seen the devil."

Radu shook his head as he sat, wishing Lazar were not here so he could think about Mehmed and indulge this exquisite pain in private. "Not the devil. Mehmed."

Lazar smiled bitterly. "I see little difference. How was he?"

"He looked ill. The siege has not been kind to him."

"As it should be."

When Radu curled up and turned away, Lazar put a hand gently on his shoulder. It did not burn as Mehmed's did, did not sear where it touched. "You still feel the same for him?"

"I always will."

"And your sister?"

Radu flinched, remembering Mehmed's careful protection of Lada. And regretting having confessed to Lazar that Mehmed and Lada had something between them that he craved. "Please, Lazar, stop speaking."

Lazar's hand moved, and Radu heard him rummaging through items in Radu's chest nearest his small writing desk. "I am writing up the reports for you. It will be a while. Do you mind?"

Radu grunted and waved. He wanted to be alone, but he did not want to have to write the reports himself. Lazar often did it for him, collecting the information. All he needed was Radu's signature. After several minutes, Lazar knelt in front

KIERSTEN WHITE

of Radu, holding a sheaf of papers so that only the bottom, where Radu needed to sign, showed.

Radu signed them all without hesitation. And then, finally, Lazar left. Radu buried his face in his blanket, heart beating to the sorrow and joy of Mehmed, Mehmed, Mehmed.

41

"W HAT I WOULD NOT give for a roving band of Huns right now." Nicolae sighed, lying flat on his back in the middle of the training ring. The dirt beneath him was packed hard by decades of feet. The low wooden walls of the ring were lined with pegs that held the equipment of the men who practiced there.

Like all days the last six months, the pegs were empty.

Tohin had left shortly after they destroyed the canyon. She had other outposts to visit, other soldiers to teach. Lada missed her. And she especially missed creating explosions. They could not even keep training with gunpowder, because there simply was not enough of it.

There was so little to do. Today, Petru and Matei were on patrol with Stefan. Lada did not know where her other troops were and found it nearly impossible to care. They were relegated to minor local duties to compensate for the lack of spahis and vali governors. Last week, they had investigated the theft of several pigs from a local farm. The thief, caught in the act, was a hole in the fence and a patch of truffles in the forest.

Even her hatred of Mehmed for leaving her had lost its spark, its flame dampened by the fear introduced with Tohin's news of the siege. Increasingly she found herself thinking of him with regret. Fondness, even. Imagining what she would do if he were here. And then she stabbed those thoughts with her sharpest dagger, cut them right out of her mind. He could do without her, she could do as well without him. He would be fine. Without her.

She stood over Nicolae, looking down at him.

"Do you want to kiss me?" she asked.

Nicolae made a strange choking noise. "What?"

"Do you want to kiss me?" She did not feel things when she looked at Nicolae, but then, she had not felt so much for Mehmed before they kissed. Maybe the secret to successfully bleeding him from her veins was replacing him. She generally found Nicolae more than tolerable, and he was good at taking orders.

"Please take this in the kindest way possible," he said, standing and walking backward to put more space between them, eyeing the knife she was toying with. "But I would sooner try to romance my horse. And I suspect my horse would enjoy it more than you."

Lada lifted her nose in the air. "Your horse deserves better."

"We can both agree on that." Now relatively certain he was not about to be stabbed, Nicolae sat on the wall next to her. The fact that she was not upset over his rejection indicated that kissing him would have done nothing to alleviate her problems.

"I think of you like a sister," he said. "Like a brilliant, violent, occasionally terrifying sister that I would follow to the ends of the earth, in part because I respected her so much and in part because I feared what she would do to me if I refused."

She nodded. "I *would* do awful things."

Nicolae laughed. "The most awful."

"And then I would steal your horse lover, to spite you."

"Your cruelty knows no bounds."

Lada stood, stretching, wishing she had somewhere to go. She could no longer retreat to the forest like she used to. A phantom voice followed her there now, whispering *whore* in her ear, the smell of dirt conjuring memories she preferred to leave buried.

"I am going to patrol the grounds," she said.

Nicolae nodded, then his jovial face turned serious. "I mean it, you know. I will follow you to the ends of the earth."

An unusual warmth spread through her chest. She looked away, trying to twist the smile off her lips. "Of course you will."

She made her way to the massive front gate of the fortress, feeling more buoyant than she had in weeks. Whatever else happened, she had her men. She had her command. And that was something, at least.

A messenger, wearing the dust of leagues on his cloak, rode a weary horse up to the gate. He pulled a bag off his shoulder and held it out. "Letters from Albania."

"I will take them." Lada grabbed the bag and called a servant. They sorted through the letters. Most were for servants who had family attending the soldiers, a few for her men from friends in the siege. It had been over a month since they had had any news, and it was all she could do not to open those letters.

Then she came to a letter addressed to her. Her heart twisted, squeezing up too high and making it difficult to breathe. Had Mehmed finally written her?

Leaving the servant without a word, she retreated to her room in the barracks. She set the letter on her desk, pacing around it, eyeing it with suspicion as though it might disappear. What would it say? What did she *want* it to say? After all this time, what could he say to make her forgive him?

Nothing. He could say nothing.

She broke the seal, ripping the edge of the paper with her force, and opened it, scanning the contents quickly. It was not from Mehmed.

The hand was unfamiliar, but the signature at the bottom was undeniably Radu's.

She sat heavily, shock making it difficult to focus on the words. Radu was at the siege? How? Why? Was he with Mehmed?

A strange sensation seeped through her, a writhing jealousy that Radu was there, where she had been forbidden, with *Mehmed*. Mehmed must have taken him, must have rescued him from Edirne. Gritting her teeth, Lada started at the beginning. The letter was brief, only a few lines long. He greeted her without preamble or explanation, stating merely that the siege was a disaster and would soon end. Then . . .

Lada stopped, dropping the letter to the floor. Then she picked it up, reading each word with care as though she could change what it said.

" 'Sickness is rampant. This is a secret to remain between us, but Mehmed has fallen ill. I do not expect him to recover or survive the journey back. When he dies you will be at the mercy of Murad, who still wishes you dead. Without Mehmed's protection I fear for you. Whatever else has transpired between us, I could not live with myself without warning you. Gather what you can and flee while no one is there to take note.' "

When he dies.

Not if.

When.

Lada looked at the date on the letter—it had been written more than a month before. Which meant that Mehmed might already be dead, might have been dead all this time. All the poison she had nurtured, the bitterness, the anger. Her last words to him. Her thought that if he did not come back he would have deserved to never know how she felt about him. She doubled over, holding her midsection, a wail threatening to tear free from her throat.

She had sent Mehmed to his death with nothing but cruelty, and, worse, it was a death that even she could not have prevented. She could not fight the plague with a sword, could not stop the assassin illness with a dagger, no matter how clever and sharp.

She dropped to her cot and curled into a ball, incapable of imagining a world without Mehmed in it. Radu was right—there would be no place for her in that world. And Radu was not threatened as she was, because he had found his own role to play.

Radu had earned his place. Everything she had now—her

home, her men, her very life—was because Mehmed cared for her. All her threads led back to him, and with his death each one would snap.

Rolling off her cot, she picked up the letter and read it again and again, willing it to change. Then she slammed it onto the desk with a scream, burying her dagger in it so deeply that the handle stuck straight up from the wood.

———

A week later, Lada was nearly ready to leave. She would steal a horse. As a Janissary, she had no horse of her own, but there were a few left in the fortress stables. All she needed was two more days. If only she had accepted or demanded extravagant gifts of Mehmed. She had almost nothing other than her payments as a Janissary. She had visited the bursar to draw her salary early, but the aggravating old fool would not budge the schedule. Stealing more than was strictly necessary would draw attention, so she was forced to wait.

It was agony.

All her men picked up on the change in her demeanor, but none could account for it. Nicolae in particular seemed nervous, and Lada feared he had received word of Mehmed's demise in his own letter, or that he suspected she would flee.

While she glared at the sun, willing it to set faster so she could escape, Nicolae put a tentative hand on her shoulder. The other Janissaries had left for a meal. She had not noticed him staying. "We can talk," he said, voice strained. "About what is bothering you."

She turned to him, eyes narrowed in suspicion. "Why would you think something is bothering me?"

"This last week, you have been . . ."

"What?" What had he noticed? Had he told the other men? She did not know whom she could trust, and the fewer people who knew of her plans, the better.

He shrugged. "You nearly broke Petru's arm sparring. And then you missed yesterday's training entirely. You either fail to respond to what we say, or you snap so sharply it wounds. I am sorry. I thought— I did not realize you were serious." He shifted on his feet, tugging at his collar. "If you want, I mean, if it is important to you, I— We could try kissing."

Lada stared at him in disbelief. Then, the strain of the last week being too much, she threw her head back and laughed. It bubbled out of her like a mountain stream from dry rock, cascading from her lips in a cold, unstoppable rush. She laughed so hard she fell to the ground, clutching her stomach, which soon began to ache.

Nicolae nudged her with his foot, scowling. "This is the most offensive rejection to an offer of romance I have ever received. And that is saying something, as I have had *many* rejections."

"You idiot," she gasped. "You tremendous, arrogant ass. You thought I would be so distraught over *you?*"

He sat beside her. "Yes, right. While I still have some dignity, can you tell me what is really wrong?"

She sighed, wiping beneath her eyes where tears had leaked from them, and sat up so their shoulders were touching. She knew Nicolae. She could trust him. "I am leaving." With a grimace, she added, "Running away."

"Why?"

"Radu wrote from the siege. Mehmed is—was—sick."

She swallowed the pain that built like a cancer in her throat, but it would not move. The letter, folded and tucked into her chemise, sat right beneath the pouch around her neck and poked into the skin above her heart. "Dying. Or already dead. He is the only reason I have any freedom or power. If he is gone, I will lose this." She gestured at the practice ring, toward the small building she had been allowed to claim as private barracks. "Murad loves Radu but still wants me dead, and no one will stop him. No one will care. So I am leaving."

"God's wounds, it is about time."

Lada turned to him, surprised. "What do you mean?"

"I only marvel that it took you this long to decide to run away! I always wondered what was keeping you when clearly you had the intelligence and ability to escape years ago."

"I—I could not have. If I could have, I would have!"

Nicolae lifted his eyebrows, scar wrinkling across his forehead. "You have had access to money and horses. You can hunt, you can track, you can fight. With a little planning, you could have been across the border and on your way home at any time."

Lada leaned back against the wall, mind churning. He was right. There was nothing that made now different from any time in the last two or three years. Except . . .

Mehmed.

She had stayed because he gave her a reason to.

"I have no home to return to," she said, avoiding Nicolae's gaze lest she see the truth reflected back at her. "Our father betrayed and abandoned Radu and me, twice. Once when he left us here, and once when he signed our death warrants by breaking his treaty. He was—" She closed her eyes, sick with remembering how she had looked up to him, how she had craved his approval. "He was never a great man, and now I know that. If I return to him, he will find some other way to barter me for scraps of power to be squandered." It was true. If she went home to Wallachia, she would be married off before she could show her father she had grown into so much more than he could have dreamed.

"Then we go somewhere else."

Lada opened her eyes, looked at Nicolae. "We?"

"This place was no fun before you got here, and it will be even less so in your absence. I told you I meant it—I will go with you to the ends of the earth. Though I would prefer the ends to be closer rather than farther, as riding makes me quite sore in a very treasured spot."

"I cannot ask you to come."

"You cannot ask me to stay."

"You have a position here. Money. Value."

"I am a salaried slave. We both know it."

Lada nodded, relief warming her like a hearth in wintertime. It would be good to have Nicolae with her.

"You should ask the other men," Nicolae said.

She shook her head. "The more we take, the greater the odds of discovery. I will not risk their lives. And I doubt they will come."

"I think you would be surprised. You chose well."

"I will consider it. We have two days. Prepare what you need to."

He stood, offering a hand to help her up, then kept his

hand clasped tightly with hers. "To the ends of the earth," he said.

"To the ends of the earth." With a tight smile, she turned to leave.

"And, Lada? I am sorry about Mehmed. I know what he was to you."

She missed a step, nearly stumbling. "That is strange," she said, eyes burning. "Because I do not think I know." All she had was how she felt, and that was such a mixture of anger, bitterness, jealousy, desire, and affection that she knew she would never untangle it to see what was at the center.

She went to her old room in the fortress to see if there was anything worth taking. It was as she had left it, untouched, a layer of dust over everything. Empty. An empty past, an empty future, and no one left to care about her in either.

"The devil take you, Mehmed!" she screamed, filled with sorrow poisoned by rage. This was his fault. She had stayed for him, had let him lull her into feeling like she had security, safety, a future. But, as always, she was at the mercy of the men in her life. And, just like her father, Mehmed had abandoned her.

"And where is the devil to take me?"

Lada whirled around, heart racing. Mehmed leaned in the doorway, mirth twisting the new form the siege had carved his weary face into. He looked haggard, his cheeks stubbled, dark circles beneath his eyes showing weeks of poor sleep. He crossed the room to her, arms open.

"You died!" She pushed him away, staring at his face. He was changed, but it was him. Alive. Healthy.

"Did I? That is disappointing. I was very much looking forward to being alive for our reunion. Though I feared *you* would kill me."

She pulled him close, letting him hold her, shaking in disbelief over her miracle. "I had a letter. It said . . . I thought you were dead." She dug the letter free and held it out. Frowning, Mehmed took it. The line between his brows deepened.

She loved that line. She had thought it lost forever. Relief and joy warred with anger. Because when he was gone, she had been left with nothing. She could no longer pretend that she had a life of her own here. But now he was back. And it left her . . . confused.

"This is not Radu's writing, but the signature is his. Whoever wrote this, it was not him. Someone wanted you to leave." Mehmed frowned at the letter as though it would reveal its secrets. "Who would wish this?"

For a few dark moments—the darkest of her life, even worse than thinking Mehmed dead—Lada wondered if Radu had been behind it, after all. She had what he wanted. It would have been a perfect way to get rid of her without killing her.

But no. She could not think that of him. Whatever else was between them, Radu would not harm her this deeply. Because she would never do it to him, and Radu was not capable of being crueler than she was.

Mehmed continued. "It would have to be someone in his inner circle. Someone with access to his signature." He looked up at her expectantly.

"You would know better than I." Her tongue was dipped in the venom left from months of waiting and a week of grief.

"I have been here, right where you left me. While Radu was at your side."

Mehmed shook his head. "He is with my father. I saw him but once. He commands a small group directly under the sultan."

"Then it could be anyone. I am no favorite of your father's, or of Halil Pasha's, or any number of men. My absence would not be mourned."

"I would mourn it. Every moment of every day."

"Did you?"

Mehmed's eyes were heavy with longing. "I did."

She turned away. "I was going to leave."

He pulled her close, burying his face in her hair. "I forbid it."

"You can forbid me nothing." But it sounded hollow and forced when she said it. She had spent the last week knowing exactly her value without him. It was a stolen horse, a single loyal friend, and a bleak and difficult future.

He moved from her hair to her ear, trailing his lips along it. Her body responded despite her resolve to be angry, to punish him.

He still wanted her. And she knew now what a fleeting and precious thing it was for a woman to be wanted in any way that made her important. She had been ready to run when she had lost this, but now . . .

She would never admit it to Nicolae, could barely admit it to herself, but she would stay for Mehmed. She would stay for the way she felt when his mouth or eyes were on her. And she would stay for the power it gave her.

His lips found hers, and she kissed him back with a determined ferocity. She touched him everywhere, his face, his hair, his shoulders, his hands, because he was here, and he was alive, and it was the first time that a man she loved had come back for her. She did not have to lose the life she had built here, the threads of safety and power she had. She had not lost him.

"Say you are mine." He trailed his lips down her neck. She arched into him, digging her fingers into his back.

"I am yours," she whispered. The words cut like knives, barely out of her mouth before he stole them, sealing them with his own lips.

42

THE CARAVAN TRAVELED SLOWER than the rest of the army, left behind to follow the trail of a hundred thousand failures beaten into the dirt ahead of them.

Radu was in no hurry to catch up.

He had received begrudging permission from Murad to attend to Kumal's contingent as they tried to keep him alive long enough to get home. Though Radu knew it would accomplish nothing toward his larger goals of aiding Mehmed's ascension, he could not simply leave Kumal behind. Not like this. Kumal had begun to improve, but he was still fragile enough that Radu feared he would not survive the journey.

Kumal had helped Radu understand his own soul, and he would not throw Kumal's away without care.

He pulled his horse to a halt, raising a fist for the men behind him to stop. He led his Janissaries, down four poor souls, and Kumal's spahis. He did not know how many Kumal's men had lost, but dreaded the unacceptable loss they faced should they be delayed.

Up ahead, a group of men roughly equal in size to their own sat on horses, blocking the road. Hand on the pommel of his sword, Radu rode forward. Lazar moved to follow him, but he shook his head. A man broke off from the other group and rode to meet Radu. From a distance, Radu thought him very young; then he got closer and Radu realized his face was simply clean-shaven. Deep lines around the eyes betrayed his age, and Radu wondered who he was and why he would go against custom by not growing a mustache or a beard, depending on what he was entitled to.

The man smiled bleakly, raising a hand in greeting. Though he was dressed in clothes more closely matched to this region, he spoke perfect Turkish. "Hello, sultan's dog. Have you lost your master?"

Radu narrowed his eyes. There was something familiar in the man's face. And then he realized—he had seen this man's portrait, altered now by the brushstrokes of age.

Skanderberg.

Radu looked over his shoulder. The wagon that carried Kumal sat like a fat beetle, unwieldy and vulnerable. Though their forces were evenly matched, Radu had seen too many caravans attacked to doubt for a second that the advantage was always with the attacker. He had something to protect—they had nothing to lose.

With a heavy sigh, he turned back to Skanderberg. "My friend is ill."

Skanderberg looked into the distance, eyes soft and out of focus. "My whole country is ill." His gaze fixed itself on Radu, taking in his clothes, his cap, his horse. "What is your name?"

"Radu."

"Simply Radu? No family?"

Radu smiled darkly. "My father sold me as collateral against the throne of Wallachia. You will understand why I do not claim him."

Skanderberg nodded. "I do. We must claim ourselves, sometimes. You should pick a new name." Skanderberg's name was a perversion of the name he had been given by the Ottomans—Iskander—and the *bey* title he had been given and then defied.

Skanderberg's mouth twisted playfully. "Perhaps Radu the Handsome."

"I was considering Radu the Overwhelmingly Weary."

"Hmm. Yes." Skanderberg rubbed his cheeks, examining the men behind Radu. "Who are you escorting?"

"His name is Kumal. He is vali of a provincial area half a day's travel from Edirne. He owns very little, is no particular favorite of the sultan's, and has no living relatives other than a younger sister who has nothing if he dies. And he will probably be dead before a ransom can be demanded."

Skanderberg laughed. "I see. So why are you risking your life escorting a corpse of no value?"

"He showed me kindness when there was no advantage to him for doing so."

With a grunt, Skanderberg pulled a beaten metal flask from his saddlebag, took a drink, and then wiped his mouth. There was no tension in his body, no sense of imminent attack. Looking at Skanderberg's men, Radu saw that their shoulders were turned inward, away from the potential fight.

They looked, instead, over the ravaged and burned countryside. Radu wondered if they were the ones who had set the fires.

"You do not seem to be taking much joy in your victory," Radu said.

"Ah, yes, my victory." Skanderberg bared his teeth, holding his arms wide. "I remain lord of a broken and burned land, my coffers empty, my people sick, my fields destroyed. And yet my pride remains intact! My damnable pride and my people's freedom will not fill their bellies this long coming winter. Some victories are merely defeat wearing the wrong clothing." He spat on the ground. "How many men would you estimate we will lose if my pride demands one last gesture of defiance against our sultan?"

"I will certainly lose the wagon. Even if you do not take Kumal, delay and hardship will mean his death. My men are tired but angry at their humiliation. Yours are bitter at the forces that cost them so much. I suspect you will ride away, as you always manage to, but with nothing gained other than Janissary blood mingling with your own men's to water your dead fields. I do not think I will survive, which will be disappointing."

Skanderberg nodded thoughtfully. "He is a kind man, you say?"

"The kindest I have ever known."

"Well then. We are late for our afternoon meal. Give Murad my regards, Radu the Handsome."

Radu tried his best to keep the relief flooding through his body from showing on his face. He merely inclined his head in respect, then urged his horse forward as Skanderberg moved to the side, signaling his men to do the same.

For the next mile, Radu tensed, waiting for an arrow to find the center of his back, but none came. He said a silent prayer of gratitude for the kindness of Kumal, which had once again saved his life.

Murad had not ceased drinking. Everyone was so constantly consumed by avoiding remarking on it that they may as well have spoken of nothing else.

Radu walked through the streets of Edirne late one night. The winter chill had settled deep into the stones of the city, radiating outward and stealing the warmth from his bones. People imitated the buildings, huddling into themselves, peering out through shuttered eyelids, suspicious and bitter with cold.

He stopped in at every gathering place he could—the mosques, the inns, the markets. Everywhere the tone was the same. The Janissary barracks, normally boisterous at mealtime, were as silent as the frost-covered trees. Radu slipped in wearing a Janissary cap and sat at the end of a table, head bent over his food.

"... gets to keep his land and income? After all the ways the spahis failed during the siege? And our pay remains the same. He should have his wages garnished to give us a portion of what ..."

"... ill, my girl says he will not last much longer. Where are we then? If we could not take Skanderberg's city, imagine what a siege on Constantinople would do to our ranks. I will walk away before I will serve under the little zealot. . . ."

He was learning nothing new. With a sigh, Radu pushed away his food and walked back into the night, staring up at the sky. Low-hanging clouds pressed down on Edirne, looming and cutting the city off from the stars. Perhaps it was just as well. Radu did not think any portents found in the stars tonight could be good ones.

When he arrived at the palace, the air tasted as sour and close as a tomb. He stepped lightly as he stole past doors where his presence would be desired, and found his goal: his own room.

His boots fell heavily to the floor in front of the hearth. The fire was low, but strong enough to warm the room.

He was so tired.

Murad requested his presence at all hours of the day and night, oftentimes demanding they stay awake until dawn. Radu had performed his poem so many times he often awoke, head aching and mouth dry, reciting it in his sleep as he had once joked he could do.

If there was any mercy in the world, tonight Murad would forget him.

A stack of letters had been left on his bedside table. He sifted through them, discarding the invitations from various acquaintances that were still pretending his return was a cause for celebration. After Kruje, he no longer had the spark for pretending to enjoy himself at gatherings. He had seen men die.

He had killed men.

And now he was right back where he had started, no closer to helping Mehmed. And Mehmed was as far away as he had ever been.

Radu paused on a letter in a shaky script, then tore it open.

It was from Kumal. Radu sat back, grinning with relief. Kumal was on the mend, slowly recovering his strength. But a sentence at the bottom of the letter left Radu both shocked and dismayed.

I expect that, by spring, I will be well enough to attend your wedding to Nazira, a joyous event we bask in the warmth of anticipating. Until then, my dear brother, take care of yourself.

Radu laughed in disbelief. Apparently Kumal did not view his survival as voiding a contract made on his deathbed. He would have to wait to tell Kumal it was impossible. He did not want any disappointment interrupting his friend's convalescence.

Radu had no idea if he was even allowed to marry. Janissaries were not, but he was not strictly a Janissary, despite his command. He supposed it came down to the whim of the sultan. Nazira held no political value, with Kumal's position dependent on the favor of the capital and no significant money to their family. He knew she could marry higher than him, though, a pashazada or another vali. Why would Kumal want such a thing for her?

A pang of bittersweet understanding rippled through him. Kumal wanted the best for his sister, which meant he wanted for her what he thought would make her happiest. All her kind attentions, her blushing smiles, her joyful radiance when he had visited—Radu was not Kumal's choice. He was Nazira's.

But how could he give Nazira his heart when it was so twisted and tangled up in Mehmed's? Hers glowed pure and open. He would have to persuade Kumal that Nazira deserved more than he could give her.

A light knock on the door startled him. A servant boy, wide-eyed and wary-looking, bowed. "The sultan requests your presence."

Radu sighed. "Of course he does." He gave the servant a beleaguered smile, and the boy's face lit up with the shared understanding between them. "Do you get any sleep these days?"

The boy shook his head. "None of us do. He wants every candle burning, constant singing, food and wine at all hours." He darted a look over his shoulder, torn between excitement over the deviousness of speaking of the sultan in this tone and fear of being caught at it.

Radu smiled to show the boy he was not worried. "I think he fears the dark. Who attends him when I am not there to keep him company?"

The boy made a face. "Halil Pasha, often. He hit me last week for spilling a drop of soup on his shoe."

"Oh, I hate him. He is a terrible man." Radu pulled out a coin from a purse beside his bed and handed it to the boy. "What is your name?"

The boy bowed, voice squeaking. "Amal."

"Amal, I am sorry you must work so hard for so little. Whenever Halil Pasha is here, find me and I will give you an extra coin to make up for the pain of enduring his presence."

Radu feared Amal's big head would fall right off his thin neck, he bobbed it so eagerly.

If Halil Pasha was perched like a carrion crow, waiting to seize on the moment of Murad's impending death, Radu needed to beat him to it.

43

LADA LAY SPRAWLED ACROSS Mehmed's bed, her head hanging over the side. "No, no, no." She pushed his hand away from where it pointed at a map of Constantinople and the surrounding areas. "Your father could see only the wall, and that is where he failed."

"But if we cannot take the wall, we cannot take the city!"

"Ignore the wall. The wall is your last step. If you want the city, what do you need first?"

Mehmed scowled at the map, fingers unconsciously tracing the wall surrounding the city. But then his gaze shifted, his expression turning thoughtful. He moved his finger from the outline of the wall to the Bosporus Strait. It was the point through which all ships carrying supplies, soldiers, and aid from Europe had to pass. "We need to cut the throat," he said. He threw himself off the bed, grabbing an inkwell and pen. On one side of the narrow stretch was a tower built by his great-grandfather Beyazid, the last point of Ottoman holdings before Byzantium land. He drew a matching tower on the other side, the side that was Byzantium territory. And then he slashed his pen across the water between them.

Lada clapped her hands together, the sharp crack echoing through the room. "Deny them aid. Meet them on the sea and the land. Make them fight you on all fronts—stretch them as thin as they go—and somewhere they will snap. Knock on every door; you need only one of them to open."

Mehmed's smile dropped away, his hands hovering reverently above the map. He touched Lada that way, sometimes, and it stirred a strange jealousy in her breast to see him look at a city with the same worshipful hunger.

"If I fail," he said, "it will be the end of me."

Lada laughed. "Then do not try, little sheep. Tend to your flock. Patrol your borders. No one ever said you had to take Constantinople. It is only a dream."

Mehmed's eyes burned when he looked up at her. "It is not simply my dream."

She rolled her eyes. "Yes, I know all about your precious prophet's dream."

"That is not what I am speaking of. My whole *country* was founded on a dream. Less than two hundred years ago we were nothing but a tribe, running from the Mongols, with no home of our own. But our leader—my ancestor—Osman Gazi dreamed we could be more. He saw a moon rise from the breast of a great sheikh and descend into his own. From his navel grew a tree, and its branches spread to cover the world. He knew then that his posterity, his wandering, homeless people, would rule the world. Is how far we have come not a testament to the truth of his vision? I have inherited that,

Lada. It is a calling and a dream I cannot deny. The tree is mine to spread, and I *must*."

Lada wanted to mock him, wanted to argue, but her soul would not allow it. She understood that idea of something bigger than you, all encompassing, impossible to ever truly leave behind. She knew Mehmed would never be whole without the city that demanded his conquest, just as she knew she would never be whole without her country.

Mehmed leaned closer to her. "I can do this. *We* can do this. Together."

"We cannot always have what we want, no matter how much we want it," she whispered.

Misreading her mood, Mehmed leaped onto the bed, nuzzling his face against her breasts and trying to sneak his hand lower along her stomach. As always, she caught his fingers, twisting them until he cried out in pain and gave up his attempt.

"You are cruel," he said, lifting her hair to his nose and hiding his face in it.

"Do you really want to discuss this now?" They had found a sort of peace, come to a truce on the matter of his harem: Lada pretended it did not exist, and Mehmed never acknowledged it. But she still refused to give him all he wanted. Holding her maidenhood to herself was the only way she knew to protect herself, to keep her heart from becoming fully his.

And she was afraid, too, that if she ever allowed him in, he would cease seeing her as Lada and dismiss her the same way he did the mother of his son. She was even more afraid of having a child, of being broken from the inside. She wanted nothing to change. She wanted to live in these sharp winter days, curled together against the evening chill, the two of them forming their own secret society. But she could not deny that every passing day made it more difficult to want him to stop.

She left the warm cocoon of his bed, seized with a sudden panic that if she did not break free right then, she would emerge different, unrecognizable to herself.

"Where are you going?" Mehmed reached out to grab her, but she twisted free of his hands.

"Training."

"You have the most deadly force in the entire Janissary ranks. What more can you possibly need to do today?"

She did not answer, but instead rushed out of his room and ran to the barracks. There, Nicolae was crouched on the floor, throwing dice with Petru, whose face indicated he was not doing well. "Ah," Nicolae said, looking up. "She graces us with her presence! To what do we owe the honor?"

"Is that how you address your leader?" Her words snapped Petru to attention. He stood, tall and straight, bowing his head.

Nicolae took his time, stretching his long body before finally standing. "I did not realize you were leading anywhere I would need to follow." His tone was light, but his meaning lashed Lada to the core. He had been ready to flee with her. And she had decided to stay without any thought of him. Things had not been the same between them since, but she filled her time with Mehmed and pretended not to care.

"When I have somewhere to go," she said, holding his gaze, her chin tipped up, "you will be the first I want by my side."

He sighed, raising a scarred eyebrow. "I hope so."

"Now, we can—"

Mehmed burst into the room, chest heaving, a terrified young boy following him. "Tell her," he ordered the boy.

The boy, who had a large head and a skinny neck, spoke. "Murad will not survive the week. Halil Pasha means to turn the city against you before you can come claim the throne. Leave now, bring only those you trust absolutely. Enter in secret. He is watching all the gates. I will be waiting for the boy to return with news. My arms are scarred by rosebushes. Yours faithfully, Radu."

Mehmed stared at her. "What does the last part mean?"

"I have been deceived by someone falsely claiming to be Radu in a message before. But no one else would know about that except us. The message is from Radu, without question." Lada paused, an unexpected ache for her brother rising in her belly. "Gather the men. We leave now. Bring extra horses to switch out."

"What about Ilyas?" Mehmed asked.

"Do you trust him?"

"I do."

Lada nodded. "His force is too big. We need to get you into the palace without notice. I will have him follow with his troops two days after us. For now, we ride hard and fast, and with only my men."

"We are playing 'Attack the City' against Edirne?" Petru asked, eyes lighting up.

Lada could not help matching his anticipation with a smile of her own, showcasing each of her tiny, sharp teeth. "Yes. We infiltrate the capital."

"But if we split up," Matei said, crouching near the fire as the rabbits Stefan had caught cooked, "we are more vulnerable. Mehmed is not exactly unknown. We need all the eyes and swords we have."

Petru, Nicolae, Stefan, and Matei, as Lada's first Janissaries, sat in on the council. Her other men were sprawled in the woods nearby, trying to sleep in the early-afternoon light. They had made good time, mainly riding at night, avoiding the towns and cities that dotted the roads.

"We cannot enter the city as Janissaries." Nicolae held his cap out. "We would be stopped, questioned. And no one will fail to notice a troop of Janissaries led by a woman."

Lada growled, kicking at the ground. "Why must I be a woman?"

"Yes, why must you?" Mehmed said, amusement coloring his voice.

"I never think of you that way," Petru said, his sincerity earning a snort of laughter from Mehmed.

"Stefan, give me your breastplate."

Face as impassive as ever, Stefan slowly unbuckled it. Though most of them wore mail for increased ease of movement, Stefan always opted for a full metal breastplate.

Lada took it and fastened it over her chest. It compressed her breasts, but not unbearably so. She took a stick from the edge of the fire, waited for it to cool, then rubbed the charcoal lightly along her upper lip and jaw line. "If we enter under cover of night, I can be a man."

"Still a Janissary, though," Nicolae said.

Amal, tiny and clinging to the edges of their group as always, spoke so softly Lada could barely hear him. "No one looks at servants."

Lada opened her mouth to argue, but she had barely looked at him this whole journey. Even his horse was old and unremarkable. No wonder Radu had chosen him instead of someone stronger or faster. Amal was the least threatening, most invisible messenger possible.

Mehmed frowned. "So I am to enter my city as a servant?"

Nicolae's smile was as easy as ever, but Lada knew him well enough to know there was none of his usual warmth behind it. "What is a sultan but a servant to his people?"

Lada handed the breastplate back to Stefan, then turned to Amal. "How quickly can you steal me the right clothing?"

He smiled shyly, then ran, disappearing through the trees in the direction of the road.

After they had eaten, the men stripped free of their uniforms. They left their Janissary caps in a pile that glowed faintly in the twilight, looking like nothing so much as a tumbled stack of skulls. They had brought various articles of extra clothing, ones that had no indication of their rank. Simple turbans covered their heads; in the dark, they would pass for servants. Provided that no one probed too deeply or touched them, discovering an incongruous layer of armor.

Lada, however, owned no clothes other than her uniform and the ridiculous dress she had used to sneak into the harem so many months ago. She had left the dress in Amasya. It was not a role she cared to play ever again, even in defense of Mehmed.

She was about to give up and make plans to scale the walls when Amal returned, breathless, holding a bundle of dull brown cloth.

"Well done," Lada said, covering her armor with a simple dress and draped sash. She tied up her hair and pulled a scarf low over her forehead.

Nicolae coughed to cover up a laugh. "You may want to shave."

She frowned, then remembered the charcoal she had neglected to clean from her face. "I suppose a bearded woman would draw notice," she said drily, wiping it away.

It was dark by the time everyone was ready to go. They had stopped half a league from the city and would go on foot in groups of three or four, meeting at an inn they all knew. Lada watched as her forces dwindled until she was left with Stefan, Nicolae, and Mehmed. Amal had gone ahead to alert Radu that they were on their way. His code phrase was to remind Radu that only an ass pulls a shield for a sled.

"I feel like a thief," Mehmed said as they crept along the trees parallel to the road, waiting until the last moment to emerge into the open.

"We *are* thieves," Lada answered. She stopped, the walls of the city coming into view. "Now we steal your city."

44

A MAN MELTED FREE FROM the wall behind the inn.
He was tall, with a face so blank and eyes so lifeless they
made Radu shudder.

"Radu," the man said, a statement rather than a question.

Radu nodded. He had left Amal behind to keep the boy
out of any further danger. "I think I am being followed."
Though the path he had taken was wandering and he had
walked with casual, aimless ease, an echo of footsteps—a hint
of a cloak—had shadowed him the whole way.

The man pointed to Radu's own finely woven cloak, worn
with a hood against the evening's chill. Radu unfastened it
and handed it over. After two quick knocks on an unobtrusive
door, the man threw the cloak over his shoulders, adjusting
his posture and gait to match Radu's, and walked to the end
of the alley. The door opened, and Radu ducked inside. Nicolae pulled him into a quick embrace, his smile a bit tighter
than normal but still a relief after the strain of the journey.

"Come, we have a room." He led Radu up an uneven flight

of stairs along the back of the building, the bright sounds of fireplace and food growing and then fading as they passed behind a kitchen. "We have a man in the main hall to watch the entrance."

"You made good time." Radu reached for more to say to block the painful lump growing in his throat, the breathless flutter of his chest, but nothing came to him.

He was about to see Mehmed.

And Lada.

Nicolae opened a door on the second floor to a sitting room filled with men like trees growing too close together. As one, they looked in his direction, hands on weapons. The men relaxed when they saw Nicolae, and the door closed behind them. Radu could not see any of them, not really, not with how hard he was looking for—

Mehmed. Leaning over a roughly made table, a lamp's light catching his face so that even his eyes seemed to glow soft and warm. He pointed at a piece of parchment spread against the table and weighted down with various weapons, long fingers tracing intrigues and plots in the air over the map.

And next to him was Lada, scowling, shortest in the room and still somehow taking up the most space. She wore women's clothing, which seemed incongruous on her.

She glanced up first. Something flashed across her face, and Radu instinctively curled his shoulders inward, bracing for a blow. Only after she looked back down without acknowledging him further did he have time to process that her expression had been one of rage, and then of sadness.

But everything else was forgotten when Mehmed straightened up and caught sight of him. A relieved smile transformed his face as he crossed the distance between them and hugged Radu. Radu closed his eyes, answering the embrace for only the briefest moment. He feared if he held on longer, he would betray himself. Instead, he pulled back, keeping his hands on Mehmed's shoulders to separate them. "Are you well?"

Mehmed nodded, gesturing to a low bench built along one entire wall of the room. He sat, and Radu followed, turning toward him.

"My father?" Mehmed asked.

"I will be surprised if he is still alive by the end of tomorrow. He has not been conscious for three days."

"What are we fighting?" Lada asked, standing nearby. Her arms were folded tightly across her chest, and she looked over Radu's head when she addressed him.

"Halil Pasha's forces are scattered through the city, watching all the entrances. The palace is guarded as always. It will be a problem getting Mehmed inside without being noticed."

Lada's frown deepened. "What does Halil think he can do? He has no claim. Even if the people here are wary of Mehmed's rule, they will not hand the throne to a pasha."

"There is the brother," Radu said.

"He is still an infant!"

"If something were to happen to me," Mehmed said, "Halil Pasha could designate himself the grand vizier and rule as regent on my brother's behalf until he came of age. Probably after he came of age as well. I do not know the boy's mother well, but she is not powerful enough to make herself his regent."

"But if Halil Pasha cannot kill you, he is out of options," Lada said.

Radu shook his head. "No. He will have another way." He leaned back, closing his eyes, scouring his memory for any hint of what Halil Pasha's larger plan could be. And then he remembered—that night, that horrible night with Salih. There had been a letter from Constantinople. What was the name it mentioned? Radu put a hand to his forehead, trying to re-create the words when all he could think of was the kiss he had wanted but not received, and the kiss he had not wanted but gave anyway.

Then it came to him. "Orhan! Does the name Orhan mean anything to you? I saw it in a letter from Constantine to Halil Pasha."

Mehmed's eyes tightened. "He is a pretender, allegedly an heir to my throne from another line. We suspect he is not even related, but Constantine has held him against us for years. My father pays a yearly tax for his upkeep so that Constantine does not send him here to stir up trouble. Halil Pasha means to set the city against me and bring in Orhan as sultan. If he can keep things unbalanced enough, he can hold Edirne and trigger a civil war, *and* keep Constantinople out of harm's way. I wonder how much they have paid the snake."

Radu blanched. "So many Ottomans would die. How can he not care what the cost of a civil war would be?"

Lada picked up a dagger from the table. "The solution is simple. We kill Halil tonight; Ilyas arrives with his Janissaries in two or three days, and the city is ours."

"It is *not* that simple," Radu said.

Lada let out a derisive huff, but Mehmed had turned away from her to face Radu. Lada recoiled as though struck, her face darkening.

"Tell me, then," Mehmed said. "What do you think we should do?"

Radu rejoiced. "I have an idea."

"I have always thought red was a better color for me than blue," Nicolae said, his mouth and nose obscured by a veil as he plucked at his flowing skirts.

"We speak of this to no one." Mehmed's voice was a growl. If anyone looked too closely at the new concubines, they would doubtless be terrified of the murder they saw in their faces.

Lada said nothing, simply waited for the last of her men to finish scaling the wall and dropping over it into the winter-dimmed gardens of the harem complex. All told, she had brought only four: Matei, Nicolae, Stefan, and Petru. Radu could not get more women's clothing than that, and the smaller the party, the less likely they were to draw attention. The others left the city to await Ilyas and inform him of the plan.

When everyone was over the wall, Lada pulled the rope back, coiled it, and tucked it beneath her sash. Though Radu did not want to, he could not help seeing the way Mehmed continuously observed her movements.

"They will be watching Huma," Radu said. He had lied about a meeting with the ailing Huma to get into the harem, but in truth they were not involving her. She was too volatile, too unpredictable, and too obvious a choice. "The shortest distance between here and the palace is the sultan's chambers. That may be our best entry point." Radu rubbed his chin, then smiled. "I am well known to be a favorite of Murad's. Follow me. And try to look like women."

"How do I do that?" Petru grumbled.

"Watch Lada?" Matei suggested. Fortunately, the snorts of laughter were smothered by the veils, and Lada pretended not to notice. Something in the way her eyes tightened made Radu wonder if perhaps it bothered her, though.

"Short steps," Lada said. "Make your body curve wherever you can. Shoulders rounded, hips swaying. Walk as though you have nothing between your legs, which should not be a problem for Nicolae or Petru."

More gruff laughter.

"And perhaps stop laughing or speaking," Radu said, shaking his head. He strode ahead, walking confidently in front of the procession. When they got to the gated entrance, he nodded at the guard.

The eunuch peered over his shoulder, raising his eyebrows.

"The doctors have suggested we try to arouse Murad's senses in an attempt to wake him. I thought, well . . ." Radu gave a sheepish grin, gesturing back at the women.

The eunuch opened the gate, and they filed through. Radu prayed silently that the eunuch would not look too closely at the "women" or their feet. He had been unable to find slippers for them, and their leather boots were hardly standard for women who spent all their lives living in a single building and its surrounding gardens.

The next door was an entrance to Murad's private apartments, manned by several Janissaries. Sweating profusely beneath his clothes, Radu gave the same explanation with the same knowing-but-embarrassed smile. He was met with shrugs, the Janissaries obviously bored with their role of guarding a nearly dead man.

And then they were inside.

"Do you want to see him?" Radu asked, pausing outside Murad's chamber doors. He looked nervously down the hall, certain that at any moment the Janissaries would realize their mistake and storm in, swords drawn. Or a doctor would come, calling an alarm. Or Halil Pasha himself would be waiting.

But they were alone, for now.

Mehmed considered his father's room, then shook his head. "I have no reason to."

Radu was strangely tempted to go in and pay his respects. Whatever else he was, whatever else he had done, Murad was the reason they were here. And Radu would not change that. Murad had taken much, but he had also given him Mehmed and Islam.

Radu put his hand on Mehmed's shoulder, squeezing once. Then he led the group through the sumptuous rooms to a little-used side chamber. It was too small to entertain, and with Murad dying, visitors were few and stuck to the main rooms.

With the door safely closed behind them, the men stripped off their disguises, some with more urgency than others. "I prefer your face veiled," Nicolae said to Petru as the young man ripped his outer clothes off.

"I prefer your mouth shut," Petru retorted.

There was an ease between them, a safeness that stemmed from knowing so much about one another. Perhaps not even liking each other, but being certain that if it came to it, they would defend one another with their lives.

Radu wondered what that would be like, a friendship with nothing else—no fears, no tangled and unwanted emotions. Kumal was more of a mentor than a friend, too much older to be a true peer. Radu trusted Lazar, but there was always a note of discomfort there, a hint of desire on Lazar's part that left Radu constantly on the defensive. He kept his other men at a distance for fear they would see in him what Lazar had, what Huma had, what Lada had. What Mehmed had not.

Radu did not know whether it was a relief or another dagger to his heart that Mehmed could not see how he felt merely by looking at him.

"What now?" Mehmed looked to Radu.

Radu felt his chest swell, his shoulders straighten to fill more space. "Now I send for the captain of the Janissaries."

Lada shook her head. "Too risky."

"It is a risk, but it is a bigger risk to leave the city's Janissaries in Halil Pasha's pockets. If he sees us today, he might betray us. But if we do not persuade him to support Mehmed, we will be fighting him in the streets."

"I agree," Mehmed said.

It was a simple matter to summon the Janissary captain to Murad's chambers. Radu did not tell the servant who was requesting his presence. Kazanci Dogan was impassive upon seeing Radu, having interacted with him enough during the siege to be familiar. Radu smiled, waving for him to follow.

To his credit, Kazanci Dogan betrayed only the slightest amount of shock upon opening the door to find Mehmed sitting on an elaborately gilded chair, wearing deep purple robes and a dark red turban. He held a sword as casually as a breath.

"Come in," Mehmed said.

Kazanci Dogan dipped his head in acknowledgment and entered the room, eyes flicking to either side as he took in the grim-faced men lining the walls. Lada still sat in the corner, one leg up on the bench, the other swinging lazily. She finished pulling a knot tight, then dropped the noose, letting it hang toward the floor as though she had forgotten it was there.

Radu felt a surge of affection for her that overcame even his anger. She really was magnificent sometimes.

"I was not aware you had arrived in the city," Kazanci Dogan said to Mehmed.

"Yes, odd that no one saw fit to tell me my father was dying. But with things poised on the brink of change, I thought you and I should come to an agreement."

Kazanci Dogan said nothing.

"During my last rule, we had discipline problems with your men. Have you been able to get them under control since then?"

Kazanci Dogan's face betrayed a flush of red. "My Janissaries do more for the empire than any other soldiers. It is my job to make certain they are taken care of."

"Of course. Remind me about the structure of the corps."

Frowning, Kazanci Dogan explained that he was the head of all the soldiers and reported to by the leaders of each division and garrison. Mehmed nodded thoughtfully.

"And you owe allegiance to the sultan and none else?"

Kazanci Dogan's voice slid out easily. "Yes."

"But the sultan is not the commander. You are."

"Yes."

Mehmed nodded. "It is good that you are separate from the spahis and their endless politics. I value my Janissaries above all else. Tell me, then: What can I do to help you lead your men?"

Kazanci Dogan's face turned shrewd. "We are tired, sir. The siege against Skanderberg was long and disheartening. Many of my men returned ill and have only recently regained their health. There is some concern that ..." He paused, as though choosing his next words carefully. "... that *when* you take the throne, they might be thrown into another ill-advised, protracted siege."

Mehmed tilted his head in surprise. "I have no desire to go against Skanderberg. That was my father's quarrel, not mine."

"Not Skanderberg."

The intelligent confusion on Mehmed's face almost made Radu smile. "Whom would I besiege? I already have an empire that needs attention, and I will need help and time learning how best to rule. I would depend on my Janissaries to be my hands in that. That is my only plan for their future."

Kazanci Dogan made an uncommitted noise in the back of his throat.

"Tell me, do you think my father has run his empire well?" Mehmed smiled at the look of alarm on Kazanci Dogan's face.

"Come now. He is dying. It is not treason to examine what we can do better. For example, how do your men feel about their compensation?"

Kazanci Dogan cleared his throat. "There have been some complaints. We shoulder a heavy burden for the empire and see other men more richly rewarded."

"I agree. My first act will be to go through my finances, determine where taxes are being misused, and divert all available funds to raising Janissary pay. I want you to think of an amount you feel is fair but generous. It is important to me that your soldiers—and you—know that no one values you or can take care of you as much as I can." Mehmed's smile dropped off, his eyes becoming as sharp as his tone. "*No one* can offer you what I can, and if anyone tried, it *would* be treason."

Kazanci Dogan bowed deeper in an actual show of respect. "I look forward to serving you when you are our sultan."

"Your *father.*"

"Yes. Our father."

Mehmed nodded. "I trust that you will keep our meeting in confidence. I am not ready to declare my presence here yet. I would like more time in privacy to mourn my father's imminent passing. Should anyone discover me, I would know who had betrayed me."

Kazanci Dogan's Adam's apple bobbed as he swallowed. "Yes, my father."

Mehmed smiled, opening his arms generously. "I look forward to watching you lead. As soon as my father dies, we will agree upon the terms of pay increase, and you can announce it to your men."

Bowing again, Kazanci Dogan was escorted out by Matei.

"Do you think it worked?" Mehmed asked, a worry line between his brows.

Radu collapsed onto a chair, relieved of the tension his body had been holding since the Janissary leader had arrived. "He is no fool. He knows you can offer him more than Halil Pasha could. And he was sincere about his men being tired. He will want to avoid fighting in the streets and a protracted civil war. He has more to gain now from an alliance with you."

"I agree." Mehmed stood, stretching. "As soon as I am secure on the throne, we will kill him."

Radu blinked in shock, but Lada simply nodded, tightening the noose.

"What now?" Petru asked.

"Now we wait for my father to die and Ilyas to arrive."

———◆———

Both events happened the next day. Amal brought word from the wall that Ilyas had arrived en force and simply marched through the gate when the guards tried to deny them entry. Mehmed watched from the tower above his father's room, the procession of white caps making a tremendous show through the streets.

"Is it done?" he asked.

Radu did not know what he spoke of, but Petru nodded. "Your father is dead."

"Then I go to meet my people." He turned away from the window, turban glittering with metal threads woven throughout. His clothes were deep purple, the traditional color of the

Roman emperors. A heavy gold necklace, glimmering with rubies, hung from shoulder to shoulder, and a cape draped down his back.

They rode out. Kazanci Dogan's Janissaries met them, gathering more as they went until they came to the great square in the center of the city and joined Ilyas. Mehmed rode at the front, sword raised, bells pealing as news of his father's death spread. After a parade around the whole city, he returned to the palace.

Halil Pasha was waiting in the throne room, murder on his face. Mehmed strode straight up to him and clasped his shoulders. Lada stood with sword drawn, directly behind Mehmed. Naked fear quickly replaced the violence on Halil Pasha's face. This had been Radu's idea, the grand plan behind all their secret maneuvers.

"Halil Pasha, my father's most trusted advisor, the wisest man in our great empire." Mehmed turned to the crowd of nobility gathered, some still hastily adjusting their finery. "Halil Pasha will serve as my grand vizier, to help guide me in ushering in a new era of peace and prosperity for the glory of the Ottomans!"

The crowd cheered. Halil Pasha's terror was replaced with incredulity, and then the sly, triumphant smile of a fox that had stolen another beast's prey. But the fox failed to notice Radu's hounds surrounding him, driving him exactly where they wanted him.

Poor fox, Radu thought.

45

MEHMED WAS GIVEN THE sword of his ancestor
Osman Gazi. He held it reverently in front of him before sheathing it and girding it about his waist. He now wore
the dreams of his entire country's history.

Lada did not know how to feel as she watched it happen.
This was not the Mehmed who had spoken so passionately
about that dream when they were alone. This Mehmed was
wrapped in silk and girded in armor, a turban obscuring his
head, his face as sharp as steel and as untouchable. He stood
on a dais, separate from all others. There was a man whose
only role—complete with royal title—was to carry around
a stool for Mehmed's feet should he require it. There was a
man who had stewardship over Mehmed's turbans. There was
a man who stood to the left of Mehmed, ready with perfume
and a fan should some noisome scent dare approach the un-
approachable.

Because that was what Mehmed had become.

Through the endless ceremonies, the naming of viziers,

the acknowledging and receiving of gifts, Mehmed stayed in the same spot and moved further and further away.

Lada wondered if the poison testers would taste the seething jealousy creeping in her veins as she stood on guard and watched Mehmed's dream take root.

Lada could not have anticipated that an even more odious and discomfiting task than watching the endless coronation lay ahead. Mehmed, in the outer chambers of Murad's apartments, met with each of his father's wives and concubines. As per Lada's demands, there were two guards stationed at each door, and one of her own men in the room with Mehmed at all times.

Today, that was her role. As woman after woman entered, starting with the lowliest who had only recently moved from servant to full harem member, Lada was forced to acknowledge the reality of this part of the throne. Her hand constantly twitched over her sword. She was not certain what, exactly, she wanted to kill.

A trembling concubine left, to be replaced by a woman Lada knew. Mara still wore clothes unsuited to the courts—a full, intricately embroidered dress with no veil. Her hair was pulled back and elaborately curled. There was no touch of Ottoman style in her entire ensemble. She did not bow to Mehmed, merely raised an eyebrow. "Good morning." She spoke Latin instead of Turkish.

He smiled, bemused. "Mara Brankovic."

"My fame precedes me." Sweeping her skirts out, she sat

on a sofa parallel to Mehmed's chair, rather than cowering in front of him.

"I am glad to see you well."

"Widowhood suits me."

Lada snorted a laugh. Mara acknowledged her with a glance, smiling coldly.

Mehmed cleared his throat, trying to regain Mara's attention. "I am not certain what to do with you." Most of the other women were being sent to various estates, depending on their rank within the harem and whom they were related to. Daughters of important families were returned, some with marriages already prearranged by Mehmed and their fathers. Radu was, even now, discussing a match with some important pasha on Mehmed's behalf. Like coins exchanged, the women passed from one hand to another.

Lada's fingers tightened around her sword hilt.

"I have had an offer of marriage from Constantine," Mara said.

Mehmed could not hide his surprise. *"Constantine?"*

"I suspect he thinks it will soften your alliance with my father and Serbia, since it was in large part due to my influence that my father stayed out of the conflict at Varna. Losing Serbia as a vassal state would be a blow to your empire, and an embarrassment to your recent ascension to the throne. Europe does not expect much from you."

Mehmed nodded, his face now carefully impassive. "I am surprised at his boldness. And his speed. Though I wonder at your wisdom in telling me."

Lada did not question it. Mara had something behind this. She was too smart to let an opportunity go to waste.

Mara shrugged, tilting her head. "God has freed me. I will never marry again. I have already written Constantine a refusal, which I will sign and send as soon as I am on my way home to Serbia."

Mara had no sword, but she had effectively used herself as a weapon. Mehmed could not harm her without risking his alliance with her father; and if he angered her, he risked strengthening Constantinople's chances at more allies. She would not be used in any way other than the one she chose.

A sudden, fierce envy seized Lada. All Mara's patience had paid off. She had written her own fate, free of the men who tried to engineer it for her.

Mehmed stood and inclined his head respectfully. "I shall make the arrangements immediately. We will have you on your way in the morning with gifts for yourself and your father, and a renewed peace treaty to deliver with my blessing."

Mara stood, dipping into a graceful curtsy. Her smile for Lada this time was genuine. Then, without expressing gratitude for the escape she had crafted all on her own, she walked from the room.

"I will miss her," Lada said.

Mehmed laughed. "That does not surprise me. She always was the most fearsome of my father's wives."

"And with fearsome wives on our minds . . ." Lada nodded toward the door, where Huma waited, supported by a eunuch.

"Concubine. Never a wife." Huma spoke with a tremble that had not been there before. Her skin was a shade of yellow that made Lada want to look away, the full body she had been so proud of before now wasted beneath her slack robes.

"Mother." Mehmed rose to help her sit. "You did not need to come."

"Of course I came. You are my son. The sultan."

Lada had expected pride, even exultation, but the words sounded as though they tasted bitter on Huma's tongue.

"But there is no question of your future," Mehmed said. "You will stay here, in the palace."

"It is not my future that concerns me. We need to discuss plans. We got you to the throne; now we must ensure that you keep it."

Mehmed shook his head, taking her hands in his. "This is not for you to worry about. I want you to concentrate on getting well."

She continued as though he had not spoken. "We can do nothing about Orhan for now, but there is the matter of little Ahmet, your half brother. He is a threat that must be addressed."

Mehmed shifted away from her. "I will make arrangements to send him to an estate in the country, where he will be safe."

Huma coughed, the sound rattling between her shrunken breasts. "Safe? You want to keep your closest rival for the throne safe?"

"He is an infant."

"He will not always be one. Think of your father, the years he wasted fighting his own brothers. They nearly pulled the empire apart. We cannot allow the same thing to happen with you and Ahmet!"

Mehmed dropped her hands and stood, glowering. "This

is not a matter of *we*, Mother. I am well aware of the perils of the future. I will keep Ahmet safe—safely away from here, safely out of the reach of any who would use him against me, safely separated from poor Halima his mother, or anyone who would put his interests above my own. He will grow up a prisoner. Forgive me if I do not wish to dwell on it."

Huma's expression matched his in ferocity, and it struck Lada how alike they looked. There was an intensity to their faces, something about their eyes that pierced whatever they set their sights on.

Then Huma collapsed into herself, giving in to her illness and exhaustion. "At least tell me you have a plan for Halima. Put her to good use."

Mehmed rubbed the space between his eyes. "Yes, yes. I am meeting with her soon. I think I will marry her to Ishak Pasha. I am sending him to Anatolia to be the new beylerbey. I want Ishak away from Halil. They are too strong together."

"Yes, that is wise. Though I still think Halil would better serve you from the top of a stake." Huma stood, holding out an arm. The eunuch who had escorted her hurried to her side. "And you are wrong about how to deal with the baby Ahmet. But you must do what you think is best."

"I will."

After she was gone, Mehmed sighed. "It is hard, seeing her so weak."

"I think she has never been weak. She frightens me as much as she ever did. And . . . she has a point." Lada's mouth curled down; she hated to agree with Huma. She even felt sorry for Halima. "If Constantinople is leveraging a distant cousin against you, imagine what they could do with access to Murad's other son. Halil will try to use him."

"I will keep him away from Halil. And by the time Ahmet is old enough to be useful, we should be done with that wretched pasha."

"Vizier," Lada corrected Mehmed, and he stuck out his tongue. "It was Radu's idea, remember. If you had listened to me, Halil would be dead."

"I know, I know. But we have to think further ahead. We are building a foundation. Each stone must be considered. We have to dismantle the wall Halil has built before removing him. Otherwise more stones would fill in the gap, and the wall would still be in my way. Radu is right about that."

"And what does wise, clever Radu think about Ahmet? Is he a stone, or a weakness that threatens the whole building?"

Mehmed did not answer.

46

THE ROYAL CLERK'S INK-STAINED fingers drummed nervously on his legs. His voice was halting and garbled, as though unused to speaking. "You want to see the tax records?"

Mehmed's face was a mask of patience. "Yes. I want to see accountings for the tax revenues."

Radu pitied the clerk, whose brow was beaded with sweat. He suspected the man had never before been called in front of a sultan.

"Which taxes?"

Mehmed did not smile. "All of them."

"All—all of them?"

"*All* of them. I want to trace every coin that comes into the treasury, and every coin that leaves it. I want to see what every state and city is making, who is in charge, how they are spending my gold, and what there is to show for it. Wages. Allowances. Payments to foreign countries. Payments made by vassal states."

"But—it will be weeks before I can gather enough information for us to go through, and it would be a massive undertaking."

"Then you had better start. Now."

The man scurried from the room as though Mehmed's declaration were whipping his heels. Mehmed sighed, rubbing his forehead. "We have lost so much time. It will take me months, years perhaps, to get everything in order. When I think of how far I could be if my father had not taken back the throne, if I had not been banished again to Amasya . . ."

Radu tasted Mehmed's anger, and his tongue dried in his mouth. Though they had never spoken of it, Radu often wondered if Lada, too, regretted what they had done. Maybe there had been another way. A way that would have let Mehmed keep the throne the first time he inherited it. They had been scared. They had been *children*. And they had made a decision that impacted Mehmed's future without consulting him.

"Are you well?" Mehmed asked.

"Yes! Yes. I am simply nervous. I meet with Kumal and Nazira today."

"Why would that make you nervous?"

Radu realized with a pang that although he and Mehmed were together nearly every day, they had not fallen back into their comfortable ease of telling each other everything. Radu had too many secrets he could not afford to reveal, and so he spoke as little as possible. It was easy. Mehmed always had people around him. Even now there were two guards in the room and a squat, thick-fingered man who held a stool for Mehmed's feet. Their presence did not lend itself to intimacy, which might have hurt Radu before, but now seemed a tender mercy.

"Did I not tell you? Kumal wants me to marry Nazira."

Mehmed sat back as though struck. The stool-carrier jumped forward, but Mehmed waved him away. "Marry her? You would leave me?"

Radu felt a flutter of something—not quite hope, but its darker, more desperate cousin. Perhaps the disbelief and hint of anger from Mehmed was jealousy. "Am I not allowed to marry? I know the Janissaries cannot, but I am not clear on what, exactly, I am here."

Mehmed's face softened. "You are my friend. You are certainly not a slave. If you want to marry her ..." Mehmed trailed off, his eyebrows lowering as he examined Radu with an intensity that made it difficult for Radu to breathe.

"I do not love her." The words tumbled from his mouth like pebbles in a stream, cold and clacking together. He did not know where they would land, but he kept talking. "I care about and for her, and Kumal has been very kind to me. I am not certain I am a good match for Nazira, though. I think she could marry higher and be better off. And my first duty—my only duty—will always be to you. No one could take me from that."

No one could take me from you.

Please, Radu thought, *please know what I am saying.*

Mehmed's eyes widened, pupils dilating almost imperceptibly. Then a smile shifted the intensity and sincerity away from his eyes. "I will leave it up to you, then. Kumal Vali is a good man. I will make him Kumal Pasha. You are free to do whatever you wish, as long as Nazira knows I require you by my side."

Radu clasped his hands together behind his back, away from Mehmed, so tightly they ached. "There is no place I would rather be."

The words caught in his throat, trying to pull more out. Radu knew if he started, he would never be able to dam the flow of honesty that would pour forth, drowning him in its wake.

So he bowed and walked from the room, breath shaking and pulse pounding.

Love was a plague.

He was meeting Nazira and Kumal in the same garden where he had first seen Mehmed.

They found Radu standing in front of the fountain, staring at ghosts, wondering: If he had not met the crying boy here, would he be able to love Nazira?

"Radu!"

He turned, still tangled in the past, and embraced Kumal. His friend was thinner than he had been. A lingering shade of death's touch deepened the shadows beneath his eyes and the hollows of his cheeks. But he was alive.

"I am so glad to see you well." Radu hugged him tightly before releasing him.

"It is only thanks to you."

Radu turned to Nazira. She wore a sunrise-pink scarf over her black hair; her soft, dark eyes turned up at the outer corners and made her look pleasantly teasing. Her lips were so full, they were nearly a circle, but she pulled them apart into a smile. "Radu."

Radu bowed. He was happy to see her, but uncertain how to act around her. Where before they had had the easy rapport of friendship, siblings even (as Radu imagined sisters who were not Lada to be), now there was a chasm he did not know whether to cross or flee from. He had wished her his sister, and she, apparently, had wished for more.

"I see an interesting shrub over there." Kumal pointed, beaming. "I will go examine it for a while, I think."

Radu could not bear to sit at the fountain, so he led Nazira to a stone bench beneath a broad tree. Its branches were bare for the winter. They sat, shielded from view. Radu did not know what to say.

Nazira stared straight ahead when she finally spoke. "I want to marry you."

Her directness disoriented Radu, who had become so used to the angling and meandering communication of the courts. "I— You are very— You see, I—"

She turned to him and smiled, putting her hand on top of his. "Radu, sweet Radu. When you look at me there is no hunger in your gaze. I have spent a good deal of time observing men and the way they look at women, and you do not look at me as a man looks upon something he desires."

Fear blossomed, its dark petals spreading wide. "You are very beautiful, and—"

She squeezed his hand, shaking her head. "It is not a hunger I welcome. That is why I picked you. You are kind and smart and you are ... alone. And you will, I think, always have to be alone." She formed it almost as a question, her eyes searching his for a truth he did not want them to find. "Do you remember our dance?"

Radu shook his head.

"At Mehmed's wedding to Sitti Hatun."

"Ah, yes."

"Half the women in the room watched you move, craving your attention, waiting for their turn. And you looked at none of them. I knew then. I understand. I understand what it is to look upon what you are supposed to have and feel nothing." She waited, then whispered, "I *understand*."

Radu realized tears had formed in his eyes. "You do?"

"I do. As your wife, I would expect only your friendship. Nothing more." She looked at the ground, and a blush spread across her cheeks. "And I would request that my maid, Fatima, be allowed to accompany me. Always."

"Fatima." Radu sat back, remembering. The way Nazira's gaze always followed the maid wherever she went, the day he found them in the gardens, breathless and flushed, their hair askew from being *chased by a bee*.

A cloud passed from the sun, bathing them in warmth and light. With it came surprising clarity. Radu smiled. "You *were* happy to have been stung by that bee in the garden. You have found happiness, then."

She nodded. "I have. Will you—please, will you help me protect it? Will you let me be your friend, your true friend who knows you and loves you?"

Radu leaned his forehead against hers, closing his eyes. He

could not help the welling of jealousy that filled him. Nazira had found her happiness and, miraculously, Fatima felt the same. But his bitterness was brushed away by genuine love for Nazira. If she had what he feared he never could, he would do whatever he could to help her.

"Nazira, it would be my greatest honor to be your husband."

She let out a burst of laughter mingled with a sob of relief and threw her arms around his neck. "Thank you, thank you, sweetest Radu. Thank you."

He placed a gentle kiss on her forehead.

When they rejoined Kumal, he took in Nazira's tear-streaked face with alarm before noticing their clasped hands.

"Brother!" He took them both in his arms. Nazira's frame trembled as she cried and smiled, and Kumal began making wedding plans.

"We can invite the sultan!" he said.

"No," Radu said, too quickly and with too much force. Nazira's eyebrows raised knowingly. Radu nodded his head, a tiny movement only she would catch. She squeezed his hand, and he was surprised by how much comfort it was to be understood.

This time when he spoke, Radu was careful to sound calm and unaffected. "He is burdened so heavily right now. He would feel guilty for being unable to attend. It is best not to invite him. I will ask him for an estate nearby, but out of the city. Closer to you. It will be healthier air for Nazira, and I can travel between her and my duties to the sultan with ease. I would like to marry in a simple ceremony, as soon as possible."

"That is my wish, too." Nazira glowed, outshining the sun.

Kumal laughed good-naturedly. "It appears you both know exactly what you want."

"We do," Radu said. But only one of them was able to truly have it.

47

EXHAUSTION PLAGUED LADA, dragging her limbs and mind down. Nicolae was occupied with scouring the Edirne Janissaries for Wallachian recruits to fold into their ranks. Stefan was training the few they had found. And so, with Petru and Matei both ill, Lada had taken a double night watch. Now, finally past dawn, all she could think of was bed.

It had been strange, standing inside Mehmed's room while he slept. He had pleaded for her to join him in his bed, teased and flirted, but she reminded him that she was all that stood between him and a knife in the dark.

And that if he did not shut up and go to sleep, the knife would belong to her.

Still, there was something discomfiting about the whole experience. It was like watching him during the coronation. He was there, he was Mehmed, but he was so separate from her. Unreachable. His face sleeping was the same as it had been during the ceremony: alien.

During the longest, loneliest hours of the night, it had

been all Lada could do to keep herself from waking him just to see the way his eyes changed when he saw her, the way his lips formed around words and intentions. She liked who she was when he looked at her, craved it. But she had resisted. And now, with her own sleep so close, she found her door blocked by a woman.

"Lada?" The woman's round face was sweetly pleasant, like a plum, with equally round lips. Her eyes were weak, too large and watery.

"What?"

"I—it is me. Nazira."

Lada frowned, her mind sluggish. The woman did look familiar.

"I introduced myself at Mehmed's wedding? I danced with Radu."

"Everyone danced with Radu."

The woman laughed. It came so easily to her, a reflex of a muscle Lada did not have. "Yes, that is true. Radu has not mentioned me?"

Red flashed before Lada's eyes, all her muscles tensing. Was this some sort of test? A trick? Did someone know Radu's true heart and feelings for Mehmed? If Halil had discovered it, he would try to use it to his advantage. Lada would not betray her brother so easily. "Radu and I do not speak much. We are both very busy."

"Oh. I am sorry. You would know my brother, though. Kumal?"

Recognition slammed into place, jarring Lada completely awake. She had never paid much attention to the women who floated around the edges of the court, but she did remember

Kumal. Kumal, the stealer of souls. The man who had driven Radu into the heart of the Muslim god.

"I do know him."

Nazira must have missed the growl in Lada's voice, because she smiled in relief. "Well, apparently Radu has not spoken of it with you yet, but I—we . . . we are being married tomorrow."

"You are *what?*"

"We have only recently decided, and we wanted to be married quickly, without fuss. There is so much else going on, and Radu must be available for Mehmed."

Lada felt dizzy, as though she had dismounted from a daylong ride and the earth still moved beneath her with the gait of a horse. "He is marrying you."

"We are avoiding the more rigorous traditions, but I wanted to spend today at the baths with my cousins and aunt. And you, of course. You are his only family." She mistook Lada's expression of confused horror for a questioning one about the baths. "It is custom to spend the day before a wedding at the baths. Radu has reserved one of the palace baths for us, so we will not be disturbed. And I hoped, since we will be sisters, that you would join us."

Who was this woman? First her brother delivered Radu's soul to a foreign god, and now, when Radu had the ear of the sultan, she swooped in to marry him? Lada knew Radu did not love her. She suspected her brother incapable of loving anyone but Mehmed. Why, then, had he agreed to this marriage? Did they have some sort of hold on him, some vicious blackmail?

If Nazira was using Radu to get to Mehmed, Lada would

need to have as much information as possible. She could work with subtlety like Radu. He was not the only one who could play that game. She gritted her teeth in an approximation of a smile. "Give me a few moments to change?"

———•———

Lada followed Nazira through a walkway over which deep green vines arched, waxy and impervious to the chill of winter. She had never been to the baths, preferring to clean herself in private rather than spend time with other women. The exterior of the building was simple, almost austere. But once they were inside, a new world was revealed. Hand-painted tiles featured a repeating flower motif that grew along the walls and climbed across the ceiling in brilliant reds and yellows accented by the deepest blues.

High-set windows let in light, which cut through the steam curling in the air. Nazira greeted several women with delight, exchanging kisses. Everyone seemed overjoyed and surprised, remarking on the speed of the engagement and Nazira's good fortune in nabbing the handsomest man in Edirne.

Lada wondered whether her own head or the tiles would break first if she began smashing her skull into them.

Her smile felt like agony.

An attendant led the women to an area that had been prepared for them, with mats for their clothes and long, soft swaths of cloth to wrap themselves in while disrobing. Lada lingered near the back, wondering how Radu did this sort of thing. Did she insert herself into conversations? Did she hope to be invisible and merely listen?

The other women did not hesitate to slip out of their clothing, laughing and talking, perfectly at ease. They were neither ashamed of nor embarrassed by their bodies. When most of them had gone into the water, Lada threw off her clothes as quickly as possible, tucking the leather pouch she wore around her neck beneath them. Then she slid into the bath from the side, rather than walk naked to the shallow steps.

She stayed there, arms folded tightly across her breasts, hoping that someone would say something damning very quickly so she could leave.

The water *did* feel nice on her exhausted, tight muscles, but she felt more than naked. She felt exposed and vulnerable. She longed for a weapon, for chain mail, for something between her skin and the rest of the world.

Lada inched closer to the other women, her hair trailing behind her. But instead of speaking of Radu's favor in the capital and his connections to Mehmed, the women spoke of his eyes. They spoke of his smile. They spoke of his charm and his kindness. Each one had an anecdote, a story of something Radu had done for them or for someone they knew. Some perfectly timed joke, some utterly captivating tale, some startling moment of generosity.

A pang in her chest made Lada aware of a strange sense of loss. Of missing Radu. Because she did not know the man they were speaking of, and she thought she might want to.

Maybe she was wrong. Maybe Radu did love Nazira. Maybe whatever he felt for Mehmed had been siphoned off and given to this sweet-faced nothing of a girl. Lada obviously did not know him as he was to this city.

But no. The way Radu watched Mehmed, the way he could not escape the current left in Mehmed's wake—that had not altered. The rest of the world was an afterthought to Radu. Only Mehmed mattered.

Lada had once mattered to him. How had she lost that?

Nazira laughed, and Lada remembered. Kumal had given her brother prayer and taken him away. And now Nazira was claiming him as well. She drifted closer to Nazira, who was partially blocked by two broad-shouldered aunts.

"We will tell you some secrets," one said, a lisp coming from where one of her front teeth was missing, "so Radu's handsome looks do not go to waste."

The other aunt gave a bawdy laugh. "Looks will count for little if he is not a good learner."

"Hush!" Nazira said, her skin flushed from the heat of the bath or from embarrassment. She put her hands over her face, shaking her head.

"Oh, come now, you are to be a wife. You must know that husbands are useless in all things unless properly instructed. Particularly in the pleasuring of their women."

Lada inched away, intensely uncomfortable. If they were going to speak of snakes and gardens, of a woman's responsibility to provide safe haven for a man's seed . . .

"Please, aunties, you are scandalizing her," one of the married cousins said, though she laughed, too, comfortable with the topic. "Wait until after her wedding night when she is no longer terrified. Then tell her how a woman can be pleased as well as a man."

"Bah," the lisping aunt said. "How long was it after your

marriage until you came to me, crying, complaining of your unhappiness with his nightly ministrations?"

The cousin laughed. "Five miserable years. Two screaming infants I had given him and gotten not one evening of joy in return. You are right, I would not wish that on my poor Nazira."

Nazira splashed water at them. "No more! If I have questions, I will write you a delicately worded letter. I have faith in Radu's generosity and *abilities.*"

Lada choked, and every head whipped around to face her.

"Oh, Lada! I am sorry," Nazira exclaimed. "We should remember Radu is your brother."

Spluttering something that resembled an excuse, Lada fled to her mat, her skin not even dry before she tugged her clothing on and gripped the pouch safely back around her neck. She would find out nothing she wanted to in the bath.

But as she ran to her rooms, trousers clinging to her legs, she kept hearing the phrase that was more of a revelation than any political plotting: *A woman can be pleased as well as a man.*

———————

"He married her? Already?" Mehmed stood, then sat back down, then stood again. "But we spoke of it only three days ago! And he did not even want to marry her! He asked for a modest estate, but when I agreed I did not think . . . *Married?*"

"Things change, apparently." Lada had tried to corner Radu to talk to him before the wedding, but he had barricaded himself behind his big eyes and empty smile, simply saying over and over that Nazira would make a wonderful wife. She had been forced to watch as they were married in

Turkish. Radu gave his life away in another tongue sealed by another god.

Nazira had blushed her way through the ceremony, a maid standing by her shoulder. And when it was over, the couple had barely touched, all the passion of two innocent children playing at marriage between them. Lada had been invited to a feast at Kumal's city house afterward, but she feared she would not be able to be civil. Not to *that* man. Not ever.

Radu had just nodded and wished her well when she told him she was leaving. And now he was married.

"It makes no sense," Mehmed said. "What does Kumal Pasha have to gain by an alliance with Radu?"

Lada scoffed. "Is it not obvious? Kumal is a pasha now. Radu has your favor. Kumal wants to be closer to you. We will have to watch him."

Mehmed shook his head. "Kumal has no ties to Halil Pasha. In fact, I have already gone over all the taxes and accounts from Kumal's vilayet. He is beyond reproach. He and his men acquitted themselves with honor during the siege of Skanderberg. He already knows I value and trust him, and he is respectful without ever courting favor. This does not benefit him. But Nazira is his youngest sister. Perhaps he spoils her, and let her pick her own match."

Lada did not want that to be true. She wanted there to be a darker purpose, a reason to hate them, a reason to punish them. But Radu was smart. If he were in trouble, he would have gone to Mehmed, if not Lada.

"Maybe ... maybe she really does love him." Lada knew Radu did not love Nazira. But if it made him happy to focus on a person other than Mehmed, it could be a good thing for him as well.

Mehmed shook his head. "Of course she would love him. Half the city is in love with him. Still, his acceptance makes no sense. He does not love her."

Lada watched him to see if there was more meaning, more understanding behind his words, but she could not tell.

He stared at the wall, deep in thought. "And she cannot make him happy."

A bathhouse conversation tugged at Lada. "What about Nazira?"

"Hmm?" Mehmed finally focused on her, still distracted. "What *about* her?"

"Why is it her duty to make him happy? What will Radu do to make her happy?"

He waved a hand dismissively. "Be her husband. Provide for her. Give her . . . children." He puckered his lips as though the word was distasteful. As though he had not already done the same.

"And children are her reward for enduring him."

"Enduring him? She is fortunate!"

"Tell me," Lada said, her thoughts of snakes and gardens and seeds and duties now muddied with steam-swirled, improbable ideas of pleasure beyond kissing. "What do you do to make your *women* happy?"

Mehmed's mouth drew taut, his eyes narrowed shrewdly. "My women? What are you speaking of?"

"Your harem. They exist to serve you. They give you sons." She spat the word out. "What do you do for them?"

"I do not wish to speak of that with you. You know I have to—"

"This is not about what you have to do! Do you like them? Do you love them? Which of them do you love best?"

"I do not know! They are— It is different. It is like the man who carries my stool. I neither like nor dislike him. He is there to serve a purpose. Why do you want to talk about this?"

"Because I want to know if you have ever, even once, thought of what might bring them pleasure! Or is it entirely a transaction, part of the business of being sultan? Are they as *stools* to you?"

His brows drew close together, his expression pained. "Which answer do you want, Lada? Which would make it better?"

She backed up. "I do not know."

He took a step forward, closing the distance between them, eyes on the floor and voice uncharacteristically tentative. "If you wanted to . . . I would do whatever you wanted, whatever you needed for us to be together. Anything."

With a sharp rap preceding him, Nicolae opened the door. Lada jumped guiltily away from Mehmed. Nicolae grinned, oblivious to the atmosphere in the room.

"We are not due for a changing of the guard for another hour, when you will accompany me to the royal treasury," Mehmed snapped, sitting down.

Nicolae bowed deeply. "My anticipation is so strong it is physically painful to wait even that long. But I am not here for you, my father. Lada, I have a surprise for you. Come out."

"Bring it in here." Mehmed slouched on his chair, scowling.

Nicolae shrugged, but his scarred face was unable to conceal his glee as he stepped aside.

A man walked into the room, broad-shouldered and barrel-chested, thick in his movements. He wore a Janissary uniform. Lada was about to shout at Nicolae that a new recruit was hardly worth the interruption, until she saw what the man's cap failed to cover.

Two ears that stuck out like the handles on a jug.

His grin felt like all of Wallachia reaching out to draw her home. "Lada," Bogdan said.

She ran forward and threw herself at him. He did not hesitate, wrapping his arms around her and spinning her in a circle. She buried her face in his neck, unable to believe it was real. Bogdan, her Bogdan, lost to her so long ago.

Alive. Here. Hers.

"Who are you?" Mehmed demanded.

Without putting Lada down, Bogdan answered in a voice deeper than the one she had known, but so very *him* that it made her feel like a child again. "I am her husband."

Lada laughed, smacking the back of his head. He lowered her, but she kept a hand on his shoulder. She had to make certain he was real and he was not leaving.

"I hardly think our marriage was binding." She took his hands in hers, his fingers short and callused. His face had broadened, his features fitting better now that he had grown into them. He was sturdy, strong, exactly how she would have imagined him had she had the heart to let herself.

"Will you *please* explain?" Mehmed asked. His face was as coldly and precisely arranged as a floor of tiles.

"This is Bogdan. My oldest friend. His mother was my nurse, and we grew up tormenting her and Radu. He was lost to me, so long ago. I thought him lost forever! Oh, Bogdan." She put a hand on his cheek, the stubble there shocking her and reminding her of all their missed time.

"You have no idea how many Bogdans I had to try before finding the right one," Nicolae said.

Lada could not restrain her smile. "Thank you."

"He seems like he will make a good addition to our corps. Big enough to sit on Petru when he gets too annoying."

"Are you quite finished?" Mehmed raised an eyebrow.

Lada's smile vanished. What was wrong with him? Why could he not see how happy she was to be reunited with Bogdan? She caught his eyes flicking to where her hand still rested on Bogdan's shoulder.

She lifted her chin, not letting go. "Bogdan, this is Mehmed, the sultan."

Bogdan bowed as was appropriate, but there was something in his movements that made the bow look as though it were an afterthought. Something he was going to do anyway, and Mehmed simply happened to be standing in front of it.

Lada pulled his hand. "Come, let me show you—"

"I want you to accompany me to the treasury," Mehmed said.

"What?"

"There are some accounts I wish to have your thoughts on."

"But Nicolae was—"

"Nicolae can show—Bogdan, was it?—where the barracks are. Go now."

"No! They will stay."

Bogdan stood, impassive, his face betraying nothing. Nicolae's eyes widened in warning. "Lada," he mouthed.

She realized she was asking them to directly defy a command from Mehmed. Her Mehmed, yes, but their sultan, their "father." If they obeyed her, they could be killed for treason. She knew Mehmed would do no such thing, but at the same time, she could not ask Nicolae and Bogdan to defy him for her sake.

"Go," she said through gritted teeth. "I will meet you later."

She watched them leave, then walked five steps in front of Mehmed the whole way to the treasury. She was seething.

"Lada," he said.

She did not turn back or answer.

When they arrived at the treasury, Mehmed was detained by mounds of parchment: tallies and ledgers and contracts. She stood by the door, supposedly scanning for threats but instead spending all her energy glaring at Mehmed's back.

Finally, the clerks left.

"What is this about?" Lada asked.

"What do you mean?" Mehmed did not look up.

"You dragged me here when you knew I did not want to come. I have not seen Bogdan in years—I thought him dead—and you decided my input on matters of the treasury mattered more?"

"Forgive me if I was taken aback to be introduced to your husband."

Lada spluttered. "He is not— It was a game between children." She looked down her nose at him. "Besides, you are certainly in no position to complain about that. How is Sitti Hatun these days?"

Mehmed burst from his chair, hands around her shoulders before she could move. She braced herself, but his face softened and his grip loosened, one hand coming up to cup her face. "I am sorry. I have not seen you that happy in . . . It surprised me, is all. I did not know how to react. I am glad you found your friend."

Lada nodded, still wary.

"You should go, speak with him, catch up. Come to my rooms for supper tonight, afterward, and tell me about it." He smiled, and she did not have time to see whether it was a genuine smile or a smile of the sultan before he leaned forward, pressing his lips to hers. The soft insistence of his mouth trapped her, and she answered back with her own.

They had not had time alone like this in all the days since they came to Edirne. Her hands and mouth informed her she was ravenous for him. He stepped back to the chair, pulling her with him as he sat down. Sitting on his lap, she wrapped her legs around him. She felt his neck's racing pulse as he drew her closer and closer. His hands danced along her body, moving to a new place as soon as she registered where they had just touched. They left a trail of fire in their wake, writing him onto her skin.

Lada heard the knock at the door as if through water, and it took several more knocks before she understood what it meant.

She drew back, gasping.

Mehmed smiled wickedly, straightening her tunic for her. "You should go."

"I should go," she echoed.

"I will see you tonight."

She floated on a red haze of lust, pondering what pleasure could be had if one's partner was willing. It lasted a single corridor before she remembered Bogdan. With a dark suspicion that Mehmed had been trying to make certain she thought of only him, she ran for the wing of the palace that housed her men.

She raced from room to room. Their ranks had swelled thanks to Nicolae's diligence, and she was greeted with barely familiar faces until finally she found the room she wanted.

Nicolae stood, talking easily as Bogdan put his things into a plain set of drawers.

Lada froze in the doorway. After the first shock of their meeting, she did not know how to greet him. They were no longer children with the ease of a lifetime spent together. What had the last years done to him?

What had they done to her?

She was struck with a sudden horror of what the Lada who had first come here would think of the one who existed now.

Bogdan regarded her without expression. "So, this is the life you have built for yourself." Though his tone lacked judgment, Lada felt herself bristle. She did not have to apologize. Not to Bogdan, and not to her old self.

"Yes. I lead the finest troops in the whole empire."

"So I see. And you answer to the sultan."

She folded her arms. "I answer to myself."

"Then why are you still here? Why not take what you can and leave?" He searched her face as though looking for something no longer there.

"I— It is not that simple."

Nicolae's scar twisted around his wry smile. "We were going to, once. And then she changed her mind."

"I did not change my mind! There were other considerations. And besides, if we had left, you would be here and I would be gone. How would we have found one another again?"

Bogdan nodded, accepting the truth of that as easily as a dog thrown a bone. "So we go now."

"Where?"

"To Wallachia."

"I cannot go back there. My father *sold* me, Bogdan. He brought me here and he used my life to buy his throne. There is nothing for us there. I will never go back to my father." No matter how much she learned—how strong she was, how clever or brutal or loved—her father still dictated her life. "Better a sultan than my father," she whispered.

"Fathers do not live forever," Bodgan said, shrugging. But he used the Turkish word for *father*. The word Janissaries used to refer to the sultan.

48

Back in the city after his brief postnuptial leave, Radu passed the dough-faced youngest member of Lada's band of soldiers. Something about him nagged at Radu. His face was so soft looking, his body so hulking. He did not match.

Radu did not care for most of Lada's men, but he could not deny they were the best at protecting Mehmed. They each had a portion of that feral, ruthless determination that made up his sister's core. Sometimes Nicolae or one of the friendlier ones would greet him in Wallachian. He always responded in Turkish.

Mehmed sat listening to Ishak Pasha speak on the status of finances in the Amasya and Anatolia regions, where he would soon be sent as the beylerbey, a local governor. Radu had told Mehmed they needed to separate Ishak Pasha and Halil Pasha, and Mehmed trusted his judgment. Radu wondered what had been decided in the few days he had been gone. He had been so anxious to return that Nazira and Fatima had teased him for constantly looking over his shoulder at the road to Edirne.

Mehmed caught Radu's eye. Some trouble betrayed itself in the sudden tightening of his eyes. But it was gone as soon as it appeared, and he went back to nodding.

On Mehmed's right was Halil Pasha. Grand Vizier Halil, Radu reminded himself.

As soon as Ishak Pasha finished speaking, Mehmed stood. "Radu! Back so soon? How could you bear to leave your lovely bride?"

It was not difficult to flush with embarrassment. The sheepish, knowing smile was more of a stretch, but Radu had had much practice. "Thank you, Sultan, for the beautiful estate. She is overjoyed with the process of making it home. I am afraid I was quite in the way, and have already been banished until she has everything precisely the way she wants it."

The men laughed knowingly. Kumal's smile was soft. Not for the first time, Radu wondered if he knew the true nature of his marriage to Nazira. But he did not have the courage to ask. If Kumal did not know, what would he think of Radu if he found out?

Mehmed gestured toward a chair near his. Radu sat, wishing he could sink down and close his eyes.

The home *was* lovely. A secluded estate, large enough to support a woman and her maid, a village within easy distance to purchase what their gardens and livestock did not supply. Nazira could not stop crying as she went from room to room, holding hands with Fatima. Radu had the spare bedroom, a warm and bright space. He did not anticipate visiting much. He held Nazira dear, but hers was a happiness so complete that it threatened to canker his soul. He did not want jealousy to cast any shade on her life with Fatima. And it had been agony for him to be that far from Mehmed.

Just as it was now agony to be this close.

A page came to the door, interrupting the conversation, which had shifted to crop plans. The boy bowed, trembling, and announced the arrival of an envoy from Constantinople.

Mehmed's eyebrows rose, though it was his only discernable reaction. Other men in the room gasped or whispered in hushed tones. Though many countries had sent envoys with gifts and elaborate proclamations of congratulations, they had not expected one from Constantinople.

Mehmed gave Radu an imperceptible glance. Radu nodded toward Halil.

His face open and at ease, Mehmed turned to Halil. "How do you advise me? Should I see them immediately or make them wait?"

Halil's chest puffed like a tiny bird chirping its importance to the world. "I think it would be wise to see them right now, Sultan."

"Very well. Send them in."

Three men entered. They were dressed in vibrant yellows, blues, and greens, and wore red boots. Each layer of elaborately stitched and brocaded clothing was styled to reveal the layer beneath, a gaudy display of wealth. Clothing was expensive, a symbol of status. The Byzantines apparently made every effort to show as much of their clothing at one time as possible. Large hats like the sails of ships covered their heads, and each man held something in his hands.

Halil stood. "I present the sultan, the Shadow of God

on Earth, the Glory of the Ottoman Empire, Mehmed the Second."

The three men bowed respectfully, though they did not remove their hats. "We come on behalf of Constantine the Eleventh Dragaš Palaiologos, emperor of Byzantium, Caesar of Rome, bearing gifts and petitions."

They were invited forward. The gift, sent to honor Mehmed's ascension to the throne, was a jewel-encrusted book, colorfully illuminated with gold leaf accents. After admiring it, Mehmed passed the book to Radu.

As always, Radu felt a thrill opening a book. There had not been many in the castle at Tirgoviste, but the Ottoman Empire was so wealthy there were many books. This one, written in Latin, told the story of Saint George slaying the dragon.

Radu knew the story from his childhood. A holy knight, wandering through a heathen land, discovered a kingdom terrorized by a venomous dragon. The king's daughter had been chosen by lottery to be that day's sacrifice. Vowing to save her, Saint George fought and tamed the dragon. He led the princess and the dragon back to the city, holding the entire kingdom hostage under threat of death until all inhabitants agreed to convert to Christianity. His holy mission accomplished, Saint George finally slew the dragon.

The book was an illuminated, ancient story of a threat. Radu looked up at the envoy to find one member, a young man with clear gray eyes, watching him intently. The man blushed and looked away.

"An interesting choice of books," Mehmed said, amusement dancing on his face.

Next, a letter from Constantine was read aloud, words as elaborate and ornate as the swirling borders of the book. Radu tried to pay attention, but there was so much circular praise he soon lost interest and let the sentences wash over him, lulling him half to sleep. It sounded like the church of his youth—in love with its own voice, cold and inaccessible.

Again he caught the gray-eyed young man staring at him. Radu did not know what it meant. Perhaps the young man was struggling to pay attention to the reading of the letter, too.

Then the name Orhan was spoken, jarring him out of the strange game of trading stares he had been playing.

Constantine had not waited long before reminding Mehmed of the threat of his pretender to the throne. Worse, he had the audacity to ask Mehmed to increase payments to Constantinople for the keeping of Orhan.

Mehmed steepled his fingers thoughtfully beneath his chin, waiting until the lead envoy member had finished reading. "My," he said, as calmly as if he were commenting on the weather, "it would appear Orhan is an expensive guest."

No one laughed. The tension in the room hung heavy, as though everyone had sucked in a breath and refused to relinquish the air. The envoys were pale. The youngest no longer looked anywhere but a fixed point on the wall. Though their faces were brave, sweat beaded beneath their hats, betraying their nerves at coming to the new sultan with such a demand.

Mehmed turned to Halil. "You have more experience with Byzantium than I do. Does this seem fair?"

Halil raised a trembling hand to dab at his brow. "Yes." He nodded to himself, as though encouraging his voice to be firmer. "Yes, I think the terms are quite reasonable. If I were to advise your grace, I would say we should agree to the demands. It is better to keep Orhan where he is, and to give Constantinople a show of good faith."

Mehmed turned back to the envoy. "Very well. Halil, my esteemed vizier, will see that you are taken care of tonight. Tomorrow we send you home with news for our ally, Constantine, and a renewed era of goodwill between our great empires."

The envoy's bows were less formal this time, their movements fast and deep with relief. The gray-eyed young man caught Radu's gaze one last time. A quick smile like a secret fluttered over his lips. Radu felt a matching flutter somewhere inside. Then Halil escorted them out, followed by his main advisors.

Radu shook his head to clear it. He was still out of sorts from spending time in the country. And this was a big, interesting development.

Mehmed dismissed most of the other men. He kept Radu, Kumal, Ilyas, the leader of the Edirne spahis, and Kazanci Dogan behind. Under Radu's advice, Mehmed had decided to spare Kazanci Dogan for the time being. They knew he could be bought, and they needed every ally they could secure.

Leaning back in his chair and stretching his arms overhead, Mehmed yawned. "My friends," he said, "I would like to discuss our navy."

"What navy?" Radu asked.

"Precisely." Mehmed's smile was a predatory fish slicing through the water. "Bring me reports on the ships we have, and, more important, the ships we do not have. And do it in secret."

The men were wise enough to keep their curiosity modestly clothed with their expressions.

Mehmed dismissed them, gesturing for Lada's soldier to wait outside the door. As soon as they were alone, the portent of bad news Radu had seen when he entered the room reappeared on Mehmed's face.

"What is it?" Radu fought growing dread. "Are you upset with me? I am sorry I did not give you more warning of my marriage. I scarcely know how it all came about so quickly. But Nazira is—"

"No, no. It is nothing to do with that. I am happy for you." Mehmed paced, distracted, his words lacking any weight. "She is lovely and a good match. And you will still be here." He stopped and looked up. A hint of fear mingled with the trouble behind his eyes. "You *will* still be here."

"Of course."

"I depend on you. I trust you as I trust no one else."

Radu smiled, lifting a hand to his heart. "And I you."

"Do you remember a man from your childhood? Lada's friend? Bogdan?"

Radu wrinkled his nose in distaste. "Yes. They were always teasing me. He was an oaf."

Mehmed scowled. "He is here."

"What? *Here?*"

"Nicolae found him."

Panic clawed through Radu's chest, and he was suddenly eight again, too timid, too quick to cry, too easy a target.

Bogdan had forced him to put on his nurse's shawl, taunting that if Radu loved her so much, he may as well be her. Worse had been the fear that, no matter what, his nurse would always love Bogdan more. No matter how hard Radu wished, Bogdan was her child, Radu her charge.

Bogdan being taken away had been one of the highlights of his childhood, because it left him unlimited access to his nurse's heart.

And Lada's.

But now Lada was not his, had not been for a long time. And she had Mehmed. And she had Bogdan back, too. A spot behind Radu's eyes pulsed with a stab of white-hot pain.

"I hate him." Radu cringed, knowing he should have censored his words better. But there was something triumphant in Mehmed's face, as though Radu had proved a point.

Then Mehmed shifted again, abruptly, turning away from Radu. "I have had news from Wallachia. It was late coming, and I wondered at the lack of a gift or emissary upon my crowning." He stopped pacing. "Your father is dead."

Radu understood the words, but they had no meaning. He shook his head, trying to clear it. His father. A high laugh echoed through the room, and only when he put his fingers to his mouth did Radu realize it was coming from him. "Do you know, I cannot even recall what he looked like? Only how he made me feel."

Mehmed took Radu's hand. "How did he make you feel?"

"Like I was nothing." Radu could not look away from Mehmed's hand on his. "And now he is nothing."

Mehmed was quiet for a few moments. Radu knew he

ought to be sad, or ask questions, but he was more relieved than anything else. Vlad no longer existed in the world, and Radu could not consider that a bad thing.

"Would you like to know how it happened?"

Radu grunted his assent.

"It was Hunyadi, on behalf of the boyars. They killed Mircea as well."

"Poor Mircea. I am certain that must have upset him."

Mehmed's face drew closer to Radu's, interrupting his view of the ceiling. His brows were pinched in concern. "Are you well?"

Radu put a hand to his forehead, pushing down against the lightness overwhelming him. "I think I am."

"I tell you this because . . . because you are the heir to the throne. You are the next in line. And, as sultan, with Wallachia as a vassal state, if that was what you wanted . . ."

Radu felt the weight of the world crash back down on him. Wallachia, with endless dark trees and fists in the forests, with fountains that brought gasping, choking mouthfuls of water instead of beauty, with winters as cold as a father's dismissal. Wallachia, with Lada back with Bogdan, not needing him, not seeing him, not caring. Wallachia, with no mosques, no call to prayer, no god that knew or cared for him.

Wallachia, with no Mehmed.

He grasped Mehmed's shoulders. "I know it would help you, to have someone you could trust on that throne. And I want to serve you, to do whatever I can to help you gain Constantinople and be the sultan your empire has waited for. I *will* do whatever I can. But please, I beg you, do not ask this of me.

I want nothing from Wallachia, as it never wanted anything from me. My home is here, with you. Please do not send me away."

Mehmed's face smoothed with relief, and he folded Radu into an embrace. Radu drew a trembling breath, breathing in Mehmed, steadying himself.

"Say nothing to Lada," Mehmed said. Radu nodded against his shoulder, and this one time held on for longer than was safe because he could not bear to let go.

49

LADA'S SKIN WAS TOO tight. There was not enough to contain everything she needed it to. It stretched and itched, phantom sensations crawling across her neck, muscles twitching in desperation.

Bogdan walked on one side of her, Nicolae the other, buffers against the chill of the evening. It was her first free night in over a week. Mehmed had demanded her presence every waking hour, constantly making some excuse for why he needed her, specifically, on guard duty. Or why he needed her advice. Or why he simply needed her.

Those particular needing sessions burned deep and low, and she shuddered.

"Are you well?" Nicolae asked.

She walked faster.

It felt right to have Bogdan next to her, like a return to how things had been. He fell into step without hesitation, her shadow, her right hand. Hers, as he had always been, even across the years.

But she was not the same person. She had grown, distorted, become something new. And the Lada she had been with Bogdan—the Lada she wanted to be around him—was not the same Lada she was with Mehmed.

Nicolae and Bogdan both stared at her, as though waiting. Waiting for what? She wanted to snap at them, to hit them, to make them leave with their constant unasked question: *Why?*

Why was she still here?

The question did not seem to exist when she was alone with Mehmed, but as soon as he was gone it covered her like boils, an itching plague upon her soul. Why was she still here? What had become of the girl who was the daughter of a dragon? Was this it, then? Had she reached the pinnacle of her potential? A command of fifty men in service of a man she loved, who ruled an empire she loathed?

"What more is there?" she snarled.

Bogdan and Nicolae both stopped, staring at her with confusion. "What more is there to what?" Nicolae asked.

She jabbed a finger into his chest. "Stop talking to me. Stop looking at me. Stop expecting me to solve this."

Nicolae's lips parted in a tentative, baffled smile. "If I understood anything you were saying, I absolutely would endeavor to obey. As it is, I think I will steer us toward a merchant who has a stock of juice that has been kept far too long and turned sour in the best possible way."

An orange haze lighting the night gave them all pause.

Fire.

Four years ago, Lada had walked these streets, imagining raining fire down on them. Her heart leaped with joy, needing to be closer, to find the fire and feed it.

"Is that smoke?" Nicolae asked.

Lada ran forward, ducking around vendors packing up their stalls for the night, Bogdan and Nicolae on her heels. It became harder to advance as they got closer to the fire. People fled past, faces white with panic. Finally, they burst into the main market.

In the center of the square, a massive bonfire greedily reached toward the sky, sparks dancing up through the smoke. Lada wondered if she had missed some sort of festival.

And then she saw what was feeding the fire. And who.

Janissaries ran wild, ripping apart vendor stalls with their bare hands, tossing everything into the flames. They were grouped around the side streets, blocking them. Lada climbed the side of the building next to her, Bogdan steadying her. She could see several other fires starting, all along streets leading toward the city outskirts.

"They are moving away from the palace." She jumped down. "How did this happen?"

Bogdan shrugged. "Revolt. There have been rumbles about it since Murad died."

"But Mehmed is going to raise the pay! He and Kazanci Dogan made an agreement before he became sultan."

"I heard nothing of a raise. If they negotiated one, no one told any of the men here."

Lada wondered now who Bogdan had become in the time they were apart. He betrayed no emotion, though. She slammed her fist into the wall. "Kazanci Dogan betrayed us. He could not keep Mehmed from the throne, but he played both sides."

"So they burn some buildings, maybe scuffle in the streets

with spahis." Nicolae's eyes glowed as they stared at the fire. "Mehmed will raise their pay, and it will all be settled."

"It makes no sense." Lada watched as the fires spread, still moving away from the palace. What did Kazanci Dogan stand to gain by letting his men revolt? He already knew Mehmed would raise the pay. Maybe he was trying to get it even higher, but . . .

"The fires," she said, her heart racing. "They are drawing soldiers to fight them."

"Yes." Nicolae drew the word out as though speaking to a child. "Fires do need to be put out, lest the whole city burn."

"Play 'Kill the Sultan' with me, Nicolae. Think. The fires are moving away from the palace. The soldiers are moving away from the palace. All eyes are moving away from the palace."

Understanding tugged the scar between Nicolae's eyebrows flat. "They are going to kill Mehmed."

"Petru and Matei are there tonight. I do not know the other men well. They could be part of it. We have to get to Mehmed."

"Streets are blocked," Bogdan said. If he had an opinion on which side they should be supporting, he did not show it. But he was right. Each street leading back to the palace was filled in by rebel Janissaries.

"I only have knives." Lada looked hopefully at Nicolae, but he shrugged, holding out his empty hands. "You have *nothing*?"

"Not all of us sleep armed, Lada."

"How are we going to get through the men?"

Bogdan walked over to a stall that had been partially dismantled. A couple of rebel Janissaries were there, but they saw his cap and nodded, whooping loudly. Bogdan reached through the stall to the heavy wooden door of the building it abutted. He opened the door, grabbed the top, and wrenched the entire thing from its hinges.

"I think he is a very different type of Wallachian than I am," Nicolae noted.

Bogdan turned the door sideways, holding the latch like a handle. Lada laughed in understanding, getting behind the door next to Bogdan. Nicolae joined them.

With a roar louder than the fire, Bogdan ran forward. Lada pushed against the door, matching his pace. Wishing she could see the soldiers' faces, she still felt the impact as they slammed into the men who failed to dive out of the way fast enough. Nicolae tripped, rolling and coming back up with a sword in his hand. Bogdan never slowed. He cleared their way with the crack of wood meeting bones with crushing force.

Lada looked over her shoulder to see two men pursuing them. She threw one of her knives and it was met with a wet thud and a scream. Stopping abruptly, she somersaulted beneath the second man's sword and grabbed the first man's from his slack fingers.

The clang of metal on metal jarred her to her core. She bared her teeth in a smile as she screamed, throwing herself at her attacker. He went for her head, and she dropped to her knees. A hot spray of blood confirmed her slash against his hamstrings.

No time to finish him. She sprinted to catch up to Bogdan

and Nicolae. They had become mired in a mix of terrified civilians and a mass of Janissaries. The Janissaries were shouting, obviously confused about what was going on and not aware of the revolt.

Bogdan threw the door aside, shoving through to get Lada clear.

"Revolt that way!" Lada shouted, pointing. "Glory and honor if you protect the sultan by my side this way!"

Finally clear of the melee, she sprinted. She did not bother to look if her rallying cry had gathered any men to her side. But the footfalls around her were far more than just Bogdan's and Nicolae's.

The gates of the palace gaped, open and unmanned. "Trust no one!" Lada shouted. "Janissaries or otherwise! Disarm everyone, secure all the doors." The dozen men with her entered the main door, swords at the ready.

She ran for a side entrance used by kitchen servants. Kicking the door open, she braced for a fight, but found none. She wound past the kitchen and up a flight of stairs hidden behind a dusty, worthless tapestry. Nicolae and Bogdan stayed close on her heels.

"How do you know about this?" Nicolae asked.

"It leads directly to the sultan's chambers."

Lada did not have time to be embarrassed about the revelation of her intimate knowledge of secret passageways to Mehmed's bed. This one was used by the kitchen staff so there was no chance of someone accessing his food between when it was sampled for poison and when it was delivered. Lada had used it to sneak down and steal food when they had stayed up late into the night talking . . . and not talking.

The hall was eerily silent behind the thick stone walls that sealed them off from whatever was happening elsewhere in the palace. Lada could scarcely breathe, images of what would await her at the end flashing before her eyes.

Mehmed dying.

Mehmed dead.

Mehmed's purple robes soaked in darkest red.

Mehmed's black eyes gone permanently dark.

Lada knew no one would ever look at her the way he had. If she lost that . . .

"Either they are already in the room and we are too late," she said, gasping for breath, "or they have not yet reached his apartments and we can still stop them. Here." She shoved open a secret door that led to the grand hall outside Mehmed's apartments. "Secure his door!" She did not wait for Nicolae or Bogdan to agree before ducking back into the hallway and running for the entrance to Mehmed's rooms. If he was dead, she had to know. She had to make them pay. She slammed her shoulder into a door hidden behind a tapestry in one of Mehmed's sitting rooms. Then she ran through, ripping the tapestry free from its hanging rod.

Mehmed stood, mouth open in shock.

Radu was barely visible in the next room, a tall, lean Janissary's hand on his arm and the man's mouth next to his ear. No one was panicking, no one was dead.

And Ilyas, not Kazanci Dogan, was standing beside Mehmed.

Lada slumped against the wall, relief robbing her of the fire that had chased her here. Other than the door that connected them to the hall containing Radu and the Janissary, the only other entrances to the sitting room were the one she had come through and the balcony. They would need to move to a more secure location. She closed the hidden door, barring it with the tapestry rod.

"What is this about?" Mehmed asked, incredulous.

"Revolt. Janissaries. I thought—I feared it was a distraction. That they were trying to assassinate you."

"God's wounds," Ilyas said, but he did not sound shocked. He sounded tired. He walked over and nodded to the Janissary with Radu before closing and locking the heavy door to the sitting room.

Lada crossed over to it, shaking her head. "We should move to a more defensible room. One without a balcony. Someone could climb in, or jump over from Mehmed's bedroom balcony."

Ilyas sighed, pulled out a dagger, and slid it into Lada's side.

50

T HE JANISSARIES ARE REVOLTING?" Radu asked, shock robbing him of coherent thought.

"It would seem so." Lazar's voice was bright, his eyes darting to the locked door between them and Mehmed.

"But we are raising their pay!"

Lazar raised an eyebrow. "We?"

Radu shook his head. "Mehmed. He met with Kazanci Dogan before Murad died. It was all arranged." It made no sense for the Janissaries to revolt now. They were being paid more than ever before. What had Radu missed? How had he failed to anticipate this move by Halil Pasha?

"Doubtless it will work itself out." Lazar licked his lips, then startled as banging echoed down the hall from the palace entrance to Mehmed's apartments.

"Is that Petru?" Radu stepped toward the door. Ilyas had sent Petru and Matei to the outer hall so he could discuss confidential plans with Mehmed. "Why is the outer door barred?"

"Ilyas must have locked it after they left. Smart. Safer that way." Lazar bounced up and down on the balls of his feet, gaze flitting between the two locked doors like a moth against a lamp's glass. "Maybe we should check Mehmed's chambers. Look out over the balcony to see what is going on in the city."

There was more banging, louder now and accompanied by shouts. Panic seized Radu. "Do you think the revolt has made its way here? What should we do?"

"Help will arrive soon." Lazar took Radu's elbow, pulling him toward the other end of the apartments. "We really need to check Mehmed's bedroom."

"That sounds like Nicolae shouting. We should let them in."

"No! If the fighting has gotten to us, they need to defend the door. We should position ourselves in Mehmed's bedroom in case someone tries to come in that way."

"Stop." Radu pulled his arm free. "We need to think this through. We should get Mehmed to a better location. The room they are in has a balcony, too. It is not safe, and only Lada and Ilyas are in there with him."

The pounding turned into rhythmic slamming. Some-one was trying to break down the door. Radu could still hear Nicolae shouting. It made no sense. If they had been over-powered, he would be dead, not shouting.

In the sitting room, Lada shrieked with rage and pain, the wall shaking as something smashed against it.

Mehmed.

Radu ran to the door, wrenching at it, but to no avail.

"Help me!" he said, casting about for some tool to unlock

it. The hall was filled with plush furniture, everything padded and soft. There were no utensils, no pens, nothing that was not gold and delicate. Radu had a knife in his belt, but it was too thick to jam into the keyhole.

"Radu."

"We have to break it down!"

"*Radu.*"

"Why is there nothing useful in this whole damn room?" Radu shouted, kicking over a cushioned footstool.

Lazar grabbed his wrist, yanking Radu around to face him. "Please listen to me." His voice was low, too calm. Lazar did not understand the trouble they were in—even Radu did not understand it. There was so much noise from so many places. He needed to get to Mehmed.

Lazar did not release him. "There is nothing you can do."

"What are you talking about? We can do something! We have to, we—" Radu stopped. Lazar did not look panicked—he looked sympathetic. Sorrowful.

It was definitely Nicolae yelling, accompanied by Petru. They were shouting for Lada, screaming to be let in. They would never do that if enemy forces were outside.

"You pulled me out of the room," Radu said, his stomach sinking as the truth settled like lead. "You do not expect help to come. You are counting on it not to."

"Let me explain."

Radu twisted his wrist free, darting for the door where Lada's men were trying to get in. It was blocked by a bar easily lifted from the inside.

Lazar tackled him from behind, Radu's head meeting the

tile in a blinding flash of lights. "Please," he said, knee digging into Radu's back. "I was trying to keep you safe."

Radu spat blood from where his lip had been cut open. "Keep me safe?"

"You were not supposed to be here tonight. You were supposed to be with your *bride*. When Ilyas told me you were back, I begged him to let me come along, to keep you out of it."

Radu squeezed his eyes against the pain and despair, arms trembling as he tried and failed to push himself up. "Why is Ilyas betraying us?"

"He is *protecting* us. You are not a Janissary. You cannot understand. All we have is each other. No one else cares about us, no one else values us as anything other than bodies to be thrown at enemies in the name of the sultan."

The muted sound of blades from Mehmed's room drew a sob from Radu.

Lazar leaned his head down, resting it against Radu's back. "I am sorry. I know you care about him; I know. But he would spill our blood against the walls of Constantinople. Ilyas will not let that happen to us. *He* is our father, not Mehmed. It has to be like this."

"No!"

"Tell me. Tell me that Mehmed will not kill us." Lazar waited, but Radu could not. He knew Mehmed's heart was set on Constantinople. "He wants it as a dragon wants a jewel— merely to possess, merely to feed his hunger. He will never be satisfied. You saw what the siege of Kruje was. It will look like a holiday compared with Constantinople. We will all die, and no one will mourn us. These are my brothers, Radu." Lazar's voice cracked, and his warm tears found their way through

Radu's tunic. "They are the only family we have. If you think about it, you will understand. You will forgive me. I love you, Radu. Please. Please forgive me for this. I would sacrifice anything for my family. You would, too."

Radu stopped fighting and released himself to the floor. Lazar's weight was heavy against his back, the same as that patrol night in Kruje when Lazar had tackled him to save his life.

Lada would die defending Mehmed. Mehmed would die. But Lazar was right. If Mehmed lived, so many of the Janissaries—his friends and companions—would die. All to take a city that threatened nothing. Only because it was their dream, because the Prophet, peace be upon him, had declared it so long ago.

Radu turned his head, trying to look back at Lazar. Still keeping Radu pinned, Lazar shifted his weight, so their eyes could meet.

"I am so sorry," Radu said. Lazar had saved him so many times—saved him with kindness as a child, saved him on the battlefield, saved him tonight. "I love you, too, my friend."

Lazar's face lifted with hope.

Radu answered that hope with a stab, his hand freed just enough to shove his knife into Lazar's stomach.

Lazar rolled to the side, hands clutching his wound. Bright blood spilled between his fingers. Radu knelt over him. He threw Lazar's sword across the room, then pressed his forehead to his friend's. "I am so, so sorry."

Lazar gave a lazy, lopsided smile. It broke Radu's heart. "You always choose him."

"I always will," Radu whispered.

Then he ran, leaving Lazar to die alone. The door to the palace hall was barely splintered despite Lada's men's continuous attempts. Radu called for them to stop, then put his shoulder under the bar. They had warped the door, and Radu let out a cry of rage as he pushed up with all his might. Finally, the bar slid free.

Radu ran straight for Mehmed's bedroom. "Mehmed is in there!" he shouted, pointing to the locked sitting room.

He scanned the bedroom, hands bloody and mind utterly focused. Long curtains were draped from the wall, held by a rod. Radu backed up, then ran and leaped, grabbing the rod and swinging his body until it tore free with a metal scream.

He carried the rod onto the balcony, too far from the room where Lada and Mehmed were. They were not dead yet. They were not allowed to be.

Radu could not leap from one balcony to the other. The distance was too great. He threw the rod across the gap, barely catching the curtain before it all followed. The rod clattered to the stone floor of the other balcony, curtain pulled taut. Radu yanked it, praying.

The rod caught, snagged on the stone railing.

Wrapping the curtain around one hand, Radu climbed onto the edge of the railing and jumped. The impact of the fall jarred his arm, nearly pulling it from its socket. He cried out in pain, then pulled himself up, every muscle screaming in protest, until his free hand found the edge of the balcony. With one last burst of strength, he climbed up.

He was in the darkness, looking in at the brightly lit room. The scene inside was a nightmare. Mehmed crouched, weaponless, in a corner. One good hit would be all it took to murder him. It was a testament to the wonder of Lada that that had not happened yet. She was all over the room, ducking and twirling and screaming. Her blade clashed with Ilyas's, denying him at every turn.

Though Radu had missed the beginning of this story, he could see the end.

Lada was bleeding heavily, every footstep smearing her life against the delicate floral patterns of the tiled floor. She favored her right arm, and her breathing was too heavy, too fast. All Ilyas had to do was outlast her, and they both knew it. She fought with everything she had, and he stepped around her with the ease of a partner in a dance.

Neither had noticed him yet. Radu went to draw his sword—

He did not have a sword.

Or a knife.

He had been so desperate to get into the room, he had not thought what he would do once he got there. Bleak surrender threatened to pull him under. He had murdered his oldest friend. Now, as a reward, he would watch his only family and his only love killed while he stood by, unarmed and useless. All his wit and charm amounting to nothing in the end. He would at least die by Mehmed's side. He stepped forward, nearly tripping on the curtain.

The rod!

Radu yanked it free of the railing, letting the curtain fall free.

Lada slipped on her own blood, crashing to the floor,

sword trapped beneath her hand. Ilyas raised his blade. He was close enough to strike either Lada or Mehmed. Radu did not know who Ilyas would kill first, and he could not protect them both at once.

He chose Lada. With a scream, Radu ran in front of his sister, holding the rod. Ilyas's sword fell on it, the force nearly jarring it from Radu's hands. Lada kicked out at Ilyas's knee, forcing him to stumble back.

Lada looked at Radu, wide-eyed with surprise. Then her focus snapped into place. "Get him to turn his back to the balcony," she hissed.

Lada stood as Radu shifted sideways, angling to put himself between Ilyas and Mehmed. Lada darted to Ilyas's other side, swinging her sword wide in a lunge so predictable even Radu could have blocked it. Ilyas took advantage of her opening, filling the space she had left.

The space right in front of the balcony door.

Ilyas's sword sliced through the air. At the last possible moment, Lada dropped backward onto the floor, screaming, "Now!"

Radu braced the rod at shoulder-height and ran forward with everything he had left. The rod slammed into Ilyas, catching him off guard. He stumbled backward, but Radu did not have enough momentum to push him off the balcony.

Lada appeared at Radu's side. She grabbed the end of the rod and pushed it like a door, hinging hard to the right so Ilyas was knocked off balance. The backs of his legs met the stone railing of the balcony, and Lada followed the swing of the rod.

Ilyas fell.

But Lada could not stop, her momentum carrying her forward. She tipped over the edge of the railing.

For one moment the world died, hanging lifeless and devoid of air in front of Radu. And then he felt the rod being wrenched from his hands. He tightened his grip, twisting so the rod was under his armpit.

"Hurry!" Lada said, and in her voice he heard the girl he had grown up with, the girl who always chose to be fierce instead of scared. The girl who was now terrified. "I cannot hold it!"

Radu pushed down on the rod, using the railing as a fulcrum. The metal bent but was strong enough to pull Lada back. As soon as she was level with the balcony, Radu threw himself forward and grabbed her blood-slicked hands. He tipped her up, falling backward with her on top of him.

She was shaking all over, trembling as he had never seen, delirious with blood loss and fear. "You saved me," she said.

"Of course I did."

She shook her head. "Not when I was falling. When Ilyas had us both on the floor. You chose me over Mehmed."

"You are my family," he whispered. Lazar had been right, after all.

He held her, stroking her hair and crying, the sound of the door finally breaking open and Lada's men pouring into the room a distant, dull roar.

51

ILYAS HAD NOT DIED in the fall, though Lada suspected that he wished he had. She was surprised to find Kazanci Dogan exonerated by the information the prison guards extracted from Ilyas. Kazanci Dogan had not been in on the assassination plot, merely encouraged to hold Edirne hostage for even higher pay increases.

It had been a simple matter for Ilyas to walk through the palace, commanding Janissaries to go into the city and put out fires. Leaving only him and his accomplice Janissary to know the truth of the mission.

Lada shifted on her seat, her side complaining doggedly when she moved and when she did not move and when she did or did not do anything at all. She did not feel like herself, head aching and tired after even modest exertion. Still, she would heal.

She glanced over at Radu. His eyes were unfocused as he stared at the courtyard.

The head gardener raised the stake, planting Ilyas. Ilyas,

who had allowed her to train with his men. Ilyas, who had given her a chance to prove herself and accepted it when she did. Ilyas, who had given her responsibility in an empire where she should have been invisible.

Ilyas, who had stabbed her.

She did not know whether to hope he died quickly or lingered in agony. His accomplice was more fortunate, having bled to death on the floor while a physician sewed Lada together with black thread.

"You did him a kindness," she said to Radu, her voice low so it would not carry beyond them to Mehmed or the gathered officials. Grand Vizier Halil was there. He had not been implicated. But he was also in charge of the rotations of prison guards who extracted the information.

"Who did I do a kindness?" Radu did not look at her, his tone lifeless.

"The Janissary you killed. The accomplice."

A spasm of pain twisted Radu's features. "Lazar. His name was Lazar."

"You knew him?"

Radu did not respond. Lada wished for some sense of what to do, some knowledge of the ways people comforted each other. Were their positions reversed, Radu would know what to say.

"Was he the first man you have killed?"

"No. But he is the first I murdered."

Lada scoffed. "He was a traitor. And you saved him the agony of prolonged death. It is more than he deserved."

"He was only there to protect me." Radu gave her a bleak

grin she did not recognize, a tortured imitation of humor. "He was worried I would be hurt."

Lada reached for Radu's hand and was surprised when he accepted it. She squeezed, once. "You saved all our lives."

"You once told me some lives are worth more than others. How many deaths before the scales tip out of our favor?"

She had no answer.

———•———

With Ilyas executed, the official story was that the Janissaries had simply revolted, behaving badly as they occasionally did. That same afternoon, Mehmed had Kazanci Dogan dismissed and publicly flogged until his back was more blood than skin. He announced a universal pay increase for the Janissaries, as well as sweeping reform in the structure of the military. Mehmed would be the head. Every thread of power and authority would start and end with him.

A few days after the attack, Lada was strong enough to join Mehmed in his study to go over the restructuring. Radu was already there. He looked haunted, moving too quickly through the outer rooms, eyes fixed ahead.

Lada remembered the hillside forest she could no longer enter in Amasya and felt pity for Radu. She was about to suggest they move to the gardens when they were surprised by the arrival of a eunuch escorting Halima.

"Halima Hatun," the eunuch announced. She bowed, straightening with a shy smile for Lada and a low wave. Lada had forgotten how pretty she was and quickly tamped down a flare of jealousy. Mehmed would not want a woman who had borne his father's son.

Mehmed stood, confusion masked with a bright tone. "Halima, to what do I owe the honor?"

"You sent for me. To discuss my future, the messenger said."

"Yes." Mehmed nodded, gesturing for her to sit. He gave Lada and Radu a puzzled look when her back was turned. "Yes, your future. Are you well?"

"I am, thank you."

"And little Ahmet?"

Her face transformed with eager joy. "He has much spirit. I think he and Beyazit are nearly the same age."

The name of Mehmed's son stabbed Lada in a place other than her side. She shifted uncomfortably, wishing Halima would leave.

"Oh!" Halima put a hand to her mouth in embarrassment. "I have not offered my congratulations on the birth of Mustafa. Two sons! What good fortune."

"Another son?" Lada spoke before she could stop herself, the words leaving her more wounded than Ilyas had.

Another son.

And this one not conceived before their first kiss, before Mehmed made her feel as though she were the only woman in the world who mattered.

Another son.

Radu was all false cheer. "With so much excitement, you must have forgotten to mention it."

Mehmed cleared his throat, not looking at them. "Yes, Gulsa had to stay behind in Amasya. It was not safe for her to travel so far into her confinement. I received word only yesterday. How did you know?"

Halima tipped her head conspiratorially. "Huma told me. She knows everything."

"Yes, she does. Well, I am afraid I have nothing official to tell you. If I can do anything for you while we arrange for your future, please let me know. You are welcome to stay here as long as you wish. This is your home."

Lada wondered why he had not yet sent Ahmet away and separated him from his mother. But even that was quickly pushed aside. *Gulsa.* Who was she? What did she look like? When had Mehmed visited her? What had he thought about while he planted his seed in yet another woman?

Halima bowed prettily, and Lada caught a flash of relief in the other woman's face that the interview was over. After Halima left, Lada kept her eyes fastened on the door. Drowning in her own pool of misery, she could not look at Mehmed. How could she continue to ignore the harem if its occupants did not stop giving birth to Mehmed's sons?

No one spoke.

As though Lada's obsessive thoughts of the harem summoned her, Huma appeared in the doorway.

"Mother." Mehmed said the word with tiredness, not reverence. "I did not send for you."

"Just as you did not send for me when Ilyas tried to kill you."

"How did you—" Mehmed sighed, rubbing his forehead. "I have taken care of it."

"No, you foolish boy. You have not. *I* have taken care of it."

Mehmed's exhaustion gave way to barely concealed anger. "What do you mean?"

"When will you realize that they see you as expendable because there is another option living under your very protection? If you can be replaced, they will try to do it. Again and again and again. And all it will take is one dagger, one poisoned meal, one moment where you are not on guard, and then my sacrifice will be for naught."

"It is not your concern."

"It is my *only* concern! But never worry, my stupid little boy. I have done what all your guards could not. I have made you irreplaceable."

Lada sat up, previous conversations with Huma humming through her mind with sudden intensity. A wrongness seized her stomach and would not release it. "Mehmed did not send for Halima," she said.

Huma lifted her emaciated shoulders dismissively. "While she was meeting with the sultan, her son was drowned."

Mehmed exploded across the room, pressing his mother against the wall. "What did you do?"

"What I have always done. Protected you."

"No. No. Tell me you did not— He is an infant."

"He *was* a threat. And now he is gone."

For the endless span of a single breath, Lada thought Mehmed would kill his mother. Then the tension fled his body. He staggered back, falling into a chair. "He was the same age as Beyazit."

"I have done what you were not willing to. I have secured your legacy. You are now free to be the sultan you were born to be. The sultan I gave birth to. *My* son. My empire."

"Get out."

"We should discuss—"

Mehmed stood. Rage gone, despair gone, he stared down at his mother with all the icy authority he commanded. "Guard."

Stefan, the Janissary on duty, stood at attention.

"Please escort Huma to her rooms. Bring as many men with you as you need. See that she does not speak with any of her attendants, and that the eunuchs are barred from communicating with her. I will send directions for where she is to be taken."

Huma shook, her thin, yellowed lips pulled back to reveal gray gums and more black spaces than teeth. "What are you doing? You cannot send me away! I am the valide sultan, the mother of the sultan!"

"No," Mehmed said. "You betrayed me. You are nothing."

"Betrayed you? You have no idea what I have done for you. How many times I have saved your life. If going behind your back to keep you alive is betrayal, then they should be banished with me." She pointed a bony, twisted finger at Lada and Radu.

Mehmed waved in disgust at Stefan. He took Huma's arm and led her, wide-eyed and shaking, out of the room. Lada thought they had escaped, but then Mehmed turned on them. "What was she talking about? What did you two do?"

Radu looked like a rabbit caught in a trap. Lada understood his fear. Mehmed would never forgive them when he found out their role in his loss of the throne during his first rule. And Huma had no reason not to tell him, not now. She had no more leverage to employ, and Lada had no doubt she would try to burn everyone down with her.

Tears filled Radu's eyes, despair pulling his head low. He was no longer the man Lada did not know. He was the boy on the ice, the boy in the forest, the boy in the thorns.

He was hers.

"Radu had nothing to do with it," Lada said. "It happened when you first came to the throne. After I killed the assassin Janissary, I knew it would never stop. Radu was certain you could be sultan. He was stupid and shortsighted, so I went to Huma. It was my idea to have the Janissaries revolt then, to contact Halil and work with him to get your father back to the throne."

Lada watched as shock and anger transformed Mehmed's face from the one she knew and loved into something too distant to touch. It was physically painful to watch. She did not look away.

"How could you? All the power Halil gained! All the years I lost . . ."

Lada lifted her head higher. "I did it to save your life. I would make the same choice again."

Mehmed sat, refusing to look at her. "I cannot—I cannot think about this right now. Not with what just happened. Ahmet. Little Ahmet." A curtain came down over his face, as though he had cut off all thoughts of Lada's betrayal until he could sort through them.

Radu put a hand on Mehmed's shoulder, but he stared at Lada. "Thank you," he mouthed.

She did not acknowledge it or the immense gratitude welling in his eyes. She owed him a debt. Nothing was more important to him than Mehmed's trust. Perhaps it would have been kinder to break that trust and force a removal. Maybe then Radu could be free of the impossible love he carried. But she could not do that to him, not when it was so easy to take this blow on her own shoulders.

"They will think I ordered Ahmet's death," Mehmed said, oblivious to Radu's feelings, as always. "Halima was with me when it happened. I will have to tell them, it was Huma, it was not—"

"No," Lada said. "They will think it was your order no matter what you say. If you claim it was your mother, it will make you look like a murderer *and* a liar."

"What am I to do?"

Lada thought of what she would do. This was a time for power, not subtlety. No one could question that the sultan was in charge. "Make it law. You know what your father's brothers did. The wars they fought are still raw wounds. Your father had to kill them all eventually. Make a decree that when a sultan is crowned, it is legal for him to kill his brothers for the security of the empire."

Mehmed had never looked at her with genuine horror before, but he did now. She stopped herself from taking a step back and steeled herself against the fear that, between this and the revelation of her betrayal, she had lost his love.

She would not be weak to avoid his judgment. That was not who she was.

"You think my mother was right to do this?" Mehmed asked.

"I think ..." Lada pushed away the image of hopeful, happy Halima glowing as she talked about her son. The son who was being murdered even as she spoke. Did she know yet? Had she learned her whole world had been taken from her? "I think sometimes when balancing a nation against a single life, impossible decisions must be made. Huma made the decision. Whether it was right or wrong is beside the point. It is done."

"If I make that law, I am already condemning one of my own sons to death."

Lada had not thought of that and cringed at the accusation in Mehmed's eyes. Did he think her so monstrous, that she craved the death of his sons? She shook her head. "If you do not make this law, you are allowing a future civil war that will claim untold thousands of your citizens."

"These are lives, Lada," Radu said. "How can you speak of them like they are matters of simple mathematics, a problem to be solved?"

Lada stood, a hand to her side against the pain of her wound. "Because thinking like that is the only way to keep from losing our minds."

"What about our souls?" Mehmed whispered.

Before Lada walked out, she paused at the door. "Souls and thrones are irreconcilable."

———————

That evening she sat next to Bogdan. They were alone in the palace barrack's mess hall. She had not spoken with or even seen him since the assassination attempt. This was the first time she had felt up to joining her men for a meal, but most of them were on duty. Mehmed trusted them more than ever, and they were all in heavy rotation.

"How are you?" Bogdan asked.

Lada gave him a flat look, wishing she were strong enough to physically punish him for asking such a stupid question. "I was stabbed and beaten by a trusted mentor a week ago."

He matched her expression with a similar one. "I was there."

She wondered if he had been scared, if he had been angry that she might die so soon after they were reunited. But his face betrayed nothing.

"I meant how is it being in mourning."

Bogdan was a fool if he thought she was mourning the death of Mehmed's half brother. She was not happy that the boy had been killed, but she could not pretend to oppose Huma's rationale. It would be hypocrisy to dress in sackcloth and ashes. Disrespectful, even.

"Is it common knowledge, then?" she asked. Radu had sent her a note that Mehmed was going to make the fratricide decree, but she had thought it would be tomorrow. She had also been hurt that Mehmed had not asked for her advice on what to say.

She wondered how long it would take him to forgive her for everything that had transpired. The fear that perhaps he would not be able to nagged at her. Where would she be then?

Bogdan shrugged. "Petru told me."

Lada frowned. "Petru was not on duty today. How did he hear about Ahmet?"

"Who is Ahmet?"

"Mehmed's half brother."

"What are you talking about?"

"What are *you* talking about?"

"Your father." Bogdan stopped, his jaw tightening. "They did not tell you."

Lada knew she was looking at Bogdan's face, but she could not see it. She could not see anything. "My father is dead?"

"I am sorry. Petru thought you knew. Hunyadi and the boyars killed your father. Mircea, too."

Lada nodded, her head bobbing up and down of its own volition. A roar filled her ears. A roar like the wind rushing along the banks of the Arges River, tearing at a tree growing sideways out of the rock. "When?"

"Petru overheard Mehmed and Radu a week ago. Right before the revolt."

"A week." Her hand darted to the pouch around her neck—but it was gone.

She had not realized it, had not felt for it since she fought Ilyas.

It was gone.

52

A<small>LL</small> R<small>ADU</small> <small>WANTED</small> <small>TO</small> do was sleep, but the knocking would not cease. He stumbled to the door and yanked it open, ready to yell at whoever was there. The ghost of his sister stood in the doorway. Her eyes were large and vacant, her face as smooth as a fading memory.

"Our father is dead," Lada said.

Radu leaned heavily against the doorframe. Lada drifted in past him. He shut the door, closing them in.

"Why did you keep this from me?"

Radu was glad it was dark so he could not see her face. "I did not know how to tell you." He reached for her hand. It felt cold and tiny in his own. "I am sorry. I know you loved him."

"I did not love him. I worshipped him. And then he betrayed us by being human—so worthlessly, weakly human. He left us here with nothing and made it impossible for us to return home."

"He terrified me."

Lada laughed sharply. "Little brother, everyone terrified you."

"That is true."

"Mircea is dead, too."

"Yes." Radu thought of the raw grief Mehmed had been consumed by after the murder of his infant half brother. Radu felt nothing like that when he thought of Mircea's death. Perhaps that meant something was wrong with him. He wondered if Lada mourned Mircea. He did not ask.

Lada spoke. "Do you remember that summer? When Father took us out of the city?"

"Yes. I was bitten by so many bugs I could scarcely move."

"I thought he would see me. I thought if we left Tirgoviste, if we left stupid Mircea, if we left behind the boyars and their ceaseless bickering, he would see what I was becoming to please him. For one day, I thought he did. It was the happiest day of my life. And then he left, as he always did."

"He loved you."

"You sound so certain. How do you know?"

"Because he tried to save you, that day the sultan claimed us."

"He failed."

"But he tried. That was more than he did for me."

After a brief silence, Lada let out a harsh bray of laughter. "I keep thinking how angry Mircea must be to be dead."

"I had the same thought!"

They laughed, and then it was quiet for a few warm minutes, safe and dark with their childhood between them. The things they had had and the things they had lost that only they could ever understand.

"I have something for you." Radu reached into a box on his side table and pulled out a locket. "That night. When the physician was sewing you back together, I found your little pouch. The one you always wear around your neck. It was ruined, but ... Well, I saved what was inside and had this made for you."

He held out the necklace. The metal locket was heavy and cold in his hand.

With a sniffling gasp, Lada lowered the chain around her neck and clutched the locket to her chest. "Thank you. I have lost too much recently."

She rested her head against his shoulder. Radu knew some of what she lost had been solely to protect him. As she had always done, in her own way. He breathed out a sigh and steadied himself to tell her he was sorry. That he loved her. That he understood her.

"The throne is yours," Lada said, puncturing the space and bringing the night with all its dark terrors back down on Radu.

"No."

"It is." Her voice rose, excitement kindling there and growing toward a fire as only Lada could burn with. "Nothing holds us here now. We are beholden to none, ransom against nothing. You could claim the prince title. Mehmed will support you, he will be glad of it. We could go back to Wallachia, together, strong, and no one could tell us—"

"No! Lada. No. I do not want to go back."

"But it is our home."

Radu shook his head, rising to sit on the edge of his bed. "My home is here."

"You mean Mehmed is here." There was no accusation in her voice, but the way she said it stung Radu.

AND I DARKEN

"Yes." He did not pretend it was otherwise, but he could not explain to her the other reasons. The mosques, with their domed towers making him feel insignificant in the most comforting way. Praying in perfect union with his brothers around him. Having a place, a life, a position where he was valued. And yes, doing it all by Mehmed's side. Even if it would never be as much as Radu needed.

As though following his train of thought, Lada said, "He can never love you. Not the way you love him."

Radu laughed, but it sounded old and brittle. "Do you think I do not know that? And still this is better than what we can ever hope for in Wallachia. How can you not see that? You have him, Lada. You have his heart and his eyes and his soul. I have seen the way you wait for him to look at you, the way you relish his attentions. You pretend you do not love him, but you cannot lie to me." He paused. Then, unable to stop himself, he slipped into a goading tone. "No one will ever love you as he does—as an equal—and you know it. You will not leave that. You cannot."

She stiffened. Radu saw her fingers curl into fists, ready for a fight. "I can. I have already started. He will never forgive me for admitting my betrayal."

Radu was reminded of her beating the boyar sons in the forest outside Tirgoviste. Those same fists had always defied everything expected of her. Now he had made her love of Mehmed a challenge to be overcome. His heart sank as he realized that by taunting her that she could not leave, he had virtually guaranteed she would do exactly that.

Maybe he had known that all along.

"Come with me," she commanded. "I will not go home

463

without you." She waited, then shocked Radu with her desperate, soft tone. "You chose me."

He had. And Lada had not asked him for something like this in so long. She was his sister, and she was begging him to choose her again. But maybe, if Lada left, Mehmed would finally choose him.

"I am home, Lada." Radu lay back and turned on his side, away from her.

53

THOUGH LADA DID NOT know what would happen, she was certain of two things:

It would hurt, and she would need to be strong.

She dressed in chain mail and the Janissary uniform, except for the cap. She left her hair down, a tangled mass of curls in defiance of both Janissary custom and feminine styles. At her hip was her sword, and on her wrists were her knives.

Her spine was steel. Her heart was armor. Her eyes were fire.

At her side were Bogdan and Nicolae. Bogdan, to remind her of what she had left behind and could find again. Nicolae, to remind her that she could lead and men would follow.

Mehmed looked up in surprise when Lada entered the reception room. He sat behind a table, robed in purple, perfectly in place in his gilded chair. His official stool holder crouched nearby, waiting. Behind Mehmed, Radu avoided Lada's eyes.

Unable to account for her appearance, Mehmed's eyebrows

rose in a question. "Leave us," he said, and the attendants scattered and disappeared.

Lada planted her feet, rooting herself. "Make Radu prince of Wallachia."

Radu shook his head, turning toward the window, away from her.

Mehmed's expression fell, then turned deliberately neutral. How long had he known about her father and kept the information from her? And why? But she would not ask those questions. They made her look weak. She was here to demand, not question.

"Why would I do that?" Mehmed asked.

"Because you need as much stability as you can get before you go after Constantinople. You have had enough problems with Wallachia allying with Hungary, Transylvania, and Moldavia. Make Radu the prince, and you will guarantee no treaty with Wallachia will be broken."

Mehmed leaned back and stretched, long and feline. "He does not want to take the position of vaivode. There is another way to strengthen the alliance with Wallachia."

No! Lada had been hoping Mehmed was not in contact with the Danesti family. If they had already agreed to work with him, her position would be irreparably weakened. "You cannot trust the Danesti boyars."

"The Danesti line? No, I am going to ally myself with the Draculesti family."

Lada bit back a growl of frustration. "With Mircea dead, that leaves only Radu to take the throne."

"He is not the only Draculesti." Mehmed's mouth curled

around a smile fighting to break free. "And thrones are not the only way to secure alliances."

"What—" Understanding slammed into her, stealing her breath. "No."

Mehmed stood, walking around the table to stand in front of her. He cupped her chin, lifting her face to his. "Marry me, Lada. It is the perfect solution."

Lada laughed.

Mehmed's smile grew, until he realized her laugh was not a sweet breeze of delight, but a brutal desert wind carrying stinging sand in its wake.

"I will never marry."

"Why? Stand at my side! Rule my empire with me!"

"I want no part of the Ottoman Empire."

Anger flashing in his black eyes, Mehmed let go of her chin. "Why do you hate my country so? Have you not been happy here?"

"Do you know me at all? I have never been happy any-where except Wallachia."

His face darkened, and he jabbed a finger at her. "You have been happy with me."

She realized, finally, that she had been less selfless than she thought when taking the full blame and sparing Radu. On some unconscious level, she had hoped that Mehmed would be unable to forgive her. That she would not have to make the choice to leave him, but that the choice would be made for her.

Love was a weakness, a trap. She had learned that from her father her first day in Edirne, but somehow she had failed to keep herself free. Mehmed and Radu stood before her, snaring her, keeping her here. And even knowing it, she recoiled at the thought of losing them.

Lada made her face stone, her heart a mountain. A mountain that would never be pierced to let cold, clear water flow. "Nothing holds me here."

Mehmed closed his eyes, rearranging his features from rage and hurt to supplication. He had so much control now, so much skill in using emotion as a tool. How they had all grown. "You have saved my life three times. I would be dead without you. I need you."

"Give up Constantinople."

"What?"

Lada lifted her shoulders impassively. "Your mindless determination to take Constantinople is what threatens your life. You have no claim to the city, no right to it, no reason to fixate on it. Give it up, and your enemies will stop trying to kill you."

"You know I cannot!" He clasped his hands behind his back, pacing the length of the room. "It calls to me, taunts me. The Prophet, peace be upon him, said it would be ours, and I must—I *must*—be the sultan to see his words fulfilled. As my people were made for greater things than traveling deserts on horses, so am I made for bigger things than maintaining a stagnant, dismissed empire. We *will* be the jewel of the world, the envy of all Europe, the new Rome. *I* will be the one to make it that way. I have to show the world what my people are. This is my calling. I cannot turn my back on it."

Lada nodded, lids half closed, heavy with the weight of the future. "We understand each other completely. I cannot give up Wallachia. I cannot turn my back on my home for what scraps may fall to me from another master's table. I did not choose to come here, Mehmed. I was held against my will."

"But now I am asking you! Choose to stay! Choose *me*."

"And be left behind when you go crusading? You would not take me to Albania, you will not take me to Constantinople. I will hate you for it, and the poison between us will grow until I turn into one of your invisible wives, as captive as your father ever made me. If you try to keep me, I will hate you, and you will lose me forever. You already know you cannot rule me. I proved that the last time you were on the throne."

Anguish and anger warred on Mehmed's face as he stopped in front of Lada and grasped her shoulders. "What would you have me do?"

And, in that moment, Lada saw her future. Her past was filled with snatching what threads she could from the men around her. Her father. Ilyas Bey. Mehmed. But before her was a knife. She would cut them all.

She did not have to accept only what was offered to her.

She would *take* what should be hers.

What had always been hers lit on her face like the sun on the mountain peak so many summers ago. "I want Wallachia."

"What?"

"Make me vaivode."

Mehmed frowned. "But that is the title for a prince."

"Make me prince, then. You know I am capable. Send me with my Janissary troops, give me the backing of the empire."

Mehmed raised a hand dismissively, but he sounded un-sure. "They will never accept you."

"I will *make* them." She waited for another dismissal, but none came, so she pressed her advantage. "Send me as prince, as a gesture of peace. No one will see it as a show of strength or aggression. They will see that you want stability, not con-quest. I will deliver treaties to Hunyadi, to everyone who has opposed you. I will spread news of peaceful Mehmed who wants only what he already has and nothing more. And you will be free to focus on Constantinople."

Mehmed's voice was soft, tortured. He did not turn to face her. "But I will lose you."

Though she had always known returning home would mean leaving Mehmed, until that moment she had never con-sidered the reality of it. It was not fleeing, or being forced away. It was *choosing* to lose him. It felt impossible. Radu finally met her gaze, and she silently implored him, holding out a hand. She could not, would not lose both of them.

He shook his head.

Huma's words from all those years ago slipped beneath her armor, piercing her heart. *What must be sacrificed to secure a future where no one can touch you?* Lada knew now exactly how much she had to lose, because she was about to cut out her heart and leave it.

The two men—the only two people—who had been con-stants in her life would be left behind. Radu and Mehmed had both given her something she could not give herself, had seen her in a way no one else had and no one else ever would. They looked at her, ugly Lada, vicious Lada, and saw something precious. And she looked at them and saw Radu, her brother, her blood, her responsibility, and Mehmed, her equal, the only man great enough to be worthy of her love.

One future—bleak and unknowable, filled with violence and pain and struggle—unfurled before her. Another, with her brother and the man who knew her and still loved her, shone like a beacon.

And so she cut out her heart and offered it as a sacrifice. She would pay whatever price her mother Wallachia demanded.

"Make me prince," she said without feeling.

54

After she was gone, Radu held Mehmed as he wept. Radu's joy at cradling Mehmed was like a kick to the stomach, overpowering and destined to linger with bruises long after it was over.

"Never leave me." Mehmed's grief-choked voice still rang with command.

Radu closed his eyes. "I will never leave you." Mehmed was in his arms, but he knew Lada was the only thing in Mehmed's heart. Radu had thought his own heart was filled with nothing but Mehmed. But he now had an aching fissure, the portion Lada left bereft when she abandoned him once and for all.

He had said this was his home. He had told the truth, and he had lied. Because Lada was his home, too, and now she was gone.

The call to prayer drifted through the walls, and the two men fell to their knees. Radu released everything to God. His pain, his fear, his loss, his secrets. His vast, unfathomable loneliness.

When they had finished praying, Mehmed was calm. His face was as hard as the sword of his ancestors. Radu followed him onto the balcony, where he gazed intently into the darkness beyond the city. Mehmed was looking north, where Lada and her men traveled to claim Wallachia.

Radu put a hand on his shoulder. Mehmed needed focus to move past the pain. Radu gently turned them both to look east.

Toward Constantinople.

55

Wallachian border

THE STORM CLOUDS THAT had accompanied their long march finally broke. After the dark dynamics and constantly shifting palette of the clouds, the flat blue of the sky looked false somehow. A promise worth less than the papers and treaties Lada carried in her bags.

They gazed across a wide, frosted plain to the mountains threatening the countryside.

"Wallachia." Nicolae's voice was filled with wonder, all teasing gone.

"Home," Bogdan grunted.

Stefan, Petru, Matei, the rest of her men—*her* men— joined them, staring at their past. It had become their future. Lada had made it that way.

Nicolae got past his reverence, grinning at her. "Well, are you ready, Lada Dragwlya, daughter of the dragon?"

Fire burned in her heart, and her wounded soul spread out, casting a shadow like wings across her country. This was hers. Not because of her father. Not because of

Mehmed. Because the land itself had claimed her as its own.

"Not Dragwlya," she said. "Lada Dracul. I am no longer the daughter of the dragon." She lifted her chin, sights set on the horizon. "*I* am the dragon."

DRAMATIS PERSONAE

Draculesti Family, Wallachian nobility

Vlad Dracul: Military governor of Transylvania, vaivode of Wallachia, father of Lada and Radu, father of Mircea, husband of Vasilissa

Vasilissa: Mother of Lada and Radu, princess of Moldova

Mircea: Oldest son of Vlad Dracul and his first, deceased wife

Lada: Daughter and second legitimate child of Vlad Dracul

Radu: Son and third legitimate child of Vlad Dracul

Vlad: Illegitimate son of Vlad Dracul with a mistress

Alexandru: Brother of Vlad Dracul, vaivode of Wallachia

Wallachian Court and Countryside Figures

Nurse: Mother of Bogdan, caretaker of Lada and Radu

Bogdan: Son of the nurse, friend of Lada

DRAMATIS PERSONAE

Andrei: Boyar child from rival Danesti family

Aron: Boyar child from rival Danesti family

Costin: A boy without shoes at the frozen river

Danesti family: Rival family for the Wallachian throne

Lazar: A Janissary soldier serving in Wallachia, friend of Radu

Edirne Court Figures

Murad: Ottoman sultan, father of Mehmed

Halima: One of Murad's wives, mother of the infant Ahmet

Ahmet: Mehmed's infant half brother

Mara Brankovic: One of Murad's wives, the daughter of the Serbian king

Huma: One of of Murad's concubines, the mother of Mehmed

Mehmed: The third and least favorite son of the sultan

Sitti Hatun: Daughter of an important emir, Mehmed's first wife

Gulsa: Mehmed's concubine, the mother of his second son

Beyazit: Mehmed's firstborn son

Molla Gurani: Mehmed's tutor

Halil Pasha: An important advisor in the Ottoman court

Salih: The second son of Halil Pasha, friend of Radu

Kumal: Devout vali of a small area outside of Edirne

Nazira: Kumal's youngest sister

Fatima: Nazira's maid

Amal: A young servant in the palace

Military Figures in the Ottoman Empire

Ilyas: A Janissary commander

Kazanci Dogan: Military leader of the Janissaries

Ivan: A Janissary with a nasty disposition

Matei: An experienced Wallachian Janissary

Nicolae: A Wallachian Janissary and Lada's closest friend

Petru: A young Wallachian Janissary

Stefan: A mysterious Wallachian Janissary

Tohin: A gunpowder expert

Political Figures in Opposition to the Sultan

Constantine: The emperor of Constantinople

Orhan: A false heir to the Ottoman throne, used by Constantinople as leverage

Skanderberg: Iskander Bey, also known as Skanderberg, a former Janissary and favorite of Murad, now holding the Albanian city of Kruje against the Ottomans

GLOSSARY

bey: A governor

beylerbey: Governors of the largest and most important provinces

boyars: Wallachian nobility

concubine: A woman who belongs to the sultan and is not a legal wife but could produce legal heirs

dervish: Religious ascetics (mostly from the Sufi branch of Islam) who take vows of poverty

dracul: Dragon, also devil, as the terms were interchangeable

emir: A leader of the Turkmen tribes, Ottoman allies to the east

eunuch: A man who has been castrated, highly valued as a servant and a prestigious slave

hajj: Religious pilgrimage taken to Mecca as one of the Five Pillars of Islam

harem: A group of women, consisting of wives, concubines, and servants, that belongs to the sultan

Janissary: A member of an elite force of military professionals, taken as boys from other countries, converted to Islam, educated, and trained to be loyal to the sultan

Order of the Dragon: Order of Crusaders anointed by the pope

pasha: A noble in the Ottoman Empire, appointed by the sultan

pashazada: A son of a pasha

spahi: Military commander in charge of local Ottoman soldiers called up during wars

vaivode: Warlord prince of Wallachia

vali: A local governor, appointed by the sultan

valide sultan: The mother of the sultan

vassal state: Country allowed to retain rulership but subject to the Ottoman Empire, with taxes of both money and slaves for the army

vilayet: Small area of land governed by a vali

vizier: A high ranking noble, usually adviser to the sultan

Wallachia: Vassal state of the Ottoman Empire, bordered by Transylvania, Hungary, and Moldavia

AUTHOR'S NOTE

While the book is based on actual historical figures, I have taken massive liberties, filling in gaps, creating characters and events, shifting time lines, and most particularly, changing Vlad the Impaler to Lada the Impaler.

Any book based in history is a vast and ultimately impossible undertaking. Because history is written by the victors—and those who are quite unhappy with those victors—major figures tend to be canonized or demonized in the records that make it through to our day.

Vlad the Impaler was a national hero, a freedom fighter, a brilliant military mind. Or he was a deeply disturbed psychopath, a vicious despot who murdered tens of thousands and literally sustained himself on their flesh.

Similarly divided accounts exist of Mehmed the Conqueror. History loves him and hates him. He was an incredibly devout, thoughtful ruler, even bordering on a religious figure, or he was a cruel predator who loved debauchery and destruction.

My goal in this book was to carve out a middle ground. In my research I set aside accounts that skewed too far in either direction and tried to focus on the truth: They were men who were born into great power, and they both did what they thought necessary to maintain and expand that power. The central aspect I wanted to explore was the path a person takes to get to the point where they can justify doing terrible things in the name of good. What motivations sway them? What stones laid in childhood become the foundation legacies are built on?

In the end, this is a work of fiction. I chose to make Vlad the Impaler a girl because it was a more interesting lens for me as a storyteller. Radu the Handsome is merely a footnote in Vlad's stories, but I did my best to breathe life into his legacy. Mehmed the Conqueror is a revered Turkish national hero, with Istanbul still a testament to his greatness and his ability to think far into the future. I have done my best to honor that, while still acknowledging that he was a real person.

Just how much interaction the three would have had growing up in the Ottoman Courts together is unknown. I've crafted a fictional history in which the formative relationships of their young lives were with each other. If you would like to read more extensively on Vlad, Radu, and Mehmed and their time, as well as the incredible legacy of the Ottomans, I recommend using your local library and librarians. Some books I found helpful were:

The Ottoman Centuries, by Lord Kinross

1453, by Roger Crowley

A Short History of Byzantium, by John Julius Norwich

The Grand Turk, by John Freely

Dracula, Prince of Many Faces, by Radu R. Florescu and Raymond T. McNally

Islam: A Thousand Years of Faith and Power, by Jonathan Bloom and Sheila Blair

Though the characters in the book each interact with religion, and more specifically Islam, in various ways, I have nothing but respect for the rich history and beautiful legacy of that gospel of peace. Individual characters' opinions on the complexities of faith, both Islam and Christianity, do not reflect my own.

Spelling varies between languages and over time, as do place names. Any errors or inconsistencies are my own. Though the main characters speak a variety of languages, I made an editorial decision to present all common terms in English.

ACKNOWLEDGMENTS

This book would not exist without my incredible husband. Noah's love of Romania and its history, as well as Arabic, Islam, and the Middle East, fed and formed this idea until it was ready to become a story. He was an invaluable resource. Also, he is very handsome and I'm quite lucky to be his wife.

Special thanks go to my agent, Michelle Wolfson, for never pausing when I tell her what I want to do next. She has been Lada's biggest cheerleader—and mine, as well.

My brilliant editor, Wendy Loggia, cannot be thanked enough. She saw the pitch for this book and instantly understood what it was and what it needed to be. Her guiding hand is on every page, and I'm so grateful to work with her. The entire team at Delacorte Press is a dream for a writer. Special thanks go to Alison Impey for the stunning cover design, Heather Kelly for the gorgeous interior design, and Colleen Fellingham and Heather Lockwood Hughes for catching all my many errors in copyedits.

None of my books would exist without my best friends

and critique partners, Natalie Whipple and Stephanie Perkins. Natalie saw me through a brutal first draft, and Stephanie saved me during an overwhelming edit. Thank you, thank you, thank you. I love you both.

Finally, endless gratitude goes to my family, for always supporting and encouraging me. And last in thanks but first in my heart, to my three beautiful children: I would cut through a mountain for you.